RESPECTANT

Book Four of the
Chronicle of the
Seer
Pentalogy

Florian Armas

ISBN 13 978-0-9939772-8-2

For my mother

5

Table of Contents

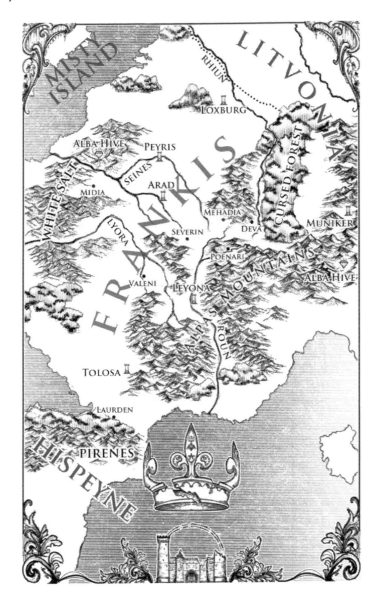

Chapter 1 – Saliné

It was dark, so dark that you couldn't see your hand in front of your face. The moon was hidden behind a thick blanket of clouds. The men waited, hidden among the trees. There were six of them, and they were patient; patience kept a man alive. Thin tendrils of white mist snaked through the trees, barely visible. The night was old and cold and bitterly damp. The assassins didn't care; gnarled hands gripped weapons, and they waited.

"Once the moon comes out, we take down the sentries," a tall man said, hearing the breathing of the shorter one, still invisible, in front of him. "Then you kill the girl. Is it really necessary to use the axe?"

"Eric, there is nothing personal in it. A dead girl is just a corpse like any other. We've been at war through spring and summer. Death was everywhere. People get accustomed to it. A butchered girl is a message. We need him angry. Angry enough to kill all of them." He gestured at a place a hundred paces away, as if the man in front of him could see his hand. "Anger dulls the mind, it's a known thing, and he will become a toy in our hands. Our lady has great plans. So, you see, it's just a formality. We need to control him, and I am the one who will pull the strings. I am Dog, and this will be a night to remember for all Frankis."

"So, it's got nothing to do with the fact that you like to use your axe."

"I did not say that. Gilia is my best friend." Dog laughed quietly, caressing the cold steel of the axe like a lover. "She doesn't say much, but she never lets me down, and there are many ways to use an axe, some of them bloodier than others. You know what I mean. The moon is coming out. It will guide me and my friend to our task." Faint light strained from the fringes of the clouds, giant fingers pointing into the camp. "The sentries are waiting for your men."

"Dog is right," Eric said, looking up into the sky. "Be merciful and kill them fast. I don't want noise. Do you know where she is?"

"I can't see her yet, but," the shorter man sniffed, "she is somewhere there. I will find her." He was called Dog not because he was both obedient and an efficient killer, though he was both of those things, but because of his peculiar olfactory gift. He was able to identify people by their scent. When he was young, children had teased him that his father was a dog. That got him into many fights, but they only strengthened and darkened him. He usually won the fights, even against older boys.

Silent shadows, two men split from the group. They hid behind a tree, then moved to hide behind the next one. Leaning on the shafts of the spears stuck into the ground, the sentries were looking the wrong way. Eyes almost closed, they were dreaming of hot meals, good wine and soft pillows. And maybe of a warm woman too. At the edge of the forest, the assassins signaled to each other in the silvery light of the full moon. They were twin brothers and well accustomed to working together, timing their moves like dancers. Moving as one, dark and swift hands closed over the sentries' mouths. In a moment, the twin brothers slit their throats, and they laid the dead gently on the ground, like they were sleeping. The forest stayed silent. There was no need for them to signal to their companions; they just retreated into the darkness.

"Dog, your time has arrived," Eric said. "It's just a girl, so I will not wish you good luck."

Barefoot, the girl walked through the grass in front of the building. It felt like silk, cold and refreshing, and she enjoyed each step. The full moon stared at her through sprinkled stardust and scattered clouds, casting everything in blue-black and silver. Her mouth curved into a wide smile, the girl waved her little hand at it. Chased by the wind coming from the ocean, a thin patch of clouds passed over the moon in a few moments.

The moon winked at me, the girl thought happily and waved again.

On the wall of the house, the guttering flame of a single torch struggled to ward off the night, and a pair of eyes glittered at the edge of the forest, a hundred paces away from the girl.

"Wolf. Go away," she said and gestured with her small knife. "You are not allowed here." The moon was her friend, and the dark forest did not scare her. Still and patient, the eyes followed her.

"Wait for me," a little voice cried behind the older girl, and she stopped, turning to wait for her nine-year-old sister. They ran together, back and forth, shimmering ribbons flowing over their bodies, like water droplets, as they moved in the moonlight. Joyfully, the girls clasped hands and danced a Hora dance, their giggles chasing away the silence of the night. On the ground, a thin curtain of white mist coiled around them, nebulous, cold fingers wrapping their toes and ankles. The girls did not care. When they stopped dancing, eyes closed, the older girl tilted her head back, feeling the night. Trembling light from the torch played on her fair face until a silent shadow came between her and the flame. She blinked at the man in front of her and, for a few long moments, she could not speak. Far away, lightning painted shining ribbons into the sky, and the thunder boomed, as if the sky were crushing down on earth. The wind sighed, swirling a few curled-up leaves around her.

"Father! she finally cried, and tears of joy ran down her face.

"Wake up," the man said.

"Father." She stretched her arms up toward him.

"Wake, up. Now!"

Abruptly, Saliné opened her eyes to see a shadow moving toward her. Tense, she tried to blink it away, hoping that it was just another dream. Silence swallowed the forest, broken only by the faint sound of the wind whistling through the trees. The shadow stopped just three feet from her, and she saw the head of the raised axe glinting in the feeble moonlight. Silent as the night, the huge axe arced down toward her. She rolled away, and the hard steel hit the root on which her head had rested only moments before. The thump disturbed the night, and she felt it like a rumble of thunder.

He is here for me. "Robbers!" she cried in a thick, almost male voice, an inharmonious disguise.

"Shit," Dog whispered, struggling to pull the axe from the hard wood. "I thought it was her. The scent..."

Instinctively, Saliné grabbed her quiver with her left hand. She rolled further, extracting an arrow, and came up into a crouch, adopting the low posture of the Assassin Dance that Codrin had taught her. The man finally freed his axe from the root and stepped back, unbalanced. She jumped forward and stabbed at his face with the point of the arrow. There was not enough light and time to find his eyes, but she managed to hurt him; the iron tip split his nose, and came half out, through his nostril. Surprised, Dog let out a muffled cry of pain. Swiftly, Saliné stabbed again as he raised the axe; then she stepped back.

"Bloody girl; you tricked me with your voice." Grunting like a mad beast, the man swung his axe in a horizontal arc, trying to cut her in two.

Saliné rolled on her back in the grass, and now men were standing, swords raised. They surrounded the assassin, who defended himself with savage swings of his axe.

"Don't kill him!" Aron shouted, but his warning came too late.

It was indeed a night to remember, Dog thought his last thought as darkness closed over him.

Weapons tight in their hands, everybody in the small clearing listened to the night. It was silent again until a wolf howled in the distance.

"Our sentries are dead."

"There are more robbers, and they are still there, in the forest." Aron spun around, peering into the night. "You men, on my left, take over the watch. The others will replace you when the moon starts to go down."

The moon hid behind the clouds again; Saliné could no longer see through the shadows, and nothing more than silence reached her ears – a silence that settled like the night's mist, shapeless and unnatural. *Why did he try to kill me? Who are they?* The coppery scent of blood drying slowly, the scent of death, came to her, and she waited for the moon to appear again, moved to find another place to sleep, far from the blood and the old root. This time, she chose to lie behind a small bush in the middle of the scattered men. Nobody asked her why, but as before, a sentry stood close to her. Blindly, she stared at the empty night, and lay down, setting her backpack as a pillow. *I can't run away in this darkness. I was lucky that they attacked before I tried. They would have caught me. How far behind us is Codrin? He will come after me. He must come.* The chill of the forest sent a shiver down her spine. Restless, she found it hard to sleep again.

Saliné opened her eyes when the first rays of sunlight were peeking over the eastern horizon, illuminating the clearing. It was not a large one. The events of the night came to her, and for a few long moments, she remained motionless, her mind blank, letting her senses swim in the new morning. Most of the men were up and, at the edge of the forest, Aron was looking down at the dead assassin. Her eyes half closed, she turned a little to face them, pretending to be still asleep.

"This is Dog, Maud's top assassin," Bucur said, his voice sour.

"Yes." Aron frowned, and nudged the body with a booted foot. "He was sent to kill Saliné. Maud wants her dead; Maud wants us dead, but she wants Codrin to kill us for her. She knows that we have little chance of surviving without Saliné."

"Maybe we should just give Saliné to Codrin."

"Are you stupid? If we do that, Maud will certainly kill us. She wants to marry her bitch granddaughter to Codrin. If we keep Saliné, in a few months, he will take the bitch and become Duke of Tolosa. Nobody will give a damn about Baldovin anymore. Maud will give Leyona to Codrin too; Devan is already on his side."

"Devan?" Bucur asked hastily, a hint of tremor altering his voice, then curved his lips in distaste.

"Octavian saw his eldest son, Filippo, during the siege of Poenari. He was fighting for the other side. You should have noticed him, son; such things are important. If we lose Saliné, Codrin will chase us to the end of the world. If we are to survive, you have to marry her. We stay hidden for a few years while you get two children on her. He will have his family too by then. At the right time, she will write to Codrin, asking forgiveness and mercy for her new family. She is a clever girl, and she will do what is best for her children and their father."

"Are you so sure that Codrin will marry the young Duchess?"

"Yes, he will, and in a few years, the Circle will crown him King of Frankis. No one can stop it now. We lost, and that's it. We go forward."

"We will pay him..."

"You will pay nothing. Try to think. Everybody will hunt us, the Circle included. We have enough problems even without your childish desire for revenge."

"The Circle knows where we want to hide."

"Do you really think we go where they want us to be? I am not a sheep to be herded. Your mother inherited a fortified house in the Pirenes Mountains. I renovated it this spring, and it's waiting for us. Dog was not alone," Aron kicked the body again, "but I don't know how many of them were there. They will not attack us during the day. I will stay behind with four guards and leave a message for Maud. That should keep us safe for a while. Go, now."

Bucur walked away briskly, crouched in front of Saliné and shook her by the arm. "Wake up. We must leave now."

She blinked and turned her head away, feigning sleepiness. "I want to see that man." She yawned, stood up slowly, and stretched her limbs.

"We must hurry."

"No one is ready to leave." Lazily, she pointed at the men around them, and walked toward the old tree root, and the fresh corpse. Aron glanced at her but said nothing. She couldn't resist testing his honesty, or lack of it. "Do you know him?"

"They were just robbers." Aron shrugged and left her alone.

They were killers. Saliné crouched to see the man better. *Maud's Dog. I have heard about him.* Then she saw the cleft left by the axe in the hard root — it was possible to fit her palm inside it. She recoiled and breathed heavily, fighting the sudden weakness in her legs. Slowly, as if in pain, she took her eyes away from the cleft that could have been in her skull. *Father warned me in my dream. Mother told me that he had warned her in the past too. Why did he not warn me that Aron would kidnap me in Severin? I could have hidden in the secret tunnel. Why, Father?* She could not know that her abduction was meant to be, and her father was not allowed to warn her. The Last Empress had agreed with Drusila that Codrin will take Marie and become the Duke of Tolosa. That marriage was needed for the future of Frankis and, further, to solve the Fracture. It was part of the Prophecy in which the first chain was Tudor, the Assassin Grand Master, the uncle she had never known. It was a strange Prophecy, revealed to the Wanderers in steps, through their Visions, during the last twenty years. One outcome of it was Tudor's defection from the Assassin Order and Codrin's training as an Assassin. Only three people knew what had really happened: Ada, the most powerful Wanderer, Tudor and Primus, the Assassin King. A paper of understanding was signed by all three and left to Primus as keeper. At his death, he passed it to the next Primus, and Ada went to explain why the defection was needed, even when Tudor was supposed to be their next Primus. What no one could explain, not even the last survivor of the initial pact, was why Tudor had to die so early. Fate.

Ignoring Bucur's stare, Saliné stood up and went toward her mare. Out of sight, she leaned her head on the horse's neck. Eyes closed, she recalled all that had happened in the last two days. The treaty between Codrin, the Circle and Aron, and her happiness thinking that Codrin would finally be able to save her, when he took Severin. Her bitterness after the Circle, and Aron, betrayed their signatures on the treaty and kidnapped her when they left Severin through the tunnel, early in the morning. And that Knight, Laurent, who had betrayed Codrin and let Aron escape. *They ran like thieves. It no longer matters. I need to think.* She shook her head and bent to pick a stick from the ground; it was about a palm in length. She cut the stick in two, along its axis, and used the tip of her knife to scratch a few marks into them.

Fearing Codrin was close, Aron would have liked to leave without burying the dead sentries, but he felt that his men would not be pleased, and they lost another hour digging with their swords. It was a mountainous area, the land was dry and hard, and filled with many stones.

When the brief ceremony ended, Saliné was the last to leave the graves, paying her own homage to the dead. Silent, she crouched beside the graves for more than a minute, her left hand playing absently in the dirt. Aron shouted the order to leave, and she mounted her horse, following Bucur, without looking back. *At least they've lost two more men and almost two hours this morning. Maybe I can do something more about that.* She remembered how she had killed Aron's soldiers while they patrolled the walls of Severin. *This time, it will be harder. I don't have a secret tunnel to hide in...*

"Wait a moment with me, Petronius," Aron said, without looking at the Itinerant Sage.

The Sage dismounted and gestured discreetly to his two guards to stay close. *Aron knows Dog too. Maud did not warn me. What was in her mind?*

They avoided each other's eyes, pretending to look at the soldiers forming up to ride away.

"You know him." Aron pointed at the body when they were alone. "Maud is playing with fire."

"There must be a misunderstanding," Petronius said, tentatively. "Let me clarify everything, when I return to Leyona, and get back to you."

"It was certainly a misunderstanding," Aron agreed, and his right arm sprang forward. His dagger pierced Petronius's chest. Behind him, four soldiers overpowered the two guards of the Itinerant Sage.

"Why?" Petronius moaned, falling to the grass.

"Nothing personal. It's just that I don't like misunderstandings. I am sure that you ... understand my position." Aron looked coldly at the Sage's body in the grass, cleaning his knife on the man's pelerine. "I am not sure that you heard me, but Maud will get my message."

In the evening, they found a larger clearing. It was well hidden among the trees, away from the roads and Codrin's scouts. Saliné found a place to sleep among the roots of an old tree again. This time it was an isolated oak, thirty paces from the edge of the forest. In the feeble moonlight, the place looked no different to the past night, and she shivered. Nervously, she pulled her mantle even closer around her body.

It did not help much, but gradually, she calmed down and fell asleep. She woke up past midnight and, eyes half closed, she looked at the sentry, who was leaning on his spear, six paces from her. Patiently, she waited until the moon slipped behind a large patch of cloud. *The moon will stay hidden for at least ten minutes*, she thought, observing the speed of the clouds. They were thinner than the previous night and allowed some faint light to pass, but she felt safe enough. Slowly, she rolled away from her sleeping place and, moving like a snail, she put the tree between her and the sentry. She thought about escape, but the men who had tried to kill her the previous night were still out there, hidden somewhere in the forest; without a horse, she would be easy prey for anyone who wanted to catch her. Five men had followed them all day, at a safe distance, and they had not bothered to hide, something that Saliné could not understand. She had seen them, everybody had seen them, and Aron had ordered extra sentries for the night.

Without knowing it, she imitated the moves of the twin brothers who had killed the sentries the night before. Her left hand closed over the guard's mouth. She slit his throat and laid him gently on the ground. The forest stayed silent.

She wiped her left hand and dagger on the man's clothes and returned to her sleeping place. Crouched there, she breathed in a regular pattern, the Assassin Cool, which Codrin had taught her, to calm herself. "Robbers!" she cried after a while and ran toward the middle of the clearing. She stumbled over a sleeping man and fell in the grass, rolling away from him before he could kill her. Fear would make him kill anyone who got too close.

Around her, men jumped up, grabbed their weapons, and gathered in the middle of the clearing, voicing their panic.

"Shut up!" Aron shouted and, in the sudden silence, he listened to the night.

Nothing happened, and they eventually calmed down, but no one could sleep until close to the morning. They woke up later than usual and buried another man. They lost two hours this time.

Later, when Aron and his troop finally vanished from sight, Maud's men came into the clearing, and Eric scratched his head. "I have no idea who killed this one," he said, pointing at the grave.

"Maybe Maud sent another team."

"She would have told me. We need to be careful. We can't afford to attack them again. You will follow Aron, to see where he is heading, while I return to Leyona. He killed an Itinerant Sage, and Maud will want his head."

Chapter 2 – Codrin

A few hours after taking Severin, Codrin walked in the long corridor, and he was the last one to enter the council room, thoughts swarming in his mind. *If I can't find her now, the only way to get Saliné back is to strengthen my position and force the Circle to return her. She may already be married by then;* he shook his head. *That does not matter to me. A forced marriage is a sham.* He glanced at the map on the wall, Mohor's map, seated himself at the table, Mohor's table, and remained silent, ignoring the eyes fixed on him until Vlaicu coughed.

I will make them pay for Saliné, for Jara, for Mohor, for everything. "Vlad," Codrin said, cursorily, "take twenty men with you and hunt Aron and his men, but don't attack them. Send couriers back from time to time, to let us know their path. From the tracks at the tunnel, they have more than half a day lead on you, and we know they rode west. Leave now; I will follow you as soon as I can." He glanced through the window: the sun would soon sink to touch the hills in the west.

"We need to prepare our defenses," Vlaicu said, his eyes following Vlad as he left the room. He understood Codrin's pain, but the new Grand Seigneur of Severin needed to focus. They had won the battle; the war would be long. Important things needed be settled. He turned his palms up, understanding, sympathetic, but firm.

Looking nowhere, Codrin sighed to himself. A long, painful sigh. He rubbed hard at his own temples, as though Vlaicu's gesture was giving him a headache, then shook his head, and his eyes became sharp again. "Attack is the best defense. Valer, are you prepared to move from Tolosa to Severin?"

"My relationship with the Duke was never easy, and with the Duchess it was even worse. News will spread that I fought for you in Poenari. I am ready to move." The Black Dervil of Tolosa was a man who did not speak much, but he was the best mercenary captain in all Frankis.

"How many soldiers can you bring in two weeks?"

"A hundred."

"You will settle in Cleuny, as my Knight." Valer was the second trusted man he had raised in rank; he had made Vlaicu Knight of Seged, which was taken from Aron, just an hour before the council started.

"Thank you," Valer bowed in acknowledgement.

"Can you find us some more Mountes?" Codrin looked at Boldur.

"After our victory, I am sure that some recrimination runs through the Chieftains, and shame, but I can't go to them. I am a still an outcast. I will write a letter to my cousin, Dragos; he was away when the Circle bought the League." The League was the council of the Mountes Chieftains, and Boldur was still bitter – they had betrayed the agreement made with Codrin and refused to send soldiers to Poenari.

"Damian will lead a squad of your Mountes on the road to the White Salt Mountains. He was born there and knows your people." *I should have enough soldiers to convince Devan now,* he pondered for a while looking at Filippo, before saying, "There is an informal alliance between Grand Seigneur Devan and me. It was made a year ago when we met at the border between Leyona and Deva." *Three years ago, he was supposed to marry Saliné,* he could not stop thinking, *and I wanted him dead. How things have changed.* "Things are not settled yet with the Circle, but we have the advantage. That doesn't mean that we are safe; they may retrieve the initiative soon. Would Deva consider a full alliance?"

"What's your next step?" Filippo asked, cautiously.

"Arad. As I said, attack is our best defense. Orban has lost many soldiers in Poenari, and there is a ferment of dissent against him. We have five hundred soldiers now. If you bring two hundred more, most of Arad will fall, and northern Mehadia, including the city, will go to you."

"I have to pass your request on to Father."

"I understand that. You should return in two weeks, with or without the new army. Vlaicu, we need more provisions. See what is stored in Severin, then send couriers to Poenari. Ban will lead the scouts in Vlad's absence. Send two squads to Arad, close to the border, and prepare the army to march in three weeks."

"What should we do with the Sages?" Vlaicu asked. "Traitors," he spat.

"I will talk to them before I leave. Then I will decide."

Codrin was alone in the council room when the guards ushered Verenius in. "Take a seat," Codrin said coldly, and nodded to the guards to leave. The treaty they had signed only the day before lay on the table, and he smoothed the document out with an imperious hand. "Read it." He pushed the paper toward Verenius.

"I know what..."

"Read it," Codrin snapped. "Aloud."

Verenius sighed and started to read out the clauses about Severin and Saliné being handed to Codrin, and about Aron leaving with all the men who wanted to join him.

"Why?" Codrin asked, and Verenius knew better than to ask what he meant.

"I received orders from the Circle. Saliné is a fine lady, perhaps the finest I ever saw, but Frankis needs more than that.

The young Duchess of Tolosa will bring you an army strong enough to unify the kingdom. She is a fine girl too."

"I will not marry her. You know that."

You are upset now, but it will pass, and you will see the truth in my words. I may not live long enough to see that. Fate. "Then we face more conflict, more dead and more lawless years for Frankis. Do you really want that?"

"As if the Sages care about that. You want power for yourselves, not a king for Frankis. All the choices for the Candidate King were wrong."

"I can't speak for all the Sages, but most of us care. I was not born a Knight or a noble. My father is a simple farmer, and the commoners suffer the most when there is disorder. They can't defend themselves. Duke Stefan was not a bad choice. He became one after his siblings were killed in battle against the Duke of Tolosa. He chose not to fight on. It was a bad decision for a good reason."

"Orban? Bucur? Were they good choices too?"

"I don't know why Orban was chosen as Candidate King. You are right that Maud is an ambitious woman, but she also wants the best future for Frankis. Except for you, she was close to unifying the kingdom."

"And you think me evil because..."

"You are strong, and you will be a better king than Bucur, but that doesn't make her plan wrong. She had the bad luck to learn too late how strong you are. If we had to choose a Candidate King today..."

"Why Bucur? What made him a good Candidate King?"

"Maud's granddaughter brought the south: Tolosa. Bucur brought the north: Peyris. In normal circumstances, that would have been enough to unify Frankis. Loxburg or Orban could not fight against the two largest Duchies."

"Duke Stefan helped Aron," Codrin whispered to himself and stood up. He went toward the window and looked out over the hills. "Why was Bucur so important to him?"

"Aron was Stefan's bastard," Verenius said, and Codrin turned his head abruptly. "Very few people know that."

"Yes, Aron behaves like a bastard, but at least I know now why. You may leave now; I have to go."

"Where are you going?" Verenius asked, still wondering about his own situation.

"To find Saliné."

"Did you find nothing of value in what I was telling you?"

"What kind of ruler would I be, if I let down friends and people I love when they are in danger?"

"There will be always tough decisions to make. Saliné is not in danger right now."

"Enough," Codrin snapped.

"You know that I am right. A ruler is not always able to take the most just decision. He must take the right one, and sometimes they are not the same."

"You are not the first to give me such advice."

"It came from a wise person."

"Wise and dead. I warned Mohor about Aron. Indeed, he took the right decision in keeping Aron as his Spatar, instead of jailing him. This treaty was a farce from the beginning." He tapped with one finger on the document, then took it, keeping his eyes on the Sage.

Verenius took his time to answer, and their eyes locked. After a while, the Sage looked away. *This is the most important moment... It will decide if I live or die.* "No, it wasn't. When we negotiated and signed the treaty, I did not know about the marriage offer from the Duke of Tolosa and your nomination as Grand Seigneur of Severin."

"Did Octavian bring that news?" Codrin asked, and Verenius nodded. "He arrived before we finished the negotiation."

Octavian wants me hanged so he can take my place as Primus Itinerant. Maud will not cry for me either. Watched closely by Codrin, Verenius struggled to find an acceptable answer. "Because of the tense negotiations, we did not time things well."

"It was your decision then?"

"I am the Primus Itinerant, so the decision was mine." *With Maud's hands tight around my throat.*

"Your decision," Codrin said and threw the paper on the table. "You may leave now. Guards!"

Verenius breathed deeply and stood up. His face blanched under his southern tan. *I have no idea what will happen to me, but I will not buy my freedom by telling him about the letter I gave to Saliné. If I die; I die.* Followed by two soldiers, he went out. They turned left along the corridor, then down the stairs leading to the cells. A path that he knew by heart already. Once Verenius was secure in his cell, the guards went to collect Octavian. Codrin had left orders that the Sages were not allowed to meet.

"Where are we going?" Octavian asked.

"Walk," one guard said.

"Where are you taking me?" he insisted.

"Walk." The guard clearly struggled not to hit him. In Severin, many knew about the power of the Circle, and how it had betrayed Mohor, Jara and Codrin, and they all hoped that Codrin would hang both Sages. It took a lot of persuasion from Vlaicu to keep the Itinerant Sages unharmed until a decision was made.

In Codrin's office, Octavian was given the same treatment and forced to read the treaty aloud. "Verenius acted in good faith," Octavian said, only because he had to say it.

"I like to think that I am acting in good faith too."

"What will you do to him?" the Sage asked, a little too eager.

"Hang him," Codrin said, looking away, but he caught Octavian's fleeting smile. "You can watch through the window."

Forcing himself to react slowly, Octavian stood up and went to the window, from where the main plaza could be seen, and where two gallows had been built. "Why two?" he asked, his voice almost a whisper.

"There are two Itinerant Sages in Severin."

"But I had nothing to do with the decision to break the treaty and sneak Saliné away." Octavian's composure had given way to panic, even though he knew that Verenius had taken most of the blame.

"Really?" Codrin asked, but Octavian was too dazed to argue. "You have half an hour to leave Severin."

"Thank you," Octavian breathed. "I apologize if..., but can I take my guards and ... Verenius's?"

"He no longer needs them. Tell Maud that no Itinerant Sages will be admitted into Severin until I say so. The gallows," he gestured at the window, "will wait there."

"We may need to communicate with you."

"I don't see the need, at least not for a while; Frankis will be a boring and peaceful place until next year. But you can use merchants or protectors if you really need to reach me. I need time to take over and organize Severin. Aron left a mess behind. The Visterie is empty. There is lawlessness everywhere. We have hanged two bands of robbers already. In spring, we may need to discuss my next steps."

"Severin is not a large city, but if you need help..."

"I was trained to rule larger cities."

"Jara told me that you were a Duke's son in Arenia."

"Don't tempt me to use the second gallows for what you did to her and Mohor. Leave," Codrin snapped. *Pierre was right. This man is a snake*, he thought, watching the Sage walking away.

From the doorway, Octavian found the courage to speak again, "I apologize for asking, but can you give an answer to the Duke of Tolosa about the marriage proposal? It will help to avoid too much traffic between Leyona and Severin."

"Marie? I saw her a few years ago," Codrin said, thoughtfully. "She was still a child. A beautiful one, as I remember. How old is she now?"

"Next year, she will be eighteen, and she is as intelligent as she is beautiful."

"I see. She was marked by the Circle... Maud will have my answer in spring." Codrin fell silent, and his face took on an expression that usually made men step back from him. Octavian's face had gone white, and his hands started to shake. He clasped them abruptly. Turning his back on the Sage, Codrin stood up and went toward the window. "Marie is no longer a child," he whispered. *I feel so old.*

I've escaped... "Thank you," Octavian said and left the room. *Well*, he mused, his hands still shaking, *it seems that Codrin took the bait.* This time, the guards took him out of the castle, where they met Vlaicu.

"You are a lucky man, Sage," Vlaicu said, his tone as chilly as the wind of a hard winter. "We saved a place for you there," he pointed at the gallows, "and we were eager to see you dancing at the end of a rope."

As they walked toward the end of the plaza, a second team of guards escorted a hooded man out of the castle.

"Wait," Vlaicu said, and Octavian turned. "Watch and remember." They stood in silence until the hanged man stopped kicking, and the rope was still. Even though Octavian wanted Verenius dead, he trembled, as if he were drenched by icy rain. "Move." Vlaicu pushed him hard, and Octavian struggled to find his equilibrium.

They walked in silence to the place where the four guards, two of them belonging to Verenius, were waiting, at the edge of the plaza. Ten of Vlaicu's men were there too, and horses for all of them.

"Escort these snakes to the border with Leyona," Vlaicu spat. "If one of them tries to run, or to return, kill him."

"I doubt that they will try," Pintea, who was leading the riders, said, "but I will be careful."

The men kept in a tight group until they passed the gate, then they spread out a little on the road. One of Verenius's guards rode up and asked Octavian about his master, his voice a mere whisper.

"Verenius was hanged," Octavian said, struggling to keep his satisfaction hidden. *It was not hard to handle Codrin after all. He is a good soldier, but he lacks political skills. That suits us well. Saliné will be dead soon, and after his marriage with the young Duchess of Tolosa, Maud should be able to handle Codrin. We will even offer Aron and Bucur to him. They are useless now. After that disaster in Poenari, who would think that the stars would align so well for Maud and me?*

Unable to speak, the guard nodded, his jaw clenched – he had protected Verenius for more than ten years.

They were close to the crossroads where the eastern road to Mehadia split from the main one going to Leyona. Behind them, a pack of a hundred riders turned with a clatter of hooves and went east. Octavian threw a glance at Pintea.

"Don't worry, Sage," Pintea said with cold amusement, "they are not coming for you. The war is over, and they are going home."

Octavian frowned, understanding both the tone and the deliberate snub. He was an *Itinerant* Sage; but he decided that he could swallow his pride for the moment. At least he was now convinced that Codrin was sending his soldiers home, so indeed Frankis would be a boring and peaceful place until spring.

The hanged man stopped moving, and Codrin shook his head. *Sometimes, I don't enjoy ruling*, he thought. Wrapped in his inner thoughts, Codrin looked over the gate, toward the mountains. A disturbing haze clouded his vision, and he started to see double. The second image parted from the first, twisted, altered. After a while, it cleared, and the landscape changed swiftly until Mehadia came in sight. *What is happening to me?* He blinked, but continued to see into the impossible distance, known and unknown places. He passed the Rhiun River, the Cursed Forest, Muniker. Then came Baia, the region where he had spent a winter in Grand's house with Vlad and Pintea. *She was a fine woman.* "Nera's gorge," he breathed. *I don't want to see it.* He closed his eyes, to avoid the place where his brother and Tudor were killed but found that he had no control over his Vision – he could see everything, even with his eyes closed. The place came to him, and a tear ran down his face, then Nera faded away as new places came in sight: Silvania, Arenia, until he found himself looking at an unknown land. *That must be Nepro River.* The river vanished from sight, and he was now inside a strange city, seeing through a closed window, into a castle. A man stood in front of the window, staring at him. "Baraki," he whispered and unsheathed his dagger. That cursed man was once the Chief of the Royal Guard of Arenia. The traitor who had killed Codrin's family, and who was now the King of Arenia. There was no person in the whole world that Codrin hated and despised more.

"You are new to this," Baraki laughed. "There is no way to fight when the Eye of the Seer is open into the Farsight. We are not in the same place. I have been wandering across Frankis to find you." His hand went to Codrin's throat and passed through it. "How did they choose a weakling like you to become a Seer?"

"What makes you think that you are strong? Betrayal? Poisoning? Night killings?"

"The throne of Arenia makes me strong. The throne of the Khadate will make me even stronger. I was told that you were in Frankis. I will come after you."

"You will come after me? No, Baraki, you will send soldiers. You are too cowardly to come after me. You almost died once, and you had fifty soldiers with you. There were only three of us."

"I will have enough soldiers."

"Yes, if you have enough soldiers, you will come. Make sure you have enough," Codrin said, and extracted himself from the building.

Baraki stretched his mind, trying to keep Codrin inside the Vision; he had not yet found out his location. Their eyes locked, and slowly Codrin retreated, feeling as if some invisible cords were trying to keep him tied to Baraki. *He is trying to find where I am*; Codrin suddenly understood and fought against the invisible tendrils Baraki placed around him. Once he was out of Nerval, Codrin felt free and, a moment later, he was back in Severin, leaning against the window, breathing hard. A fierce headache and a wave of nausea made him shiver. He clamped his mouth shut to avoid retching and staggered drunkenly before managing to steady himself and walk on weak legs across the room until his sense of balance returned. Like an old man, he threw himself into a chair. Head in hands, he groaned, trying to understand. "I need to learn how to manage that... Power? But who can teach me?" he muttered, voice cracking.

"I can."

Codrin raised his head abruptly. The strange pain surged, gnawing at his mind, and his breath quickened, wheezing through his nostrils. His eyes blurred, and almost blind, he moaned his pain and fear. It took a while, but when his eyes cleared, he saw a woman, her white dress absorbing the light of the fading sun through the window. Shadowed, her face remained hidden. "Empress, I don't know if you need to, but if you do, please sit down," he said, struggling to gather his mind. The pain was still there.

"A woman likes to be treated courteously." She seated herself in the chair across the table, looking at him. A change in the light on her dress finally revealed her face. "Questions?"

"Is Baraki a Seer?"

"You are asking much better questions this time. Yes, he is a Seer."

"Why did you choose him?"

"Wrong question. He is the Seer of the Serpent."

"The Fracture..." Codrin said, his voice hoarse.

"Yes, it will come. Perhaps."

"What is different now from what happened when my father defeated the nomads. Baraki?"

"He may become the next Khad of the eastern nomads, but it's not only that. Twenty years ago, the Serpentists found some powerful Talant artifacts. Then they found the Sanctuary, which was built by the Talants in Nerval. Mordanek, their Great Priest, had exceptional powers and opened the Sanctuary. He made it into a temple for the Serpent. Did Dochia tell you about the Maletera?" She looked at Codrin, who shook his head. "It's a tool which can pervert one's mind, making you a slave. She was almost killed in Silvania, when Meriaduk, the High Serpentist Priest, used a Maletera, trying to enslave her. She saved Ada, the Second Light of Arenia, too. You know Ada, even when you did not know that she is a Wanderer. We were lucky that Dochia is so strong. Losing both her and Ada would have been a great loss for us. The Maletera is also a tool enabling communication at long distance. Dochia destroyed a second one on the road to Nerval, but Meriaduk has more. And there are artifacts which can kill people at a distance, through the strongest armor."

Dark magic? I thought it was only a story for children. But I thought the same about Seers. "How can we defend ourselves from such weapons?"

"That is Dochia's task. She is now in Nerval to seal the Sanctuary and the artifacts. Enough of that. How do you think that you went to Nerval?"

"That was Nerval? I thought it might be, but I was not sure. I've never been there. I suppose that Baraki used his ... Seer power to draw me there."

"He can't do that." The Empress shook her head.

"Then?"

"Then?" A trace of amusement flashed in her eyes.

Codrin closed his eyes, and his feverish mind recalled everything that had happened during the dream-like journey. "Somehow, I went there," he said, just to say something. "Was it my ability?"

"A good question. Seers have this ability through the Blue Light, to see beyond what the eye can perceive. Dochia detected it in you, a few years ago. You are not alone in having the Blue Light, a few Assassins have it too, but only the Seer has the Farsight."

"Am I a Seer?" he breathed, and she nodded. *Since when am I a Seer?* "I don't feel anything special."

"Except that you can fly from here to Nerval. Usually, it's a four-month journey; if you are lucky."

He stood up abruptly and walked around the room. "Can I go anywhere?"

"Almost, and always within a certain radius. You are untrained."

"But I went to Nerval."

"You went there only because Baraki opened a channel for you, and you fell into his trap."

"He was looking for me." Codrin stopped walking and looked at her. She nodded. "And he is able to search as far as from Nerval to here."

"He can't do that on his own, but Meriaduk has the Map. A Talant artifact that can show any point on the continent. A Seer can use that to his advantage, but control of the Farsight is more difficult. By using the Map, it's more like trying to see in the night using only moonlight. At the moment, Baraki can see things in a twenty-mile radius."

How far can I see? "Do you think that I can find Saliné?"

Marie of Tolosa was meant for you, not Saliné. Drusila will take care of that. You need the power of the duchy behind you. Sometimes, you are blind. "Farsight is a potent tool, but its power depends on how you train it. Use it for personal gain, and it will not serve you well, and anyway, I doubt that you can use Farsight at more than two thousand paces yet. That's less than you can do using normal sight, but on the other hand you can see through walls or over hills. You must train. Don't complain that you don't know. Barakis's intrusion has already opened the path for you. You know how to do it."

Before Codrin could voice his irritation, the Empress was gone, and he was looking at an empty chair. *I will use the Farsight to find Saliné. La naiba with the rules, as Dochia used to say.* He let his mind wander over Severin. Once. Twice. At the third attempt, the Farsight came to him, and he could see the land from a hundred feet above. Suddenly tired, he stopped and shook his head to overcome a burst of dizziness and pain. *Less than half a mile... My Farsight is not strong. I will try again later. Now, I must leave.* Codrin stood up and, walking slower than he would have liked because of the persistent lightheadedness, he left the room and the palace. Twenty men, their horses and Zor were already waiting for him and, in a minute, they were storming out of Severin. To his surprise, Verenius was taken out of the jail and ordered to go with them. Walking toward the gate, he saw the gallows and the man hanging there. Without knowing why, he shivered.

Since Codrin had invaded Severin a week ago, his scouts had gone from one village to another and caught two large bands of thieves, men who thought that no one was in charge, and they were free to prey on the peasants. To stop the lawlessness, he decided that all the robbers, twenty in total, would be hanged in the villages where they were caught. The one he had hanged in the plaza was an exception.

Chapter 3 – Codrin

Codrin and his men rode at a fast canter for three hours, on the western road, up to the place where a scout was waiting for them. Aron had left the road there and headed through the forest. Night found them still in the forest, and they camped when the tracks on the ground were no longer visible. No fire was lit. They set off again early in the morning when the first cherry glow of dawn was creeping over the hills. An hour later, they found Vlad and most of his scouts on the bank of a small river, its water going up to a horse's knee.

"They went into the water. I've sent scouts along both banks of the river." Vlad pointed west, downriver, which was the most probable path for Aron, then east.

"You should look for a small black ribbon in the water," Verenius said, and at Codrin's questioning look, he told them about the letter he had given Saliné, and the ribbons tied to small stones that he had planted in her saddle. He smiled sheepishly at the end of the story.

Saying nothing, Codrin went downriver, walking along the bank, occasionally stepping into the shallow water. Vlad went upstream. Sixty paces on, Codrin bent abruptly and picked out a small black ribbon from the water. "We go this way," he pointed downriver, and most of the scouts mounted and rode with him. Two of them stayed behind to wait for the team which had traveled upstream. Fifteen minutes later, they met the second squad, sent out by Vlad an hour earlier.

"We know where they left the river," the scout leader said, and they followed him along the bank to the point where the tracks showed that many horses had turned into the forest again.

Vlad sent four squads of three skilled scouts to ride parallel to the main group. It was a tactic that Codrin had copied from the Arenian army. He mixed both Arenian and Assassins ways in their training. The outriders were not slowed down by the need to follow the tracks on the ground and had more scope to search for unexpected things. At noon, one squad returned and reported riders ahead.

"There are two riders, wearing the colors of Leyona," the lead scout said, "and they are coming your way. They are not riding hard, and they will be here in less than ten minutes."

"I will hide, with Pintea and Lisandru," Codrin said. All three were dressed in dark blue and all fought with two swords, like the Assassins. "Vlad, interrogate them." He walked away, then turned. "Verenius, come with me."

"I will wait there." Vlad pointed to a place where the small road through the forest, more a path than a road, curved abruptly, and hid most of his men behind some thick bushes. He kept only five soldiers with him.

Five minutes later, they met the riders and surrounded them, before they knew what was happening. The two frightened men unsheathed their swords.

"I would not do that," Vlad said, and reluctantly the men from Leyona sheathed their swords. "You could have been dead by now. I am not fond of Leyona, and nor am I fond of the Circle's men." He pointed at their insignia. "But that's not enough reason to kill you. Who are you, and why are you here?"

"My name is Eric, and I serve the Master Sage. I am travelling."

"I am looking for Aron, one of your Sages."

"What business have you with him?"

"An unpaid debt. A large one. Did you meet him? He was headed that way." Vlad gestured at the curve from where the riders had come.

"In a manner of speaking."

Vlad frowned, but chose to remain silent, moving his horse closer to the man in front of him, and at his discreet sign, his men tightened the circle.

A second team of scouts returned, and its leader approached Vlad. "There are six graves at the edge of the forest, about five miles from here. There is a circle drawn on one of the graves."

"Who died there?" Vlad aimed his question at the Leyonan riders.

"Some men, perhaps," Eric said, and his lips drew back in a sort of bitter grin.

"Hang him," Vlad ordered, pointing at the second rider.

"Wait!" Eric cried. "An Itinerant Sage, and some guards."

"Petronius?" Vlad asked casually, and Eric nodded while his gray eyes flashed, unable to mask his surprise. "Who killed him? Aron?"

"Yes."

"Why?"

"I don't know."

Vlad sensed that the man was still hiding something and pondered how much pressure he could apply. "Were Bucur and his wife to be there too?" he asked, his eyes cold and staring, half-concealed by the droop of his eyelids, and again Eric nodded in haste. "Where are you going now?"

"Leyona, we need to report the death of Petronius."

"Where is Aron going?"

"I don't know."

"How will the Circle react if we catch Aron?"

"In a favorable way, if you deliver him and his son to us. After killing Petronius, he is now an outcast. Maud wants the girl too. She wants to protect her, and the Master Sage is a generous woman."

"My impression is that Aron does not have much money left to pay his debt. He left Severin in a hurry. Once we capture them, I will send a man to Leyona, to contact the Master Sage. I will require five thousand galbeni. And, Eric," Vlad looked straight at him, "don't play games with me." Their eyes locked, and the Circle's man nodded. "Let them go," Vlad said, after a few more questions, and his scouts pulled back.

They found the graves and the head of a small black ribbon sticking out of the freshly dug soil of one of them, almost invisible. Codrin pulled the ribbon, which was tied to a piece of wood this time, and there was a word scratched on it with the tip of a knife: Dog. There was another stick carved with the word Pirenes, at the edge of the grave, signaling that Aron was taking Saliné to the southern mountains. One of Eric's men had stepped on it by mistake and covered the ribbon completely. Codrin played the ribbon between his fingers, having the feeling that Saliné was there with him. *She thought this was important for me to know. Why Dog? Does Aron have dogs with him? There are no dog prints. Maybe dwarf Canteli dogs carried on horses?* The small dogs were famous for their sense of smell and strident barking. They were famous for their price too. *I can't attack Aron directly, Saliné would be in danger. Aron and Bucur would not hesitate to harm or to kill her, if they had to. I must surprise them during the night. The dogs might detect us.* It was logical, but he was not pleased by his logic, it contradicted his feelings, and continued to play with the ribbon. *Why was Eric here at the same time as Aron? This is just a path in the forest, not a road. And why did Aron kill Petronius? Aron is a bastard, but he is not a stupid bastard. Perhaps Maud planned something against him. Dog is Maud's top assassin. Not many people know this. Saliné used a capital D. Why Dog?*

"Verenius, what do you think of this?" He gave the ribbon to the Sage. "Man, or animal?"

He doesn't know that Eric is the chief of the Circle's assassins. Dog was the famous one, Eric worked in the shadows. "Man."

"Why were they here? Dog, and the other two." Codrin gestured back toward the path they came into the clearing on.

The only reasonable guess is that Dog tried to kill Saliné, but I can't tell Codrin that, at least not now. He needs a calm mind. "I don't know, but after this affair with Petronius, Aron is no longer the Circle's man. Neither is Bucur. That bodes well for you." He returned the ribbon to Codrin.

"And that means that Aron will not take Saliné where the Circle wanted them to be. That's both good and bad." He put the ribbon in his pocket. *I must hurry. I will think about this later.* From Eric, they knew that Aron had left the place two hours after dawn. *We are getting closer.* Codrin was now convinced that they were less than six hours behind Saliné. *Soon, I will reach her, and Aron will pay for everything. And Bucur too.*

The next day, they found another grave where Aron and his men had camped. Codrin searched for another message from Saliné. There was nothing. *Whoever did this, it delayed them,* he thought, looking at the grave. *Saliné? She has killed Aron's men before.* "Ride!" he shouted and mounted his horse.

At the end of the fourth day, they were close to Rochil, and ten miles north-east of the city was Windcross, a large crossroads where the roads going north and south met the one coming from the east. While not a large town, Rochil was a rich one – both the intersection of the roads and its natural harbor gave it a natural advantage.

Nightfall found them still among the small mountains through which Aron had led his small force. They were at the edge of the plateau, from where the path went down abruptly through the scree, and there was no way to go down in the low light — the sun was already drowned in the sea. They ate in silence and sat in silence.

Codrin searched for an isolated place on the ridge and leaned against a black stone, three feet tall, its western side still warm. He knew he was very close to Saliné, maybe less than three hours ride. *Let's see if it works.* Eyes closed, he tried to use his Farsight to search for her. It did not work, but he persisted, forcing himself to try, even when he did not fully know how to do it. After a while, his strained eyes started to feel the pain, and he decided to take a break. Freed from the effort, his mind wandered back to Severin, to their cherry tree, and good old memories came back to him. He saw a younger Saliné playing with Vio. It was his second day in Cernat's hunting house, more than four years ago, but he felt it like it was yesterday. Focused on Saliné, he smiled. After a while, there was a subtle change in what he was seeing. Caught in his thoughts, he was slow to realize it. There was now an older Saliné in front of him, dressed in her riding suit, sitting alone in an unknown room. *I am using my Farsight...* Realization came with the sudden pain in his head. He ignored it, fighting to keep the Vision, which stretched further than his previous attempts. *Seven or eight miles,* he thought and moaned; the pain was also stronger than before. A man entered the room. *Bucur.* The image blurred, and he almost lost his Farsight. Without really knowing what he was doing, he left the room, flying backward, keeping an eye on Saliné, the same way he had left Baraki a few days earlier, through the window. He moved further away. In front of him was the Albatross Inn in Rochil, a city he had visited only once. A moment later, he was back again on the ridge, and saw Vlad looking curiously at him.

"Tomorrow, we take the road and go directly to Rochil." He pressed his fists to his temples to alleviate the pain. It did not help, and blood ran down from his nose. It was dark enough that Vlad did not see it. *She is so close. Only seven miles. Tomorrow I will free her.*

"Are you sure? Our scouts did not find them, and Windcross is in front of us, perhaps ten miles from here. There are plenty of places to go from there."

Seven miles as the crow flies from here to Rochil. How many miles on the road? Ten? Twelve? "There is something that you should know. I have no idea why, but I am Fate's Seer of the Realm now, and I can see things from far away. I know it sounds strange, but trust me, and keep this to yourself; no one else must know about it. I saw Saliné and Bucur at the Albatross Inn in Rochil. I know the place; I stayed there two years ago."

Under the faint light of the dawn, they moved on the steep slope leading down from the ridge. It took them more than an hour to reach the road, when the first golden spark spread along the horizon – the path led east again – and another hour of hard ride to reach the still sleeping town. The gate was not yet open. Codrin knocked on the hard wood until a guard finally came, annoyed by the intrusion.

"What do you want? Don't you see that the gate is closed? It will open in half an hour."

"A girl was kidnapped three days ago and brought to Rochil last evening. She is in danger. Let me enter with five men." Codrin stretched out his hand and placed a galben in the man's palm.

The guard blinked and tested the coin with his fingers, without looking at it. *This is my lucky day. A galben will pay for two nights with my whore. But this man is pressed. He can pay the wine for one evening for me and my men too.* "I need another galben for my men." He got it and opened the gate.

"Vlad, you stay here with the rest of the men. Stay out of sight and watch the gate. Pintea, Lisandru and you three," Codrin gestured quickly at his men, "come with me."

They rode like a storm through the silent streets, and the few people out and walking leaned hastily back against the walls. Their horses' hooves scraped sparks from the old cobblestones, metallic noise chasing the silent morning, echoing between the walls, waking the still sleeping town.

"Keep my horse ready," Codrin said and dismounted in front of the inn. "Pintea, come with me." There was a man standing guard in front of the door, but he moved quickly away, as soon as the two men walked toward him, and let them enter. There was no one in the saloon. Codrin went to the counter and banged his fist on it. "Innkeeper!" he shouted, and a burly man came out from a room behind the counter. "A girl with auburn hair, dressed in a dark blue riding suit, was kidnapped. I have information that she is now here."

The man looked at him, pondering how much he could extract for his knowledge. A second look at Codrin changed his mind. "They left an hour ago. Go to the harbor. Look for the Sea Lion."

"Thank you," Codrin said and stormed out of the inn.

It took them fifteen minutes to reach the harbor. Already far, Sea Lion was heading toward the high sea. Codrin closed his eyes. He had no way to reach the ship, there was no other ship in the small harbor, only boats. He took out his spyglass and searched the Sea Lion: on the stern, he saw Saliné. She was alone.

"Lisandru, take my banner and plant it there." He pointed at a tall pole on the edge of the quay.

The young man halted his horse close to the pole and, while Pintea kept it in place, he stood up in the saddle, placed an arm around the pole and unfurled the banner in the moderate wind.

On the ship, Saliné was looking at the quay, knowing that whatever chance she had to escape had disappeared when the ship set sail. She saw riders coming to the quay, but they were far away, and she ignored them at first. Then she saw the banner. *Codrin.* She smiled sadly through her tears and waved.

Codrin waved at her too, but she could not see his gesture, and even with his spyglass, he could not see Saliné's tears running down her face, stolen by the breeze, small, salted drops landing in an ocean as large as her sorrow.

You came too late Codrin, but at least you tried.

Shoulders slumped, Codrin stood with the spyglass stuck to his eye. Slowly, Saliné became a point, then the ship became a point, lost in the distance. Unaware of anything around him, he watched, gripping the spyglass with one hand and the sea wall with the other.

Vlad placed a hand on Codrin's shoulders and said, "There is nothing more we can do now. We need to go."

Codrin forced himself to stand up straight and take a deep breath. Eyes closed, he saw Rochil on the map in Severin and cursed it. He had lost Saliné again. And later, when they asked around the harbor, he was not able to learn where the Sea Lion was heading. Half of the people he asked said south, the other half said north.

Chapter 4 – Io Capitan

The Mother Storm hit their ship in the evening of the same day they left Rochil, under Codrin's sad scrutiny. The wind came from south-west, danced in a frenzy, then turned north. Like a fish caught on the hook, the ship followed the wind, and for three days they traveled farther and farther from land. Even Dolgan, the tough captain of the ship, one of the only five captains given the title of Io Capitan on both the ocean and Southern Sea, prayed to Fate, his eyes fixing the compass while there were still some traces of light. In the sailors' world, the Io Capitan was the equivalent of the Wraith for the protectors or the Black Dervils for the mercenaries, and in the old Alban language, Io Capitan meant 'I the Captain'. The compass was an Alban relic, and had been his family's pride; only a few remained in existence after six hundred years. There were old maps too, but no one had gone so far west for many generations. Dolgan's father was a captain, and so were his father and his father before. Their stories were passed from father to son, and there was one which made Dolgan tremble. The story of the Misty Island, a deserted place where the water and wind were poisoned.

Keeping his hands steady on the helm, Dolgan closed his eyes. The darkness was now so deep that eyes closed or eyes open made no difference. "Farno, Matais, Paulus," he whispered backward a long list of ancestors, and continued up to the ninth one, Marin. "That was the one... That was the one who went to the Misty Island. Most of his men died, touched by some plague. Only Marin and three sailors escaped from a crew of twenty. How did they manage to escape and return? He was a tough man, an Io Capitan too."

Eyes still closed, he worked his mind to remember the Jurnos, the family journal that was buried in the cellar of his ancestral home. Each time a new generation took command of a ship, the novice captain, the Novo, was brought to the cellar by the elders, the journal was unearthed, and he was given one night to read it. The next morning, the Novo would bury it again, before going to take command of his ship. Years later, when the captain had retired and become a Veteranis, he would go again to the cellar, to write his story in the Jurnos, if he had one to share. Not all the captains experience trouble or wonder worth leaving to posterity. Eight more captains had lived and died after Marin, but only two had added a new story to the Jurnos, and they were far less important and terrifying than the dark tale of Misty Island and its dangers.

Something clicked in Dolgan's mind, and he remembered what he had read twenty years ago, when he was the Novo. The plague, and even worse the descriptions, the drawings. Even after so many years his stomach churned. Hours after being touched by the plague wind, the men started to rot alive. They could no longer eat or drink, and they withered in atrocious pain. Their hair fell out; their bodies shriveled. Rotten, their flesh fell too, revealing their bones. Within three days all were corpses. "I don't want to go there. I prefer to die by drowning, rather than by the plague." He strained his muscles and turned the wheel a notch. It was a tough decision. The storm tried to wrestle him, but Dolgan was a strong man, and the ship changed course, heading a little more to the west. Its hard timbers complained and trembled in the wind. *It may shatter*, Dolgan thought, but the ship resisted the assault of the storm, at least for now.

Chased by the gale, they continued west-north-west for two more days, and Dolgan rarely left his place on deck. The wind of the storm tore at him, biting deep, but the knowledge that if they did not make a landfall soon, they would all be dead when the ship reached the end of the ocean, the end of the world, bit even harder. The ship shivered in a sudden squall, leaning to port at a dangerous angle, pulling him away from his worries, and Dolgan held on to a spar near the wheel until the deck returned to an almost horizontal position, timbers squealing. *More turns like this, and all my worries will sink together with the ship.*

The sudden shock threw people out of their beds, and they struggled to recover in the darkness. Saliné occupied a cabin with Aron, Bucur and their Spatar. None of them had eaten since they left the Albatross Inn. Their stomachs empty, they still had the impulse to retch from time to time. In the first two days, they tried to wash the vomit from the floor, then they gave up, and the room smelled worse than a military camp latrine. Strangely, they became accustomed to the stench. Of all of them, Aron was the most affected by the rolling and pitching of the ship, and he remained in his bed, more unconscious than not. After the most recent shock, he was now lying in the middle of the room, his clothes soaked in whatever vomit was on the floor. A rat scurried in the shadows cast by the hanging oil lantern on the wall. It sniffed at him and went away. Bucur was able to grasp the foot of the bed, and was now lying along it, unable to stand. For whatever reason, Saliné and the Spatar had fared better and, grudgingly, they climbed into their beds.

When the ship recovered, Dolgan forced himself to consult the map deeply engraved in his mind. There were precious old maps in his cabin, but after so many years, he no longer needed them. It did not take him long to recall what he already knew; there was no land toward the west, and soon the ocean would fall off the end of the world. The Misty Island was not a land; it was a coffin. The worst of the worst. The sailors were accustomed to the idea of drowning; they were not accustomed to the horror of rotting alive.

There's more storm to come, Dolgan thought, *and perhaps things that no one has seen for centuries. And a lot of unknown sea. I fear the unknown, and I dream of it. Perhaps the unknown will put some land in front of us. Any land but the Misty Island. The tiniest isle with a bay to shelter us from the storm. I've set myself against the sea all my life and I've always won. I always will.*

Dolgan was hungry, and his body ached from gripping the wheel for so long, but he could trust no one else to steer the ship now. With the next lighting, he forced his eyes to check the compass and his brain to calculate an approximate direction. He failed. The cut of the cold wind stopped his mind from wandering and kept him awake. To sleep now would be more than foolish, it would be death. *You'll wake from that sleep in the deep seas, among mermaids*, he thought, stretched his arms, one by one, to ease the cramped muscles in his back, and pulled his cloak tighter around him. *They say that the mermaids are beautiful and treacherous. I would like to feel one in my arms. Are they warm, like a woman? Or cold, like a fish?* There was nothing to see through the darkness, yet in his mind he saw that the sails were trimmed, and the wheel was secured. He saw a mermaid too. He could not decide if she was warm or cold. Patiently, he settled back and prayed to Fate for his tiny island.

"Go below, Captain. I will take this watch." The Secondo was pulling himself up by the railings, his face discolored with fatigue, eyes sunken. He leaned heavily against the rails to steady himself. "I dreamt of land, sunny and calm, and a young woman making food for me, then coming to my bed. Venison and that good wine from Tolosa. I don't remember what was better, the woman or the food. All I had when I woke up were more worries and foul stench. There's a strong reek of death below decks. I'll take the watch. What's the course?"

"Wherever the wind takes us." *Go to sleep for an hour. Even for fifteen minutes, Dolgan, and you'll be fresh for another half day.*

"Where's the haven you promised us? Fate knows that there is no land from here to where the water falls off the end of the world. We'll all die."

"You are drunk with fear. Hold your tongue and go back below. Sleep." *If you can.*

"Drunk from too much water," Secondo mumbled, framed in the low light of the sea lantern that hung above his head, swaying with the pitch of the ship. He shrugged and left the captain alone.

I'm tired. I'm so tired. Dolgan closed his eyes and opened them quickly. *But I feel something. The fingers of my left hand are itching. There is something there, in front of us. Death perhaps.*

The lightning brought the world to life. It was a thick thing, like the vein of a great god.

"Land ahead. Turn to port. Turn to port!" the watcher cried.

Dolgan felt the cry more than he heard it at first. Then, in the howl of the wind, he heard the wailing scream of the lookout again. He unlocked the wheel and turned it hard to port. He exerted all the strength he could muster as the rudder crashed against the current. The whole ship shuddered. With the next flash of lightning, he saw: the coast was barely half a mile ahead, great black towers of rock pounded by the angry sea. The foaming line of surf stretched left and right, broken here and there. The wind was lifting huge swathes of spume, hurling them at the blackness, at the ship. The ship began to swing with increasing amplitude as the wind grew stronger. The storm carried the ship as if it were a toy, and all the ropes of the three masts took the strain, singing from that immense tension, and they were making headway, parallel to the rocks, when he saw the great wave thundering through the night. "Wave!" Dolgan shouted, though no one could hear him.

The sea fell on the ship and water flooded the deck, cascading away through the gaps, and he gasped for air. Another wave roared across decks, and Dolgan locked both arms through the wheel. In the cabins below, people rolled across the floors, dancing to the tune of the waves, most of them unable to feel anything. The shock brought the unconscious Aron into Saliné's bed, and his heavy body ended up half covering her. She placed her arm around his neck, trying to strangle him. She tried and tried, but in her weakness, she wouldn't have been able to strangle a rat, never mind this hulk of a man. Resigned, Saliné tried to push him from her and out of her bed. She was too weak for that too. Aron went away on his own, when the next wave turned the ship in the opposite direction. Saliné had to cling to the bed with all her feeble strength. She was lucky at least that this wave was smaller.

Water foamed along the deck and took one sailor with it, then brought back the corpse of the one who had fallen into the sea before. Eyes straining, Dolgan searched desperately for a channel to escape from the rocks. There was no steady line of sight, everything came to him in spurts, lit by sporadic flashes of lightning. There was a crack, a wild shudder as the keel scraped the sharp edges of the rocks below and he saw the oak timbers burst apart and the sea flood in. He shook his head at the darkness, and the fantasy vanished from his mind. The ship resisted but, like a wounded bull, it was fighting to escape his control. Then he saw the channel and pushed all his will into turning the wheel. "A palm's width. A palm's width is all I need. Fate, give me that. Give me that palm."

In the mouth of the channel, the sea became mad, driven by the storm, constricted by the rocks. Huge waves smashed at the jagged land, then reeled back against the ship until the waves clashed among themselves and broke into all four azimuths of the world. Driven by Dolgan's desperation, the wheel turned in time and, like a giant toy, the ship was swiftly sucked into the channel. Soon, the strait broadened and the ship slowed, but ahead the rocks seemed to grow abruptly, towering over them. The current slid by on one side, taking the ship, trying to turn it and pass it to its doom. "I won't let you win!" Dolgan cried and fought to turn the wheel, his muscles knotted against the strain. Driven by the sea, the ship fought back. The wind suddenly changed course and the sea became his ally, speeding the ship through the gap, into the bay beyond. A fresh vein of lightning revealed the almost calm sea. Dolgan howled his victory and collapsed over the wheel. *I hope that my beauty can carry us back from here.* His last thought before darkness swallowed him.

Chapter 5 – Maud

They were riding too slowly for Octavian's taste, and no one was willing to talk. The guards of the Circle were still in shock at Verenius's death. He was the second Primus Itinerant to be hanged by Codrin. Octavian did not share their grief, but he understood the need to put a mask of sorrow on his face and keep silent too. The ten soldiers from the escort Codrin had provided ignored them. With Mohor's death and the kidnapping of Saline, Vio and Jara, the Circle was not popular among his men. The Sage wished he could fly and get to Leyona as fast as possible. Pintea had a different order: delay, to give Codrin enough time to arrange his pieces on a chess board as large as Frankis.

With the death of Verenius, the position of Primus Itinerant was now his. Octavian glanced at the riders around him. *Are they doing this on purpose? I am becoming paranoid,* he almost laughed. *Why should they want to delay me? And why should they care about my need to hurry? They even don't know it.* The journey toward the border between Severin and Leyona could be accomplished by a determined rider in a day, or at most in one and a half. At this speed, it would take them three days to make it. *I did not expect Codrin to fall so easily into our trap. He may be a good soldier, but he is an inexperienced politician, or perhaps just too young. In the short term, both will work to our advantage. Given the new circumstances, Maud will be more than happy to marry her granddaughter to him. She is not interested in a mere man; she wants a King for the girl. Aron was a stubborn mule, and we had to play him with caution, but Bucur was even easier to handle than Codrin. He was not stupid either; just too dependent on Tolosa and Maud.*

Two days later, they finally arrived at the border, and from there Octavian could set his own speed. He arrived in Leyona in the evening, and his impatience was again put to test; the guards at the gate were slower than usual. With Codrin's victory in Poenari and the taking of Severin, the new Grand Seigneur of Leyona was being more cautious than usual. In front of the finely sculpted door which guarded Maud's office, Octavian breathed with relief. Two sentries stood guard, but he was a known entity, and they let him enter without questioning him.

To his surprise, he found Laure, Maud's daughter and Duchess of Tolosa, and Laurent in the office too. In that brief moment, when those inside were still half aware of his presence, he thought about the unusual closeness between Laure and Laurent. The next thing he observed was that Laurent wore the insignia of the Itinerant Sages. "My ladies," Octavian bowed slightly, "Laurent."

"Octavian, finally," Maud said and flashed a smile at him. "Tell me that you have good news."

"Yes, Maud, I have very good news," he could not help bragging. "Important news."

"Tell me." Maud overrode his caution, and that unsettled him; Laurent was still a new member of the order, and some things should have been discussed only in higher circles.

"As you know," he gestured at Laurent, "we were able to secure Aron's and Bucur's leave from Severin. They took Saliné with them. The next news is of a different and sadder nature. Codrin reacted badly to Saliné's departure and killed Verenius. Hanged him. That young man has a sick predilection for hanging our Primus Itinerants."

"One day, he will be punished for that," Maud said coldly.

From her reaction, I should not delve any deeper into this subject. "I wonder if there is news from Aron by now."

"None yet. You must be tired and hungry. We should talk again, after you have refreshed yourself."

There was no time to talk when they met again, without Laurent this time, as the guards announced Veres, the Grand Seigneur of Midia. Maud, Laure and Octavian shared a laugh and, suppressing her mirth, Maud signaled the guard to let the man enter. She raised three fingers, and the guard understood that she needed three minutes of delay.

"That pompous nothing. Snail, the Grand Seigneur of Midia. I wonder what he wants. I am sure we will have a pleasant talk. More funny than pleasant, I suppose. I still don't know if he is called Snail for his slow mind or body."

"Maybe both," Octavian offered, and they laughed again.

Entering, Veres bowed, and his eyes moved from one woman to another; he did not know any of them.

"The guard said that you wanted to talk with me," Maud said, her voice flat, her eyes still glimmering with amusement.

"Lady Master Sage, Octavian, Lady," Veres bowed again. It pained him to bow in front of a woman, even more so knowing that he needed her, but even he understood that Maud represented the power of the Circle. She nodded, inviting him to speak. "I tried to reach the Candidate King in Severin, but the roads were blocked by that vagrant from Arenia, and I thought that you might want to hear the news I bring." He stopped and glanced at Maud, who nodded again. "After the siege of Poenari, Bucur suspected Pierre, the Spatar of Tolosa, of treason, and asked me to punish him. I did so, and Pierre is now dead. Bucur promised to give Midia back to me before the end of the year."

With some effort, Maud avoided looking at her daughter. "Where did this happen?"

"I waited until the army of Tolosa went south and ambushed Pierre from a ridge. My man planted a bolt in his chest."

"Did you see him dead?"

"We had to run, but there was a bolt in his chest."

This one is not a man, Maud thought, looking at Veres. *This one is a tool, and as with any tool, he begs to be used. That is his reason for existence.* She closed her eyes, trying to remember everything about him, from the reports she had received from Aron and the other Sages. *He is stupid and violent, mostly with women. He is too weak to fight men. I think that this is exactly what we need.* "Veres," she said and set her lips in a warm smile, "you are one of the few faithful men that we can fully trust. We, meaning the Circle and the Candidate King. And I think that Fate has sent you here today, as we have a particularly important mission, and you are the perfect man for it. You are twenty years old, aren't you?" she asked, and Veres nodded, surprised and pleased at the same time; Maud's detailed knowledge about made him feel even more important. "That's the perfect age to marry."

Deflated, Veres frowned. Marriage was the last thing he wanted; he was expecting something significant, something to match his self-importance. *There is no glory to gain from this.* He tried to protest. Maud's sharp glance quieted him, his mouth closing as fast as it opened.

"There is a young lady at the court of Peyris, who is creating problems for us, both the Circle and the Candidate King. More problems for us mean more delays for you in recovering Midia. She is not without qualities, and she is the granddaughter of the former Duke Stefan. Unfortunately, she is acting against us, and we need someone to control her. I think you are a strong enough man to control her and, in time, she will add a good dowry to your possessions."

The words *Duke* and *possessions* invaded Veres's little mind, and he completely forget his previous worries about the lack of glory. "Yes, Lady Maud, I think that I will be able to serve Bucur and you well in this."

"You will leave tomorrow for Peyris. An Itinerant Sage will accompany you. You don't need to worry; he will negotiate everything for you." *You don't need to think.* "Take some rest now; we need you in good shape tomorrow."

"What do you think about Pierre?" Maud asked her daughter when the door closed behind Veres.

"We were not friends, and I did not expect his death, but it suits us. A new Spatar will be more malleable to my will."

"Pierre was right about Poenari and, sometimes, malleable people don't make good advisers."

"Or maybe he lost because he wanted to prove his own words. As it looks now, from Veres's story, Bucur and Aron thought the same."

"Who will be your new Spatar? Joffroy?"

"No, he is as stubborn as his father was, and he is the one I told you about; he is too close to Marie."

"Ah, that thing about Marie would explain your worries. And mine. Octavian?" Laure looked at the Sage.

"Bucur was wrong; there was no way to take Poenari. I am sorry, Lady Laure. We made a mistake, and we have to learn from it. What good will Pierre's death bring?" He shrugged, meeting Laure's eyes. "Probably nothing, but we will see."

Laure considered this but did not speak her thoughts. Pierre was a capable man. And a thorn. "What is this game with Peyris? I suppose that's about Cleyre."

"We have a strange situation there. Cleyre is undermining Albert, and for the moment, we want to keep him in place as the Duke of Peyris. We do not contemplate her ruling there, or at least not until we have a new King. The Duke himself is a kind of older version of Veres. He is not violent, though. At our suggestion, Albert forced her to marry an old man, who has just died, and no one knows why. She is free again. But the strangest thing is that we have tried twice to *solve* her situation." Maud used her forefinger to tap twice on the table. The faint, muffled sound strangely filled the silent room. "Twice," she repeated in a low voice. She tapped again. "The first time, we hired a team of five mercenaries, but they never reached Peyris. We still don't know what happened to them. The second time, a Triangle of Assassins protected her and dispatched a team of twenty hardened mercenaries as if they were children. Who hired the Assassins and why is still a mystery. They are expensive at worst and often money alone is not enough to buy them. Maybe the old Duke foresaw this and made plans to protect his granddaughter. If so, he was doing the right thing; Cleyre is his only descendant intelligent enough to lead the Duchy. We will never know if Stefan planned to grant the Duchy to Cleyre; Reymont moved a little too fast against him, and I hate it when poison replaces control of the situation. The Assassins left one mercenary alive to spread the word that Cleyre is under their protection, and now, no one dares to touch her. Veres is known for his violence against his lovers. Of course, he has to pay women to love him. We must find an isolated castle and keep him and his new wife there. At least until spring. She will have something else to think about than taking Albert's place. This will free our hands in the north and, later, we may help her take Peyris. She will be a wiser woman by that time and willing to cooperate with the Circle. Now we need to concentrate on Codrin. He acted like an idiot with Verenius, but he is still young. And full of anger because his girl vanished. What did he say about our proposals?" Maud asked Octavian.

"Nothing, really. He says he needs time to think about it and will answer in spring. At least that means no more wars this year. By spring, we may be able to undermine his position. Devan would be a good start. His son fought along Codrin in Poenari."

"I know about Devan." Maud closed her eyes for a few moments. "This idea that Codrin will do nothing until spring? It doesn't match what we know about him. I was expecting an attack on Orban, who is weak now; he has lost a third of his army."

"Nonetheless, that's what I learned from Codrin, Vlaicu and a captain who is one of his four young wolves. Codrin has already disbanded his army. I saw them breaking camp when we left Severin. Perhaps his losses were higher than we know, and he needs time to build another army. This frees us to act in the north. Which Itinerant Sage will go to Peyris?"

"Laurent; he played his role well in Severin and delivered Saliné to us," Maud said.

So, he is Laure's lover, Octavian thought. "The last days on the road, there was not much to do, and I thought about Poenari again. It was an isolated place that only old men still knew about. Laurent was there several times, and he did not inform us how strong the fortress actually is."

"He thought we knew that already, and he did not think we would try to take it by siege. He was expecting us to have someone inside who could open the gates for Bucur, like he opened the tunnel in Severin for Aron to leave."

Octavian pondered for a while. *I need to learn more...* "There are some restrictions on us, in Codrin's land. Sages are not welcome until spring."

Before they could continue, the guards announced Eric, the man Maud had sent on a special mission. *This is an interesting evening*, Maud thought. *Laure and Octavian will learn more now.* She glanced at Eric, and signaled him to sit at her desk, next to Octavian. *Something is wrong.* "Tell me, Eric."

"My Lady, I don't bring good news. We failed, and Dog is dead. Even worse, Aron killed Petronius and his guards."

What? Maud gripped the edge of the table. Eyes closed, she breathed deeply. Once. "Let's take your tidings one by one. Dog, first."

"As planned, we killed the sentries, and Dog went for the girl. I think that he was too confident in his abilities. The girl was awake and sounded the alarm."

"He still had time to..."

"She stuck an arrow in his face, and that delayed him. Aron's men surrounded Dog and gave him no chance. We were at least lucky that they overreacted and killed Dog instead of taking him alive. They would have tortured him to learn more and then killed him anyway."

"Who is the girl?" Laure asked.

"Saliné. I had no choice. She is a fine girl, but we need to clear the path for Marie. Aron recognized Dog, and then he killed Petronius." Maud looked at Eric this time.

"Yes, my Lady."

"He is not an idiot, but he lacks subtlety." Maud closed her eyes for a moment, rubbing her chin. "Aron will certainly not go to the place we provided for him."

"My men are following him. There was one other thing, a strange thing. We met a band of ten men, looking for him. Some large unpaid debts, they said. They were tough men, and they promised to bring him here for five thousand galbeni. Saliné and Bucur were included in the price too."

"Tough men don't come cheap, it seems. I would be willing pay that money but, as we planned with Petronius, a ship is waiting for Aron in Rochil, and who knows where it will sail? For sure not to Bardaux, as we agreed. You may go, Eric. You too, Octavian."

"Mother," Laure said, when the two women were alone, "don't you think that we are going too far, by trying to kill Saliné?"

"I don't feel particularly proud of the assassination attempt, but we are in a kind of war with Codrin. That young man is as stubborn and inexperienced in politics, as he is experienced in making war. Any other man would have accepted the proposal of marriage to Marie, become Duke of Tolosa this year and King of Frankis the next. He wants to think until spring. That's childish. Lose a kingdom because of some infatuation for a girl? Another year lost, and who knows what could happen before spring? He may not give up until Saliné is dead or married and with children. We don't have time to wait until she gets children."

"Aron probably thinks the same: force Saliné to make children with Bucur in the hope that the children will shield him from Codrin."

"I no longer care about Aron or Bucur. Drusila told me that a Fracture is coming. The nomads will invade the continent. We need a kingdom united under Codrin to have any chance against them. I wish I had known more about the Fracture and Codrin's abilities before we elected Bucur as the Candidate King, but at least the death of Petronius frees my hand. I will ask a Conclave to demote Bucur and make Codrin the Candidate King, not necessarily at the same time. Until then, the marriage must be arranged. Even with his skills, alone, it will take Codrin years to unify Frankis. With Tolosa behind him and Peyris weakened, we may have a King next year." Feeling suddenly tired, she put her elbows on the table, resting her chin on her clasped hands. "I need to write some letters."

"You want to find out where Aron is?"

"Yes, I will write to any Seigneur who has a harbor on the ocean. They must locate Aron. And Saliné." Maud paused. "If we find her, I will keep Saliné until spring. If Codrin accepts the marriage and the Duchy of Tolosa, I will release her."

"That sounds better," Laure said. "I am teasing you," she added with a faint smile, seeing Maud's frown. "We have a free hand in the north until spring. Maybe we should use Manuc while he can still do something; the Duke of Loxburg is old but strong."

"I wish I could make you a Sage, daughter, but Duchesses are not allowed in the Circle." This time, it was Maud who set a tired smile on her lips. "The Duke is an old man indeed, the only one still alive from the old generation, and his son is not... Well, his son is not Albert or Veres, but he is not much better either. Manuc will be the obstacle we raise in Codrin's path. He is capable enough and has a larger army. Technically, Codrin is stronger than before the siege, but his strategic position is weaker now. In the next war, he can't afford to hide in Poenari. He must defend his land and fight in the field, army against army. Manuc and Orban have seven times more soldiers than Codrin. That should be enough to convince him that Tolosa is his only way to gain the crown. We need to offer Manuc a bone, something he wants, perhaps a part of Peyris. Soon, Reymont will convince Albert to replace Nicolas as Spatar. Nicolas is to close too Cleyre. Sandro, the second Spatar, is weaker, and the army will find itself without a capable commander."

"And maybe we will free Cleyre after a while, to enhance the chaos. Will you send Laurent to Peyris and Loxburg?"

"No," Maud shook her head, "we need a more skilled negotiator, and there are some things we need to clarify about what he actually knows of Poenari. I stopped Octavian from asking awkward questions to protect Laurent, for now. He has a lot of potential. Though I don't like his persistence in trying to get into your bed."

"It will not happen. At least, it will not happen while Baldovin is still alive." Laure's lips twitched in a dry smile, and Maud smiled back. "There is not much love between us, and my husband is sick and less than a man now, but I will not cheat on him. Laurent has to wait as long as it takes."

Maud looked away for a while, almost dreaming, eyes half-closed, rubbing her nose thoughtfully. A thought struck her, and her eyes snapped open. "Codrin is an anomaly."

"In what sense?" Laure asked, cautiously.

"In the sense that no one expected him. He is not a center of power that grew organically, from whatever base. He appeared from nowhere and stormed Frankis. And he is not the only anomaly."

"His young wolves."

"Yes, capable men are attracted by strong leaders, but they appeared from nowhere too. I don't understand." Maud paused, and the fine lines of her face deepened with her frown.

"We know about them." Laure shrugged. "We use them. The process should have been started earlier, but anomalies are hard to predict, and even harder to control. We will find a way."

"It's not easy to handle such men. They don't have past allegiances or obligations. They are like newborns, without a history that can be used to control them."

"Codrin is a Duke's son, and he was formed like any other noble. There are patterns, and they can be used to lead him in one direction or another."

"Codrin is not a Duke; he is the legitimate King of Arenia. In the longer term, the game is larger than Frankis," Maud said, frowning even harder. "We learned that a bit too late."

Chapter 6 – Saliné

"Sebastos," Dolgan murmured, and pressed two fingers of his right hand over two on his left – the forefinger and middle. They formed a cross, the sailor's sign of gratitude to Fate at the end of a dangerous voyage. The harbor was not yet in sight but, white with snow, the hazy hints of mountain peaks behind it melted in the distance into the light blue sky. He had seen them a hundred times and more, and he knew that before noon, he would be able to drink his favorite wine in the White Ship Inn. He deserved it. And he had a story to write in the Jurnos. His elder son and the many sons who came after him would read his story, and they would remember him, as much as Marin, the Io Capitan who saw the Misty Island and survived, was remembered. *I have justified my title of Io Capitan.* A new island which was not shown even on the oldest maps, and he had discovered it. Erie, as its inhabitants named it, was a paradise of lush green. Now that the danger was only a memory, he could afford to be proud and enjoy his adventure. *Such a Mother Storm, and I lost only three men.*

He was already fretting when the ship moored in the harbor, but he had to wait patiently until everything was unloaded, including the two passengers who he, several times, considered throwing into the water, as an offering to calm the storm. Nastos, the sailors called such horrible specimens. When all was done, he bowed to the lady, which he liked, saluted the soldiers and turned his back to the nastos, ignoring them; he knew well that Aron wanted to speak with him.

Recognizing the snub, Aron cursed coarsely, but Dolgan walked away, his mind already set on the good wine at the inn. In a burst of rage, Aron stepped forward, ready to hit the captain from behind. He stopped at the last moment. It was not just that he had fewer men, though they were trained soldiers; it was also that his head was still bandaged to cover the wounds from when he rolled unconscious on the floor of the cabin. That, and the bandage on his left hand, where three fingers were missing, eaten by rats.

"Stay away from the captain, rat-shit," one of the sailors whispered under his breath. While Dolgan used the derogatory term nastos term for Aron, the sailors called him rat-shit, a reminder of where his fingers had vanished; when an animal eats, it also discharges.

Aron boiled inside, but wisely chose to pretend he hadn't heard the sailor.

It did not take long for Guiscard, the warden of Castis, to find Aron and his people. The wind was strong on the shore, and they stood huddled together, almost hidden by the remaining four horses. Three of the animals had died during the first storm, and the others had been left on Erie Island. The islanders had taken them in payment for food and repairs. They did not use money in Erie. The last four, belonging to Aron, Bucur, Saliné and the Spatar, were the best. While Aron was thinking about money, Saliné had a different attachment; her mare had been a gift from Codrin. The horses were thin and weak now, and not ready to ride, but at least they had survived. It was a less than three days sail from Rochil, and Dolgan had expected to land in Sebastos well before the autumn equinox. Instead, the ship arrived two weeks after it. Aron and his people looked miserable, the memories of the nightmare on the sea still reflected in their eyes. The emptiness of their stomachs was clear too. Just when things seemed to be turning out well again, a new storm had hit them, three days ago. It was smaller, a mermaid's breath as the crew called it, but that did not save them from seasickness. They also looked different from the locals, obviously from the north, tall and blond.

"Sir Bernier, I assume," Guiscard, the warden said and bowed briefly to Aron. He was not a tall man, but that was common enough in the south: people here were shorter, their skin had an olive tan, and their hair was black. He was not tall, perhaps, but there was a not so hidden warning in his appearance; the warden was a man few dared to cross. "I am Guiscard, your warden in Castis. My lady," he bowed to Saliné. "Castis will shine because of your presence."

"Thank you, Lord Guiscard." Saliné curtsied. "You are most kind."

"I am no lord, my lady, just a simple warden. Please follow me." With an ample gesture of his right arm, he included everyone in the invitation.

Trying to hide his tracks from the Circle, Aron had used his second name in his correspondence with the warden. While he was the Knight of Seged, the main part of his wife's dowry, which was adjacent to Seged, was called Silon. In Castis, he was now known as Bernier, Knight of Silon. It was good choice, as the people of Castis were under the protection of Silon, and they did not ask many questions. Bucur would also use his second name, Claudin, and for Saliné, Bucur had played a game, and called her Vio. The servants and soldiers in Castis were already aware of the new names, as were the soldiers who accompanied them. Aron knew that his cover would not survive for long; money could buy his men, and betray his secret, but just a year would give him enough time for more preparation, and Saliné would be pregnant by then.

"Yes, I am he," Aron said, his voice weaker than he would have liked to acknowledge. He coughed, but that brought no improvement. "We are ready... We will be ready to travel tomorrow. Find us a good inn. And we need more horses. How far is Castis from here?"

"Four days, more or less. In half a day, we arrive at the mountains and, from there, the road will not be easy. You can see them from here." He half turned and pointed at the white peaks lined up to the south. "The White Ship Inn will take you in. The innkeeper is a friend of mine."

"If it's hard going, we will need ten horses."

Sebastos was a small town, sandwiched between sea and mountains. For all his efforts, in three days, Guiscard could find only five horses, and the price made Aron pull at his hair. At least both men and horses were in good shape by then. Still, some men had to go on foot, and that delayed them even more. The road to Castis took more than a week, and it was a mid-autumn when their new fortified house came into sight, high in the mountains.

The mountain road turned again on the steep curve, but when they rounded it, a valley lay before them, and a village built alongside a narrow stream.

"That's Lower Valis, Sir," the warden said. "The village belongs to you."

"It doesn't look much." Aron cupped his hand over his brows to avoid the glare of the strong southern sun.

"There are twenty-seven houses. That's a good number for a mountain village. The next village, Upper Valis, is larger, it has thirty-five houses."

"You know my lands well."

"Well, sir, it's not so hard to count up to thirty-five." The warden smiled thinly. *And with only two villages...* He kept that thought to himself.

"Do they have a church?"

"There is one in Upper. Usually, we call the villages Upper and Lower. It's easier."

"Is it consecrated to Fate?"

"We all worship Fate north of the mountains, Sir. Only the savages in the south are pagans."

"What do they worship there?"

"Who really knows, Sir? Goats, maybe," the warden said, and Aron laughed, pushing his horse on faster.

There was a crossroads between the villages, and as they reached it Saliné urged her horse on until she caught up with Guiscard, some twenty paces away from all the others in the group. On their long trip, he had been friendly, and even brought her berries, making Bucur frown. "Where does this road lead?" she asked, pointing at the one in front of them – they were turning right for Castis.

"Laurden, my lady. On the maps it looks close, but it takes almost three days to get there, the road is sinuous and not easy. Two days more and you are in Tolosa. The road to the Duchy is longer, but also easier. If you are willing to learn more, I will tell you later." He kept his word, and by the time she retired to her room, Saliné knew a good deal more about the area. She did not just ask about the road between Castis and Laurden. With his rich warm voice, Guiscard was a good storyteller, and the mountains carried many interesting stories.

They found the church in the middle of the second village, and the few extra houses did not make Aron feel better. Unconsciously, he touched the purse at his waist. Guiscard went to the small house next to the church and came out with the priest: an old man, in his early seventies, his white hair an unruly mane.

"Sir Bernier." The priest bowed briefly. "We are pleased and honored to again have a Knight on the land. My lady." His voice was warmer when he addressed Saliné.

"We will have a wedding tomorrow." Aron gestured at Bucur and Saliné. "My son and Lady Vio. Come at noon. Are there any women to make some food and serve it to my people?"

The priest turned and counted all the soldiers behind Aron, then observed the two soon to be married. "A fine wedding it should be, with such a handsome couple." The priest smiled warmly at Saliné, who responded mechanically. *She is not thrilled by the wedding, and she seems to be a fine lady. Delicate and strong at the same time.* The priest was an old man, and through his long life had dealt with all sorts of people, troubled ones included. His keen eyes scrutinized Bucur next. *An arrogant young man, even more so than his father. And cold, the kind of killer who takes lives between two mouthfuls of wine. Guiscard may be right that she has been kidnapped, but I don't know how we can help her.* On the road, it had not escaped the warden's notice that Saliné was closely watched during the night, by two guards. *I may learn more tomorrow, during her confession.* "I think that we can arrange something, but mountain people are not rich, Sir. I am afraid that the meal will be less than you are accustomed to."

"We will make do." Aron opened his purse and gave three galbeni to the priest, who looked suddenly uncomfortable.

"I apologize, Sir, but there is not much need for gold here. These are poor people. Do you have the equivalent in silver?"

I wonder how poor they really are, and how much revenue they will bring me in one year, Aron mused, and searched his pockets for silver. "We will see you tomorrow, then."

The night was closing upon them when they finally arrived in Castis. Before she rode through the gate of her new prison, Saliné had a last look at the snowy peaks, still glittering like amber in the sunshine. Down here, it was almost dark, but up there, she could see the shining remains of the sunny day, and a sad smile settled on her face. That did not escape Guiscard, either.

After a dinner in which the venison felt like ashes in her mouth, Saliné found a reason to leave early. Entering her room, she found Gria arranging Bucur's clothes in the wardrobe of the second, smaller room. *These are not my rooms; these are* our *rooms. Bucur lied to me again. Does he feel pleasure in small things like this? Small man, small pleasures. He will not wait for the wedding;* she shook her head, *so I must be ready today. A bit earlier than I had planned.*

"Where are my things?" Saliné asked.

"I serve Bucur and Aron," Gria said, a malicious smile on her lips.

"You serve the house, and from now on, I am the lady of this house. Men have their own world. You belong to the women's world. Mine. If you think that Bucur or Aron will take your part, think again. After a happy night, men are easy to lead, and I will lead Bucur as I please. A child will come too. A week or a month will be enough time to make my husband listen to me. I will not throw you out of Castis straightaway. I will throw you out in midwinter. You are not a stupid woman; think on it. I want my things here, and I want a plate with venison for two people and a loaf of bread. I doubt that I will sleep much this night, and after midnight I get hungry. The last thing I will want to do is walk to the kitchen. After that, you will prepare my bath. I am sure you know why I need it."

After her bath, for a while, Saliné looked at the half moon through the window, thoughts and memories tumbling in her mind. Some of them were pleasant. Some were not. The unpleasant ones were stronger, and her mood was sour. Bucur entered without knocking, but she sensed him sneaking in, and turned to face him. His visit did not come as a surprise; Saliné already knew that he would not wait for the wedding to claim her body. *He drugged and raped me once. This time...* She let nothing show on her face when their eyes met. Her feelings were the only things that still belonged to her.

Bucur's eyes wandered around the room, and he saw the food on the table. "Are you expecting guests?" His face twisting into a wicked smile.

"I thought that we might need to eat." *That food is for me, Bucur. I doubt that you will be able to eat after...*

"We ate just three hours ago, and I am not hungry for food. I am hungry for you, now. Later, you may be right. My dear Saliné, tomorrow the priest will finally perform our marriage ceremony, but I already consider you my wife. In fact, I have considered you so for a long time now. You know that." His face formed a smile; his blue eyes did not. She smiled coldly too. Keeping his eyes on her, he came closer and fumbled with the ties of her bathrobe. Still smiling, he pulled it away, exposing her soft skin, and leaned down, kissing the top of her shoulder. Saliné closed her eyes as Bucur slid the bathrobe off her body. It landed at her feet, leaving her clad only in her shift, as he wrapped his arms around her, pulling her closer.

Feeling nothing for the man in front of her and unable to reject him, Saliné decided to close her mind, and let nature follow its course. She kept her eyes closed too, her head back against the wall, as his mouth touched the tender skin of her neck. It wasn't long before his hands moved to her lower back, feeling its roundness through the silk, until they slid further down and raised her shift, gripping her naked bottom. Bucur leaned back, keeping his eyes on hers, and after several moments of pause pulled her shift farther up, revealing her belly, then her breasts, then her shoulders.

"You are such a wonderful woman, Saliné." He studied her beauty, up and down, with a deliberate slow rudeness, in the low glow of the candles, light and shadow playing on her skin. She was naked and, snapped out of her trance for a few moments, she felt naked. As if guessing what was in her mind, Bucur undressed. His smile, Saliné thought, was an altogether evil smirk. It passed out through his eyes, drinking in her body. Her curves pleased him. His lecherous stare made her nauseous.

Keeping his eyes on her, Bucur touched her face with a finger, played with her lips, parting them and went down, trailing along her neck, to find her breast. His mouth went to her other breast, and she closed her palms into fists, nails pressing into her skin. Feelings were not involved in their interactions, and they both knew it.

Eye closed, Saliné leaned against the wall, and let her mind fly faraway to Severin, imagining that she was in the arms of the man she loved, and she abandoned herself to the pleasant tension in her body. When he thought her fully subdued, Bucur lifted her and walked toward the bed. *You did not want me. I saw it in your eyes, but now...Your breasts are swollen and hard and you are wet as a cheap whore, from my touch. Yes, my dear, I will make you feel like you never did before, until you will want me day and night in your bed. Then my punishment will strike you.*

Before she realized, Saliné was on her back in bed, staring up at him. Laying beside her, he continued to play every trick he knew on her body. And he knew many. When he could no longer restrain himself, Bucur abandoned his play and moved to part her knees.

"Give me a moment," Saliné said and moved away from him, until she could reach the wall with her right hand.

Bucur frowned, as his fingers already sensed her ready, but he said nothing and restarted his game. *You want to play me,* he thought. *I know this game better than you.*

"Come," Saliné whispered after a while. "I am ready now." *It will end soon...*

He rolled over her, his hands tense against the bed, and finding his position, he thrust forward. Both moaned in a twin voice.

Chapter 7 – Saliné

After a night of bad dreams involving money slipping between his fingers and Maud's hard stare, Aron woke up early and went to the kitchen. He disliked eating there, among the servants cooking and eating too, but there was no other choice. Built on a side of the house, with a separate entry from the large square terrace, the kitchen was at least spacious enough for three tables. There was a second terrace, on the first floor, above the lower one. The double terrace was the only feature that relieved the architecture of the house, which looked like an ugly cube. There were three doors on the lower terrace, going into the main part of the house, down into the cellar and into the kitchen. *Maybe I should enclose the lower terrace*, Aron thought. In the kitchen, he found Gria and one more servant of the four he had sent to Castis just two weeks before Codrin started the siege of Severin. Their faces revived memories he wanted to forget. Everything was going as planned, then everything crashed, and he hated Codrin in a way he had never hated anyone before. And Aron was accustomed to hate. It was a way of living for him, a way to escape the thought that he should have been the Duke of Peyris, not that weakling Albert. *One day, I will make Codrin pay. The day he will no longer expect it. It may take years, but I am a patient man. I've waited fifteen years to take Severin from that weakling, Mohor.* He shook his head and sat at the main table. The hard wood of the table was scratched from years of clattering plates and looked older than the house itself. It had been stained by drink and oil. The surface had also been carved into in several places, by some bored soldiers who defended Castis over the years. One was phallic in nature. Some things were just universal. The other two tables were in even worse shape. The view did nothing to improve Aron's mood.

Gria knew well that morose look in his eyes, put the food of the table and tried to vanish.

"What's this?" Aron asked. "Yesterday evening we ate the same thing."

"There is also milk." She proffered a jug made of brown clay. "We have some stored food, Sir, but the variety is not great. The warden said that food is scarce in the mountains."

"Send him here." Absently, Aron started to eat the venison, which was warm, but still had the taste of re-cooked food.

"Yes, sir," Guiscard said and sat at the table before Aron could give him permission.

Impertinent man, but I still need him. "Gria told me about some issues related to the ... variety of food." He gestured at everything on the table.

"I am afraid, Sir, that our main issue is quantity, not variety."

"You received enough money."

"Enough is a relative term, Sir. In your letters you did not mention coming with nine more soldiers. Food is scarce here. There are now seventeen soldiers, five servants, your faithful warden, and three members of your family."

"How long do we have provisions for?"

"Three months at best, and winters are long here. Hunting may add another month; there are plenty of deer, and we have a few more weeks to hunt. If we are lucky, we may find a bear. Snow and storms come early in the mountains. In fact, one of them is brewing now. A big one. We call them Mother Storms."

The name of the storm made Aron grimace, and he involuntarily looked at the bandage where his fingers were missing. *Curse that storm and Dolgan.* "The sky looks almost clear." He glanced through the window, but all he could see was the decrepit wall of the precinct – built only ten feet from the kitchen, it obscured everything. He remembered the view from the two places where he was accustomed to eat, the valley in Severin, or the small mountains of Seged. That did not enhance his appetite.

"The winds are strong, here; now it is sunny, but in an hour, rain will come from the ocean, then it will be sunny again. In the afternoon, it will snow hard and the wind will uproot old trees. On a day like this, we stay home in front of the fire and drink wine." *If we have it.*

"How long have you been here?"

"Since I was born, Sir. My father was the warden before me. Three years ago, he was killed by robbers, when they attacked the villages."

"Does that happen often?" Aron asked, ignoring the pain in the man's voice.

"From time to time, savages from the south cross the mountains."

There was nothing else to ask, and Aron finished his meal in silence. "Let's go and look around the area. I want to see the gate first."

The gate was a massive wooden thing. There was nothing on it to prove the rank of the owner of Castis, but it was sturdy. And partially rotten. Aron used his dagger to test the wood. In places, it entered a palm's width into the beams. He kicked at the gate nervously and tried to close it. He couldn't. "I asked you to carry out renovations."

"You asked me to renovate the house, Sir. And anyway, there was not enough time to repair the walls, the barn and the gate. Nor was there enough money. If the need arises, we can bar the gate with planks."

"How long will it take to rebuild everything?"

"We have good carpenters in the village, and they will be happy to work here, but they are few. In one month, we can repair the gate. There are no masons. We need to bring them from Laurden. That means spring; they will not come here at the end of autumn."

"What is Laurden?"

"A Seigneury. Castis pays allegiance to S'Laurden."

I know nothing about Laurden. Aron shook his head and went out through the gate to survey the wall. To his surprise, he found a stable being built outside the wall. "What idiot built the barn outside the wall?"

"One without sufficient money, Sir. There is a smaller stable inside. It can keep three horses, and you have four of good quality, but the inner courtyard is rather small. When there is no danger, I suggest you keep all the horses here."

You are suggesting too much. You must learn your place. "How long will take to raise a wooden palisade around the barn?"

"A year with the carpenters we have, but we can bring more from Laurden. That will cost. The revenues from the villages will not cover it; they will not even feed all the people you have now. Your revenues will pay for food for half a year," the warden added before Aron could ask. "And hunting may provide food for another two or three months."

Aron glared at the warden but said nothing and returned to the precinct. On the terrace, he met two of his soldiers and the Spatar. "Go and wake up the lovers and bring them to the council room; there are decisions to be made. And they need to be awake for their wedding," he said to general laughter. *I don't think I can afford a Spatar anymore, but I will clarify that in spring. Here, money seems to vanish fast and appear slowly.*

"I heard her cries and moans all night," the Spatar said, when the laughter subsided.

"Claudin knows how to please a woman." *It's what Bucur knows best. It seems so strange to call him Claudin...* "You will come to the council room too," Aron said to the warden and walked away at a brisk pace.

The soldier went upstairs and knocked at the door. Then he knocked again. "Sir Bucur. I mean Sir Claudin. Lady Sali... Lady Vio. Sir Bernier is waiting for you in the council room. Sir Claudin." This time he used his fist to bang on the hard wood. *They are sleeping heavily. It's not easy to please such a beautiful wife. Lady Saliné has a well-trained body.* He grinned, imagining himself in her bed. *Well-trained women need well-trained men.* "Sir Bucur. Open the door." He was worried now, too worried for false names. He tried the handle but found that the door was locked. *I would have done the same.*

"Why are you shouting?" Gria asked behind him.

"They are requested downstairs."

"They are busy, I suppose. Most people are in such situations." She took a key from the link at her waist and unlocked the door. "Come," Gria said, her voice mischievous. *Let him see the bitch naked. She thought to put me in my place. We'll see.*

Lying on his back, Bucur was alone in the large bed. *Where is the bitch?* Gria wondered. *Perhaps in the second room, trying to dress.* "Wake up, Bucur," she ordered and went to the other room, which was more a large wardrobe than a room.

"Sir," the soldier said in a low voice. "Sir, you are needed downstairs." He shook Bucur's shoulder. "What's this?" He frowned and shook him again, harder. Something felt wrong, and he pulled the blanket away. Eyes wide, he looked at the knife in Bucur's chest. "What will I tell Aron?" His voice became a faint whisper. *He died making love. That would be a pleasant death.* Bucur's had died instantly; Saliné had pierced his heart at his first thrust, and his blood stayed more or less where it was – the bed bore hardly a stain. He also wondered why she had left such a strange and expensive knife stuck in Bucur. When they still lived in the hunting house in Severin, both Vio and Saliné had received a set of five Assassins throwing knives from Codrin. They were unusual, almost a palm long and a thumb's width broad, with no covering on the handle. Thin blades, shaped with two quillons and a thumb raise, perfectly balanced. Aron knew where she had got the knife, and Saliné left it stuck in Bucur's heart as a message for him.

"What are you waiting for?" Gria asked. "Vio must be downstairs already." Then she saw. "The bitch killed him." Swiftly, she covered her mouth. *She could have killed me too.*

The soldier went to the slightly open window and saw the sheets, tied to a piece of wood, taken from the unused fireplace, which was longer than the window was wide. "She went out through the window."

Aron and his men were already gathered in the council room, waiting for Saliné and Bucur, when the soldier came inside like a storm. "Sir," he said and moistened his lips.

"I told you to bring those idiot lovers here," Aron snapped. "I don't like to wait. She can come naked if she can't dress in five minutes. It will make the meeting more enjoyable."

"Enjoyable indeed, but it will be not easy to make decisions staring at her breasts," the Spatar said, and both he and Aron guffawed, while Guiscard forced himself to smile.

Go, go, Aron gestured at the soldier with his left hand, his mouth still full of laughter.

"Sir," the soldiers said again and stopped, struggling to continue. "Claudin is dead," he said, finally.

Aron froze, his mouth open wide, like he had been caught in the act of laughing at a weird joke. Eyes fixed on the soldier, he forced his jaw closed, before saying, "What? How?"

"He was stabbed."

"And the bitch?"

"She is gone, Sir. She climbed down from the window, using a set of bed sheets."

"Sound the alarm," Aron growled and stood up abruptly, throwing his chair against the wall. It fell into pieces. "You come with me," he gestured at both Spatar and the warden. "We start the hunt now. Tell Gria to prepare my son for burial."

When they arrived at the gate, Aron turned toward the Spatar. "Who was on watch last night?"

"Csaba, Sir. I will go to find him."

News about Bucur's death spread, and the soldiers hurried to gather at the gate, like a flock of headless geese.

"Where is Csaba?" Aron asked when the Spatar finally returned.

"We couldn't find him." *Did he run away with Saline? I will have problems. I already have.*

"And all morning, none of you thought to ask where he was?" *I have to leave this, for now, but I will hang the one who was on watch after Csaba. The warden said that I have too many mouths to feed.*

They lack discipline, Guiscard thought. *I doubt that Bernier will survive long here. And now I am sure that Vio was kidnapped. I hope she escapes. She is a fine lady. But,* he shook his head, and glanced furtively at the sky, *the Mother Storm is coming.*

When they led out the horses, the soldiers found Csaba in the stable, under a pile of straw. The warden pressed his fingers to the dead man's skin. He was already cold and almost stiff. *She seems to be a good fighter and must be far away by now. But not far enough...*

When all his men were mounted, Aron looked at them before speaking, his eyes on fire. "I want her alive and unharmed. The first night, she will be mine, and then she will be your servant and your whore. She will belong to all of you." He kicked the horse angrily, keeping the halter tight, making him turn abruptly. "Find her! Grab her! Spread her legs!" Aron growled, and his men cheered.

On the road down, they met the priest and two women coming to Castis, carrying provisions in a small cart, pulled by a mule that looked old and bored. The warden nodded at Aron, who nodded back, and dismounted to talk to the priest. Guiscard took him away from the two women.

"As things now stand, we will have a funeral, not a wedding," Guiscard said.

"Did they kill the girl?" the priest asked, his voice filled with sadness.

"It was the other way around. The girl killed the groom and vanished."

"So, you were right about lady Vio being kidnapped. Try to help her." The priest looked at the sky, and worry surfaced on his old face. "She has chosen a bad day to escape."

"She is new here and doesn't know the mountains. She did not have too many options. I will delay them as much as I can, but I can do nothing about the Mother Storm. She looked like a clever girl to me and may have a chance. I think that she left before midnight. It's not easy to walk during the night, but we had almost full moon, and the sky was clear. Go and prepare the funeral." Glancing again at the sky, the warden mounted and pushed his horse to a gallop.

When they arrived at a small gorge, Guiscard pushed his horse to the fore and turned, making the column stop. "The road in front may be dangerous for us. From what you told me, Lady Vio has a bow, and she is good with it."

"What do you want us to do?" Aron snapped. "To go back, as if nothing happened? And she is no lady. She is a whore."

"No, Sir. There is a parallel road, and we will not lose much time." *That's all I can do for you, Vio. It will take twenty minutes more to reach the other road.*

Saliné decided to let her mare rest and graze on the small meadow beside the stream. Contrary to her expectations, the road went abruptly up into the mountains for many miles, and that tired the horse. She was expecting to go north and down, toward Laurden. Instead, she went south and up, and Guiscard had warned her about the savages living there. Between the high peaks, the view was majestic, but she had no eyes for beauty. Looking at the grazing horse, Saliné felt famished too; she had eaten nothing since the last evening. She opened her backpack and took out a piece of cold meat and bread. *As I told you, Bucur, the food on the table was not meant for you.* She started to eat, her mind wandering back to the last night, and she felt again her knife enter Bucur's chest, at the same moment he had entered her. *It was so easy...*There was only a single moment of panic, when he had laid her on the bed, and she could not reach the knife hidden in the compressed space between the mattress and the wall. Her mind came back to the present, and feeling an itch, she rubbed her neck. She found dry blood. *Bucur's. I was not hurt. He died instantly. He will not pester me again. I need to look forward.* She shook her head, yet her mind went back again. To the day before when they had arrived at the crossroad from where they turned right.

Why was Guiscard so eager to teach me about the road and the area? Did he guess that I was a prisoner? She glanced at her mare and decided to give her more time to rest. *I am just as tired. She will warn me if danger comes.* Saliné did not fear Aron, not yet, but there were wolves and bears in the mountains and maybe savage robbers; she had certainly seen animal footprints on the narrow road. Eyes closed, she lay on the grass, between two bulky roots of an old pine, bared over the years by the strong winds; her pelerine was thick enough to shelter her from the cold ground, and Saliné fell instantly asleep. When she woke up, her first instinct was to look for the sun. It was partially cloudy now, but the sun had not moved far, it was still early in the afternoon. *I don't think that I slept more than an hour.* She was still tired after a night without sleep, and restless walk through the darkness. There was anxiety gnawing at her too, something that she tried to ignore. Stretching, Saliné became aware of a strange quiet – or perhaps a sense of disquiet – in the tall rocks, covered with lush vegetation, on both sides of the valley. The cicadas had stopped singing their almost metallic tune. The birds were silent too. Hairs rose on her neck. She tensed but showed no physical reaction. She casually shifted her stance, carefully placing her hand on the pommel of her dagger. *I am worrying over nothing.* She shook her head yet, unconsciously, she felt the static tension in the air. The calm before the storm. *There is nothing there.*

Slowly, she mounted her mare, and let her dictate the pace. Half an hour later, the road finally turned north and slightly downhill, and she breathed a sigh of relief. "Let's go faster," she said and pushed the mare to a moderate canter. The road wound down like a giant snake and, after a long curve, she found herself face to face with Aron and his men, less than a hundred paces separating them. For a few moments, everybody was stunned, and they stared at each other with unconcealed animosity. Except for the warden, who looked amused. There was a three hundred feet deep precipice, between them.

"Gallop!" Aron shouted, his voice salivating from the feeling of catching her soon, and his men followed him at once.

The warden captured Saliné's attention and pointed at the sky. She looked up and saw the few clouds flying at high speed. *Is he warning me about a storm?* She bowed slightly to thank him and started to ride again. He did the same, knowing that in twenty minutes the riders will stop, their horses exhausted from the gallop up on the steep slope, a common mistake for any newcomer. There was a three-hour ride between them and Saliné, around the precipice, and she was safe from Aron. Guiscard could not say the same about the impending storm.

I hope that she understood my warning about the storm and finds shelter, he thought. *There is only one safe place; the Blue Cave, but it's not easy to see it from the road. It's large enough to shelter the horse too, and the Mother Storms pass as fast as they come. Tomorrow, we will have a clear sky. Maybe she will be lucky; she seems determined and well organized.*

Lulled by the rhythmic beat of hooves on the rocky ground, Saliné let her senses wander. The sigh of autumn leaves falling.

The sound as they rustled from here to there in the gentle breeze. The distant cry of an eagle. The overwhelming scent of resin. All different and similar to a string of memories that felt distant too. Her own heart beat strong and alert, ready to burst into action should danger approach. *Is a storm really coming?* Everything looked so peaceful around her, and the feeling of freedom lifted her mood. In an hour, she forgot about the storm. The hailstones assaulted her from nowhere, making her lean forward to protect her eyes. The sun vanished, and the darkest clouds she had ever seen gathered, covering the top of the mountains. She was on a plateau, open to the wind. Half a mile in front of her, the road wound toward the forest. *I need to get there*, she thought, *the trees will offer some protection.* Rain came before she could finish her thought, or start to ride and, in a few minutes, darkness fell over the meadow; it was like late evening. It was cold too.

Close to the edge of the plateau, where the forest filled the gentle slope, the rain had turned to snow. Her view restricted by the hood, Saliné failed to notice until a gust of wind pelted icicles into her face. She was foreign to those mountains, and she was foreign to mountains in general. The small rocky hills around Midia or Severin could not really be counted as mountains. Here, everything was different, grandiose, savage, and the large mountain chain topped by the dark clouds was breathtaking even through the low light. She was breathing hard, but not because of the view, which she ignored. The day before she had eyes for the mountains; now she needed to survive. The snow was a hand deep already, and the road here was so potholed that she had to walk down the slope with her mare at halter. She whipped off the hood, to shake out her long hair from the ice clinging to it, then pulled the hood back. The breeze, crackling with frost, smelled so different to any place she had been before – rusty and salty. Even a foreigner could now see that a Mother Storm was brewing up here, between the mountains and the ocean. It was coming her way. It was already here.

She peered up, shielding her eyes against the dense snow: the mountains were gone, and she could not see more than a hundred feet in front of her. Saliné shivered, both from the lack of perspective and from the cold. It was suddenly so cold, and she could not understand neither the cold nor the storm. In winter, usually, the cold comes after the storm when the sky cleared. More crystalline icicles formed and clung to her hair and her clothes as she trudged through the snowy vastness. The snow seemed to petrify the surrounding forest and leave behind an inert silence that haunted her. There was no easy path to follow through the snow, and it had been like this for the most part of the last hour. She only knew that she had to go down, through the forest. At least she could still see the trees flanking the path through the icy whirlpools of snow surrounding her. Without the trees, there were no markers, and she would have to stop or risk falling over a precipice. A sudden gust of wind picked up, howling through the forest. The air crackled. Snow sizzled, and blew into Saliné's face, blinding her.

As she trudged through the snow, the night's events came back to her. It seemed so far away. She felt no joy from killing Bucur; she felt joy from feeling free. Free, for the first time in years. *Free to die.* Saliné shook her head. The wind picked up with her last thought. *It's getting worse.* Determined, she walked further, snow crunching under her boots. Soon, even that sound vanished, as she ploughed through knee-deep snow. Her only company was the howling wind. That, and the howling wolves. *They are still far away,* Saliné encouraged herself. The cold, the wind and an abrupt sense of loneliness cut through her, but she felt more and more numb. She was tired. She wanted to sleep. Her steps became less frequent, then they became erratic. Bent against the wind, she hit a tree with her shoulder, but she hardly felt the shock. Exhausted, she leaned against the thick trunk. *I am tired. I need to sleep.* Slowly, she slid down, her back scratching the rough bark of the pine tree.

For a few moments, a figure came to her, an unknown man, smiling at her, his eyes and hair black. The colors were crisp and pleasant. The smile was pleasant too. *I was not dreaming. That was a Vision. It's only the second time I've had one, if I don't count the dream when Father warned me about Dog. Mother told me that my Light is stronger than hers. Vio's Light is much stronger, perhaps even stronger than Dochia's. Mother was afraid that the Wanderers would try to kidnap Vio. Why did this Vision come to me now? It's pointless. I will die here.* She was now seated in the snow, her legs half covered by it, her head leaning back against the tree. The mare touched her gently and snorted. The cold moved further inside her. Drained and hopeless, Saliné was falling asleep.

Chapter 8 – Saliné

Saliné opened her eyes, slowly. It hurt. She moaned and forced herself to look around. Blurry at first, the world around her began to have contours, then colors. The pain continued, but the place she found herself in was warm and pleasant. *I've died.* There was no other way to explain the warmth after the long agony in the frozen forest. She blinked through the pain. *The afterlife probably doesn't look like this.* The room looked real, a place inhabited by humans, not by spirits; flames were dancing in the fireplace, logs were singing in the fire, and the pleasant scent of resin filled her nostrils. *This is not heaven; this is a real room. Maybe I am still alive. But how did I get here?* She forced herself to think, to remember, but nothing came to her. *I am here, however it happened.* Involuntarily, she shook her head, and pain overwhelmed her. Her view darkened, and she panicked, feeling like the room was moving away from her. She wanted that room desperately; it was the only thing that proved she was still alive. That and a vague feeling, somewhere between a memory and a presentiment.

It was hard to keep her eyes open and harder to move. Pain forced her to give up the attempt to stand, and she was content to observe the things around her. The room was unfamiliar but rich in furniture and paintings, and that alleviated her fear that she was back in Castis. *How did I get here?* She recalled some faint memories of a man, or two men, lifting her from the snow and tying her to a horse, like a useless bag. *Was it a dream? But I am here... What happened to my mare? I hope she survived too. Codrin gave her to me. She is the only thing I still have from him. Her and my flying knives... I have one flying knife less. And one enemy less.*

The door opened with a faint noise, and she tried again to move, pain and fear fighting for control over her weak body and mind. Unable to stand and defend herself, Saliné pretended to be still asleep. Surprise might help if things went bad. Closing her eyes eased the pain too.

"I never saw a more beautiful woman," Eduin said, absorbed by Saliné's fair face and auburn hair; its unruly fall around her head make her even more attractive.

"You are not yet married, and a mistress can help during the cold winter nights. I'm not saying you have to," his father laughed, seeing the frown on his face, "but consider it; I may be tempted too."

"Father, she is so young, nineteen, perhaps not even that."

"Young and fresh. I did not say you should force her; that would be an unacceptable breach of hospitality, and seduction is always more interesting. The negotiations for your marriage will end in spring, and the wedding will be in autumn. Laure is pressing us. I agree, her niece and your future bride is less ... agreeable than this girl, but her dowry is very agreeable, and it will enlarge our lands considerably. There is still plenty of time for you to learn more about women. I don't remember you complaining about your previous two mistresses."

My future bride is much less than agreeable, and it's not just her looks. That woman is a shrew. "This girl is different." Still frowning, the young man measured Saliné again. *She is not fat, but she is heavy, and I think that I felt some muscles,* he remembered the moment lifting her from the snow. *Trained for fighting?*

"What's so different about her, except that she is strangely beautiful? I see a head with auburn hair, and that tells us that she is from the north. We need to know how she came to be here. She has a charming mouth. I can imagine pleasant breasts under that dress, and long legs under the blanket. Where the women you had before so different?"

"I can't tell you why, but she is different, and she is dressed in a fine riding costume. She is clearly not a commoner. I am glad that I went to Siecle and found her."

"You disobeyed my orders." The voice of Foy, the Seigneur of Laurden, became cold, even angry.

"What kind of Seigneur would the people think I was, if I hid like a coward behind my men? Savages from the south attacked Siecle. I had to go there. You did the same at my age."

"Perhaps. So, you think she is different because she wears an expensive riding suit."

"That tells us things about her status, nothing about the woman."

"Then why is she special? And don't tell me that story about a strange feeling telling you to go there and find her. Men don't have the Light."

"I don't know, Father. Whatever you think about the Light..."

Before Eduin could finish, there was a knock at the door, and a servant entered with a letter. "A courier from Lady Maud," he said, and Saliné twitched involuntarily. The movement would have betrayed her, but both men had turned away, toward the servant, and ignored her. Pain had not, and she suppressed a moan, biting her lip.

"You may go," Foy said to the servant, taking the letter. "My dear aunt Maud. I've never received a pleasant letter from her. Her writing is so much like Maud herself, cold, biting, and nasty. Intelligent, though. Hmm," he said thoughtfully. "It seems that the Candidate King and Queen have vanished somewhere south of Frankis, and no one knows where they are."

"I forget their names."

"Bucur and Saliné. They are important names. Try to remember them. I know nothing about the girl, but I heard in Tolosa, from Pierre, that the man is a scoundrel. Maud wants us to search for them and... This is interesting. She wants the girl."

"Why should we give her the girl?" Eduin's mind was still set on the beautiful stranger he had saved from the deadly storm.

"Because dear Maud is the Master Sage of the Circle, son. And dear Laure, her daughter and my second cousin, is the Duchess of Tolosa, our big northern neighbor. She acts like a Duke, as Baldovin is so weak. It's not his fault, he is ill most of the time. Pierre, the Spatar, is the only real man there, but there is not much love between him and the Duchess. He opposed that military misadventure in Poenari, but she ordered him to go anyway. It ended badly, and I bet that Laure is biting her nails right now. That's a pity, she has such nice fingers."

"Joffroy told me that his father was wounded on their way back from Poenari. He suspected the Circle."

"No way, Maud is too intelligent for such a blunder. If she wants someone dead, then he is dead. That's why you can't refuse her. But I need to know why she wants the girl. Sometimes it helps that we are so far from the main centers of power, sometimes it's a disadvantage. If we find the Candidate Queen, I may be able to negotiate some further advantages, like the dowry for your bride. What name did your damsel in distress use in her delirium?"

"Vio. Did you think she is...?"

"You think she is special, and she may be, but a Candidate Queen doesn't ride alone into an uninhabited area, and into a storm. Did she say any other names?"

"Mother and Corrin, or something like that. Probably her brother."

"Or her husband, or her lover. Let's go, I think that you have ogled her enough. Maybe she will wake up tomorrow."

"I will ask the servants to leave her something to eat. In case she wakes up during the night."

"That's a good way to impress a girl. Write her a message too."

"Thank you, Father, that's a good idea."

Her tension dissipated after they left, and Saliné felt asleep instantly. She woke in the morning, her eyes opening onto a man and his warm smile. *The man in my Vision,* she thought, unable to speak.

"Good morning, Vio. I am glad that you are awake. I am Eduin." *Why is she scared?* As it had happened in the forest, during the Mother Storm, Eduin had the sudden impulse to reach for her hand and calm her. He stopped himself and pretended to shift his position in front of her bed.

Eduin, the man who came yesterday. Maud's relative. I must be careful. She closed her eyes, opened them again. The man did not vanish, and his smile grew wider. And warmer. "Good morning, Eduin. I don't remember what happened to me, but I assume that you saved me yesterday, during the storm. Thank you, you are most kind." *I hope you are kind enough to skip the part about the mistress.*

"You are welcome, but actually it happened two days ago, in the evening. Do you feel strong enough to come and eat with us?"

I have slept for almost two days... "I don't know, if..."

"There is only one way to find out." Eduin grinned and, stretching his right hand out, clasped hers. "Let me help you," he said and pulled her up gently before she could react.

To her surprise, there was almost no pain left in her body, and she stood up easily. Unwillingly, Saliné found herself face to face with the man, who she thought must be in his early twenties. Despite her reticence, she found him handsome and somehow trustworthy, though the conversation about mistresses still lingered in her mind, in a wrong way, as it was Foy who had brought the issue, but she was too tired the day before, and some of her memories were distorted. *Eduin was in my Vision that happened during the storm*, she thought again, still trying to find a reason for that. Even if it stayed hidden for a while, there always was a reason behind a Vision. *Fate warned and helped me. Is my Light stronger than I thought?* "Thank you," Saliné finally said, when the silence had gone on too long. "I can walk by myself." Her hand was still in his, and she freed herself gently, feeling his thumb playing along her skin. She frowned briefly but said nothing.

"Are you sure?" he asked, jokingly. "I am ready to help you walk, even to carry you in my arms."

"Thank you, but that won't be necessary."

"Come then, my father is waiting for us."

"Eduin, where am I?"

"You are in Laurden. My father is the Seigneur of Laurden."

And Maud's second nephew. Guiscard was right, the road did lead to Laurden. Why did he warn me about the storm? He knew that I killed Bucur.

Entering the room, Saliné found herself facing Foy S'Laurden, the Seigneur of Laurden, and a girl, with a delicate fair face and black hair. Her eyes moved between Foy and Eduin, finding some physical resemblances, except for the father's dark brown hair, and the son's black curls. Involuntarily, she compared them to the other father and son who had marked her life: Aron and Bucur. There was the same ruthless determination in Foy as in Aron, yet she had the feeling that the man was not evil. When she thought of Eduin, she remembered his mistresses. That was so much like Bucur, and her lips twitched. *Maybe he is not so wicked*, Saliné encouraged herself.

"Did I pass the test?" Foy asked, and his eyes crinkled with mirth.

"You passed it two days ago, Sir, when you sheltered this stranger in your house. I thank you for your kindness."

"What do you think, Eduin? We have a girl who knows how to speak for herself." *She doesn't speak like a commoner, and Eduin was right, her riding suit is expensive.*

"You know my thoughts already," Eduin said, and offered Saliné a seat.

"My son thinks you are special, Vio. Are you?"

"I am just a girl."

"That's quite plain to see, but what more can you tell us about this girl?

"My father was the Half-Knight of Debretin," Saliné said. "I was going to Valeni, where Lady Agatha, a distant aunt of my mother's, had arranged a good marriage for me." Debretin was in Arad, more a fortified house than a castle, and as she did not know until now about Laurden, she did not expect them to know about Debretin, which was much smaller and further north of Arad.

"Do you know the man?" Eduin asked, a bit more eagerly than he meant to.

"Yes, he is a kind man, who I like. We met two years ago, when I visited Valeni with Mother."

"As a young man, I was once in Valeni," Foy said. "I attended Lady Agatha's wedding."

"My grandmother was there too. A sad story, Lady Agatha's husband was killed soon after the wedding, and she never remarried."

So, she did not lie about Agatha... "Yes," Foy nodded, "a sad story, but Valeni is far from here."

"Our ship was caught in a storm from the north, and we landed in Sebastos. We hired two people who knew the roads."

We? Foy thought, looking at her.

"My mother hired two protectors to guard me. I suppose that they are dead now. It's a strange thing, but I don't remember much of what happened in the last few days."

"It happens sometimes when you are in shock. You were unconscious and freezing when we found you," Eduin said.

"Thank you, again, Eduin."

Foy looked at her and frowned thoughtfully.

I should have said Sir Eduin, Saliné suddenly worried. *It's too late now.*

"The men you hired brought you much too far south." Foy was still thoughtful, feeling that her reactions were not those of the daughter of a Half-Knight; he guessed that she was trying to mimic a lower status, but everything in her stance worked against her. *Why would she do that? The higher the status, the more chance of being treated well.* Maud's letter about the missing Candidate Queen resurfaced in his mind, but he chose to ignore it.

"They knew that we were strangers, maybe they just wanted more money," Saliné said, injecting some sadness into her voice. "I suppose that is of no matter now."

"My dear niece." Foy turned toward the girl, who was studying Saliné with a strange intensity. "What do you think?"

She is a Wanderer, a thought whispered to Saliné. She felt a strong pressure from the Light, and a hidden meaning in all that happened. And in all that will happen.

"You know what I am," the girl said, a glimmer appearing and vanishing in her eyes.

"What should I know?" Saliné asked, hiding well her surprise.

"That I am a Wanderer. I am Idonie, the Twenty-First Light of the Frankis Wanderers." *I was right about her Light; this complicates matters.*

"Yes, I knew that you are a Wanderer," Saliné whispered.

"So, you are special." Foy's thick brows drew together, and he looked between the two women, a touch of worry on his eyes. Matters related to the White Light were always complicated.

"I have some Light, but that doesn't make me special. There is not enough of it to make me a Wanderer."

"But you know about the Wanderers," Foy insisted, "and there are not many people who know about them."

"In my family, we know about the Wanderers. My mother is a Helper." She pondered for a while. *It may help me to know a powerful Wanderer without revealing who I am.* "I know Dochia." She saw Idonie react, and unwillingly, their eyes locked for a few moments. Surprised by the strong interaction between them, both looked away.

"Idonie had a Vision about you arriving in Laurden, that's why she came here, this morning."

"Wanderers have Visions," Saliné said, a touch of irritation in her voice.

"Vio," Foy said gently, "we just want to know more about you and understand Idonie's Vision. From what I understand, there is always a purpose in them. You have nothing to worry about. Let's eat now. We will have time to get to know each other." Foy nodded at her, smiled and, looking down at his dish, he proceeded to eat.

Saliné calmed, but she could not be light-hearted. For the first time in her life, she was surrounded entirely by strangers, on foreign ground. A guest of strangers and a prisoner of chance. Recalling that Eduin had saved her made her look at him out of the corner of her eyes. She found that he was doing the same. He winked at her and, blushing faintly, she looked at her plate, and began to eat. Once her nerves had settled, she realized how hungry she was. She still forced herself to eat slowly, though breakfast struck her as being both different and delicious. *Because I am so hungry*, she thought, amused. *Last time I ate was before the storm, and my mare... What happened to her?* "Eduin," she said suddenly and stopped, realizing that she had interrupted him.

"Yes."

"I don't know if... What happened to my mare?"

"A beautiful horse, indeed. A perfect riding animal for her mistress. I will take you to the stables after breakfast."

"Thank you. She was a gift from... From my mother," Saliné said gratefully, dropping her eyelids and drawing a deep breath, annoyed by her inability to recall what had happened during the last two days. And afraid about what she could have spoken in her sleep.

"I will be happy to show you the castle too."

"Thank you. Will you help me get to Valeni? My wedding is supposed to be in a month from now."

There is no wedding planned to happen in Valeni, Idonie thought suddenly.

"Laurden lies in a large valley, surrounded by mountains," Eduin said. "They are not tall mountains, but after the Mother Storm, all the passes are blocked. There is no way to leave the valley until spring."

Saliné merely nodded, trying to take in the implications. Once breakfast ended, and the daily routine claimed Foy and Eduin, she thought would prefer to attend to their affairs without a stranger meddling. She went to her room with Eduin's promise that he would come later and take her to the stable.

"Son, I don't remember the northern passes being closed so early. Winter is not yet here, and tomorrow it will probably rain," Foy said, when Saliné was gone. His hazel eyes glittered, and his intelligent face showed a trace of amusement.

"Perhaps, but the roads are already dangerous for young ladies. We can't risk."

"Started to change your mind about a new mistress?"

"No, but the winter is long; a bit of distraction would do no harm."

"What do you think now, Idonie?" Foy turned toward his niece.

"There is always something behind a Vision. A meaning. Vio may be an important person, or she may become important for the House of Laurden. It looks to me that Eduin thinks the latter."

"Am I so transparent?"

"Men are always transparent in this kind of situation." They grimaced at each other, as they had so many times in their childhood, and burst into laughter. "Whatever Foy thinks about men and Light, there is a bit of it in you. Being a man and untrained, your Light acts erratically. You went to Siecle against your father's will, and that doesn't happen often. On the road back, you had that impulse to take the western road to Laurden, which is longer. You found Vio there. You risked your life to save her. There is a meaning in all this, but I don't see it yet. Keep her here until spring. She is *safe* in Laurden, and we will know more by then. You may want to keep her safe from Eduin too." She turned to Foy and made a mock pleading face.

"Do you think so badly of me?" Eduin asked, frowning heavily, but his eyes were laughing.

"I received a letter from Maud. She was asking about the Candidate King and Queen," Foy said.

Idonie's face changed, and she was lost to them for a while. "I've had a new Vision," she said after a while. "There was nothing in it about the Candidate Queen, but Arnauld may cause problems for Vio. He will come to the Winter Solstice Party." *Why have I the feeling that Vio is related to the Candidate Queen? And what made the Candidate King run from Severin?* Idonie belonged to the second Wanderer Hive in Frankis, the smallest one, built in Pirenes Mountains. News about what happened in Severin arrived there two days after she had left the Hive to visit her family. She knew about Codrin from Dochia, and that he was important to the Wanderers. She did not know that he was the new Grand Seigneur of Severin. Neither knew Foy. Severin was a small place, and too far from Laurden. He will learn about it later.

"I invited him," Foy said, "and your brother is always a problem where beautiful girls are concerned."

"No surprise here, he is Eduin's cousin after all." Idonie jumped from her chair, when Eduin sprang toward her, and they ran around the table. She let him catch her, and he embraced, then lifted her, turning her in the air twice. "I miss Laurden," she said after Eduin released her, like he was playing with a child, "my big cousin here, and my family. Sometimes, it's not easy to be a Wanderer." *I will never marry and have children. Eduin is a kind man. I would have like a husband like him. Joffroy...* she sighed, remembering the man who once she dreamed of marrying. *Maybe Vio is meant for Eduin.*

When she was sixteen, and her parents started to search a husband for her, she had suggested Joffroy, the son of Seigneur Pierre, who was the Spatar of Tolosa. They had met in Laurden the year before, and they liked each other. For a reason still unknown to Idonie, her father pushed her to marry Cambio, the son of a powerful Knight in the south, and their neighbor. Later, she thought that perhaps her family did not think she could marry into a Seigneur's family. Even though her uncle was a Seigneur, Idonie was just a Knight's daughter. Negotiations went on over the course of a week, in Laurden. One evening, Cambio tried to rape Idonie, and it was Eduin who saved her. She cried a lot in his arms that evening. Her father continued the negotiations, as if nothing had happened, though she asked him to stop the marriage negotiations.

"We don't marry for love, Jaquine." Her father brushed away her complaints about Cambio. We marry out of duty. Love will come later, as it came between your mother and me." She was still Jaquine then, not Idonie; she took her new name when she became a Wanderer.

A week later, she has chosen to join the Wanderers. He parents were furious, but they could not afford to oppose the powerful order. The day she left her home to join the Wanderers, she told them the reason she had accepted the Wanderers' offer; she could not marry the man who tried to rape her. They were shocked, because they did not think of things from that angle, but it was now too late to agree with her. She later heard that Joffroy was also unhappy when she joined the Wanderers, but two years later, he started to court another girl. It felt strange to Idonie that she resented such a normal thing; the Wanderers could not marry, and she was lost to him.

Both Eduin and his father sensed that she was wandering, and they thought that a new Vision was coming to her. There were two Visions occupying her mind, but they were not new. Idonie knew that Saliné had killed a man; she saw their last moments together, and she also heard the conversation between Guiscard and the priest, when they said that the girl had been kidnapped, and the man who kidnapped her forced her into his bed before the marriage. Her past bad experience with Cambio made her hide both Visions from Eduin, and even more from Foy. With her Wanderer senses, she felt that Saliné was a kind woman, with a sad past, who deserved better and, just like Eduin, Idonie felt she was important too.

"So, you took care that Vio has everything she needs." Idonie went out from her inner trance and turned toward them.

"Yes," Foy said, surprised by her half-amused tone.

"And will she have only that riding costume to dress in?"

"Dress... Why? If you ask me, she doesn't need to be dressed..." Eduin could not continue as Idonie slapped the back of his head, and he let out a cheerful peal of laughter.

"Men, they only dream of naked girls. Take good care of her, Eduin, or I will have some *nasty* Visions about you."

After she visited the stables with Eduin and Idonie, and saw that her mare was well looked after, Saliné went to eat lunch in the kitchen, with the servants; no one had told her where to eat, and an unexpected courier delayed Foy and Eduin. It was a separate place, built in the left wing of the castle, a kind of kingdom inside a kingdom where Norma, the Chef of the palace, reigned. Norma knew that Saliné had eaten with the S'Laurdens in the morning, but she said nothing. She took care to arrange a separate table and treated Saliné like an important guest, not a servant.

"The Mother Storm I got caught in, was it a particularly strong one?" Saliné asked when she felt confident that she had formed a small bond with Norma. "I've never seen such a storm before."

"It was of normal strength, but it came a month earlier than usual."

I am always lucky, Saliné sighed. "I suppose that Laurden is now cut off."

"Not at all. Tomorrow it will probably rain. The passes are fully blocked only deep in winter, but they can be dangerous for a few weeks before."

Eduin lied to me, but if he thinks to force me becoming his mistress... Maybe I can leave in two or three weeks. I need to recover first, and preparations may take a while. Laurden is a Seigneury, not a small place like Castis. "I suppose that you have hard winters here." Saliné found refuge in the usual small talk about weather. Norma kept her entertained with a few stories, and that improved her knowledge of Laurden and its owners.

The S'Laurdens gathered for lunch later than usual. Waiting for Saliné, they did not start to eat. After a while, Eduin got up and went to her room, only to find it empty. He asked some servants, then some guards, and they asked more people, but no one knew Saliné's whereabouts, mostly because almost no one knew her. Seeing Eduin's anger, a young guard panicked and called the alarm. Armed men ran through the palace, patrolling the designated areas, none of them knowing what the danger was, and what should they look for. Hearing the noise of marching men, Foy left the dining room in a hurry, fearing that Saliné had run away.

Soon, patrols ran through the city, the gate was closed, and Foy asked for horses, thinking that the bird had already flown. Eduin was already in his fighting gear, when a young servant from the kitchen came out and asked what was happening.

"Lady Vio is missing," a soldier whispered. "We are going out of the city to find her."

The servant, a seventeen-year-old girl, took off at a run. She saw Eduin, ready to leave the palace, and ran even faster. "Sir," she gasped, catching him only a few steps out of the palace.

"I don't have time now," Eduin dismissed her, and walked hastily away.

She swallowed her fear and acted quickly before things could degenerate further. "Vio is in the kitchen!" she shouted.

Eduin stopped; the soldiers stopped, and every sound died in front of the palace. He turned slowly toward the servant. "What?"

"Yes, Sir, Lady Vio is in the kitchen."

Eduin looked at her, and the girl tried to make herself small under his intense star. Then he laughed. "Take me to her." Feeling her fear, Eduin placed a reassuring arm on her shoulder, and turned her gently toward the kitchen, to where they walked together. "Stop what you are doing and tell Father the news," he said to the soldiers.

He found Saliné eating alone at her table, Norma keeping her company, in a chair next to her, telling stories about the palace and the town. "What is the meaning of this, Norma? Since when do my guests eat in the kitchen?"

Norma tried to answer, but Saliné placed her hand over hers. "I came here, Eduin," Saliné said gently, though there was firmness in her voice. "I was hungry, and what place better to eat than the kitchen? And Norma is a fine storyteller. I have enjoyed her company."

"My apologies, Norma. I think this is my fault. Vio," Eduin said, "I should have told you to come and eat with us. Someone raised the alarm, because we thought that you ... that you were lost in the city," he said sheepishly.

"I suppose I should be grateful for your concern." There was a hint of amusement in Saliné's voice.

"Please come with me, Vio, we are all hungry, even if you are not." Eduin extended his arm, and clasping her hand, pulled her gently to her feet.

"Thank you, Norma," Saliné said, led by Eduin as they walked together – it did not feel unpleasant. She would have been surprised to learn that Eduin did not even realize what he was doing. She took care to slip her hand from his just before they left the kitchen. It looked natural, as if she needed to detach her hand to pass through the door.

Norma looked on in knowing amusement. *They make a good pair.*

In the evening, Eduin and Idonie came to Saliné's room, bringing Martha, the dressmaker, with them and three everyday dresses. They were of fine quality and, while they were a bit short, they fit her surprisingly well – Martha did not have much work to do. Unknown to both Saliné and Eduin, they had belonged to his mother. The dressmaker knew, of course, as she had been making clothes for the S'Laurdens since she was a young girl, fifteen year ago, but Foy told her to keep quiet about it.

The day she left Laurden to visit her family, Idonie took Saliné aside, and they walked together in the garden, which was now white with powdered snow and gleaming in the sun. "There was a man in your life, Claudin," Idonie said. "I don't know much about him, but I know that he did not deserve you. He kidnapped you and tried to rape you. In Laurden, you have nothing to worry about. Uncle Foy may look tough, but he loved his wife and never remarried when she died. He feels lonely. I will see you again next year, and I wish you good luck." She opened her arms. Saliné did the same and they clasped hands. "I have not told Foy and Eduin; what we say now stays between us."

"That man killed my stepfather, drugged and raped me when I was still a child and sold my mother. I am not ashamed that I killed him; I just wish I had done it earlier. Thank you, Idonie."

"Oh, poor you." Idonie embraced her. To her surprise, Saliné felt comforted, and she responded with the same warmth. It was both odd and welcome for her to feel such warmth from a stranger; the S'Laurdens, she decided, were not unkind people.

"Do you think that Foy will let me go to Valeni?"

"Vio," Idonie leaned back until they were eye to eye, "there is a reason for your arrival here, but I am not yet able to grasp it. My feeling is that everything will be revealed in spring. You are a strong woman, but please don't try anything until then. It may be dangerous. I will return as soon as I learn more."

For a moment, Saline thought to ask Idonie if she would carry a message for Codrin; she was a Wanderer after all, and Codrin was under their protection. Then she remembered that both Foy and Idonie were related to Maud. *Perhaps I will find a merchant who goes to Arad.*

Silent and dreaming of Severin, Saliné leaned on her elbows against the windowsill. *I could have been in Severin with Codrin,* she sighed, *planning to free Mother and Vio.* Her eyes followed the road in the low light of the morning storm, starting from the almost invisible stones at the gate and flowing downhill, vanishing through the heavy, whirling snow. It was the beginning of her fourth week in Laurden, and the storm outside continued unabated. She felt calm, almost like being at home, and the feeling surprised her. Now and then, she pondered about the strangeness of the situation, but didn't dwell on it. If she didn't include the storm that had almost killed her, and of which she remembered little, Saliné found that the mountainous area during a winter Mother Storm was even more spectacular. Nature unleashed both attracted and frightened her. The thought that she could so easily have been a frozen corpse in a ravine, or food for the wolves, made her shudder, and there was also a more insidious fear besetting her: Idonie's knowledge. For a few days, after the Wanderer had left Laurden, Saliné both wanted and didn't want her to return.

Eduin and Foy entered the room, and they stopped abruptly. Caught in her inner thinking and the roaring of the storm, she ignored the small noise of the opening door and their footsteps. Five feet behind her, the men glanced at each other, smiled, and continued to eye the gentle slope of her torso, as it descended into a rounded bottom, outlined by the stretched material. They'd never seen finer curves. In the south, the dresses were tighter on a woman's body and, being bent over, Saliné offered a wonderful view. From time to time, she swayed to left or right to the tune of the wind, and that enhanced her curves even more. She looked delicious.

Involuntarily, Eduin changed his stance from one foot to the other. A floorboard complained with a loud creak, and he bit his lip, wondering what excuse he could offer without looking stupid. He didn't get long to ponder. Saliné swiveled, bent and, touching the floor with her left hand, rotated her flying body, her legs hitting Eduin behind his knees. He fell before he knew what was happening. Then she leaped again, and her knife touched Foy's neck. In that moment, she realized who they were, and stopped herself from killing him. Her eyes widened. Her face stiffened. She stepped back, dropping her knife, and raising her hands.

"I apologize," she said, barely intelligible, breathing fast, in ragged gasps. With all her effort, she couldn't make them slow. "Please don't sneak up behind me again. You saved my life, and I am grateful, but this is still an unfamiliar place for me, and I need to be on my guard. I might have killed you."

Foy appeared calm, but he let out a long silent breath. An experienced soldier, he had assessed her as she took Eduin down, and was convinced that she would stop in time. "That I have to agree with, lady Vio, we came uncomfortably close to having my throat slit. I am glad that it escaped unharmed. I happen to be fond of my neck." His timbre and cadence were distinctive, and behind his dark humor, for the first time, there was a touch of appreciation in Foy's voice. His appreciation of her wasn't new but letting her know about it was. There was also a trace of a smile on his lips, frozen. "I apologize for sneaking up on you."

He did not try to defend himself, and he called me lady... "Well, I can only guess why you two did that, and sometimes a woman appreciates such attention, but there are times when it is too much." Saliné smiled ingenuously, and both men burst out laughing.

"Caught red-handed." Foy's laugh became louder, and his powerful baritone voice filled the room. "Would you mind telling us who taught you to fight with such skill?"

"My mother and a friend."

"Is his name Corrin?"

Saliné hesitated for a moment, and Codrin's face came to her as if he were there. Sometimes, an eidetic memory is not helpful. She pressed her nails into her palm to calm her mind. "Yes."

"I would like to learn that move," Eduin said.

"I can teach you, but you are tall and strong. That move is better for smaller people."

Eduin came closer. She panicked, and tried to step back, but the wall blocked her. Eduin ignored her obvious tension and moved even closer, their bodies almost touching. His palm touched the top of her head, which was at the level of his brows. "I wouldn't exactly call you small."

"Still, I am smaller than you, and I am also lighter, and I did not say that you can't learn it or use it; I just said that it may be less useful to you."

"Then we have agreed that you will teach me."

"Yes," she said, gracefully acknowledging his well-laid trap.

"Dinner time." Eduin placed an arm around her shoulders, escorting her toward the door. He let his arm drop before Saliné could feel too uncomfortable.

They soon began a routine of training three times a week, and though she was reluctant at first, Saliné found herself enjoying it. Eduin was an entertaining man, and he never overstepped the mark, not even when their bodies touched during training. She also found it useful to keep herself in shape. Her main worry was not to show him too many of the Assassins' secrets; she had promised Codrin. She showed him things that Jara and Cernat had taught her before Codrin came into her life, and some simple tricks from the Assassins Dance.

"Her level of training is remarkable," Eduin said to his father, after two weeks. "And the way of fighting too; it doesn't resemble our way at all. It makes me think of the Wanderers. Vio mentioned that she knows one of them, Dochia."

Foy was thoughtful, and his fingers drummed the table. "Idonie said that she is the most powerful Wanderer in Frankis, and part of their Council. That's all she was willing to say."

"Idonie is a fine girl, but the Wanderers have their own rules."

"I have never asked her to break the rules, and I never will. The Wanderers never do anything without a reason. If Dochia trained Vio, she must consider her ... special." Foy looked at his son, his eyes crinkling with silent laughter.

"So, you finally believe me," Eduin grinned.

"When did I say that? Young men are unreliable, and even unstable, where beautiful girls are concerned. See how much you can learn from her, then pick a few young soldiers and train them."

Eduin was attracted to Saliné, but he also tried to stay away from her. She could be no more than his mistress, and she looked too proud to accept such a relationship. He kept his feelings to himself, unable to see that whatever charm or magic she held, it worked against him.

Chapter 9 – Dochia

Dochia's new life in Nerval was both different and hard to bear. Meriaduk, the High Serpentist Priest looked like a snake to her, and she had to pretend to be a loyal Serpentist acolyte. It was the task Ada, the Second Light of the Arenian Wanderers, and the strongest living Wanderer, had given her. She was ordered to come to the Sanctuary and help Codrin to stop the Fracture. After years of collecting information through Visions or by using spies, both Wanderers and Assassins had come to the same conclusion: this Fracture was about the nomads using Talant artifacts to conquer the continent for the Serpent God. It was not enough that the Khad of the nomads could muster an army of two hundred thousand riders; they had now things like the Maleteras to help them communicate at distance. And Dochia still did not know what other artifacts Meriaduk had been able to bring to life in the Sanctuary.

There was also the issue of Ai's magic powers sneaking around and inside her mind, which was so similar with what the Maletera did to her; yet she could not complain about Ai, at least not yet. The young woman – Dochia guessed that she was young, even very young, as they had never met – seemed to be strange but kind. And powerful too. Dochia still remembered the moment when Ai spoke directly in her mind for the first time, on that day when she entered the Sanctuary, to meet Meriaduk. The magic in the Maletera was evil, dirty, like

Meriaduk, who used it on her. Ai's magic was not. At least not yet. And they never spoke, in the real sense of using sounds, when there were people around Dochia. The Wanderer, who had quite a logical mind, could not understand the reason for that rule, as Ai had enough magic power to speak at distance, making herself heard physically even when she was faraway. And Dochia never knew how far Ai was when she spoke to her. The elusive young woman could be in the next room, or in the next building, or Fate knew where. Or the Serpent.

"Why won't you speak to me when other people are present?" Dochia asked her for the tenth time. They were alone, and she could hear Ai's voice filling her room. There was no point from where she could identify the voice, it was everywhere in the room, another kind of magic that made Dochia wonder.

"It's dangerous," Ai said, again.

"Why is it dangerous?"

"Because it's dangerous."

At least Ai never tried to take over her mind; as Meriaduk had done, using the Maletera, and left her unconscious for three days, when she was in the Alba Hive of Silvania. It was only Dochia's strength that saved her from having her mind corrupted and becoming a slave of Meriaduk. The memory of Splendra, the Third Light of the Frankis Wanderers, was still fresh in her mind. The poor woman had acted like Meriaduk was always in her mind, telling her what to do. And even fresher were the memories of the servants she saw in the Serpent Temple, what Meriaduk called the Sanctuary. Most of them were enslaved by the Maletera, and they could not oppose Meriaduk's will, or that of his most trusted priests. They took any woman they wanted at will. The women never resisted. There was pain and disgust in their eyes, but they never resisted. Dochia once heard a woman complaining to another about the dirty things one pervert priest did to her. The woman stopped talking when she came close; Dochia was an apprentice priestess, working for Meriaduk, and hated by the servants, as most of the priests were. Ai was not like Meriaduk, never tried to enslave her, yet Dochia still feared her. A little. Or maybe more than a little.

"When will I find out why it's dangerous?" Dochia asked. In time, she had realized that sometimes, by reformulating the question in a slightly different way, she could convince Ai to give her more clues, like being rewarded for something she could not yet understand.

"When you are ready."

I will never be ready.

"Let's go, now, Dochia. I want to show you another part of the Sanctuary."

"How large is the Sanctuary?" That was another question which never received an answer.

"Very large."

Dochia opened the door of her room and went out into the corridor, knowing that from now on, Ai would speak in her mind again. She asked once if Ai was always in her mind, even when they were not speaking to each other.

"What should I do that?" Ai answered with her own question. "There are more interesting things to learn than your thoughts, and it's time-consuming. Why do you fear me? I always let you know when I enter into your mind."

"But you can enter without letting me know."

"I could try, but I think that you would sense it. You have a strong mind, and you are trained. I never met a Wanderer before. Are all of them like you?"

"We are as different as people in general are different."

"Turn to the right," Ai said in her mind, and Dochia started, the memory of the past conversation fading away.

She turned right. As Meriaduk's acolyte, she had a large room close to the core of the Sanctuary, and she knew this section well enough to understand that they were leaving the central area. After a while, she turned right again, into a different corridor. The length of these passageways always unsettled her; the most impressive one she had seen was almost three hundred feet long. Even the Royal Palace in Muniker, the largest construction she had ever entered before coming to the Sanctuary, was a small place compared to this. The main dome alone, which Meriaduk called Prainos, would host half of the Royal Palace.

"Turn left now," Ai ordered, and Dochia obeyed and walked for another minute. "Wait."

"Why?"

"There are two priests in the next corridor."

Dochia was surprised; that was the first time that Ai had let slip a negative thought about the Serpentist Priests. Did Meriaduk try to enslave Ai? Was she able to overcome the Maletera too?

"I can hear you." Ai's voice was childish and exuberant, like she was amused by Dochia's thought. "Ask me to open the door."

"What door?" There was no door in front of her.

"Just ask me."

"Open the door," Dochia said, and a crack appeared in the wall in front of her. It was just a slit at first, into which she could barely squeeze her hand. It widened slowly, making little noise, leaving an empty space, resembling a door. Dochia felt her throat dry with fear. There was fear in her eyes, fear in her mind. She felt paralyzed, and she had to muster all her long training just to keep her legs moving. Eyes closed, she breathed deeply a few times and forced herself to step through the door. The door closed behind her, and Dochia turned quickly, deep fear gnawing at her. The door was no more, and her hands fumbled over the wall, trying to find the crack and open it. "Ai, open the door," she rasped, not realizing that she was speaking aloud. The door opened, and Dochia's breath slowed down. In a few moments, she was calm again.

Dochia understood magic; after all, she was able to see the future. It came to her with almost no effort. She knew that a Seer was able to fly over the land with his mind and see faraway places. And he could *control* his Farsight. She knew about the unclean magic of the Maletera, which could control minds, and was so similar to Ai's magic; but what had just happened was different, this was touching something material, opening a hole in a wall, then filling it back in. She knew of no magic that could create a door in a wall. She knew of no magic that could directly affect the material world. For the Wanderers, magic was always about the mind. The implication of what she had seen was staggering.

"What do you want me to do?" Dochia finally asked.

"There is no one here, so we can speak normally again. Turn right and walk to the end of the corridor."

"Why are there so many corridors?"

"Because they needed them."

"Who needed them?" Dochia looked left and right and started to walk again.

"The people who built the Sanctuary."

"Were they from the Talant Empire?"

"There was no such Empire, but yes they were from what you call the Talant Empire."

"Then what should I call them?"

"Turn right now."

Why is she keeping so many things secret? Dochia turned, and another door opened in front of her. It was like before; the door wasn't there until it was there. She entered the new corridor, and the door closed behind her. This time, she strained to hear the closing door; Dochia had no terms yet with which to describe the magical process, but it was opening and closing. The sound was faint, resembling heavy cloth rubbing over wood. The *door* didn't look like a door, and it didn't sound like a door either. "How can I open a door without you?"

"You can't."

"I can't, or I am not allowed? What can I do if I am caught here, and you are away?"

"You can't be caught here when I am away," Ai laughed, "because you can't enter here. After you learn more about the Sanctuary, I will teach you how to open some of the hidden doors."

Hidden doors... There are special places where you can pass through the walls, Dochia thought. *Perhaps the material of the walls is weaker or thinner, so the magic can make the hole. Or the wall was made by magic and you only need to know where and how...* "Does Meriaduk know how to open the doors?"

"He knows how to open some of them." There was a sudden irritation in Ai's voice that surprised Dochia. It was the first time she had felt such an emotion from the invisible young woman.

"I apologize, if I upset you."

"You did not upset me, but what you will see now upsets me," Ai said, and another door opened on the right. Dochia entered a small room which had no doors. "Ask me to open the door."

"Open the door." Through the new door, Dochia entered a new room, a square one, thirty feet wide. Passing through it, she saw that the wall was no thinner than the rest of the structure, so it was perhaps a magic wall, not a real one. She touched the wall; it felt solid. She shook her head, then searched through the new room: there were two open spaces in the opposite wall, like it was missing its doors, and she heard voices.

"Go to the space on the left and look outside, but don't let yourself be seen. Meriaduk is there."

Fifty paces from the opening, Meriaduk was standing in front of a table that looked more like a long bench, only three feet wide. There were five priests with him, and all six of them had their back to Dochia. Two of them were Vicarius, his most powerful and loyal priests. There were only seven Vicarius in the temple. On the table, there was a fourteen-year-old boy, his hands and feet tied to the table. There was a belt tying his waist too. And there was a strange sound, something invisible was whooping, quite loudly. They were in a dome that Dochia had never seen before. It was smaller than the main one, but was still a hundred fifty feet in diameter and seventy-five feet high.

Dochia did not know the boy, but she saw the blood running from his nose, mouth and eyes. She saw his small body contorting in pain. She heard his cries. And she saw a Maletera in Meriaduk's hand. He was holding it a foot above the boy. "No," she whispered, and unsheathed her dagger.

"Don't interfere, Dochia," Ai said in a low, urgent voice which stopped her.

"But they will kill him, and he is so young." Dochia shook her head, and tensed her body, ready to attack Meriaduk and his five priests.

"He can't be saved; his mind is already gone, but if you get closer, they will learn that you have the blood too, and next time you will take the place of that poor boy. And you can't take all of them with a dagger. They have some powerful weapons."

"What does it mean that I have the blood?" *I need to learn more about the weapons...*

There was a short pause before Ai said, "The Sanctuary responds to people's blood. If one's blood is strong enough, that person can do things here. Like reactivating a Maletera."

"Are they ... closed? Sleeping? The Maleteras."

"In a way, and you need someone with strong blood to wake and command them. Meriaduk's blood is strong enough to command them, but not strong enough to reactivate them. He needs help from other people who have the blood. People like that boy, or people like you."

"Does he know about my blood?"

"He knows that you have the blood, as the Sanctuary let you enter without being helped by a priest, but he thinks that you have weak blood, because you are not from Nerval. He can be really stupid sometimes. If you go close to that table, he will know. There are things on the table which can read your blood, even at a distance. They are called Blood Sniffers, and they will warn him. Once you become a novice priestess, he will test you and then he will know, but by then you can no longer be used like that boy. Priests are never used that way. Meriaduk can't rule without them."

More dirty magic. Why did the Talants create this? What kind of sick minds did they have? "I still don't know what it means, to have the blood."

"It means that you are the offspring of the people who built the Sanctuary; that's why this place recognizes you, Meriaduk and his priests. You can't be a priest if you don't have the blood."

That's why Ada sent me here. But how did she know about this? She told me about the Sanctuary, but she did not seem to know much about it. She knew that I would meet Ai. "There must be many offspring out there. I am from Frankis, Meriaduk is from Nerval."

"It's not that simple. Not all offspring have the blood, and there are three more Sanctuaries on the continent. Let's go now."

"How can I stop this?"

"What do you mean by *stop this*?"

"Stop them from killing children. Stop the Maleteras. They are evil. No one should be allowed to do such things. Those who created the Sanctuary had sick minds. I want the Maleteras destroyed."

"I am glad that you said that."

"Then help me destroy them."

"This is what I am doing, Dochia, helping you close them again. The Maleteras are only things, and things are not evil. They can be used in a good way. It's one's mind which makes the choice between good and bad."

"How is this helping me?" Dochia asked, ignoring the talk of the *good way*. She needed more time to think about it. *Maletera can be used for communication.*

"If you want to fight something, you must learn its powers. You must understand the Sanctuary, and how the Maleteras and other things work. Let's go now; they will soon move away from the table."

Taking her eyes from the dying boy, Dochia finally saw the box on the table. Made of glass, it was almost invisible and going as long as the table, a foot square in section. Looking more attentively, she realized that there were two boxes, each covering almost half of the table. There was an open space in the middle, ten foot long, where the body of the boy lay. *He is dead*, Dochia thought bitterly. *One day, I will make Meriaduk pay for everything.* At fixed intervals, she saw objects in the boxes.

"Are the things in the glass boxes all Maleteras?"

"Some of them are, but there are different things inside. There were a hundred Maleteras, and twelve were activated. Thirteen now. But five of them have been lost."

"I destroyed one of them," Dochia said.

"The one on the shore of Kostenz Lake? I am glad that you did that, there was no way for you to disable it."

"Taking over people's minds is a terrible thing. Do they have other powers too?"

"Communication, but you already know that. We have to go now."

There was urgency in Ai's voice, and Dochia walked briskly toward the opposite wall. She stopped, waiting for the door to open. "Ai, open the door." She was still startled by the sudden hole in the wall but walked through it without hesitation.

Guided by Ai, Dochia returned to her room, memorizing the path through the maze of corridors, and the approximate positions where a door could be created to get into the next corridor. She could not open the doors, not yet, but she was beginning to learn more about the Sanctuary, and she had a powerful motivation to do so.

"How are they using the blood to ... reactivate the Maletera? I saw no blood on it," Dochia asked after closing the door of her room.

"The blood gives power, but it's the mind which opens the Maletera or other things in the Sanctuary. Meriaduk takes over the captive and merges their minds under his control. His mind is not strong enough to open a Maletera, because his blood is not strong enough. Most children die at the first attempt. Adults, depending on their power, can be used two or three times."

"How many times could he use me?"

"More than the others, your blood and mind are strong. In some ways, you are even stronger than Meriaduk. In others, you are weaker."

"Is he stronger than you?"

"In some ways, yes. In others..."

"How old are you?" Dochia asked on impulse.

There was a moment of pause that was uncommon for Ai. "I am seventeen years old."

That's why you are hiding, Dochia thought, and from that moment she fully trusted the girl. "Thank you, for trusting me, Ai. I will tell no one about that. And how long have you been in the Sanctuary?"

"I was born here."

Should I ask about her parents? Are they still here? Or alive? I can't ask. "There were too many bad things to see today," Dochia sighed. "I will go to meet Umbra, Mira and Irina." Her guards were living in a small, rented house at the edge of the city, where they took care of Umbra, who was not allowed in the Sanctuary, not that he would have liked it. Umbra never went in a room without windows, and the Sanctuary was built underground. Their house was close to a forest that entered in the city like a protuberance, and there was an old pine in the backyard. The place behind the house was not overtaken by buildings; not because some rulers felt the need to have a park in the city, but because in spring it became a swamp. The forest and the old pine helped Umbra to fly in and out of the house without being seen.

"I wish to meet them too. Umbra especially." There was a childish eagerness in Ai's voice that made Dochia smile.

"You can come with me."

"I can't leave the Sanctuary, Dochia. Would you trust me enough to bring Umbra to a room here, far from Meriaduk?"

"I will ask Umbra; it's his decision to make. He is a friend. Well, he is more than a friend to me."

"I apologize; I should have thought about that, but a talking bird... It's so strange. Exciting. A bird which thinks and talks, not one which simply parrots human words. I did not know that such birds exist."

"You can open and close walls, but you are puzzled by a talking bird," Dochia laughed. "I will pass your invitation on to him."

The Sanctuary was built deep under the city, and there were several ways to leave it. All the stairs led up inside recently built structures, domes which protected the exits. One of these exits was close to her guards' house, a small one, with a sturdy wooden door and an iron lock. Several keys always hung on pegs inside the structure. Thirty feet underground, there was one of the magical doors which had greeted Dochia on her first journey inside the Sanctuary. This magic she could understand better. The door was there, visible for anyone to see, and when the priest who greeted her waved his hand, the door opened. Dochia learned that she could master that kind of magic too, though she did not understand how. She simply waved her hand, and the door opened. This door looked no different to the others, yet there was something different about it. When Ai revealed the door to her, she found that no one had used it for a long time; there were no footprints in the dust covering the floor.

"Apart from you, no one has the blood to open this door," Ai told Dochia, when she first ventured out through the door. "Keep this to yourself."

"Then why did they build this exit? Dochia asked.

"Mordanek, the Great Priest of the Serpent, had the full blood of the builders. He was able to open all the doors. It was him who reopened the Sanctuary after almost four thousand years."

What can be opened, can be closed, Dochia thought. *This place is too large to destroy.*

It was cold and sunny when Dochia went out, her mind still invaded by images of the poor boy on the table. Lost in her inner world, she walked through the streets and arrived at the house without realizing it. When she opened the door, the real world returned.

Why did Ada send me here? Killing Meriaduk and Baraki will not solve the Fracture, others will take over. And it's an impossible task. I will never be able to kill them both. Ai talked about closing the Sanctuary. Is this the solution? Mordanek opened the Sanctuary; others may come, as strong as him, and do the same. But it may not happen soon. Is this the key? Delay the Fracture until someone can close the Sanctuary?

Chapter 10 – Kasia / Dochia

Thin and small for her sixteen years, Kasia could hide in many places. She sat quietly in one of the watch-holes – a hidden niche built into the thick walls on the front of the house, facing the street. All the houses in Nerval had thick walls, to ward off both winter's cold and the frequent attacks of the robbers. From the niche, a child could watch the street for signs of danger. Kasia wasn't on duty; the watch-hole was simply one of the few places where she could find solitude. She liked solitude – it felt safe. The cold autumn rain continued to fall. Sometimes, Kasia imagined she was like the rain or the wind, free to go anywhere. Free of danger. She started when a hand grabbed her shoulder.

"Your brother wants to see you."

That was exactly what she did not want. Iovon, her brother, was both a robber and a merchant, but when he bought something, from time to time, it was more extortion than buying. And he always used her when he wanted to obtain a cheaper price. Kasia had the White Light, though she would not have called it that – she did not know what it was – and she was able to feel if the other merchant, who was being forced to sell, would accept the deal or not. Iovon needed a façade of respectability. During the night, his men would rob a merchant of his money, and the next day, he would offer a deal to the man they had robbed, buying his merchandise at the lowest possible price, and Kasia would nod to him when that price was reached.

Mesko, she thought. *Why is Iovon doing this?* Mesko was a friend of their father, and Kasia had played with his daughter until a year ago, when she vanished without a trace. She was a beautiful girl, and everybody thought that she had been kidnapped to serve as a concubine, or a whore for some rich man. Half a month later, they found her dead, and Kasia cried for many days for her friend. *How could Iovon do this?* She waited in the doorway until her brother nodded to tell her to sit in a corner of the room, behind Mesko, who could not see her.

"I offer you fifty galbeni for all the packs of cloth in your storehouse. You cannot sell them, and you know it, and you need money to pay Krisko." Fifty galbeni was less than a tenth of the merchandise's value.

"I can't sell at that price," Mesko growled.

"Fifty-five?"

"No."

"Sixty." This time Iovon was offering what he really wanted to pay, and he looked discreetly at Kasia. She shook her head. "Sixty-five. I am doing you a favor."

"The cloth is worth more than five hundred galbeni."

"If you sell it in time, certainly, but Krisko will come to collect your debt in a week. How much will you sell in a week? Ten galbeni's worth? Twelve? If you can't pay the debt, Krisko will take everything in your warehouse, and in your house too, and never bring you cloth again. You will be bankrupt. He will also take your last daughter into his bed. It does not matter that she is to be married in a month. Sixty-seven." He glanced again at Kasia, who shook her head. She knew that Mesko was ready to accept, but she wanted to help him. "What do you think, Kasia? You are a fair girl. Give him a price."

Mesko turned, startled to see her in the corner.

"Seventy-five galbeni." In her Vision, she saw that Mesko had to pay Krisko eighty galbeni.

"Eighty-five." Mesko wiped the perspiration from his face.

"Eighty," Kasia said, and nodded at her brother,

"That's my last offer. Take it or leave it." Iovon extended his arm toward Mesko, who grimaced, but clasped the hand. "Good. Bring the cloth to me and collect the money from Gresha."

"Why did you rob him?" Kasia asked when she was alone with her brother. She realized her mistake when he slapped her.

"I have the feeling that you cheated me. Without me, you would be selling your skinny body in the street. Mesko is fair game, as everyone is these days. He was Father's friend, not mine."

"He helped us when we were almost bankrupt."

"He helped Father, not me. Cheat me again, and I will throw you out in the street."

"I did not cheat you. He owes a hundred galbeni to Krisko." *Well, only a little.*

"Get out." He slapped her harder this time, and she fell to the floor.

She rolled away and scrambled on all fours through the door. Iovon's kick missed her bottom by a thin inch. In the hall, she jumped to her feet and ran out of the house, into the street. She slowed down beside Mesko. "Your future son-in-law told the robbers where you kept the money." Before he could answer, she was already gone.

"I am sure that she cheated," Iovon muttered to himself, looking after her through the window until she vanished from sight. He didn't see her speak to Mesko.

"Iovon," Gresha said from the door. "You have visitors." He turned as two priests entered the room.

"The Serpent be with you," one of them said, and Iovon bowed deeply. "We have a proposal for you," the priest added, before he could give the standard answer.

"Yes, priest, how can I help you?"

"You are a merchant. Not like the others, but still a merchant. In a way. We want to buy something from you."

"Of course." Iovon's voice was suddenly hoarse, and a bead of perspiration ran down his face. *They know...*

"You will receive two hundred galbeni."

"Thank you for your offer, but what do you want to buy?"

"Your sister. She will serve the Great Serpent."

"My sister?" *She will serve in your bed, but I can't refuse you. Why should I, anyway? That little whore cheated on me.* "When should I bring her to you?"

"Tonight. Here is the money. There is a vial in the bag too. Get her to drink the content. After that, you should forget that she ever existed." The priest put the bag on the table, and both priests left the room, and then the house.

"I told you that we don't need a Maletera to convince Iovon; he is a greedy coward," the older priest said. "Kasia's mind will be more receptive to the Serpent and the Maletera once she knows that her own family sold her. We still don't know why that happens, but who are we to question the Serpent's ways?"

Kasia woke up the next morning in a place she didn't recognize. She moaned; she felt sore all over, and now she started to remember. She felt strange after dinner, like she was sleeping with her eyes wide open. She saw Iovon carrying her to the carriage, then to the Temple. She remembered the priest undressing her, and... *He raped me...* Tears ran down her face, and she tried to stand, the pain made worse by her shame and anger.

"You are awake," a man said, and she recognized the voice of Meriaduk, the High Priest. "Your maidenhood was offered to the Serpent this night, and you will serve tomorrow. You will receive food, and you will be purified. Stand up."

She obeyed, even as she realized that she was naked under the blanket, and he stood in front of her, raising her chin. Then he kissed her. She wanted to resist but realized that she could not do it.

"Good, now you know the power of the Serpent. Dress yourself."

❧

The next morning, another priest came for her, and she followed him through the Sanctuary until they arrived in a great hall build like a dome. For all her sorrow, she gasped at its size. Meriaduk was already there, in front of a long table, with four priests.

"Ah, Kasia," he said, "it's time to serve the Great Serpent. Take off your dress."

She wanted to protest, or to run. Instead, she pulled up her dress, which was all she wore; everything else had been taken by the priests during her *purification*, which had all taken place in one bed or another. *I did not fight them. I just obeyed them and let them have me. Why?*

"Lie down on the table," he ordered, and she obeyed.

The priests tied her hands and legs and placed a restraining strap across her waist. Their hands touched her everywhere and, through her anger, she only could look as they groped her. The Serpent needed her anger to open the Maletera. One of them squeezed her breast harder, and tears swelled in her eyes.

"There is strong magic in her blood," Meriaduk said, examining the scale on the Blood Sniffer. "The Serpent brought the girl to us, and we can use it to activate two Maleteras. Or maybe I should open one of the rooms we can't access. No," he shook his head, "she does not have strong enough blood to open the room I want. Bring me a sleeping Maletera."

Too numb to feel fear, Kasia looked at the small sphere the priest held in front of her eyes.

"Serpent, hear the prayer of your humble priest. Help us to activate the magic of the Maletera."

Kasia's eyes widened, and she felt pain like nothing she had felt before. And she screamed.

When Meriaduk loosened his grip on Kasia's mind, she was almost unconscious, and blood ran from her nose and her eyes.

"It is done. The Great Serpent answered to my prayers." Meriaduk took the sphere in his hand, looking at the pulsating colors on its metallic skin. "We have a new Maletera. Take the girl to the Healing Room. She is strong; in a few days, we can use her to activate a second Maletera."

"Can we have her?" one priest asked, staring at Kasia's naked body.

"Not today," Meriaduk said, thoughtfully, "and not tomorrow, but then she's yours to soften up for the next opening. I need her here in a week. Go now, I have duties to attend to."

༺༻

"Wake up, Dochia," Ai said, and a burst of light chased the darkness from the room. "Dress yourself. You need to leave the Sanctuary."

I can't leave. I need to stop the Fracture. "Why?" she asked as she struggled into her clothes.

"You will see. Please hurry. You need to return before the morning."

I misunderstood... "I am ready. Can I leave the room now? What time is it?"

"Yes. It's a half hour after midnight. Turn to the right."

For a few minutes, she walked along familiar, empty corridors, then she had to ask Ai to open a door, and went into an area she didn't know.

"It's here," Ai said as Dochia stood before a door she had never seen before.

"What's inside?"

"A girl. Her name is Kasia. She was used two days ago to activate a Maletera, and she survived the ordeal because of her strong blood. They will use her again in five days. She will die."

"I am a good healer, but I don't have my pack with me."

"This is the Healing Room, it's better than any healer."

"Do you want me to take her out?" Dochia asked, a trace of hope in her voice.

"Yes. This is a secluded area, and very few people know about it. I know a corridor which leads from this one to the gate you use to go home."

"How do we open it?" After testing the knob and finding it locked, Dochia eyed the sturdy metallic door, knowing that there was no way to force her way in. She still hadn't got used to the waste of steel. There was more of it in the Sanctuary than in the whole Frankis.

"You have to ask me."

"Why?" *To underline my weakness?* "Unlock the door," Dochia said when it was clear that Ai would not answer.

"First you have to ask me to stop seeing you. As you know, I can remember everything and put it in someone else's mind. You don't want Meriaduk to know that you entered the Healing Room."

"Ai, stop seeing me." *Meriaduk can force her too...*

"I am blind now, and the door is unlocked."

Tentatively, Dochia touched the knob, and the door opened without a sound.

After two days in the Healing Room, Kasia was conscious again. She was still in pain and a bit weak, but she felt her will returning, and she knew she would try to defend herself.

Such a young girl and they want to rape her. They have already raped her. Dochia shook her head.

"There are some white pills in the box on the table," Ai spoke inside her mind, and Dochia went toward it.

"Did you come to use me for your pleasure, priest?" Kasia rasped.

"No," Dochia said and sat on the edge of the bed, close to the frightened girl. "I think that you are in pain."

"Ah, you want to be sure that I can stand the next torture session. To make that ... *thing* work." She knew the name of the Maletera, both from Iovon's and Gresha's stories and from the priests, but she was unable to remember. Her mind closed on itself and refused to do it.

"No, Kasia." Dochia stroked the girl's hair.

"You like women," Kasia spat. "You are no different to the men who raped me when they *purified* my body."

"I am sorry if I frightened you. I have come here to free you. Please take this pill," she put it in Kasia's hand. "It will help with the pain."

"By killing me," Kasia said, but she swallowed the pill. "I guess it's better to die than be raped and tortured."

"In a few minutes, you will feel better, and we can leave."

Kasia looked at the strange woman in front of her and, for the first time, she saw a woman, not an instrument of the evil Meriaduk. "But you are a Serpentist Priestess," she said hesitantly, pointing at the metallic brooch on Dochia's chest.

"Yes, I am an apprentice priest, but I am also more than that. Lie down and tell me when you feel well enough to walk." She took Kasia's hand in hers, and the girl answered by gripping it. Gently, Dochia stroked her hair with her free hand while the girl stared at her from wide blue eyes.

"I am ready," Kasia said after a while. *Can I trust her? I have no choice. I prefer to die than be* purified *and go on that table again.*

"Walk around the room."

The girl obeyed, under Dochia's close scrutiny. "I can walk," Kasia said. "I think I can run too, if needed." She arched an eyebrow, and a shy grin flashed across her tense mouth.

"She seems fine," Dochia said to Ai. *"Do you think we will need to run?"*

"Perhaps. On the streets. They can be dangerous at night. We will see how she is when she walks through the corridors. She can rest in the small room by the gate, if she needs to, before you go out."

"If we can leave the room, open the door."

"The corridor is empty. Turn to the right."

Day or night, Nerval was a dangerous place, but their journey to the house was short and uneventful. Two days later, Kasia became an apprentice Wanderer; Dochia felt the girl had a strong Light and tested her.

Chapter 11 – Dochia / Kasia

It was Baraki's first visit to the Sanctuary. Like every other visitor, he was speechless at the vastness of the main dome and felt his lips parting on their own will. With some effort, he closed his mouth before the priests smirked in his face. Pretending to be unobservant, Meriaduk did what he did best, manipulate his guest.

"What you see now is a map of the world," the High Priest said, preparing to rotate the red sphere in front of him, the size of a child's head.

Before he could do so, Baraki turned abruptly toward Dochia. "What is a Wanderer doing here?" he barked.

"She is an apprentice priestess. Let me show you the Map."

"How did she get here? We can't allow the Wanderers to plant their Lights in Nerval."

"I was tested with the Maletera," Dochia said and gave Baraki a long look. "Were you tested too?"

"I am the Seer of the Realm," Baraki boasted. "And I did not permit you to speak. How safe is the test?" He fumbled with the ends of his moustaches and turned toward Meriaduk.

"No one can hide from the power of the Maletera."

"We should test Baraki too. Half a year ago, he was supposed to be the Seer of Fate. A famous man in their camp." *Infamous would be the right word. Poisoner. Traitor.*

"You bitch," Baraki growled, and advanced menacing toward Dochia. His advance was slow.

"You are too old for such games." Dochia released the barrette, and one of her daggers flashed into view. Baraki slowed even more. Then he stood still. "And why are you afraid of the test, Baraki? A Seer should be fearless. And the Seer of the Serpent has nothing to fear from the Maletera. It's the tool sent to us by our God. I would have expected you to volunteer for the test, to show us that you are no longer working for Fate." *You are the main danger for the Realm now, Baraki. You have the army of Arenia, and you want the nomads too. Perhaps less dangerous if Meriaduk can control you through the Maletera.*

Test Baraki... That is quite a good idea. Why did I not think about it before? Meriaduk pondered and took a sharp intake of breath.

Baraki's face stretched tight, skin turning red; his mouth standing rigid.

"I can alleviate your worries, Dochia." A voice spoke at the same time as an unfamiliar face appeared in her vision. The apparition was not like Ai, or the working of the Maletera; it was more like the appearances of the Last Empress. "I am Nabal, the Last Emperor. Baraki is the Seer of the Serpent."

"You worked with the Last Empress. You were..." Dochia felt a frisson of fear, and she paused, as though wondering what she could say that he did not know.

"You have a strong mind." *And you kept your will after being tested...* Nabal frowned, and the High Priest was brought in the vision too. "Meriaduk, aren't her reactions impressive for someone whose mind was touched by the Maletera?" One corner of his mouth curled up in a cold smile. His eyes narrowed.

Meriaduk shrugged his shoulders, squeezed his lips together like he was thinking about it. He was pleased by Nabal's tightness. They were allies. They were not friends. "Dochia has more liberty than the others, and in six months, she will become a full priestess. She serves me well. Why is Baraki afraid of being tested?"

"There is no need to test the Seer." *You want to bypass me and deal directly with the Serpent, but you are too weak. Mordanek was the only one able to do that, but you are still trying. He was strong enough to reopen the Sanctuary. You can't even activate a Maletera; you can open just a few doors,* High Priest.

"You achieved much with the Last Empress," Dochia said. "You divided the Alban Empire between you." As she spoke, Meriaduk vanished from sight, and she was alone with Nabal, in the vision.

"That's quite an old story. We worked well together, indeed, but she is too anchored in the past. The Serpent promised us a faster path than Fate. We need it. In the last four thousand years, the world has become a stagnant place. All the new civilizations have built on the previous ones, and they have built less and less. Nothing new has been created. Things can't go like this forever."

"Maybe we should try a more … peaceful path."

"We need to purge some old bones from the continent. We need fresh blood, fresh rules and fresh rulers. You have strange thoughts for an apprentice priestess of the Serpent."

I must be careful. "There is no need to waste useful resources; the population is still a fraction of what it was during the Empire, and Baraki is not really a builder."

"Oh, no," Nabal laughed. "He is a destroyer. Why do you think we chose such an old Seer? We don't want him to destroy too much."

"With the Arenian and Khadate armies under his command, he doesn't need much time."

"Perhaps. Meriaduk was right, you have an interesting mind, and we may collaborate in future. I will keep an eye on you." Nabal smiled coldly, his eyes fixed on her, and she frowned at him, but he only smiled wider.

I should have kept my mouth shut, Dochia thought when Nabal had vanished, and her mind returned to the dome. Baraki threw a murderous stare at her, but kept his mouth shut. *Did Nabal tame him?* she wondered.

"The Map," Meriaduk said, and flashed a brief smile at Baraki. "What place do you want to see?"

"My Farsight can see things twenty miles away," Baraki boasted and looked at the High Priest the way you look at an insect in the grass.

"My Map can see the whole world. What place do you want to see?" Meriaduk did not even bother to hide his condescension.

"Frankis."

The High Priest moved his finger on the smooth surface in front of him, then rotated the red sphere. "That's Peyris," he said, the voice of a teacher speaking to a small child, and the city appeared as being seen from the peak of a high mountain. "We can see a city, a mountain, or an army moving on the ground."

"An army," Baraki whispered, rubbing his chin. "Can we see a person too?"

"Perhaps. What person to you have in mind?"

Baraki opened his mouth. And closed it.

"I think I know," Meriaduk chuckled without humor. "You are afraid of Codrin. He may become soon the Seer of Fate. Nabal told me. You don't have the mind of a king, Baraki. You have the mind of a usurper. There is too much fear in you."

"Can you find him?" Baraki swallowed his pride.

"I can show any place that we already have on the paper maps. If you know where Codrin is, I can show him to you. Why are you afraid of him? The Seer of the Serpent must be fearless."

"You know nothing about war and ruling, priest. There is no need to send an army when a team of Assassins can eliminate him. The army will go after his death and conquer the land for me. Take care of the Sanctuary, I will take care of the continent."

"For the Serpent." *You are just a tool Baraki. I represent the Serpent here, and there is no need for you after the land is taken. Even Nabal agreed with this.* "You will conquer the land for the Serpent." Meriaduk's voice roughened as he spoke. "I will give you a chance to find Codrin. The Map can link you to the place it shows. Use your Farsight and find the young man you fear so much."

The veins on Barakis's neck bulged, and he pressed his tongue into his lower lip. His face reddened. "Stop babbling and make the link," he snapped.

"The link to Peyris is already done. Use your *mind*. The Seer *should* have such a thing. A tiny one perhaps."

Eyes locked, the Seer and the High Priest glared at each other in icy silence, the atmosphere heavy with their seething fury.

"Stop them." Nabal appeared alone in Dochia's vision.

"They act like brainless bulls, but they must agree on their own will." *Pray that it never happens.*

"Why?"

"Such old bulls don't get tamed until they break a horn or two. That's not much damage, and they need to learn together. You will see. Old people know many things, but they are afraid to learn new ones. Give them the opportunity to make some useless grand gestures now, or we must build walls between them."

"Be careful, Dochia," Nabal warned and vanished from her vision.

Baraki's eyes were bulging, but he was the first to look away, and Meriaduk smiled thinly. Mouth tight closed, the Seer of the Serpent concentrated on his Farsight. One minute passed, then another one. "I can't," he blurted. "Something is blocking my Farsight."

"I blocked his Farsight," Ai chuckled in Dochia's mind. *"He is as bad as Meriaduk, and I felt that you wanted to stop him."*

"Perhaps the dome is blocking you." Dochia struggled to suppress her amusement, looking at Baraki. "It was built deep underground and has no windows."

I never had issues, even when using the Farsight in the deepest cave. Is this place different? Baraki blinked at her for a moment, then he scowled. *But I can use her excuse.* "You are right." He spoke fast, his words almost unintelligible.

"I will give you a tablet," Meriaduk said, and picked one from the table on his right. "It is linked to the Map, and you can use it from your room. The Serpent has great powers, Baraki. You just started to understand them. One of my priests will teach you how to use the tablet, but there is no way that you can use it *alone*." The priest flashed a large smile, looking at the Seer with a cold amusement, which seemed calculated to make him even more uncomfortable.

Baraki paused to think with his mouth half open. Then he snapped it shut, before saying, "Very well."

"Don't worry, Dochia," Ai said when she returned to her room, sensing her worries, "Nabal can enter only the two largest domes in the Sanctuary."

"Why?" Dochia asked surprised that such a powerful entity could be restrained. Nabal was an Ascendant Wanderer.

"The Sanctuary is a special place."

You are teasing me again. "Is the Empress able to come here too?"

"Yes, with the same restrictions as Nabal, but why would she?"

"Perhaps to gather information."

"She was here in the past, trying to convince Mordanek, the Great Priest, to close the Sanctuary."

"She failed, then." Dochia felt anxiety pressing on her. "And I suppose that Nabal can visit our house outside the Sanctuary."

"Yes."

"I should not have provoked him."

"What you did today will prove useful in the future. I feel it. There is some rivalry between him and Meriaduk. Nabal may find you useful, and there is a limit to his power to wander around the world. Usually, he needs an anchor to reach your house or any other place on the ground. He needs to connect to you, or to other people in your house. And maybe to Umbra too. He can't do this without the person who is the anchor knowing what's happening. Their powers are more limited than you think. The Gods took care of that. At least in this, both Fate and Serpent think the same. People are weak. A weak man or woman with too much power is dangerous."

"Are you sure?"

"Yes, Dochia. That's how it works. To travel without an anchor requires a level of energy that drains any Ascendant Wanderer. He would not be able to spy more than a few seconds on you, and he will feel like an exhausted old mule. He is a mule," she chuckled, and Dochia smiled despite her tension. "The same is true for the Empress too, though she is a little stronger than Nabal. Even in the upper spheres there are limitations. And there are rules."

Some people enjoy breaking them. Dochia shrugged but stayed silent.

Once the commotion following Kasia's escape from the Sanctuary had died down, twice a week, on a sunny day, Irina, Dochia's youngest guard, took her for a walk in the forest behind their house. She was not much older than Kasia, and they got on well together. It was mid-autumn, and the leaves of the maple trees and beeches in the forest had exploded in myriad warm tones: red and orange, violet and tangerine. Kasia had not visited this forest before, as their house was on the other side of the city, but she was used to the vivid colors of autumn covering the land. For Irina, Nerval autumn forest was a marvel — there were no maple trees of this kind in Frankis. The forest was not a crowded place. Now and then, children and old people came and went, looking for firewood. In the summer, they hunted for mushrooms too but, there were no mushrooms in autumn. It was too cold. Nerval was built at the edge of the taiga, the large blanket of forest covering two continents.

"Training?" Irina asked, scanning the forest; there was no one around them.

"Training." Kasia smiled; she was smiling much more than in the past. She was far from a trained Wanderer, but her skills were improving. When Dochia had tested the girl, she found good coordination and speed in her. And a strong will too. In the house, or in the forest, Kasia trained hard and never complained. Any girl walking on the streets of Nerval knew the value of being able to defend herself. It was a dangerous city. Lawless. And the Wanderers taught her things that even the best fighters of Iovon did not know. Perhaps even the guards in the Sanctuary did not know such defensive movements.

After an hour, both girls were tired, and lay on the grass. Content, Kasia smiled. She saw Irina as the sister she had never had and, for the first time since her parents had died, she felt part of a family. Still smiling, Kasia picked up a large maple leaf from the ground. "These are my favorite autumn colors." She spread her palm, mimicking the lobes of the leaf, which was twice the size of her hand. The leaf was mostly a palette of violet nuances with tangerine borders. "I want to kill Meriaduk with my own hands." She tightened her palm in a fist over the leaf. *And my brother. He sold me to that monster.* She did not voice her thought, unwilling to let Irina think she was obsessed with revenge.

"You are courageous," Irina said, her eyes joyful, and tapped Kasia's head. "But that's not your task. Meriaduk is too strong. We should return, now."

I will become strong enough to kill him. "I would like to stay a while longer. This is the best part of autumn in Nerval."

Irina scanned the forest again, but they were still alone. "Mira has to go to the market and wants me to wait for Dochia. Don't stay long."

Alone, Kasia walked absently, letting the warmth of the day bathe her. It was one of those rare days that felt more like late summer. Perhaps the last one before the first freeze would touch Nerval – the Fools' Summer, people called such days. Caught in her own thoughts, Kasia was slow to notice the four men advancing through the forest; now she was on her guard. Pretending to be unaware, she changed course slightly, walking a little faster. They changed course too. She walked further, her eyes ranging left and right, searching for an escape. *The bush*, she thought, and changed her course again. Once the dense bush was between her and the men, she ran. After a while, she turned her head, but the men were not yet in sight. Too late, she saw the other two men blocking her path, and too late she recognized them. A hard punch in the stomach forced the air from her, and she fell to her knees. Another blow on her chin, and she felt nothing more. The men pulled a bag over her head. It was long enough to cover her thin body completely. They tied the bag, and one of them carried her like a rolled carpet on his shoulder. She recovered consciousness when they dropped her like a piece of merchandise on a hard wooden floor. Rough hands pulled at her, dragging her out of the bag, making her kneel.

"Little sister, I did not expect to see you so soon." Iovon looked at her with a cold smile on his lips. "I had to return the money when you ran away from the temple." He came closer and slapped her hard.

Without looking at him, Kasia touched her bloodied lips. "What kind of man sells his own sister? You are worse than a rat. Or a pig. Worse than both." Her voice cracked, and her lips pained, but she felt better.

Iovon slapped her again, only this time he slapped the air. She ducked, her left hand stuck to the floor, and her foot sprang up, kicking him in the crotch, a move that Irina had taught her. Iovon wailed, and fell to his knees, next to her, his eyes wide. Before the stunned men in the room could react, she jumped to her feet, and kicked his face with her heavy winter boot. This time, Iovon fell in silence, and lay on the floor, unconscious, among three lost teeth.

"The priests will not like it if you harm me," Kasia said, looking around at the four men in the room. "And if this worse than a rat *brother* sold his own sister, how long until he kills or sells you too? Eh? Tell me."

"Take Kasia upstairs and lock her in the small room," Gresha said.

It took Iovon ten minutes to wake up, and he needed Gresha's help to sit in his chair. "I will kill that bitch," he mumbled, feeling something wrong in his mouth. He tested the gap between his teeth with his tongue and anger exploded inside him. "I will kill her. Now." He tried to stand, but Gresha's arm kept him seated.

"I've sent a courier to the temple, to tell the priests she is here. They may come to take her this evening. You don't want to mess with them."

"Since when are you telling me what to do?"

Gresha shrugged. "You told us that you had found a man for Kasia, not that you sold her to the priests."

"I don't need to explain anything to you."

"The men are not pleased. We do bad things, but we don't sell our people, much less a relative." Gresha was their cousin.

"Get out," Iovon snarled, his face locked in a frown of deep suspicion.

Confined in the small room, Kasia sat on the floor, leaning against the wall, arms clasped around her knees. "Iovon will give me back to the priests," she whispered. "They will torture me again and use that evil thing on my mind to find out what happened. They will torture Dochia, too. Because of me." Her last words ended in a bitter sob, and she pressed her head on her knees. *How could I be so stupid?*

The man they sent to the temple returned late in the evening. The soldiers at the gate did not want to receive him without having an appointment from a priest. Relieved, Gresha went up to talk with Kasia.

"My man was sent back by the priests. He will go again tomorrow. I brought you something to eat," Gresha said, guilt in his voice and, crouching in front of her, he placed a plate of food on the floor. "I cooked it myself."

"Your man?" Kasia asked, surprise on her face, and some hope too.

"We decided to replace Iovon. You were right; we have flaws, but we don't sell our people, not even to those bloody priests."

"Then you will let me go. Please, Gresha."

"I am sorry, Kasia, but I have to return you to the temple."

"But they think I am dead."

"No, they don't. Three weeks ago, they came here looking for you. I can only promise you that I will get you out of Nerval if you escape again. You should not come here. Hide in the old warehouse. I will find you a place in a village and pay for your food."

"I will not be able to escape again!" she shouted and grabbed his hands. "They tortured and raped me. Six priests raped me day and night. They laughed, saying that pleasing them would purify me. Now, they will kill me. Please, Gresha. Just let me go, and you will never see me again."

"I am sorry, Kasia, but too many of our men saw you in the house, and the priests are bound to have a spy here. They have spies everywhere, and they will kill all of us, and our families, even the little children, if we don't send you back. You know that." Shaking his head, Gresha stood up. A single tear ran down his face. Kasia saw it, and she started to sob.

Dochia arrived in her room at noon. During the day, she could enter and leave the Sanctuary through the three main gates, and there was no need for Ai to help her. The Wanderer had strong enough blood to use those gates, as did many other priests and acolytes of the Serpent.

"Ai," she called, knowing that the young woman was always listening.

"Yes, Dochia."

"Umbra has agreed to meet you."

"When?" There was an eagerness in Ai's voice that made Dochia smile.

"Would tomorrow evening work for you?"

"Yes. Do you know why he agreed? I know that it will not be easy for him to enter in a confined space, without windows."

"Perhaps he wants to see a new kind of magic, just as you do," Dochia laughed.

"I don't think that we are similar," Ai said, thoughtfully.

"And that makes both of you even more eager to meet."

"How is Kasia?"

"She is in good shape. I left her training with Irina. Our young girl is making good progress."

"Training is good. Soon, she must return and start to train here."

"Is that really necessary?" Dochia forced herself to stay calm. To breathe long and slow.

"You are tough, Dochia, and the blood is strong in you, but it's not strong enough for what you need to do. Kasia has strong blood too. You need help, and Kasia is stronger than you think. She is still young, indeed, but so were you once. Train her well. We should bring her here in two or three months. I will prepare a hidden room for her. Don't worry; it will be in an isolated area where Meriaduk and the other priests can't go."

"Would Kasia be able to leave the Sanctuary without you?"

"No. At least, she can't leave the hidden place without me, but she can leave the Sanctuary through the secret door. That door she can open. She has the blood."

"Ai," Dochia said gently. "Don't you see the flaw?"

"The flaw you are thinking of is not real. I will always be here, until the Sanctuary is closed."

"Accidents can happen."

"There will be no accidents," Ai said, slightly irritated, letting Dochia know that, when all was said and done, she was alone in her room.

❧

Close to the midnight, loud knocking disturbed the silence of the home that was now Kasia's prison. Most of the men were already sleeping, after a hard day. They feared and hated Iovon. Now they only hated him. They hated him even more.

"I hope you are not troubling us for nothing," the sentry snapped, coming to the door. "Who is there?" His angry voice reverberated through the small hall and passed through the thick door.

"The Serpent be with you, son. Open the door." The voice, coming through the hard wood, was not angry; it was icy, and the sentry felt it whipping him.

"Yes, priest." He opened the door and bowed deeply. As he did so, he saw the great silver insignia carried only by the Vicarius.

The Vicarius touched the man's brow in benediction and entered, followed by two more priests, who acted as his guards. A Vicarius never left the temple without guards. They were as important in Nerval as they were hated. Only Meriaduk was more important and more hated than them. In contrast to the warmth of the past day, the night had brought the first frost of the autumn, and the priests were dressed in rich, hooded pelerines, marking their rank, over their woolen clothes. Cold, the wind entered the house with them, through the open door. The sentry shivered from both fear and cold.

"Thank you, Vicarius," the sentry breathed. He was elated by the benediction; the priests were usually sparing with them, and coming from a Vicarius made it even stronger. Afraid to ask the reason for their visit, he waited patiently.

"It has come to our attention that you are holding a young bird that flew the Serpent's nest, a few weeks ago."

Who betrayed us? the sentry worried, sensing danger in the priest's frosty tone, a hoarse whisper, as if he had caught a cold before coming here.

"Yes, priest; the girl is here." It was Gresha who spoke his time, walking through the hall, and the priest turned toward him. Seeing the insignia, Gresha bowed until his head was level with his knees. "Vicarius, please forgive me; I did not know who you were."

"Who are you?"

"I am Gresha, the new leader."

"I wonder why we were not told about the girl. Rise."

"We sent a man to the temple, but he was turned away by the guards."

"Had your man no mouth to speak his duty? Or is that just a convenient excuse?" The priest fixed a pair of ferocious eyes on Gresha, who stepped back as far as the wall behind him permitted. All he could see of the Vicarius were vicious eyes and a large, blond moustache.

"I swear by the Serpent that we sent a man to the temple today," Gresha breathed. *I should have waited for a few more days, before taking the lead, and let that piece of shit deal with this.*

The Vicarius pulled a Maletera from his pocket, and both men in front of him froze, terror in their eyes. "Bring me to the girl. You," he pointed at the sentry, "leave the hall. My priests will take care that no one disturbs us until this little affair is done. Pray that I don't want to see you again."

The man tried to move, but his feet did not obey him, and Gresha had to kick him hard, before saying, "Yes, Vicarius. Please follow me."

The man left the hall walking on all fours and opened the back exit door with his head under the guards' mocking gazes, while the Vicarius and Gresha climbed the stairs.

Kasia could not sleep, yet she was not really awake; she was in a state of mind filled with unwanted things. Perhaps she was afraid of sleeping. The stairs squeaked outside, and she started. Her trained ear heard two people coming up. *They have come for me.* She panicked and realized there was no escape. *There is one*, she finally thought, and a sad smile spread on her lips. *At least this will keep Dochia safe.* She moved fast toward the window and reached for the lock to open it. The first one was easy to open but, because of the cold winters, all the windows in Nerval were doubled. She grabbed the knob of the second window, listening to the footsteps climbing stairs. *They are almost here.* The lock was stiff, and she could not open it. She tried again, shaking it with both hands. It did not open. She smashed her elbow into the glass, breaking it. A shard cut through her arm, but she ignored the pain; she would be dead soon, and pain no longer mattered.

"Here," Gresha pointed at the door in front. "It's not locked."

"Guard the door. I need to fix her mind before we leave." The Vicarius waved the Maletera in front of Gresha's eyes, and he leaned against the wall, unable to speak, terror overwhelming him. His wide eyes followed the priest through the door. *Poor Kasia*, he thought. *It's not my fault. That idiot Iovon made this mess.*

There was a muffled cry in the room, then a brief fight, then silence. Gresha would have liked to listen through the closed door, or even to go in and interfere, but he thought better of it. After five long minutes, the Vicarius left the room, without looking back. Her shoulders slumped, Kasia followed, a few moments later, walking like a somnambulist. Gresha saw no life in her eyes, and he said a muted *I am sorry*. Void of will, the girl did not react in any way. Her left arm was bandaged.

"A little wild, your bird," the Vicarius said, his voice still hoarse. "She tried to jump through the window and cut herself on the broken glass. We need her in good shape in the Temple, to please the Serpent, and I lost precious time bandaging her. Keeping her safe was your job, Gresha. You are lucky that I arrived in time. This is your second failure. The Serpent doesn't like failure." Playing absently with the Maletera between his fingers, the Vicarius fixed his ferocious eyes on Gresha, who pressed himself against the wall, eyes half closed.

Downstairs, the guards grabbed Kasia by the arms and pulled her out of the house. She offered no resistance. Before he left, the Vicarius turned toward Gresha.

"The girl's escape from the Temple was a kind of ... embarrassment. I am counting on you to keep your mouth shut, even if other, lesser priests come to inquire about her. You will speak only if Meriaduk requests information about this case. Until then, you must forget everything. Make your men understand that too. Carelessness may *endanger* their families. You know in what way. Ah, and Iovon. I want you to dispose of him. Make sure that his body is never found. Be careful, Gresha. No more failures; one body or two, it doesn't matter much to me. The Serpent bless you."

"Yes, Vicarius." Gresha bowed deeply and stayed like that until after the priest had vanished into the night, his steps slow. Hearing nothing, he finally straightened and unsheathed his knife. Then he closed the door. "At least this I will do it willingly. For Kasia, not for that bloody priest." *I wish I could kill the priest too.* The thought was so wicked that Gresha did not dare to voice it, and he shook his head to dislodge the blasphemous idea.

Chased by the cold wind, the priests and the girl moved quickly through the city, and when the house lay far behind them, Kasia straightened and looked around her, saying, "Oh Dochia, I would have never thought of such an escape. I will be in your debt all my life." She embraced the Wanderer and stifled a sob.

"You are more resourceful than you think, Kasia." *She tried to kill herself to keep me safe.* Dochia gently stroked the girl's hair, before embracing her too. "Your time may come sooner than both of us want to happen and, next time, it may be that you are the one who saves me."

"Are you not afraid of the Maletera?"

"What Maletera?"

"The one you carry in your pocket."

"That is just a sphere made of stone, and another lesson for you. It's all about perception. Sometimes the object in one's mind replaces the real thing. You just need to look confident, as if you really have it. Perception is a powerful tool, able to shape its own reality." For a few moments, Dochia stopped both speaking and walking, and her hand moved over her face. "That bloody false moustache was making me itch," she laughed, placing it in her pocket.

Two months later, sensing that Kasia's memories of her painful experience in the Sanctuary had started to fade, Dochia thought it was time to take the next step she had agreed with Ai. "We need to start your second round of training," she said, tentatively. Kasia's fighting training was going well, and the girl showed both native talent and willingness to learn.

"In the Sanctuary." The girl's eyes narrowed, and her nostrils flared, fear and resolution etched together on her face.

"When you feel ready."

"I will never feel ready, but I will do everything you want if I can help other children escape." *And kill Meriaduk.*

Chapter 12 – Cleyre

Cleyre was not expecting guests so early in the morning. Not that she really had guests, but Reymont's spies came from time to time, to check on her. The Secretary would have liked to kill her, but he was afraid of the Assassins. The fear that Codrin had planted in his mind was still there. No one dared to defy the invisible order of the Assassins. For three weeks now, she had been confined to her room. Sometimes it was Albert and Reymont who came to see her and to ask, with false joviality:

"How are you today, Cleyre?"

Sometimes it was Nicolas, the only one she still felt she could trust. The Spatar of Peyris had his own worries; Duke Albert did not trust him. Or more to the point, Reymont, the Secretary of Peyris and the Hidden Sage of the Circle, did not trust him. There were rumors that Nicolas would be soon replaced by Sandro, the second Spatar of Peyris but, confined to her room, Cleyre had not heard them.

She wished that Costa would come and see her. He was not allowed, and Reymont, unbeknownst to Cleyre, had punished her friend. Costa had been demoted and was no longer allowed to lead a company overseeing one of the city's gates.

The man who entered her room was unknown to her. He stopped in the middle of the room and stared at her, a wicked smile on his lips, the kind of reaction a man has when he buys a good horse or a woman when she buys new jewelry. He was tall and thick and moved clumsily. Two guards in Peyris colors followed him. Hidden in the corridor, Reymont watched, laughing silently.

"You have the wrong room," Cleyre said coldly. "Leave."

Saying nothing, the man hit her hard in the stomach, knocking her down.

"You will be my wife, and you must learn to behave."

"I will not marry you," Cleyre said, rising to one knee.

The man struck again, but this time she was prepared and ducked under his arm, moving away from him.

"Stop her," the man said.

"You will not touch me," Cleyre growled at the soldiers.

"My dear, Cleyre," Reymont said, entering the room. "Why are you always trying to make things difficult? The Duke had arranged your marriage. Grand Seigneur Veres, here," he gestured toward the man, "will be your husband. He will soon own Midia, which was his father's castle." *An oaf as your husband and the mirage of a castle, that's exactly what you deserve, little bitch.*

"I won't accept this marriage," Cleyre said defiantly, knowing there was not much she could do.

"I am afraid that you have no choice." Reymont's mouth smiled, his eyes did not. "Take her."

This time the soldiers obeyed the order, dragged her out of her room, and forced her to walk from the palace until they arrived at the Ducal Church in Peyris. The Duke was there, along with the priest and his acolytes and some servants from the court.

"My dear niece, you look lovely, today," Albert said, a smile on his lips; one that he thought charming, though most people thought it only exaggerated his stupid looks. "I'm sure it will be a wonderful ceremony. Proceed." He nodded at Reymont first, then at the priest.

The priest started his long discourse about Fate and her dedication to family. "Cleyre Peyris, do you take this man as your husband?" he finally asked.

"No," Cleyre said flatly, and the priest's eyes widened.

Before someone else could react, Veres hit her hard in the stomach, and she doubled over in pain.

"Young man," the priest said, helping Cleyre back to her feet, "this is the Church of Fate, and violence is not permitted here. I understand her reticence to marry a man like you."

"Mateus, marry them," the Duke said.

"She does not accept the marriage."

"Who cares about that? Just marry them. I order it."

"I am afraid that I can't do such thing. It would be against Fate. Marriage requires mutual acceptance and willingness. This man must be educated first. He has brought shame to the church with his violence."

Veres grunted and, as always when he was thwarted, a dark anger filled his mind. He stepped forward to hit the priest. At the last moment, the guards restrained him.

"Bishop," Reymont said, nodding at the Chief of the Church in Peyris.

"Mateus, this marriage was ordered by the Duke. It is a political matter of great importance for the Duchy. The will of a stubborn girl can't prevent the will of the Duke. She is not allowed to endanger the Duchy with her foolish behavior. I order you to marry them."

"I apologize, Monsenioris, but I can't bless this marriage. The man is not fit for it. He must be educated." His voice was calm, but hard lines creased Mateus's cheeks, and he poked a finger at Veres.

"From this moment, you are no longer the head priest of Peyris. Leave the church."

"As you wish, Monsenioris, but the Church of Fate will only lose by enacting such a sham marriage; you are abusing your power, and disregarding Fate," the priest said calmly. His eyes were somber, shaded by lowered brows, and he walked away, ignoring the Duke.

Encouraged that some still had enough courage to oppose both a sham marriage and the Duke, and still hoping, Cleyre bowed slightly to the priest, who answered with a sad smile. It took the Bishop another two hours to find an obedient priest and then Cleyre found herself married, for the second time, against her will.

Once the ceremony ended, she was escorted to a carriage where a coffer filled with her clothes was already waiting, and ten minutes later, she was leaving Peyris, followed by her new husband and twenty-eight soldiers, three of them given to Veres by Aron. There was an old woman in the carriage too. Cleyre ignored her.

Veres spent the entire journey watching her, a lascivious look in his eyes. Cleyre ignored him and, as he had been advised by Reymont, Veres tried to ignore her too. He couldn't. Twice Ferko, the captain who the Secretary had sent to escort them, had to intervene to keep Veres away from her. He was a tough soldier, and Veres, with all his desire to have her, did not dare to confront him. Cleyre was not easy to impress, but this loathsome man's gaze made her skin crawl. They arrived at the obscure Eagle's Nest fortress in the evening. Of all of them, only Ferko knew the place; he was an old hand who fought for more than twenty years for Peyris. It was an isolated fortress, in a narrow valley at the foot of the White Mountains. Ferko did not like the place, but Reymont had promised him Knighthood, if things went well. He did not like the guardian's role either. Veres was supposed to tame Cleyre without harming her. During the journey, Ferko started to doubt that. Veres had the subtlety of a bull in rage.

"Without harming her too much, that is," the Secretary had said. "I want her to ... heed my advice when she returns. I represent the Circle in Peyris. You should not forget it either, Ferko."

The old gate screeched when one of the five soldiers guarding the place opened it. Inside, both Cleyre and Veres grimaced at the sight. Apart from being decrepit, the place was as functional as it was ugly. She was not an expert in fortifications, but even for her it was clear why Albert and Reymont had chosen the place. It was easy to defend. Thirty-three soldiers could keep a large army at bay.

After dinner, Veres had ordered her to her room under guard, through corridors thick and smoky with the haze of greasy torches, and there was no way she could escape. He had her trapped. Cleyre knew that he was coming for her, and her eyes searched the room for something she could use. The window had metal grates. There was only a bed, a table and two chairs in her room. The chairs were chained to the table. Just to do something, Cleyre searched the bed too. She found nothing under the mattress or the bed sheets. She listened hard, but the walls were so thick that she couldn't hear the voices of the guards in the hall. On the road, she had recognized two of the guards; they had fought under her father's command once, and they nodded discreetly at her, when their eyes met. That was all. Her father was dead, there was a new Duke, and they did not want to risk their lives for a girl in disgrace. *Maybe later*, she thought, hopefully.

She sat on the edge of the bed, waiting; she realized Veres had come for her when the door rattled. Old iron hardware creaked in protest as he lurched into the room. He was half drunk, and his eyes sparkled blearily, seeing her. She could smell it on his breath from where she sat. Cheap wine.

"Undress," he said.

"Now that we are married, maybe we should talk, get to know each other better," she said and stood up.

His fist went for her belly, but this time she was prepared. Cleyre was an agile woman, and she had some fighting training. She ducked, and Veres almost fell on the bed, propelled by drunken momentum. She restrained herself from hitting the back of his neck, at the last moment. She was glad that Veres did not see how her arm sprang toward his neck, then pulled back.

"Let's sit together and talk," she said again, but Veres was too furious now to listen, and listening to women was not his strongest point.

Since the day they were attacked in the hunting house in Severin, and he had been too scared to defend Jara, even when his younger sisters jumped to help her against the assassins, he hated them, and he hated all women. He had built his life on the perverse thought that women were weak and stupid and meant to serve him. Sensing his potential as a tool, Aron had taken care to enhance his feelings and shape him as he wished. With a normal childhood, Veres might not have been more intelligent, but he could have been different.

Boiling with rage, he went out and came back again with two soldiers that wore the colors of Severin. She retreated toward her bed, but there was no way to escape. One of the soldiers grabbed her by the hair and threw her into the bed. The other one chained her to one of the iron bars of the bed. It was a very flexible chain, resembling a ten feet long snake, thinner than her small finger, and she realized that everything had been planned from Peyris.

One day Reymont will pay, she thought; but she was wrong this time, it was Dizier who had planned this. He had been given to Veres as an advisor by Aron, and he acted as what might be called Veres's mind.

"Undress," Veres barked again when the men left the room. *If I give up now, that will only embolden him.* "Would it be so hard for you to talk to your wife?" She stood up slowly, trying to avoid a harsh reaction from him.

"You have to obey me," he said, and for a moment, she thought that maybe he would just continue to grow at her. She was wrong. Veres tried to hit her again, and she ducked again. He grabbed the chain and pulled. She fell straight into his chest. Before she could react, he hit her in the stomach and her breath disappeared. He threw her on the bed again. While she was still fighting for breath, he tore her undergarments to shreds and climbed on top of her. She resisted the impulse to scream, fighting him with every ounce of strength she had. But Veres was too strong and too big; he quickly overwhelmed her and trapped her under his body. He grunted with pleasure, as she bit her lip to avoid screaming.

The agony went on long into the night. When Veres wasn't raping her, he was beating her. By the time morning arrived, he had taken his wife three times and beaten her so badly that her eyes were swollen shut. With the dawn, he dressed calmly and left her chamber as if nothing was amiss. The second night was not much different, except that Cleyre did not even try to speak to him.

Then he stopped visiting her. He still wanted to, but Maro, the old woman who Reymont had set as his spy on Cleyre, spoke to Ferko, and then Dizier spoke to Veres.

"Sir," Dizier said to Veres, "if Lady Cleyre dies, Peyris will not need you anymore."

"She must obey," Veres said.

"Any woman must obey her husband, but there are other ways to make them understand. Lady Cleyre has had a harsh lesson, maybe it is time for a ... gentler approach."

"She must obey," Veres repeated but, in the end, he agreed to leave her some time to recover, and in future to beat her more gently.

Ferko was a hard-bitten soldier, but he did not expect what he saw in Cleyre's room, and for a while he could do nothing but stare.

"Captain," said the soldier, the one that had known Cleyre since she was a child. "She is Duke Stefan's granddaughter and Sir Paul's daughter. We both fought under his command."

"I know that," Ferko growled, "but I thought her intelligent enough not to provoke Veres."

"You thought wrong," the old woman said, "and whatever they promised you, it will vanish, if she dies. She is still like this from last night. Unconscious."

"Treat her."

"I am not a healer, but I will do what I can. It won't help if he comes again during the night."

"He won't."

Ferko spoke to Veres, his tough hand gripping the young man's shoulder and, already tamed by Dizier, Veres agreed to stay away from his wife's bed for a week. He was not interested in talking, so he did not bother her at all.

For two days, Maro kept changing the compresses on Cleyre battered body. From the first moment Cleyre became conscious again, she decided to ignore the old woman; she was Reymont's spy and in league with the ones who had brought her to this state.

When she felt that things were better, Maro asked for a bathtub and hot water. Ferko complained but conformed to her wish.

Cleyre said nothing when the old woman helped her undress and sit in the bathtub. It felt good, and even better when Maro scrubbed her skin.

"Maybe you should change your approach with Veres," Maro said.

"He enjoys hurting women. That's why your friend Reymont forced me to marry the pig."

"Reymont is my relative. That doesn't make him my friend."

"He trusts you."

"Yes, he sent me here to look after you."

"And a fine job you are making of it." Cleyre pointed at the bruises all over her body and her still swollen eyes.

"I may be your only friend here," Maro said, still scrubbing her skin.

"You can't be friends with both Reymont and me."

"I thought we'd established that he is my relative, not my friend. Would it be so hard to cooperate with both the Secretary and the Circle?"

"But we have cooperated," Cleyre snorted. "Our cooperation started when Reymont paid twenty mercenaries to kill me. I was lucky that a Triangle of Assassins was on hand to keep me alive."

"So, it's true then."

She wants to learn more about the Assassins. Wrong, Reymont wants to learn more. "Yes, it's true. They let it be known that I was under their protection. That's why your... cooperative relative came up with this new idea. Grandfather cooperated with Reymont too, and got murdered for it. Poisoned."

"I thought that the Duke..."

"Your relative is good at hiding his tracks."

"It will not help you, if Reymont learns what you think."

"I know that you will tell him, but it doesn't matter anymore. Barring a miracle, I will not escape alive from here."

"You will," Maro said and left the room. She returned a few minutes later with a potion. "Drink this," she pushed the cup into Cleyre's hand.

Cleyre looked dubiously at the cup, sniffed it, then tasted the potion. "Bloody Moon," she said and drank the bitter tisane.

"All things considered, I thought you probably don't want to fall pregnant with that husband of yours."

"You thought well."

"You know about Bloody Moon potion."

"I am not exactly a virgin. Thank Fate for that. Do you realize what would have happened if that animal had been my first man?"

The week Veres left her alone, she planned and planned, and the only logical outcome was that she needed to kill him. That would not set her free, but Albert would at least have to find her another husband. *That will take time*, she thought; *especially if my intended knows I killed his predecessor. And I would need to act like a ... submissive wife.* The only thing she could think of was to strangle Veres with the chain tied to her leg. It was long, thin and flexible enough to be a tool of death. She tested it against the pillow.

When Veres returned, Cleyre's wounds were not fully healed, but she felt confident and smiled at him when he entered.

Chapter 13 – Codrin

I was so close to saving Saliné, Codrin thought for the hundredth time. He shook his head and returned to his work. While he was riding on the road from Rochil to Severin, he had decided to fight for her and to work hard and keep his failure out of his mind. Work helped him. It kept his mind busy. One by one, his councilors entered in the council room which had once belonged to Mohor. It was not easy for him to work there, as every object carried memories that he wanted to keep at bay, but it was the most convenient place, with the cache of maps and its central position in the castle. Of all his councilors only Mara and Sava were not there, and he missed both. Mara for her subtle knowledge of his working habits, and Sava for his quick mind and sense of humor. Sometimes, it seemed that Mara knew better than Codrin what he needed. When the others were finally settled, he placed the letter from Mara on the table.

"Pierre is almost fully healed and has left for Tolosa. Despite the efforts of our people in Poenari, we still don't know who tried to kill him. Until we learn more, or we return, Poenari remains a closed city, so your families are safe there." *And my son too.* Of all the men in the room, apart from him, only Lisandru and Julien, who was Sava's son, had relatives in Poenari. Damian was still on the road, coming back from the Mountes in White Salt Mountain, and he was expected to return a few days later. "Vlaicu, how many soldiers do we have now?"

"Five hundred and fifty are already here. As Vlad mentioned this morning, Phillip will arrive tomorrow from Deva. He brings two hundred and fifty more soldiers. We were expecting only two hundred."

Codrin knew the numbers well, but he also knew that talking about the extra troops would raise morale. He had never had eight hundred soldiers under his command, and that brought his men a new degree of confidence. Until now, they always fought against greater numbers. His new army would soon be almost equal to Orban's.

"What about provisions?"

"Most of them are already here. Phillip is bringing his own provisions."

"We leave in three days. Split the army and the convoy with provisions into five groups. It's not possible to move the carts through the forest, so they will follow the small roads north toward Arad." Codrin stood up and went to the large map on the wall. "We will go this way." He traced a secondary route from Severin to Arad. As well as being less used, it was also longer, as it went north-west for a while, before returning east toward Arad. "Twenty guards will join each convoy, and they will travel like caravans, not like an army. The remaining soldiers from each five groups will travel through the forest. Even on minor roads, we may encounter Orban's patrols. Each caravan must deal with them peacefully and be prepared to tell a story about their journey to Peyris, Loxburg and other large cities in the north. Each caravan will have a different destination to give if they are asked. Only in case of emergency will the soldiers in the forest attack Orban's patrols. I want to move like a ghost, unseen."

"What about the scouts?" Vlad asked.

"We will split them up too, but they will remain under your direct command. We will set a certain distance between the caravans, so the scouts' areas will overlap. Your scouts will also be our couriers. To begin with, two hours distance between the caravans should be fine."

"It sounds like a good plan," Vlaicu said.

Codrin smiled briefly, knowing that Vlaicu would be disappointed by his next decision. "You will remain here. I need a strong man to defend Severin with a few soldiers."

For a few moments, Vlaicu frowned, but he saw the sense in Codrin's decision. "You want all the glory for yourself," he grinned. "When you say few, how few do you mean?"

"Forty soldiers, and you will have Ban here too. Before we leave, you should gather a hundred more men, old men, young men, like we did during the Mehadian campaign. They will camp outside Severin, close to the gate. Their presence will fool any spy into thinking that my army is still here. You are my Spatar, and at a certain point, I may need you. Ban will stay behind to defend Severin. Damian has not returned yet, so we don't have any news from the Mountes." Codrin looked at his men, one by one, and saw that there were no more questions. "Let's get ready."

The crossroads was now just two hours in front of them, and then they would turn east, toward Arad. Codrin was riding at leisure, with twenty-five soldiers, one mile in front of the first caravan. To an observer on the road, there was nothing to connect his group and the caravan following them, there was no sign of the hundred soldiers riding through the forest, and the scouts were out of sight. It was a warm, sunny day, and the ground under the trees along the road was broken with shadow and slashed with bright sunlight, shifting as the branches moved in the wind. People, going north and south on the road, were content. Why think of evil things on a day like this?

Before the road emerged from the valley, toward the crossroads, a squad of scouts galloped out of the forest and approached Codrin. "Incoming riders in fifteen minutes," their leader announced. "Twenty soldiers, wearing the colors of Peyris."

"Keep watch on them," Codrin said, and the scouts vanished again into the forest. "Vlad, send two men on each side of the forest, to warn the soldiers. Blue Alert, I don't expect trouble."

That was the lowest level of alert in their army; the soldiers would remain hidden, but ready to intervene.

Once they saw Codrin and his soldiers, who wore no colors, the riders from Peyris slowed down and came almost to a stop, a hundred paces away from them.

Codrin already knew who was in front of him; he had used his spyglass. "Vlad, come with me," he said and pushed Zor forward. "Spatar Nicolas," Codrin bowed briefly. "It looks to me like you are in a hurry. We will not delay you."

"The Wraith of Tolosa. I did not expect to find you here."

"Where would you expect to see a Wraith?" Codrin laughed, entering the skin of his other self, Tudor.

"Are you free?"

"That depends."

"Ah, a Wraith always means business. How many men do you have?"

"Enough."

"How many is enough?"

"Twenty-five."

Nicolas's horse reared a little and skittered nervously. It took him a few moments to calm it down. *I never heard of a Lead Protector, or even a Wraith, having so many soldiers, and they all look tough. Maybe they can help me.* "Do you remember Cleyre?"

"How can I forget such a beautiful woman, or the strange things that happened when I last met her?"

"We need to talk." Nicolas dismounted abruptly and passed the halter of his horse to one of his soldiers. Codrin did the same, letting Zor free, and they walked a few steps away. "Cleyre has been made prisoner, in a place that is hard to take. I am afraid that she will be killed."

"Who dares to provoke the Assassins? She is under their protection."

"An idiot. I am not even sure if they told him about the Assassins and their pledge." Nicolas stopped, but Codrin asked him nothing. "His name is Veres."

"The Snail?"

"Yes, the very one. Do you think you might help me? I was going to Severin to ask Codrin for help, but the sooner we act, the better." Nicolas pressed his tongue into his lower lip, his eyes fixed on Codrin with badly dissimulated expectation.

"Do you think that we can take the place with forty something soldiers?"

"No, it will take at least five hundred soldiers and two or three months to lay a successful siege."

"And what do you want me to do with forty men?"

"You are the Wraith; I am just a soldier. You must find a way. Ask the price, and I will not negotiate."

"Where is the place?"

"The Eagle's Nest, a small fortress in the White Salt Mountains of Peyris, forty miles from the border with Arad. Less than two days' ride from here."

"I don't know the place."

"The area is isolated, almost uninhabited. There are thirty-three soldiers there. Thirty of them are from Peyris."

"They would listen to you."

"Some of them might listen to me if I am able to get in. Their captain is not my friend, and he answers directly to the Duke. He was promised Knighthood for keeping Cleyre there. In fact, I am not even sure that I still am the Spatar of Peyris. I left the city in a hurry, and things may have changed." *I was the Spatar of Peyris for nine years. It was a different Dukedom. The strong men died, the weak one survived.* Nicolas sighed to himself. A long sigh that went out in silence.

"Why Veres?"

"Maud sent him to marry Cleyre, but in truth she just wants her dead."

"You mean that they...? Codrin felt a stab of anger and struggled to control his voice.

Nicolas's keen eyes sensed that Codrin was troubled. *Strange his reaction*, he thought. "Yes, he even beat her in the church, to force her say yes. Despite that, she kept saying no, and they still married her. Look, Cleyre trusts you, and she told me that I can trust you and Codrin, even with the most delicate political matters, or with her life. I hope that she is right. There are a lot of nervous people in Peyris right now, and we may soon see a rebellion aiming to replace Albert with Cleyre, but we must free her first. It will bring a good reward."

"Let's go and see the Nest. Is it on the road going north from the crossroads ahead of us?"

"Yes. How much do you want? My purse is open."

"For a job like this, I will deal directly with Cleyre, and we never talk money."

Nicolas squinted his eyes for a few moments. *A Wraith working without payment. That's the strangest thing I've heard in a while. What am I missing here? Are they … lovers? He is not weak, but I would prefer Codrin as her husband and the next Duke of Peyris.* "Fine, I will send three couriers to warn Codrin. He may still help us."

"I will take care of that. He is not in Severin right now. Let me prepare my men. There are a few more in the forest. I need an hour. Rest your soldiers until then."

One mile behind, the next group of riders on the road was led by Phillip and Boldur. "There are some new developments, and I will ride to Peyris," Codrin said, when he reached them. "Phillip, you take command of the army. Boldur and Valer will second you. Send couriers telling Vlaicu to join us."

"I smell a fight," Boldur said. "A different one."

"You have a good nose. At the crossroads ahead, you will continue north. When you pass the border of Peyris, there is a large forest right to the east."

"I know it," Boldur said.

"You camp there and wait for me. I will return in a week."

Within the promised hour, Codrin rejoined Nicolas, bringing fifty men with him, making the Spatar scratch his head, though it was still covered by his helmet.

Chapter 14 – Codrin

"Open the gate!" Vlad shouted, knocking at the wet planks. The sound echoed soggily into the night. He waited patiently, but there was no answer from inside. "Open the gate!" he repeated and used the hilt of his dagger to knock. He stuck his ear to the wood. *Nothing.* He started to bang the gate with his dagger, in a rhythmic way. One minute passed, then another. Rain hissed on the stones of the wall above, falling water splattered on the slippery cobbles, then trickled down into the cracks in the road.

"They are probably sleeping," Codrin whispered. "I wouldn't be surprised. Snail is in charge."

"What do you want?" an angry voice finally asked from inside. It sounded half asleep and muffled through the thick wood.

"I have a letter for Seigneur Veres."

"Could you not find a better time to deliver it? It's an hour before midnight." The guard opened the small window of the postern. It was too dark to see much, but he could heat better.

"We are soldiers. Do you think that Seigneurs and the like give a damn for what we want, and when we want to ride? The letter is from his mother, the Grand Signora of Arad. She sent us on our way at midnight; we have arrived at midnight, and the road was dangerous. Some robbers attacked a caravan not far from here. They killed almost everybody."

"Wasn't his mother in Severin?"

"She was, but now she has found a more powerful husband. I am sure you've heard about Orban. His horse is more important to him than a hard-working soldier like you and me. We are wet, and we saved two boys from the caravan. They are the only survivors. Them and two small barrels of wine from Tolosa."

"They have good wine there."

"I never drank better. It was meant for the Duke of Peyris. We all feel like Dukes now," Vlad laughed. "Open this damn gate; we are freezing our asses off in this bloody rain."

"You can't deliver the letter today. Seigneur Veres is occupied with his woman and has asked to not be disturbed."

"Why should I care about his woman? Let us sleep in the barn, and we'll share some of the wine with you. It warms your blood better than a woman."

"We are not allowed to open the gate during the night."

"How many of you are there? We can share the wine. One barrel for you, one for us. Just give us a place with some dry straw."

"Seven people. A full barrel, you said?"

"Forty jugs of the best wine you ever tasted."

"How many of you are out there?"

"Four men and two boys, the poor little mites we saved from the robbers."

The guard closed the window, and his voice went quiet. Silent, Vlad stuck his ear to the gate again. Their voices muffled, he could hear men speaking inside, but he was able to understand half of the words and to deduce the other half.

"I am from Tolosa," one man said. "It's a sunny, dry place, nothing like this wet hole. We should call this place the Swamp, not the Eagle's Nest. There is no better wine than ours."

"I don't know, man, we are not allowed to open the gate, starting three hours before midnight. It's close to midnight now."

"And who will know? The captain didn't come to inspect us this evening. He did not want to dirty his boots. The food came late, and it was cold. We deserve some good things. Since we came here, we've had only bad food and awful wine. The *Grand*

Seigneur is interested only in his woman; the captain is worried about his rheumatism. Nobody cares about us, and nobody will know what we did. And they have a letter from his mother. Snail will be happy tomorrow."

"Fine," the man who seemed to be in charge finally said. "Everybody, spears and crossbows. I don't want any surprises. They will come in one by one and leave a barrel here. I will open the gate," he said to Vlad through the window. "You will come inside one by one, and you will leave a barrel here with us. Understood? We have four spearmen and two crossbows, so don't try anything."

"Fate bless you, man. After all this rain even my bones are wet, and my sword is rusted. You heard the captain." Vlad shouted his last words. "Arrange yourself in a line. The horse with the wine in the middle of the row."

The gate creaked loudly, and the men at the gate cursed, afraid of waking the captain. Vlad was the first to enter, followed by Damian. Codrin and Nicolas were the last. Pintea and Lisandru walked with their knees slightly bent to look shorter, one taking the horse by the halter, the other one keeping a hand on the barrels, which were tied with ropes to the large horse. On the wall, one small torch was playing a dim light in the tunnel.

"I know you," one man said and stopped Vlad, pointing the spear at his neck. He was one of the three soldiers Bucur had given to Veres. In a swift, but natural move, Codrin and Nicolas put the horse between them and the guards.

"I am a protector. Many people know me."

"Are you from Severin?"

"Yes, I was there for a while. Lady Jara knows me, that's why she trusted me with the letter."

"But you worked for Codrin."

"That's right," Vlad spat. "I *worked* for him, but since he is now a great man, he no longer remembers the little people who worked for him in the past."

The horse carrying the wine finally arrived in front of the gate leader, and his eyes sparkled; the barrels looked larger than he expected, and he touched one, his fingers trembling slightly.

"Boys," Vlad said, "unload one barrel. You are caravan people; you know how to do that stuff."

Lisandru, who was the youngest, untied the ropes of the barrel on his and the gate leader's side. "Could you please help me?" he asked one of the soldiers close to him, a tremble in his voice. "We are not as strong as you."

Two men answered his plea, instead of one, and they carried the barrel with the care a mother gives to her child.

"Where is the barn?" Vlad asked.

"It's not far from here; I will give you a man to escort you there."

"Thank you, man, you are a good-hearted soldier."

On the path toward the barn, Codrin and Nicolas walked together, trying to assess the place, in the low light of a few torches stuck here and there on the walls.

"Last time I was here, my bones were fifteen years younger. That should be the entrance into the main house," Nicolas whispered, pointing to a sturdy door on the left. A small torch was stuck in a sconce, and a sentry stood just under it. "The barn should be on the right and the barracks too."

"There is no place for your horses in the barn," the soldier said. "You can leave them in that hut." He pointed to something on his right, though no one could see what he was pointing at. "You can sleep there." This time he pointed at a smaller hut which was visible, with piles of fresh straw in it.

"Thank you," Vlad said. "We need some sleep now. Enjoy the wine."

"Show me where you think the captain sleeps," Codrin said to Nicolas, when the soldier had gone.

"See that small window with a lit candle, ninety paces from the gate, on the left? There is a stair going to a terrace. That's the best room, apart from the ones in the main house. I think the captain sleeps there, but I can't guarantee that, and judging by the light, he may not be asleep. Old, grumpy Ferko has some sleep issues. We must be careful; his sword is still young."

"Lisandru, come with me." Despite being the youngest, Lisandru was the most advanced in Assassin's training of all Codrin's men, and he moved with the agility of a lynx.

"What are you planning to do?" Nicolas asked, uncertainly.

"I will tell him that we have two urgent letters, one from Veres's mother, and the other one from the Duke of Peyris. Before we go, all of us should dress in Peyris colors. Give me the name of a captain from your army, someone Ferko doesn't know well," Codrin said, after taking off the pelerine and replacing it with the insignia of a captain from the Duke's army. "A captain who would not raise suspicion by carrying important letters. A tall one," he added.

"Ferko's sight is no longer what it was. Use captain Velasque's name."

"Describe Ferko for me."

"He is only fifty-five years old, but his hair is almost white. He is missing a finger on his left hand, and he has a ring with a black gem on his right. There is nothing else..." Nicolas shook his head in the low light.

"I need a bit of time to prepare myself," Codrin said and walked away. Out of sight, he leaned against a wooden pole and stared at the lit window until it melded in his vision. Eyes closed, he could still see it, and he let his mind float free. The Farsight came easier, this time; the more he trained as a Seer, the easier it became to let his mind flow, in that strange trance. Soon, he found himself in front of the window, passed through it, and looked at the white-haired man sitting at the table with a glass of wine in his left hand. A finger was missing. Codrin returned from his trance, and it took him a while to orient himself again in the half darkness.

Getting to Ferko's room took a while. They had to avoid the light spread by two torches on the walls, and sometimes he and Lisandru had to go on all fours. In front of the door, Codrin breathed deeply. Once. "Cover me," he whispered to Lisandru. "Some soldiers may leave the guard room, and no one must see me from the gate." He knocked at the door, gently, careful not to disturb the night. After a minute, he knocked again, a little louder.

"Who is it?" a morose voice asked from inside.

"Captain Velasque from Peyris. I have two urgent letters from the Duke and Seigneur Veres's mother."

"What is so urgent? And how did you enter in the fortress?"

"How should I know, Ferko? I am just a captain, like you, and I rode day and night to get here."

The door opened, and Ferko loomed in view. "Velasquez?" he asked, a touch of doubt in his voice.

"Yes," Codrin said, and his dagger pierced the man's heart. He caught the falling body in his arms, embracing it, and entered the room. "Close the door," he whispered to Lisandru. Inside, he arranged Ferko's body in the bed and waited a few minutes before taking the dagger out of his chest. A small flow of blood followed and quickly stopped. He covered the body with the blanket. The old man looked like he was asleep. "You have never slept better, Ferko. One bastard less to help the Circle punish a defenseless woman. It's a pity that you were a soldier once." Before going out, Codrin extinguished the candle and, three minutes later, they were back at the barn.

"Now it should be easier to get inside the house," Nicolas said. "I think I know the sentry at the main door of the house, but the gate is our biggest concern."

"Yes, we take the gate first, but we will wait until the wine does its job. We will attack at midnight. We can rest until then. Pintea, you are on watch. Wake us up at midnight," he said, though he knew that no one would sleep.

"Wake up!" Tulis shouted. "Wake up you lazy worms, our shift starts soon. I know that you want to sleep, and so do I, but that dirty old gate is waiting for us. The cold, dark, unpleasant gate of the Eagle. She is our precious lover."

Some men jumped from their beds; some woke up slowly. Tulis waited patiently for a minute, then walked briskly toward a man who was still sleeping. There was a carafe of water close to the bed. Without hesitation, he poured the water onto the head of the sleeping man.

"Alert, we are under attack!" the man cried and jumped out of his bed.

"There is no alert, Albi, you sleeping rat. Get dressed; we need to be at the gate in ten minutes."

Albi looked daggers at him, water still dripping from his hair, but said nothing.

"Next time you don't get up in time, I will use a lump of wood to wake you. Move."

Morosely, the six guards left the dormitory and went to the hall to pick up their weapons. Still yawning, they took four spears and two crossbows from the wall, standard gear for a gate squad from Peyris.

"Line up," Tulis ordered, and the men formed a row in front of him. The chief walked slowly, scanning his men one by one. "Close your mantle." He touched the neck of one soldier with his stick.

"It's dark..." The soldier shrugged.

"We now serve that *great man* in there." Tulis pointed in the direction of the main house with his stick. "But we are still soldiers of Peyris." Each word was accompanied with a strong tap on the soldier's helmet, and the soldier complied quickly, trying to avoid another knock on the head. "Good, you look like soldiers now. Torches."

The two men who were the torch bearers for the night took them from the designated place, went back to the dormitory and lit them in the fireplace.

"Let's go," Tulis ordered when the torch bearers returned.

The guards turned smartly to the right, and left the barracks through the large door, just as the horologe announced the coming of midnight. The wind blew, making them curse the night shift, Tulis and all the command line up to the Duke of Peyris. The wet cold enhanced their swearing imagination. In front of the barracks, they gathered in line, waiting for Tulis, who came and reviewed his soldiers again, though there was not much to see in the trembling light of the torches. He was both an old hand and an irritating pedant. There was nothing the soldiers could do.

"You should eat something," Veres said to Cleyre, his mouth full. "I like round women. You are a bit skinny, right now." It was his first visit for a week.

Beaten and raped again, just a few minutes before, Cleyre could not answer. During the last week, she had made plans to escape, but Reymont and Dizier had taught Veres to be careful. There was nothing in the room to help her. She was also almost naked, dressed only in a silk shift that barely reached her knees, one strap cut, revealing her breast. Veres did not leave any of her other clothes within reach. She was at least lucky that it was still warm. From time to time, she ate something. Only when she was alone.

"I am an important man." Veres pressed a finger to his chest. "I have done dangerous things for my friend Bucur, the Candidate King, and for Maud, the Master Sage of the Circle. For them, I killed Senal, the Secretary of Severin, and Pierre, the Spatar of Tolosa. I am a hard man, and they know it. Soon, they will make me Grand Seigneur of Midia. The title belonged to my father, but he was weak and lost it. I will not lose it. They told me that you are an intelligent woman, though I don't know why. You must negotiate a good dowry. Do you understand?"

I must please the idiot. "Yes, Veres, I will receive a good dowry, which will make us even stronger."

Satiated, Veres came to bed, and groped her breast. "A bit of sleep and we are ready to do it again. Are you ready, wife? I like that fire in your eyes when I am inside you. It warms me." He grabbed her arm, despite her desire to ignore everything he was doing to her, she moaned from the pain. Her wrist was swollen, and bruises were everywhere on her arms and body. "I am afraid that I did not hear you," Veres said, and twisted her arm harder. A cry escaped her, and tears ran down her face. "You have a nice voice. Sleep well, wife." He lay back, their almost naked bodies touching, and fell asleep in a few moments.

Cleyre tried to move away from him, but she stopped, fearing that her move would wake him. She closed her eyes and tried to ignore his body and her pain. In his sleep, he passed an arm over her and cupped her breast. She could do nothing, not even raise his arm. *I have to wait*, she thought. *I can't strangle him with an injured wrist. Next time, I should be more careful.*

That evening, when Veres returned, Cleyre was ready. She had practiced, against the pillow, how to strangle him with her chain. When he ordered her to undress, she smiled and tried to comply, pulling her shift off slowly. It backfired. Seeing her naked breasts, Veres reacted like an animal, grabbed her arm and threw her onto the bed, twisting her wrist again. When he had finished, her wrist was swollen, and her arm useless. A few tears ran down her face. He did not see them.

Codrin reached for Flame, his short word, and gripped the rough handhold tight. He sensed it was almost time, and slowly unsheathed Shadow, his long sword, too. The strange sword produced a short hiss, and the blade vibrated in his hand, acknowledging him. That released some tension. The man behind him did the same and the next. Night fighting was particularly dangerous. Accidents and surprises were commonplace. In Arenia, it was almost an unwritten rule that night attacks were never undertaken unless under desperate circumstances. *That's what we face now*, Codrin thought. The Assassins were different; they often used the cover of the night for their stealth attacks. Sometimes, he had issues in reconciling both strategies.

"We go now," Codrin whispered when the horologe rang for midnight.

One by one, they slipped like ghosts through the night, avoiding the places lit by the torches on the wall. There were only three torches, luckily. Close to the gate, Codrin stopped and used his Farsight to investigate the guardroom: the men were not dead drunk; they were in that foggy state of mind which begs for more wine. For the first time, he observed that he could not hear anything while he was in the Farsight trance. *Maybe because I am untrained*, he thought. He returned to his body and kept his eyes closed for a few moments. There was always an unpleasant moment until his mind recovered from that strange duplication of self. Involuntarily, his hands tightened on the hilts of both Shadow and Flame.

"Vlad, Pintea, open the gate," Codrin ordered. "Damian ready your bow. Just in case. Nicolas, Lisandru, take care of the door. Keep those merry fellows inside." They are still enjoying our wine, he wanted to say, but stopped himself. There was no need to spread the news that he was the Seer of the Realm. At least not until he was better trained. Stirred by unexpected noise, his thoughts stopped abruptly, and he turned: soldiers were coming around the corner, coming toward the gate, and they had two torches.

In the low light, there was a moment of confusion on both sides, the flickering lights playing games on everybody's face.

"Enemy with crossbows. Triangle. Charge." Codrin was the first to react. His keen eyes had seen the spears and the crossbows. Their only hope was to reach the guards before their bolts and spears could fly.

"Alarm!" Tulis shouted.

At the triangle command, Lisandru and Pintea ran toward Codrin and, forming an Assassin wedge, they charged together. The bow tight in his hand, Damian ran too, until he was in a position from where he could see the men with the crossbows. He sent two arrows in swift succession. Hissing through the night, each of them arrived a moment after the guards released their bolts. There was a small delay in the way the guards reacted too. The first guard's bolt hit Codrin in his left upper arm. He gripped his short sword, Flame, harder, keeping it only for an emergency; it was a rare fight which went as planned. This one was no exception. The second guard's bolt hit Damian in the right shoulder, and he let his bow fall, pain coursing through him.

It hit the bone, Damian thought, teeth gritted from the pain running through his body. His eyes searched the guards he had shot at: one was dead, the other was hit in his right shoulder too. On both sides, there was no one able to shoot anymore. Clumsily, he unsheathed his sword with his left hand and joined Codrin.

Unable to use his left hand, Codrin slowed, and Lisandru took his place at the apex of the Triangle. They clashed with the spearmen just when they were lowering their weapons, ready for close combat; the enemy was too close to throw their spears now.

Busy with their wine, the men in the gate room, heard the first cry of alarm and ignored it. The second shout half woke them up, and they ran to pick their weapons. It took them longer than usual, and even longer to reach the door. The chief grabbed a torch, opened the door and found himself in front of the Spatar of Peyris. The former Spatar of Peyris, but he did not know that.

Codrin twisted to his right, letting the spear come by him unchallenged. The guard cursed and pulled it back, rotating it to the left at the same time, trying to hit Codrin in the side. It was too late. Codrin was now facing him, and Shadow bit into the guard's neck. With an anguished cry, strangled into a gurgle before being fully formed, the man fell into his knees, clinging to life, his hand trying to stop the blood flow. His face was flushed with terror, and a thick spattering of blood marked his neck in an angled track from side to side. He lost this fight too, and fell, face down, his head hitting the ground with a dull sound.

One guard jabbed his spear with the speed of an arrow. At the front of the wedge, Lisandru deflected the spear with his small sword and lunged with the long one. Both attacks had been so fast that only the final result was visible. The point of the spear was deflected safely behind Lisandru, whose body was extended in a tight forward stance, the point of his sword stuck deep in the guard's neck. The man fell on his back, his mouth open in a wordless howl. Lisandru instantly jumped forward, behind the remaining guards.

Pintea deflected two spears at the same time and half stepped back. He did not try to kill; there were two guards in front of him, and his task was to keep them busy. Like Codrin and Lisandru, he fought with two curved swords of differing lengths. He wheeled them swiftly in front of him, the air whooshing with danger. Involuntarily, the guards' eyes followed them.

His arms and hands covered in his and the dead guard's blood, Codrin moved to the right to intercept Tulis, who had called the alarm and now attacked, sword up. Despite the slick smears of blood, the rough surface of the hilts of both his swords prevented Codrin from losing his grip. Seeing the bolt in his opponent's arm, Tulis grinned wickedly and landed a powerful vertical blow to take advantage of the wound. Instead of parrying, Codrin ducked and slashed his chest en passant. Tulis fell before understanding what had happened to him. Blood poured from the long gash, and his sword fell from his limp fingers as he died. It hit the stones with a metallic noise and rolled further. Slowly, Tulis hit the stones too. There was not much noise until his helmet crashed on the road.

In the doorway, the chief of the gate room finally managed to speak. "Sir Nicolas. There was an alarm."

"You are drunk," Nicolas said sternly. "Stay inside, there are other people to take care of the intruders."

"But, sir."

"Go inside," Nicolas snapped, and pushed the man back. He closed the door and stood in front of it. Codrin glanced back in time to see the door closing, a tangerine line of candlelight narrowing and blinking out.

Almost blind in the low light, Vlad finally managed to open the lock of the postern gate. The old thing screeched badly when he pulled it. Opening the gate, he went out and whistled three times. Eyes squinted, he tried to see something into the night. There was no moon, no stars, only the cold rain washing his face, and nothing to see. Three whistles came from the darkness, and he breathed with relief.

Alerted, the guards were now pouring out from the barracks. Codrin was glad the door did not let more than two men pass at once. They were still sleepy and disorganized, so most of the time only one man came out at a time. They gathered in groups of seven and, once formed, each group ran toward the gate.

Attacking from behind, Lisandru cut the two spearmen, kept busy by Pintea, down in swift succession, and now there was no one left alive from the first group of guards. He moved back toward Codrin.

"Pintea, take the bow from Damian," Codrin said.

The second group of seven guards was coming around the corner, almost running. Lisandru was already there, and the first man fell with a desperate cry. Beyond the corner, the guards stopped abruptly, collided against each other, and stayed hidden for a few moments until another one took command and organized them. They moved back from the corner and came into view twenty paces away, all six at once. Pintea released two arrows quickly, and Lisandru burst into the middle of the spearmen, cutting left and right, Codrin and Damian covering his back. Across the space in front of the gate, men were shouting wildly, cries of pain and screams of fear. There was no way to distinguish between them. In the commotion, Codrin's men were all silent, like death herself.

Codrin took a moment to look around him. "Back," he ordered, as more guards appeared, their crossbows prepared to shoot. They retreated and took cover around the corner again, Lisandru peering past them. He rubbed sweat and blood off his face with his elbow. It was not his blood.

Five men entered through the open postern, inside the gate tower. "You two," Vlad said, touching them. "Open the main gate. "Sandor, ready your bow. They have crossbows and spears. Follow me."

The noise coming from the inner courtyard finally woke Veres up. "What happened?"

"A guard fell from the gate," Cleyre said and touched his face gently. "Sleep, now. I want you in good shape." *Sleep, dear husband, and let them take the fortress.*

"I am in good shape," he said, and turned toward her.

She placed her good arm around his neck and kissed him fiercely. Grunting, Veres cupped her breast and rolled over her. Gritting her teeth, she forced herself to moan loudly to the rhythm of his thrusts, and the cries from the fight vanished from his mind.

Twenty feet from the corner, Sandor joined Pintea with his bow and nocked quickly. Vlad and two more men ran to replace Codrin and Damian, and there were now four swordsmen in good shape waiting for the guards to come. Leaning against the cold wall, they waited.

The remaining twelve guards reacted too, and they moved back and farther away from the corner, formed up and turned to face the intruders. They had only one man armed with a crossbow, and he fell, pierced by two arrows at once. The guard was tall and stocky, a bear of a man and, clutching the shafts of the arrows, he howled with all the power of his large lungs. The sound echoed so strongly from the surrounding walls – the courtyard was only thirty feet wide – that it stunned all the men, who stopped fighting for a few moments. His howl died in a strangled growl. The fight started again, filling the night with vile noise. Even Veres thought he had heard something, but Cleyre moaned even harder, and that pleased him.

Lisandru and Vlad crashed into the spearmen, covered by the other two swordsmen. Codrin and Damian moved forward too, together, keeping two spearmen busy, on the left side of the melee.

That was when sixty riders finally passed through the open gate, and they surrounded the fighting men.

"Stop fighting!" Codrin shouted. "Drop your spears and surrender."

Reluctantly, the seven surviving guards dropped their weapons.

Veres finally finished, and a niggling doubt passed through his mind. "Why did you cooperate just now?"

"You are my husband."

He frowned, some vague memories of noise outside coming to him, and went to the window. "You bitch," he growled, seeing riders everywhere, and walked menacingly back toward her. "You tricked me."

She moved toward the wall, leaning her back on it, knees gathered at her chest. Veres tried to grab her, but she kicked out and thrust him away from the bed. He fell on his back, and stood up, his face disfigured by rage.

"You will pay for that," he growled and pulled her by the chain. She tried to resist, but he was too strong, and when she was close enough, Veres grabbed her hair with his left hand and punched her with his right fist. After the third punch,

Cleyre was already unconscious, but he did not stop beating her. "I will kill you, bitch." He raised his fist for a final blow.

Inside the house, Codrin let his Farsight fly, and searched it, room by room. He finally saw Cleyre, and he saw Veres too. His mind shut off abruptly, and he stayed blind for a few moments. "I am fine," he said in response to Vlad's worried glance. "Follow me." His eyes lit with an inner fire, he ran toward the stairs and climbed, taking five steps at a time. He burst into the room, walked three large steps forward, and his boot exploded in Veres's ribs. Codrin threw him to the floor, kneeled over him and punched until Veres looked even bloodier than Cleyre.

"Codrin, you will kill him," Vlad said and caught his arm from behind. "Not that he doesn't deserve it, but not like this."

"I forgot myself," Codrin said and stood up. "Thank you, Vlad. Throw him in a cell. Take his clothes too, but no food, only water." He saw the chain on Cleyre's foot. "Chain him." He went to check her chain, but he needed a key to open it.

"The key is in Veres's pocket," an old woman said from the door. "I am..."

"Maro, I know," Codrin cut in. "Reymont's spy. Which pocket?"

Ignoring his question, the old woman went to the soldier carrying Veres's clothes and came back with the key. She unlocked the chain and pulled it away. There was a wound on Cleyre's leg, where the metal had bitten through her flesh when Veres pulled the chain. Maro went out, found a carafe of water, which she had left in the corridor, and returned to the room. Saying nothing, she started to clean the blood from Cleyre's face, who was still unconscious. Two soldiers dragged Veres's naked body out of the room, and Codrin signaled to everybody but Vlad to leave the room too, then he watched the old woman closely.

"Vlad," he said after a while, "take charge outside. I will stay here. Send Nicolas with my healing kit."

Maro began to clean the blood from Cleyre's neck and shoulders, and Codrin sat at the edge of the bed. He gently stroked Cleyre's hair.

"I hope I did not come too late," he whispered.

"She will survive. Cleyre is tougher than most men think." The old woman glanced briefly at him, still cleaning Cleyre.

He started to move his fingers gently over her skull, looking for concussions. He found nothing and moved to assess her shoulders and clavicles, then her arms and ribs. They seemed fine; nothing was broken. The swollen wrist was a problem, but not a major one.

"You know what you are doing," Maro said, and moved to clean the wound on her leg. It was fresh, so she was not worried.

Ignoring her, Codrin found a sheet and covered Cleyre's almost naked body.

"Are you her lover?" Maro asked.

"I thought that Reymont would find better questions to ask."

"No, not Reymont, it was just the curiosity of an old woman. You seem fond of her."

Nicolas came in, and seeing Cleyre's swollen face, he stood, shocked, in the doorway.

"What a delicate Spatar," Maro laughed. "I bet you would have fainted seeing her before I cleaned her up."

"Maybe I should hang you, to see if I can survive the view." Nicolas entered the room and gave the Assassin healing kit to Codrin. "I don't know what this is. Vlad asked me to bring it here."

Codrin opened the kit and cleaned the wound on Cleyre's leg with alcohol. For the first time, she reacted, moaning slightly. "Cleyre," he said and shook her gently, but she did not answer.

"You no longer need me." The woman stood up, and took her carafe, ready to go.

"Maro, you will not leave your room without my permission. We need to talk later. Nicolas, set two guards at her door." Cleyre moaned again, and Codrin turned toward her. "Wake up, Cleyre." He stroked her hair and waited.

Maro left the room, followed by Nicolas. *Who is this man?* she thought, seeing for the first time the bolt in Codrin's arm. *He gives orders to the Spatar of Peyris. I did not know that*

Cleyre had a secret lover. I hope that she will speak for me. That man is tough, and he may want my head, and Nicolas may feel the same.

Ten more minutes passed until Cleyre finally opened her eyes. Seeing Codrin, she started. *I am dreaming.* She closed her eyes and opened them again, slowly, painfully. Then she smiled. Her smile looked bizarre on her swollen lips and face. It was not pretty, but not ugly either. "Hold me, Codrin," she said, her voice barely a whisper. "I need to be in the arms of a man, to wash away the touch of that snail. Just hold me."

"He's gone, Cleyre."

"He's gone for now, but he will never leave my mind."

Soon, she fell asleep in his arms, and Codrin stayed on the edge of the bed, unmoving, for the rest of the night, leaning against the wall. He did not leave her even when Vlad removed the bolt from his arm and bandaged him. From time to time, Vlad and Nicolas came and went, talking to him in low voices.

They are lovers, Nicolas thought, the third time he came into the room. *But he saved her, so I can't complain. Tudor may be not as strong as Codrin, but he is strong too.* Lost in his thoughts, Nicolas looked at them, and something tilted in his mind. He frowned and went back to the time Tudor came to Peyris to tell him that Cleyre had been attacked by Bear's mercenaries and that a Triangle of Assassins had saved her. *What a fool I am. There were no Assassins. It was Tudor and those two young men, Lisandru and Pintea, who killed Bear's mercenaries. He spread the news about the Assassins to protect Cleyre. Clever. Three men against twenty, and only one mercenary escaped. No wonder everybody believed him. Even Reymont didn't dare try another assassination attempt against her. That's why they came up with Veres.* He left the room, his thoughts reeling. *How did Tudor know that Cleyre would be attacked? He must have spies at the Black Dervils' quarters. He is more than a Wraith Protector, he is a Political Wraith, whatever that means. And Cleyre knew it.* He wondered how this would affect Cleyre's chances of taking Peyris. It still looked bleak; Nicolas did not have enough men, and neither did Tudor.

Chapter 15 – Codrin / Cleyre

At dawn, Cleyre woke up unable to fathom what had happened to her. The night seemed so far away, in a different life that came to her in a fragmented way. Then she remembered. And she breathed relieved for the first time in weeks. Then she smiled. Codrin was still sleeping, leaning against the wall, holding her in his arms, his head touching hers. Her hand moved to feel his face, and he started from the light sleep only a hardened soldier knows how to sleep.

"I did not want to wake you. Thank you, Codrin," she said, and then she saw the bandage on his arm. "You are hurt." She gestured to the bandage without touching it.

"It's nothing serious."

"And your men?"

"One of them got a bolt in the shoulder. In four weeks, he will be ready to fight again. A few got small cuts. It ended well. For us."

"Oh, Codrin." She tried to embrace him, but her injured left wrist made her moan.

"Don't strain your wrist. I will bandage it later. I am sorry that I could not come earlier."

"You came. You were the only one who came. I felt lost. I felt forgotten."

"Nicolas came too. He told me what had happened, and where they took you."

"So, he did not betray me in the end."

"No, and he still knows me as Tudor. It's better it stays that way for the moment. There are some developments around Peyris and Arad right now. I was ready to take Arad. My army is hidden on the border between them. I met Nicolas in Arad, and revealing myself could reveal my army too, or at least warn my enemies that something is happening."

"Do you know about Costa?"

"He is not a prisoner, but something close to it. He is not allowed to leave Peyris."

"Would you help me to return to Peyris? It's a hard request, I know." She let a guilty smile touch her lips, then withdrew behind her tired pale eyes.

"Cleyre, the only way you can return there is as Duchess. I am not yet sure if it's the right time. I am not sure it isn't either. I may be able to defeat Albert's army, but I don't have enough men to lay siege to Peyris. If we can't take the city, you will come with me to Severin."

"Severin? I had a Vision that you won in Poenari, but I knew nothing about Severin."

"Life would be too easy, if we know everything in advance." He looked instantly apologetic, remembering what happened to her. "I should speak more carefully."

"It's fine," she said and stroked his cheek. "What is Nicolas thinking?"

"You will find out soon enough, but now I am thinking that you need to eat. It feels like I am holding a child in my arms."

"I feel like a child," she smiled. "Protected, and, well, as happy as I can be now. Will you tell that old woman to prepare a bath for me? I feel filthy."

"Do you trust her?"

"She is Reymont's spy, but she is not as bad as him. She helped me; I don't know yet why."

"While you bathe, I have to leave you alone with her. There are no women in my troop, but I will place two guards at your door."

"I will survive. What happened to Ferko?"

"He is dead."

Cleyre nodded, and there was neither anger nor satisfaction in her face. "And...?" She did not finish her question on.

"Veres is in chains. I wish I could hang him, but his mother is the woman who sheltered me when I first arrived in Frankis. I can't execute him without at least talking to her. I am sorry."

"I don't like to kill people, but I don't want to see him again. The memory is quite enough," she whispered.

There was a knock at the door, and a soldier entered. "The old woman is making noise in her room," the soldier said. "She wants to bring Lady Cleyre her potion."

Let her come, Codrin gestured, then turned to Cleyre. "Maro read my thoughts about food."

"She's not bringing food. It's a special potion. The last thing I want is to have Snail's child."

"I did not know about such things."

"Why should you? As far I know, men don't get pregnant." Cleyre laughed yet, later, Codrin got the recipe from the old woman. Like any trained Assassin, he was also a healer who understood that any concoction could help someone, sometime.

Maro was content to give him the recipe for the Bloody Moon potion. She had seen how Veres, who was a large man, looked when the soldiers dragged him out of Cleyre's room. She feared a man who could do that so easily, even with a wounded arm; he looked strong in a way that she had not seen in anyone before. The old woman survived three Dukes and had seen many things in her sixty-two years, and Peyris did not lack tough fighters. *Why does he need the Bloody Moon?* she wondered when Codrin left her alone. *Maybe he has more mistresses. Does Cleyre know? She has had other lovers in the past. Perhaps she will not marry him. He seems to be a man of power.* Maro asked Cleyre his name, but she got no answer. *He looks like a southerner, yet he is taller. A Knight? A Seigneur? Patience, Maro. Patience.*

Properly dressed after her bath and breakfast, Cleyre looked like her former self again. Almost. She was thinner, her face was still swollen, and she still felt weak; there was pain everywhere in her body, and her dark red dress contrasted with the pallor of her face and her blonde hair. Her left arm was tied in a sling, but she felt alive again. Nicolas was the first to visit her room after her transformation.

"Oh, now this is my Cleyre," he smiled, forcing himself to ignore her bluish, swollen face.

"Thank you, for saving me, Nicolas. I am glad that there still are people who will not betray me."

"There are more than you think now. And less than I'd hoped. But it was Tudor who saved you. He had both the men and the right mindset to take the Eagle's Nest. I would have never thought to bribe the guards with a barrel of good wine from Tolosa. Of course, he is a Wraith, but he seems more than that too."

"That is how you got in?" Cleyre smiled. It pained her, but the sparkle in her eyes made her look almost healed. "Yes, he is a resourceful man," she said prudently, remembering Codrin's wish to keep his two identities separate.

"What do you want to do now?"

"To claim the Duchy. It will not be easy, and there is no guarantee that I will succeed. Anyone who helps me might come to a bad end; the Circle is against me." She paused and looked away through the window, to let Nicolas make up his mind.

"Damn the Circle, I am with you, and I can bring between six and seven hundred soldiers. They will not be enough," he sighed.

"Thank you," Cleyre said and placed her hand over his like a seal for an unwritten agreement. "Beginnings are always hard, but I have seven hundred more soldiers than I had yesterday, when I had none. And one fewer chain." Involuntarily, she glanced at her foot. She shook her head and forced herself to suppress the awful memory.

Thoughtfully, Nicolas looked at her. "There is something I need to talk to you about. It will not be an easy subject." He paused for a while, to find his words, and she waited. "It's about Tudor. He is a strong man, and it seems... It seems that there is a relationship between you two. But he has less strength than you need now. Would you consider marriage to Codrin? If he is with us, Peyris will be yours sooner than you think. And he would make a redoubtable Duke; no one will dare to attack us. In a dangerous world, strong alliances matter more than our feelings. And as we both know, Codrin is a man of quality."

"You think that Codrin would agree to marriage. With me."

"Why not? Cleyre, you are a desirable woman, beautiful and intelligent and, in a year, you can bring him four thousand soldiers, and a much stronger power base than he has now. Both of you have strength and, together, you can dream of more. Frankis is still without a King."

"We shall see..." she said and stopped, as Codrin entered her room.

"I have to leave." Nicolas stood up, nodded discreetly to encourage her, and left them alone.

Codrin seated himself in the free chair and fixed her with an appreciative look. "You are quite a sight in that dress. Until now I always seem to see you in riding costumes."

"Or almost naked in a torn shift," Cleyre laughed.

"You are a sight for sore eyes, no matter how you are dressed. Nicolas seemed a bit ... strange."

"He is uneasy about the future, like all of us are. He also thinks that I should claim the Duchy, even though our army is still small."

"How small?"

"He can bring six to seven hundred soldiers."

"That would make almost one thousand five hundred, if I add my men."

"Have you decided to help me?"

"Yes. We have been helping each other for some time, already. I don't see why we should not continue."

"Thank you, Codrin. If you want to go further, Peyris will be behind you. If it's up to me," she added.

"Did you have a Vision?"

"A brief Vision. You were talking about the kingdom, but I am not really sure what you meant."

"I hoped for a clue from you," Codrin said, rubbing his chin. "I get the impression that Fate teases me with the Visions she sends. Like she is trying to put me on a different course. I really don't know."

"By seeing into the future, we have a great advantage compared to most people, but you are right, sometimes a Vision decides our next step, and who knows how it came to us? Or why. Would you consider telling Nicolas about Codrin?"

"His army changes my plans. I can't hide from him anymore if we are to talk about battles and taking Peyris. Do you feel well enough to leave tomorrow, in a carriage?" He looked at Cleyre, who nodded. "Good. I will get Nicolas and Vlad."

"It seems that we all agree that Peyris needs a new Duchess," Codrin said when they gathered. He was sitting at the table with Cleyre, while Nicolas and Vlad sat on the edge of the bed.

Nicolas frowned when he saw Codrin sat in the chair he thought was his to take but said nothing. *I was expecting Cleyre to lead the discussion.* "Let's see if we agree on the means too," he said, looking at both Cleyre and Codrin. *She can't tell him right now, but I hope that she considered what I said about her marriage. And I can't let Tudor lead this. It may create problems later.*

He is rattled by something, Codrin thought, and his eyes strayed around the room, registering both Cleyre and Nicolas. *I think that she knows what it is.* "Cleyre told me that you can bring six to seven hundred soldiers."

"Yes. We will make our plans starting with *her* soldiers. The best course of..."

"I can bring eight hundred more," Codrin cut in. "That will be enough to defeat any army Albert can gather. It may not be enough to take Peyris, though. We need help from inside."

"Eight hundred..." Nicolas said, staring at him through narrowed eyes. Unconsciously, he rubbed at his own temple, as though Codrin's words were giving him a headache. "How can a Wraith have eight hundred soldiers?"

"They don't belong to the Wraith; they belong to the other me, Codrin."

"What do you mean?" Nicolas asked, then blew out a deep breath. He understood well Codrin's words, but his mind was not yet prepared to comprehend it.

"Nicolas," Cleyre said gently, "Codrin and Tudor are the same person, and there are only a few people who know about his twin identities. You are one of them now. He was forced to play this game. Things have changed lately, and Tudor will soon vanish."

Nicolas exhaled suddenly. "You knew..."

"Yes, and I am sorry for misleading you, but this was not my tale to tell. Codrin's life depended on secrecy. And my life depended on him."

"Well..." Nicolas shrugged, "I guess that I have to get used with that." *And I don't have to worry about her marriage anymore. Codrin will be the next Duke of Peyris. Damn, if he will not be the next King too.*

"It should not be hard," Codrin smiled. "Tudor and Codrin look quite similar."

"Well," Nicolas repeated, "I suppose you already have a plan."

"Not exactly. We must rely on information you can provide. It would be preferable to take your capital without a fight. That would make it easier to unify the Duchy. In times like these, there will be factional thinking, and it will be helped from outside. Don't forget the Circle either."

"What do you mean by taking it without a fight? They will not give the Duchy..." Nicolas protested, still unable to consider Tudor as Codrin and their leader.

"We will do some chest beating, parading the army to scare Albert and some of his vassals. There are always people who wait until the last moment before joining a party. And Albert is not exactly a fighter, so we might not meet on the battlefield. Parading our army may help some of his people join the undecided, and some of the undecided to join Cleyre. Taking the city would be a different matter, and that will be mostly your action, but one step can bring the other."

"How long this will take?"

"The longer the better, but I don't think that we can afford more than three or four weeks. We are past the equinox, and winter is coming. Bad weather may come even earlier."

"Where will your army join us?"

"It will not join you, exactly, but I will give you a hundred mercenaries led by the Black Dervil of Tolosa. The moment they learn about my presence here, the Circle will act. We don't want that. Loxburg, Orban and all the Seigneurs around Peyris will be persuaded to join Albert and attack us. Together, they can bring more than five thousand soldiers. Our best chance is to keep this as an internal issue for Peyris, Cleyre against Albert, and even then, some may try to interfere. We will follow you through the forest but stay hidden. You will parade your army south of Peyris, through the roads that pass close to large forests. We will join you in battle, if there is one, but I hope to avoid that."

"This is only a preliminary phase," Cleyre said and stood up. Struggling to gather her thoughts, she tried to walk around the table, but the room was too small, and she returned to her place. "If I am right, you hope to drive Albert out of Peyris."

"Albert, or most of his army. Everybody considers him weak, and if he stays there and hides, many will think to join you. He must do something. Reymont will act, in the end. Of course, they may surprise us and do nothing, and then we have to decide how to take Peyris."

"I don't think you can bribe the guards at the gate with a barrel of good wine from Tolosa," Cleyre said, amused, but there was a note of hope in her voice.

"No," Codrin laughed, "Peyris is not a small fortress built in a forgotten place. I think Nicolas knows better what your guards at the gates might do."

"Costa," Nicolas said, abruptly, and a moment of silence filled the room. Cleyre began to say something, and thought better of it. Codrin did not speak either. "With some luck, he might be able to open the gate for us."

"I don't like to depend on luck, and I don't want to expose Costa in such a desperate act." Cleyre closed her eyes for a few moments, trying to visualize the western gate. It looked so imposing and impenetrable, though it was the smallest in the city.

"Nobody likes it. How many soldiers are guarding the gates?" Codrin asked. "Let's say the western gate, which is the smallest," he added.

"Twenty-five, whatever the size of the gate. If there is an emergency, the number can grow to fifty. And there is always a captain to lead them."

"Costa." Codrin looked at Nicolas.

"When I left Peyris, he was no longer allowed to command a gate. They thought him too close to Cleyre."

"You had something in mind, though, when you mentioned him."

"An attack against the gate from inside, like we did it after we got in here."

"Does Costa have enough men?" Vlad joined in for the first time.

"He has his own company, but how many of them will join in a fight against the Duke, I don't know." Nicolas turned his palms up; he had nothing more to add.

"Vlad is right, we need to find out, and if necessary, we need to sneak people inside, to help him take the gate," Codrin said. "We will leave tomorrow, but first I have something unpleasant to do." He nodded at Vlad, who went out and returned a moment later. "They will bring Veres here," Codrin said, looking at Cleyre, and she flinched, but said nothing. *You need this, Cleyre.*

Ten minutes later, two soldiers brought in the prisoner. He was chained; his face was swollen, and no one had washed the blood from him. Supported by two tall Mountes, Veres, who was a large man too, looked like a crumpled doll.

"Bring him here," Codrin pointed at the middle of the room, and the soldiers dragged him over. "Snail, you always had a disturbed mind, but now you have gone lower than I thought possible, even for you."

"I am under the protection of the Candidate King and the Master Sage," Veres said. "I demand to be freed."

"Ask them to free you, then. Maybe I should hang you." His voice flat, Codrin looked at Veres, in the indifferent way one looks at the worm in the grass.

"That would be a good idea," Nicolas said.

"You can't do that," Veres breathed. "Bucur will hang you too."

"Aron and Bucur killed an Itinerant Sage, and they have more pressing issues now than helping their adopted fool. They vanished without a trace, and Severin belongs to me. You are less than a common thief. Cleyre, what should I do with him?" Codrin looked at her this time, his eyes no longer indifferent but warm and heartening. *You need this, Cleyre.*

"He is an animal." She struggled to keep her voice under control, and even harder to look at Veres. Jaw clenched, she repressed a burst of evil memories, and turned a tough stare upon him, so that he nearly recoiled.

"See, Veres? No one gives a damn about you. Beg her for your life, or I will hang you."

"Please Cleyre," Veres sobbed. The soldiers let his arms free, and he fell on his knees.

"Take the snail out. He makes me vomit," Cleyre said.

"Vlad, you know what to do. He will stay chained all the time, on the road to Severin and in the jail there. He will be treated like any other robber or rapist."

"I still think that hanging him would be better," Nicolas said, as the soldiers dragged Veres out of the room.

"I know his mother, and she is a fine woman. It's only because of her that I have let him live."

"You seem to be close to many people in high positions."

"Sometimes it's my luck to know them, sometimes is their luck to know me."

Alone again with Cleyre, Codrin kissed her hand. "I know that upset you, but I thought it was necessary."

"I have mixed feelings right now, but some of my pain vanished when I saw him kneeling at my feet. The pain inside." Cleyre patted her chest. "Does that make me an evil woman?" She shrugged at her own question, one which did not require an answer from Codrin. "Some medicine is bitter." Her thumb played over his fingers, in a tacit mark of agreement. "And I hear that you are a good healer. Maro told me that."

"What should we do with her?"

"We will keep her until I am able to find a maid. Then we will free her. Or maybe I will keep her. I will see. She is a strange woman. Intelligent."

Damian's wound stopped him fighting for a month but did not stop him riding. He was sent with five men to Severin, where he would become Ban's deputy, during Vlaicu's absence. Veres was with him, chained on his horse, and they met Vlaicu halfway to Severin.

"Snail," Vlaicu spat, glaring at him. "Good that you caught him. He has to pay for Mohor's death."

"He has to pay for more, now." Damian's lips drew back in a sort of grin, the one that usually comes from tasting rotten food.

"There was some fighting." Vlaicu pointed at Damian's right arm, held in a sling across his chest.

"We took a fortress to capture Snail and free Cleyre Peyris. Don't worry, you will have your own battles. You are going to capture the Duchy of Peyris. It may prove more of a headache than taking the Eagle's Nest, and more rewarding too. Great things are taking Frankis by storm. You will see. People may be even write some songs about us." Damian burst into laughing, and the men laughed along.

"Most of the songs I know have bad words." Vlaicu grinned and pushed his horse forward.

Chapter 16 – Octavian

After more than three weeks on the road, Octavian was cursing his position as Primus Itinerant of the Circle. As soon as the Conclave elected him, Maud sent him to Peyris and Loxburg. He could not use the shortest road through Severin; there were gallows waiting for him there. The road through Deva was longer and passed through the mountains. For three days, a cold autumn drizzle wet him to the bone. From Peyris he went to Loxburg, and from Loxburg, he was now heading back to Peyris. It was raining again.

At least I convinced Manuc, he bragged inside, to lift his morale; the Duke of Loxburg was not an easy man. *And Peyris is now in sight. A hot bath, and tonight, I will sleep in a bed. That's some consolation,* he almost laughed. After a last steep curve, out of the forest, the large city was visible in the valley, as was the Seines River, its water glinting in the sun. It was still raining, but the clouds were finally broken. *I had forgotten how much I love Peyris.* A gust of wind caught his sodden cloak and set it slapping around him. *Fate take Maud.* He spurred his horse to a faster canter. The wind gusted again and whipped the rain into his eyes. His wet cloak did no good against the cold; his shoulders and back ached from the weight of his ring-mail. He cursed Maud again, and pushed his horse faster until the gate of Peyris came in front of him.

"What's new?" Octavian asked, before seating himself in a chair before the fireplace in Reymont's office, which he was taking over for himself. He was the Primus Itinerant after all.

Recalling his own title made him feel good. Then he recalled Verenius's hanging body, and a brief grin touched his lips. Waiting for the wine, he sat motionless in the chair, his eyes moving slowly from one corner of the room to the other, to memorize everything. He thought of Loxburg again, then shook his head. He was too tired to spend his time thinking of that stubborn Duke.

"Cleyre is enjoying her honeymoon." Reymont laughed, and gave him a glass of wine. "Nicolas is causing some problems, but he has fewer men than he expected."

"But more than *you* expected. I was informed that more than eight hundred soldiers are marching with Nicolas right now. You told to me that he would not have more than five hundred. It doesn't matter; in fact, it may serve us even better."

"Did Loxburg agree with our plan?"

"He can't agree with what he doesn't know. Our plan is known only to us. But he has agreed to attack Peyris with more than three thousand men. If all is well, he will be here in less than two weeks. How is Albert?" Octavian's mouth twitched, and he repressed a curse. He was supposed to meet the Duke that day. The fat man and his long list of complaints always indisposed him. *I met women who were more a man than him.*

"Hiding under his bed. He is afraid of his own shadow."

"Good. That will make it easier to convince him to leave Peyris."

"I don't think he would agree to..."

"Then think how to make him agree," Octavian cut in. "It should not be so hard. Loxburg must not lose many soldiers, and the taking of Peyris will make him ... famous."

"And then?"

"In three or four weeks, you will free Cleyre, divorce her and make her ready to marry Loxburg's son. He is average in everything, mind and looks, but after Veres, he will seem quite the charming prince. Anyway, Cleyre must be a different woman by now. Would *tamed* be the correct word to describe her?" Octavian asked, and sipped some wine, just to stifle the smile on his lips – he knew what Cleyre's return would mean for the Secretary of Peyris. There was a moment of silence, and the sound of the rain falling on the window became louder.

"Why did you agree to this?" *If Cleyre becomes Duchess, I am dead. She will hang me.* Reymont's shoulders slumped under the strong pressure of panic filling his mind. Beneath his wrinkled forehead, his eyes reflected the terror gnawing at his entrails.

He is too weak. Reymont's reaction disturbed Octavian. "Because I had no choice. Manuc knows how to negotiate," he said dismissively, trying to keep his voice calm. *He babbles like an old woman. Just when I was enjoying my wine.*

"I suppose so. We received a letter from Dornan." Reymont recovered faster than the Primus Itinerant had expected.

"Ah, yes, Itinerant Sage Solis convinced him to join Loxburg. Dornan will bring six hundred soldiers."

"Why?"

"To make Loxburg look more important. The new Chief of the north."

"And if he really wants to become the Chief...?"

"Manuc is old," Octavian shrugged. "And soon, he will join the other two old Dukes in the afterlife. That was a great generation; it has been followed by some dwarves, but maybe I am too tough on Baldovin. He is not stupid, just sick. Sometimes, it brings the same consequences." He shrugged again, then sipped some wine. "If Manuc doesn't understand that things are moving in a new direction, he will leave us like the former Duke Stefan – another man who did not adapt to the changes around him. Old people are like that. Unfortunately. I gave to our Hidden Sage in Loxburg the poison you used on Stefan, that one which kills without leaving a trace. It works well, doesn't it? If things go to plan, both dukedoms in the north will disintegrate. Then we will reform them to our needs. Just in time. But for the moment, we need a strong Loxburg to convince Codrin become the Duke of Tolosa through marriage."

"Bucur?" Reymont asked and raised an eyebrow.

"Ah, you did not know. He killed an Itinerant Sage, and the Conclave stripped the Candidate King title from him. Keep this to yourself; there are few Sages who know about the Conclave and no one outside the Circle." *Drusila may know it, though.* Octavian frowned; he disliked the woman, and he was not sure that such important information should be given to the Wanderers. *She is Maud's sister, but still a Wanderer bitch.* "For the moment, we don't want this to be known. I think you understand why."

"When Loxburg comes here," Reymont said, hesitantly, "should we open the gate of the city?"

"Of course. I don't want Peyris to be ruined. The new kingdom must be powerful, and it can't be powerful without strong provinces. That's why we arranged for him to come with almost four thousand soldiers, Dornan included. The surrender should look real, or Codrin will know that everything is a set up. He *must* fear Loxburg. Like in any conquest, some bad things will happen here, rapes, robberies, but everything should be controlled. Loxburg doesn't want *his* city to be ruined."

"He hates Peyris, and wants Loxburg to become..."

"He *hated* Peyris, but only because it did not belong to him. It was the capital of Frankis, and whoever sits here dreams of being the next King. Loxburg is no exception. And the negotiation for surrender will be led by us."

"Will you stay here?" Reymont asked, both appalled and relieved.

"Of course, my dear Reymont. How could I miss such an important event?" *How could I miss sleeping for a few weeks in a bed and drinking good wine? The sad thing is that we can't count on you for such delicate talks, but I can't tell you that. You are getting old too. Odbald, the second Secretary, will take your place. It will happen sooner than I thought before today.* "I hope that you are comfortable with my wish to stay longer in Peyris. I like this wine." Octavian nodded at his empty glass, and Reymont refilled it.

"That thing with Cleyre," Reymont returned to his worries. "It's just something temporary, until the Duchy disintegrates."

"You have it wrong. The disintegration will be temporary. Once we have a King, we need able people to rule. Cleyre has a lot of potential."

"And I have a lot of hanging potential, if she becomes Duchess."

"Don't worry, Reymont, you will move to the Royal Court. We need capable men to rule there too. Codrin is young, and it appears that his military abilities are rather better developed than his political acumen. That suits us. He will rule, led by our people. Maud, you, me... And our beautiful and intelligent Marie will help us from his bedroom. If you don't mind, I would like a few moments of silence." Eyes half closed, he looked a little as though he might be ready to sleep, but he just wanted to silence Reymont. During the evening, Octavian stayed mostly silent, and Reymont finally understood that the Primus Itinerant was not in a mood to talk much.

"Nicolas's army is camped not far from the southern gate," the guard informed Reymont, two days later.

"The real game starts now." Octavian rubbed his hands gleefully after the guard left him and Reymont alone. Reymont was now a guest in his own office. "Let's enjoy our time with the Duke. He always surprises me. Never in a good way." Amused, Octavian squinted at the Secretary. The Duke's office was close by, and Octavian entered without knocking. "Duke Albert, we have an unwelcome guest outside the city." Without waiting for an invitation, he took a chair, moved it close to the window, and sat in such a way that he could see both the Duke and the sunset. Albert looked at him from glazed eyes. "Nicolas and his army are at the gate of Peyris."

"How many men does the traitor have?" Albert asked, agitated, beads of cold perspiration running down his face. He tried to stand, but his legs did not listen to him.

"Eight hundred. Duke, let's go and observe what's happening out there before night falls. Your soldiers want to see their Duke on the wall, amongst them."

"Isn't that dangerous?"

"Nicolas is a long way from the wall."

Arriving on the parapet, behind the merlons, Albert's agitation only grew, and both Octavian and Reymont kept silent, leaving him to his fear. With smiling eyes, they looked at each other.

"What should we do?" Albert finally asked, then his lips puffed, as from a blow to the stomach.

Octavian blinked at Reymont and nodded.

"My Duke," Reymont said, "we pondered a lot about the situation, and the safest thing is to move you out of Peyris."

"What?" Albert turned abruptly. "Are you mad? These walls protect me better than anything else will, and we have almost two thousand soldiers. One thousand here, and another thousand in the north-east, halfway from the border with Loxburg. Why should we leave Peyris?"

"Because we are not safe in Peyris. Nicolas would not have come here without a plan. He can't take the city with eight hundred soldiers."

"And?"

"We think that he may have some men hidden in the city, perhaps in the palace, waiting to act. These traitors are a great danger to you. They may try to kill..."

"Do you think so?" Albert asked abruptly, then sucked his upper lip. He looked like an overgrown child.

"Why else would Nicolas be here?"

"Yes, yes, I'm sure there are traitors in Peyris. They are everywhere. Find them. Hang them," the Duke said nervously, wringing his hands.

"We are working on it, but it will take time."

"How much time?"

"We don't know yet, maybe a month or two. You can return after we catch them all. That's the safest thing to do."

"Where should I go?"

"Amiuns fortress. It's stronger than Peyris, and it's not far from here. It's also smaller, and we can control the people better there."

"I need to think," Albert said and turned away. By the time he reached the stairs, he was already running, forcing the guards to run after him in their heavy armor. Luckily, he was too fat to run fast or too long.

Octavian bit his lip, and Reymont pinched his nose to stifle their laughter. Their reactions did not escape to the soldiers on the wall, who were split between amusement and scorn.

We need a Duke, the captain of the wall thought. *Fate take this puppet and his puppeteers. Our only chance to survive is Cleyre.*

❧

Under the cover of late twilight, two discreet shadows approached the house. They did not try to pass totally unobserved, just walked carefully, watching their backs and whoever crossed their path. The autumn was in full swing, and the days were shorter. People still filled the streets after sunset.

"I think this is it," the taller man said and opened the small gate of iron. Peyris was a safe city and people did not close their gates so early. Silently, the second man followed him. "There is light in the house, so he must be at home."

"Or maybe the servants are at home."

The tall man shrugged and knocked at the door. They were both right; a servant opened the door, and his master was at home. "We came to see your master."

The servant raised his lamp to see them better. The light was not strong, and the men were half hidden by their cloaks. "Who are you?"

"Altera is far from Peyris," the tall man gave him the password.

"Three riding days from here," the servant said.

"I wish it was. The road was longer."

"Follow me."

They went in, but neither took off his cloak. The servant pretended that he did not see that. He entered the small office, closing the door to the guests. The strangers waited patiently, and the servant came out in less than a minute. He held the door open for them and closed it after they entered. He walked briskly away and returned with two armed men who remained to guard the door, ready to interfere if something should go wrong inside. In the office, both men lowered the hoods of their cloaks.

"I was not expecting visitors," Costa said, but he was smiling, and they clasped their hands.

"Neither was I expecting to visit Peyris," Vlad laughed. "Nicolas and *Tudor* sent us here."

Costa nodded, pondering for a while why Vlad had mentioned Tudor. "Sit," he pointed at the chairs in front of his desk. "I don't suppose you came here just to drink my wine." He took two glasses from a cabinet and filled them from a bottle that was already open.

"Your wine is good," Emich, the second Knight of Nicolas said, "but it isn't worth the risk of sneaking into Peyris past Albert's guards."

"I am afraid I will not like the news you bring me."

"Oh, noon the contrary," Vlad laughed, raising his glass in salute. "You will certainly like the news; Cleyre is free."

Costa drank his wine in one shot and sighed. "That is the best news I have heard in a while. How, who...? Tell me."

"The Wraith of Tolosa found a solution to her problem. It involved a barrel of wine to bribe the guards at the Eagle's Nest's gate. We met Nicolas while he was going to Severin, and he took us there. We had spent most of the summer in the south and didn't know what had happened."

"*Where is she now?*" *Codrin saved Cleyre, and whatever chance I still had to marry her is gone now. I could do nothing for her. Fate. But at least she is safe. This is what really matters.* Pleasant memories from the past came to him, filling him with regret. He sighed.

"A small house, hidden in a forest not far from here, guarded by fifty men," Emich said. "She is safe there."

"Veres?"

"In chains, heading south. The Wraith took care of it. This is from Cleyre." Emich proffered a letter to Costa.

He is being taken to Severin... The Circle can't reach Veres there, but who needs him anymore? With impatient fingers, Costa opened the letter and read it slowly. His eagerness did not escape Vlad.

'Costa,

What they will ask from you is dangerous. You know the situation in Peyris. Codrin and Nicolas are keen to attack, but I don't want to lose you, or other good men, in an attack that is likely to fail. If you think we can't take Peyris as things stand, just write back. There is no need to explain it all, just send me a letter, even an empty one.

Cleyre'

"The second part now. The part I will not like," Costa said and filled all the glasses again.

"We want to take Peyris," Emich said.

"With eight hundred soldiers? That won't happen." *It's me they want, but how can I...?*

"It could happen if we take one of the gates. The western one."

"And you want me to..." Costa stood up abruptly and went to the window. There was no more light, and he blinked at the darkness. After a while, he turned and leaned against the wall, waiting for them to tell him more. They didn't. "From the fifty men in my company, I can count on fifteen at most. For the others, I would be a traitor."

"Like us, you serve the Duchess, and they are the traitors. I know, it's just a difference of perspective," Emich laughed. "It will not matter if we lose. As it looks, you don't have enough men to take the gate. Just to be sure that we understand each other; if you have an answer for Cleyre..." He pointed at the letter.

Costa pondered for a while and read the letter again. Going back to his chair, he rested his elbows on the table. He pressed his thumb to his nose. His eyes were intent. "I think we can do this. But I'll need your help."

"That's why we are here," Vlad said. "We can bring you more men. How many do you need?"

"Twenty-five. Most of the night guards stay in the gate room, and some are stationed on the walls, from where can shoot at anyone trying to attack the gate from the city."

"How many crossbows and spears have they?" Vlad asked.

"There are five crossbows and fifteen spearmen in each company. My company is not allowed these weapons since I was demoted. You must bring both."

"They are watchful at the gates; they are searching every cart, and it will not be easy to bring the weapons in, but we will find a way. It makes no sense to attack the gate without crossbows. We will need two days to prepare everything."

"I also have news," Costa said. "Tomorrow, Albert will leave the city with five hundred soldiers."

"We had hoped to capture Albert, but five hundred fewer soldiers will make our task easier. If we take the gate..." Emich said with a shrug.

"You have only eight hundred men. It will be hard to take the city even if we capture the gate."

"Once we enter Peyris some of them will change sides."

"True," Costa nodded, "but most of them will only change sides after the winner is known."

"True." Emich nodded too.

"Seven hundred more soldiers will arrive just before we attack the gate," Vlad said.

Emich didn't know why Vlad was saying this, and he felt uneasy. *Is Vlad trying to fool Costa? It may be a good strategy, but it may backfire.*

Codrin's army is growing, Costa thought. *Emich doesn't know about the army and doesn't know that Codrin is the Wraith of Tolosa. Perhaps Nicolas and Codrin don't trust each other. That's not good.* "An army of one thousand five hundred strong sounds better."

Vlad felt the uneasiness in both Costa and Emich and pondered before saying, "The men we will bring inside the city need a place to gather before taking the gate."

"There is a stable behind the barrack between the South and West Gates. The barracks and stables will be more or less empty; they belong to the soldiers that will leave with Albert. Tell your men to gather behind the stables. We will attack at night, one hour before midnight and the change of guard."

"I will be here to lead my men."

"And I will lead my men," Emich added.

Costa sat motionless, his eyes moving slowly from one man to the other. Then he smiled. *At least I am not alone. Codrin and Nicolas are men of character.* "We are a strong team. Let me open another bottle."

"Salut," Emich said and raised his glass. "To victory, and to our Duchess."

"Salut," the other two answered.

"Octavian is here," Costa said after a while and frowned at his glass as if the name of the Sage gave him a bad taste. "We may be able to solve that issue too."

"No." Vlad shook his head. "Let him play his game."

"Is he working for you? Is that why is he taking Albert out of Peyris?"

"He is working for the Circle, but with some information we provided for him," Vlad said, cautiously. "We didn't know about Albert leaving, but there are several games afoot right now."

"The Wraith knows how to play his game. From what Nicolas saw in the Eagle's Nest, he may even become our Duke. Peyris will be safe." Emich did not see the pain in Costa's eyes and raised his glass again.

Albert's convoy left Peyris early in the morning, with the speed of hunted men, even when they had no idea how close Codrin and Nicolas were to learning of their escape. Five hundred soldiers, Octavian and Reymont accompanied him. The Sages would return after the Duke was settled in Amiuns. The Duke also wrote to his Spatar and ordered him to move the second part of the army back from the border with Loxburg, and closer to the Duke's refuge. The Sages did not want to leave with him, but Albert insisted and, this time, they could not get round it. The trip to Amiuns and back to Peyris would hopefully take less than five days, and they would arrive before Loxburg. Even the fat Duke rode a horse, something he had not tried for some years. After a two-hour ride, Albert almost fell from his horse, and even his panic could not keep him in the saddle. They had to wait almost an hour for the carriage.

Amiuns became a crowded town with so many soldiers and servants pouring in. And the castle was small. They arrived in the morning, and a day later Albert was still complaining.

"How could you bring me to such a place? This is not a castle fit for a Duke." He pointed angrily at Reymont and Octavian with his fat forefinger.

I have to bear this toad for a while, Octavian thought. *Hopefully not for long.* "My Duke, we all share your discomfort, but an uncomfortable castle is preferable to a luxurious grave. Don't you think?"

Albert opened his mouth, closed it, opened it again and closed it again.

Toad, or fish; it's all the same. "I am glad that we are in agreement." Octavian smiled and left the Duke's small suite, followed by Reymont. "You have no idea how that creature rattles my nerves."

"What? Only five days with him and you are rattled?" Reymont grinned.

"You are used to it. Anyway, we will leave tomorrow for Peyris. It is time to open the gates for Manuc. At least he is a real Duke."

"Won't you reconsider Cleyre's role?" Reymont asked, tentatively.

"I've already told you that we are under the agreement with Loxburg, and that you will move to the King's court when the time is right."

The Sages left Amiuns the same day Codrin attacked Peyris.

Chapter 17 – Siena

Siena burst into Nard's room, and she started to speak before he could recover from the intrusion. "This is it," she said, elated, tapping the old book in her other hand. "The Sanctuary, a place where the Talants preserved things, some of them so powerful that it's difficult to imagine them. Magic. Magical things." She shook the old book vigorously, barely missing his head.

Since Sybille, the Third Light of the Frankis Wanderers, had given her the Talant dictionary, Siena had spent most of her time studying it, without telling anyone except Nard, who had become her lover. Even her sister, Amelie, didn't know. There were some similarities between Aron's third son and Bucur; both knew how to court a woman. Nard had been a prisoner in Poenari since Codrin conquered Aron's stronghold, Seged, but he was not confined to a cell. Sensing that Nard was not as bad as Aron and his other son, Codrin allowed him to move freely inside the fortress.

"What kind of magic?" Nard asked. He had started to learn Talant language, but he was well behind Siena.

"All kinds of magic." Siena smiled, a feeling of power sweeping through her. "I am glad that Sybille gave me the dictionary, not Codrin." She chose to forget that her cousin had given her the manuscript for Codrin. It belonged to Dochia, and Ada, the Second Light of the Arenian Wanderers, had received a Vision that Codrin needed to learn the language and find the Sanctuary of Hispeyne. Siena convinced Sybille that Codrin did not deserve the dictionary, that he could not be trusted, though this was not about the manuscript; it was more a rebellious reaction, because she resented his takeover of Poenari.

"Look what he did to Mara," she said to Sybille during her previous visit. "He let her fall pregnant and refused to marry her." That day, Sybille was in a hurry to return her Hive, and she left the manuscript with Siena until she could learn more about Codrin. The Wanderer didn't understand what had happened between Mara and Codrin and wanted more time before deciding about the dictionary. From the Alba Hive, Sybille was sent by Drusila, the First Light of the Frankis Wanderers, to Litvonia, so she could not visit Poenari again for a while.

"Do you really think that magic exists? Nard asked, half skeptical, half willing to believe.

"How do you think the Wanderers can see the future? They use the White Light. That's powerful magic too. I am going to see Grandfather. I have a surprise for him. I know now what Poenari was, four thousand years ago. It was not built to be a fortress. I will leave you to guess. I already gave you some clues." She smiled and stormed out of the room, leaving him alone, beset with weird thoughts.

Siena burst into her grandfather's office with the same exuberance and enthusiasm; Bernart did not react as Nard had. He had more composure and a poor sense of hearing. "Yes, Siena," he smiled at her.

"Grandfather, I know what Poenari was during the Talant Empire."

"So, you have learned that it was not a fortress."

"You knew?"

"I was not sure, and my idea was so strange that I did not dare tell anyone. Let's see if we have come up with the same explanation." He stood up and went to a small library shelf containing long thin tubes of paper, and took one of them out, followed by Siena's questioning eyes – she already knew everything that was hidden there: Poenari's most secret documents. Some of them many hundreds of years old, some even older. He opened the tube and extracted a roll of paper.

"Help me," Bernart asked Siena and unrolled the paper with great care; it was fragile. The sheet was large and looked like a sort of map. She used four small objects to pin the corners of the map to the desk. "This is Poenari," he pointed at the map. "The map is very old; it was drawn long before the Alban Empire crumbled. This is the main wall." His finger moved in a semi-circle on the map. "These are the basalt ridges that form our eastern and western defense walls. From the valley, they look like towers. The Albans built the top of the wall and the city, but the main wall was built by the Talants. You know all this; I mention it only to give you some perspective. So, what was Poenari built for?"

"It was a dam," she said fast, and a smile settled on her lips, and Bernart ruffled her hair. "All the dams in Frankis put together are smaller than this one. But there are plenty of lakes for fishing and not much cultivable land in the area. Why make such a large dam? Even in Alban times there was no need for such a thing. Why did they build it?"

"More than a thousand years ago, someone translated an old Talant document that contains an answer. I don't understand much of it. The dam was built to create magic. A kind of ghosts. The Talants used them as servants."

"Ghosts?" Siena asked, confused.

"From what we could infer, the ghosts were able to make light, or could move carts without the need for animals."

"Well." That was all Siena could say, then she suddenly remembered what she had learned about the Sanctuary in Hispeyne. "You are right, Grandfather. This is magic. Something similar to the White Light of the Wanderers. The Talants used a lot of magic for transport, weapons, and Fate knows what else."

"That may be," Bernart agreed. "The walls here look like they grew from the ground in one piece. There are no stones and no mortar in them, only that strange material, resembling stone and iron. Tomorrow, show me where you read about the dam. But let's play a game now," he said with a mischievous smile. "Close your eyes and imagine yourself on the wall. Can you see the lake and how things were when the Talant Empire was still here?"

"How can I do that?"

"Maybe this can help." Bernart smiled gently, understanding the confusion in her mind. A long time ago, when he had learned about the dam and what it could produce, the same confusion ruled his own mind. It was troubling to learn that such powerful things existed, and he rejected the idea at first. He had seen paintings of carts that were as large as a small house. They were not pulled by horses, but from the painting it was clear that they were moving; their wheels were as wide as a man's height. *Maybe Siena is right, and this about magic, not ghosts. Ghosts, magic,* he shrugged.

The old man brought another tube from which he extracted another sheet, which was different from anything else in the library, and she knew most of their archive by heart. It was a very old painting, but in some places the colors were still vivid. Involuntarily, Siena touched it, and remembered, from previous experience, that it was not paper at all. While it was flexible, it had a much harder consistency than paper, and in the places where the painting had faded, the thing was translucent. She rubbed gently at a colored patch and felt no paint there at all; the thing was flat, like printed paper.

With her new understanding, she looked at the painting: Poenari did not yet have the small wall on top of the dam, and behind it, there was a long lake, narrowing into the distance. "It's so hard to comprehend how large it is," Siena whispered, trying to understand. Everything looked like the painter had viewed the dam from the top of a very tall mountain, but there was no such mountain around Poenari. "This part, with all those hillocks; that's missing now." Her finger moved across the painting, from the wall toward the end of the lake, and she felt pleasure touching the smooth material.

"Something destroyed the hillocks, leaving only the ridges that are now the eastern and western mountain walls of Poenari. The small river, which filled the dam, now flows five miles from the wall. Lerin River is here now," he tapped the map in an area where no river was painted.

"What could destroy such a large ridge?" Siena muttered.

"We don't know, but in the document I mentioned, it's written that it was blown up during the White Salt invasion that destroyed the Talant Empire."

"Only magic could do this. Very strong magic." *Was it magic that destroyed the Talant Empire? Are there such strong weapons in the Sanctuary? They can help me.*

"I can't wait to tell Codrin everything."

The smile left Siena's lips. "Maybe we should not tell him everything."

"He is the Seigneur of Poenari. In fact, he is a Grand Seigneur now. And he is a man of quality. I don't think we should hide such important things from him. We are fair people, here."

"Yes, Grandfather," Siena said, meekly.

The picture of the dam made her even more eager to learn everything about the Talants, or at least everything she could learn from the few books in their hidden library, to which only Bernart, Siena, her sister, Amelie, and Codrin had access. *Only I know the Talant language. Nard has just started to learn it too. Should I tell Grandfather? No, I will wait until I learn more and surprise him. I know where the Sanctuary is, and I don't know. The place is described in the book, but without a map...* She closed her eyes, searching for a solution. *How stupid I am. We have old maps; we just have to learn how to read them.* Those maps were indeed different, colored and covered with many strange symbols. She ran to the hidden library, then she ran back to Bernart's office to pick the key. The old man was no longer there, so she did not need to explain herself.

The maps, which she had first seen a long time ago, were still there, and judging by the dust, no one had touched them for some years. There were only six maps; she quickly found the one marked Hispeyne, and unrolled it on the floor, in front of the window. For all her knowledge, she still scratched her head. It did not help that the colors were now faint and that in places the writing had disappeared. Reading the names of places, or at least what she thought were names, told her nothing; they were all too strange.

She went out and returned with some scraps of paper. She copied all the words written in a rectangle in the left upper corner of the map. One by one, she wrote the Talant words and their equivalents from the dictionary: Legend, city, river, lake. She extracted more than thirty words. Once again, it surprised her how many words were similar in both languages: city, which they called satul, river was riul, mountain was munty and lake was lac. The list of similarities was quite long. There were words for which she could find no equivalent, words which she really struggled to pronounce and could not guess at the meaning of.

That night it took her a long time to fell asleep; the magic able to move carts swirled in her mind. *What about weapons? What could we do with magic weapons?*

Alone, hidden even from Nard, she spent most of the week trying to find every passage about weapons in the old Talant books. Fortunately, there were only thirty-two such books in their library, so she was able to read through them relatively fast. Some of them she had to leave aside; while the letters were the same, she could not understand even one word. *The Talants must have had several languages*, she thought. Unfortunately, only two of them described weapons, and they were too strange, and most of them were too large to be carried by a man or woman. What could she do with a weapon that looked larger than a horse or a cart? When she felt confident enough, Siena went to Nard again.

"I know more about the magic weapons," she said, and opened the book at a picture. They were alone in his room, late in the evening. "This one uses a sort of ... Red Fire. It throws a bolt of fire that kills several men at once, even when they have armor. And it fires at a faster frequency than a bow."

"But if we don't have magic..."

"I have some White Light. But they wrote here," she tapped the book, "that the magic is already suffused in the weapon. You need only to open it. With two such weapons we could destroy any army that laid siege to Poenari. No one would take Poenari from us." Siena still dreamt of great balls being given in the large hall, and imagined herself the Signora of Poenari, giving the starting signal, dressed in a sumptuous light blue dress.

Nard knew what she really meant. "Codrin is not that weak."

"What could he do against such weapons? Nothing. Think, Nard. Think. We can be the masters of Poenari, not just prisoners."

"You are not a prisoner," Nard said. He needed more time to think. He was indeed a prisoner, one lucky enough to walk free in the fortress. Things could change, though, and while Siena was dreaming, he knew that few men could stand against Codrin.

"I am," she said firmly, and laced her arms around his neck. "Don't be afraid, Nard. Those weapons will bring us freedom." Pulling his head closer, she kissed him, and that stopped Nard's thoughts. At least for a while. Then she undressed, and his thoughts took a longer pause.

"We will leave in one week. I will sneak you out through the tunnel. We need to take provisions for a few weeks, and I will take a hundred galbeni from the Visterie. No one will know. At least not straightaway," Siena said, early in the morning, while she was dressing. "I must go now. Our little plan must remain secret." She kissed him once more, ready to leave.

"Wouldn't be better to leave next spring?" Nard asked, thinking of the winter ahead.

"Sybille told me that it's much warmer in Hispeyne. They don't really have winters there. Well, they have, but it looks like spring here, no snow and no ice.

I don't think I like this, Nard thought, watching her leave. *If Codrin captures me again... But perhaps she is right about the weapons. And if she is not right? We could stay in Castis, in the Pirenes Mountains. Mother had a fortified house there. It was supposed to be mine. Third sons get almost nothing. Even when Raul died, everything went to Bucur. Raul was different... We got on well together. We both took after Mother. Bucur took after Father, that's why neither of them likes me. Let's hope Codrin doesn't catch me. Even if we get the magic weapons, we still can settle in Castis. Or perhaps she will give up.*

Siena was determined, and three days later, she came into his room again. "Look," she said, her eyes glinting. Swiftly, she emptied her bag on the bed. A string of metallic sounds followed, and gold glittered in the low light of the candle. "Ninety-two galbeni and fifty silvers. We are rich. We leave in two days, through the secret tunnel." She kissed Nard, before he could say anything, and left the room in a hurry. Nard was in an even greater hurry to hide the coins before someone came in and saw them.

The evening before the night of their escape, Siena went to see her grandfather. She found him dreaming, his eyes open.

"I had a Vision," he said, "Codrin is going to Peyris."

"So what?" she said, and her dark eyes glittered with derision. "He does what he likes, without asking us. We should do the same."

"Siena," Bernart said sharply. "Codrin is our Seigneur, and he has restored some of Poenari's past glory."

"I will restore even more of it," she said, irritated, and left the room, followed by her grandfather's sad smile. Seeing his smile, for the first time she thought about how her departure would upset the old man. *I will leave him a letter. And he will be happy when I return Poenari to him.* Yet his sad smile haunted her, long after she arrived in her room. *He will change his mind after I make him the Seigneur of Poenari.* She shook her head to convince herself. Opening one of the old books she would take with her, she moved her finger over the drawing of the weapon she hoped to find in the Sanctuary. That strengthened her resolve. *On my way back, I will contact Maud. She is against Codrin, and our magic weapons will enhance my status. What if I convince her to replace Bucur with Nard? They are brothers after all. Maybe I can be more than Signora of Poenari.* Eyes closed, she started to dream about the Royal Court of Peyris.

A little after midnight, Siena and Nard entered the secret tunnel, which no one had used for more than forty years and, with the first light of the morning, they left Poenari.

Chapter 18 - Codrin

For two days, Codrin's men quietly entered Peyris through all the four gates of the city. In the end, he had settled for thirty-five soldiers, twenty of them from Nicolas, men who knew the city. They were led by Emich. Twelve of them were Codrin's scouts, led by Vlad. Lisandru and Pintea joined them too. The attack on the West Gate would be led by Costa. The men entered the city in groups of two or three, at irregular intervals, joining caravans or other groups. They settled at several inns in the city, like anyone else with business in Peyris. There were no problems, even the cart transporting the bows, well hidden among merchandise, passed without a hitch. They did not try to bring spears, though. On the evening of the planned attack, men moved out of their inns, walking toward the West Gate via five different streets. Some of them spent some time for a fake drink at inns on their way. As Costa had suggested, they gathered behind the empty stable, seven hundred feet away from the gate. Costa was waiting for them, with twelve men. The day before, he had had fourteen soldiers, but two were caught trying to sneak into the main barracks and reveal Costa's treason. One of them, Costa killed himself, and that made him bitter – he had considered the man a friend.

"We have to wait for the last patrol of the day to go to the gate," Costa said to a small group of seven, the ones who would lead the assault. "One patrol comes and goes every hour. We need to capture the last one and replace the soldiers with my men. Usually, there are three guards in a patrol. The rest of my men will move along the wall, from the left. I will lead them. Once the patrol inspects the gate, the men inside will open the door of the guardroom. We need to take the room. Vlad, five of your men should come to the gate along the wall, from the right."

"Lisandru will lead them," Vlad said.

"Two streets lead to the plaza in front of the gate from opposite directions. We can't use the street that goes straight to the gate, they can see us from far off; there is a full moon tonight. This will help us as much as it helps them. Emich, you will come through the street on the left. Your men know the gate, and they will launch the first assault, after we enter the guards' room. Vlad, you have the best archers. Find a place from where they can shoot at the guards above the gate. They should do this when Emich attacks, to cover him. Then there are the arrow slits in the gate, and the men with crossbows behind them. It's hard to shoot at them, but once the guards over the gate are down, you must try your luck. At least you should be able to slow the rate they shoot at. Try and make them keep their heads down. The rest of your men should help Emich."

"Pintea will lead the archers; I will support Emich," Vlad said.

"We go when the horologe beats one hour and a half before midnight. The last patrol of the day should be at the gate one hour before midnight. At midnight, they change the guard, and there is no patrol. The patrol will come through the main street, and we have to replace the guards far enough from the gate, so they do not see us." He stopped, listening as the horologe sent its metallic ring through the night. "We go now."

Codrin lay on the ground, a hundred and twenty feet from the gate. Behind him, there were a hundred men armed with crossbows. It had taken them half an hour of crawling to get inside a small depression in the field, which offered some cover. Most of them were Nicolas's men; Codrin was relying mostly on bowmen. A bow allows a faster firing rate than a crossbow, but also needs a better trained man and a good position. This time, he needed men to shoot from the ground and at a distance, over the wall. Five hundred feet from the gate, along the road, Nicolas was waiting with a hundred riders, all dismounted, hidden behind a line of bushes along the road. They would storm the gate once Costa's men defeated the guards and opened it. Five hundred feet further on, there were four hundred riders led by Vlaicu, hidden in the forest. They would be the second troop to storm the gate.

Eyes closed, Codrin entered the city, using his Farsight. *Nothing*, he thought, and returned. He was still unable to hear anything when he used his power.

The Swann Inn was one of the best in Peyris. The owner came from Tolosa and had married the daughter of the previous innkeeper. He brought with him not only recipes from the south, but the best wine from Tolosa too, and that red liquid made him famous in the city. After a good wine, even ordinary food tastes better. It was late in the night, when even the most dedicated drinkers had left the inn. Well trained in emptying wine glasses, some of them walked almost normally. Some of them slid along the walls, keeping a hand on them for balance. And there were others, the real sponges, who walked in a zigzag, from one side of the street to the other. Sometimes, they fell. Sometimes, they managed to avoid it.

"Look at that one," one guard laughed, pointing at a man struggling to find his way, twenty paces in front of them. "How long until he goes on all fours?"

"I wish I were in the Swann right now, instead of wandering on the streets. Do you want to bet on him?"

"Why not? Two silvers apiece. Tomorrow, we have a day off, and one of us will have enough coin to get drunk at the Swann. I will say twenty steps. The one who gets closest wins."

"Thirty steps."

"Fifteen," the third one said.

"One, two..." they started to count, moving closer to the drunkard. "Twenty..."

"You are out, Lesot," the other two laughed, and the man cursed.

"Twenty-four, twenty-five, twenty-six."

"Blast you, man," the one who'd bet on twenty growled. "You won, and I am now poorer by two silvers."

"Help me," the drunkard begged, as the guards came up behind him.

"Yes, I will help you," Lesot spat, and punched him in the ribs. Ready to join him, the other two did not see a shadow moving with surprising speed from the wall. In the blink of an eye, he was behind the guards, and his two curved swords sliced through the air. The guards fell soundlessly. It was a masterly move; before his last step, the shadow man had crossed his arms and swords in front of him. When both hands sprang to their proper positions, his swords of unequal length cut two wide arcs through the necks in their path. Lesot did not get to admire their finesse; he was dead too, and the drunkard bent quickly to clean his dagger on the dead man's clothes. Three more men in Peyris colors came from near the fence and carried the bodies away, lining them up along the fence, face down.

"Thank you," Costa said, as Pintea sheathed his curved swords. "We take it from here; you can return to the archers." Eyes closed, he leaned back his head and waited two more minutes, listening, then walked away, toward the gate.

A hundred fifty paces behind Costa and his men, a courier, bringing a message for the captain of the West Gate, saw the attack on the guards, under the strong light of the full moon. Only fifteen years old, he was walking almost stuck to the fences, trying to avoid the drunkards leaving the inn; most of them were going toward the city, away from the gate. That was lucky for him; the two soldiers Costa had left behind, close to the inn, did not see him. He took in the scene, and then he ran away, toward the barracks, using the drunk men as his cover.

As they entered the plaza, Costa turned toward the three men behind him. "Good luck, Marcou. I'm going to join our men at the wall. We will attack the moment they open the door of the gate room for you."

The false patrol continued to walk at leisure through the open space, toward the West Gate, while Costa moved stealthily along the walls of the houses bordering the plaza, almost running. Just a hundred paces away from the city wall and his men, Costa stopped suddenly and listened to the night: he could hear boots hitting the ground in a rhythmic cadence. *Running men... We have been discovered; they have sent a second team to the gate.* He threw caution to the wind and ran toward his men, who were waiting at the foot of the wall.

Marcou heard the noise of running soldiers too, and half turned: the soldiers were just entering in the plaza. "Don't turn round," he ordered his men. *We are trapped.* "Walk normally. Our best chance is if they ignore us. We look like a patrol, and it's only thirty paces to the gate."

Codrin was using his Farsight, letting his mind fly around the gate and inside it. Somehow, he found it easier to train when he had a real objective, and he was more than motivated; taking the gate of Peyris was more dangerous than taking the gate of the Eagle's Nest. *Ah*, he thought, *finally. Costa is entering in the plaza. They have replaced the men in the patrol.* He watched everything, learning how to change perspective faster. Each change pained him, as if a knife were stabbing into his brain, but at least the pain did not last. Then he saw a twenty-five strong group of guards entering the plaza, just as the horologe beat the hour before midnight.

"First line, shoot over the wall," he shouted, and watched patiently until the flock of arrows flew over the wall and hit the ground in front of the running guards. *Too short.* He waited a few moments, watching the guards advancing through the plaza. "Second and third line, shoot over the wall." *Tomorrow, I will have an interesting time explaining why I ordered this.*

The arrows followed the same trajectory. This time, they hit the troops full on, and only eleven guards were left standing. Disoriented, they stopped running for a few moments. Five more arrows came from the side street, and four more guards fell. The remaining men ran toward the gate.

"Charge!" Emich moved forward and attacked the remaining guards in the plaza. From above the gate, arrows flew down at them and a man from Emich's troop fell. Then another.

"Shoot at will at the guards on the wall," Codrin ordered, and a hundred arrows peppered the wall above the gate.

"To the gate!" Costa started to run even before finishing his order. *How did Codrin know when to shoot?*

"We are under attack!" Marcou shouted, knocking at the door of the guardroom. "Open the door! Faster!" The door opened suddenly, and he barely had time to step back before it crashed against him. He grabbed the door and pulled it wide open, dragging the guard who had just opened it – his hand was still gripping the handle.

"What are you doing?" the guard asked just before he died, stabbed by the man behind Marcou.

"Make way!" Lisandru shouted and jumped inside the room, his two curved swords unsheathed, moving them like the wings of a windmill. He killed three men before they knew what was happening. A moment later, Marcou and Costa came in behind him. The room was thirty feet across and there were twelve guards still alive. One of them charged his crossbow, aiming at Lisandru. Parrying a sword thrust, he slipped aside, trying to put someone else between him and the bolt. An arrow came from the door, piercing the neck of the man with the crossbow. From the corner of his eye, Lisandru saw Pintea, who was already nocking again, and another arrow flew. In less than a minute, all the men in the guardroom were dead.

"Emich!" Costa shouted. "Open the gate, I will go after the men at the arrow slits."

Looking back from time to time, the men grunted from the effort, and it took them four long minutes to unlock and open the heavy gate. Emich and another soldier took two torches from the sconces on the wall, and they painted two circles of fire through the darkness.

"Make ready!" Vlad shouted. "Riders are coming from the barracks."

Pintea moved forward with his five archers. "Shoot at will," he ordered, while Vlad organized the men behind him in an inverse V shape. "We move forward when the riders are thirty paces from us. Stand. Steady. Now!"

Followed by two of his men, Costa climbed the stairs, three steps at a time. A man appeared in the doorway of the upper room, a crossbow in his hands. Five feet away from the guard, Costa half turned, to offer a smaller target, and a bolt hit him in the left shoulder. He stumbled, then pressed forward, cutting the hand on the crossbow, then finding the man's neck. He stepped aside, hiding behind the wall, and his men did the same. "Two archers are still alive. We need to take them."

"Ride!" Nicolas ordered, seeing the torch signal through the open gate. The Spatar and his men were already mounted, their horses trotting nervously in place, five hundred paces from the gate. The battle cries from the city carried far through the night, even before Emich could open the gate.

"Vlad, make way for our riders!" Emich shouted, and slowly, Vlad and his soldiers retired toward the walls, pressed hard by the mounted guards.

Nicolas stormed through the gate and found himself in a good position; the city guards were lined up to fight Vlad's men. They cut through the guards and entered the plaza, where fifty more riders were still ready to fight.

"I am Nicolas, the Spatar of Peyris," he shouted, turning his horse two times. "Put down your weapons and return to the barracks."

Accustomed to obeying him, more than half of the guards stopped fighting. The ones who continued to fight were surrounded quickly and surrendered when Vlaicu entered the city. His four hundred riders split in two wings and surrounded everybody in the plaza, friends and foes.

"Lisandru, come with me," Pintea said. "Costa went up there and has not returned." They passed through the guardroom and climbed the stairs leading to the first floor. "What happened?" he asked, seeing Costa and his men hidden behind the walls on both sides of the door. He frowned, seeing the bolt in Costa's shoulder.

"There are two more with crossbows inside."

"Do you know their positions?"

"The same position as ours, but on the other side of this wall." Costa tapped the stone with the hilt of his sword.

"The gate is taken, and our men are inside the city."

"Did you hear?" Costa asked. "I am captain Costa, and I serve Duchess Cleyre. We have taken the city. You are the guards of Peyris, not of Albert."

"You killed one of us."

"He put a bolt in me. Think about it."

"How do we know that you've taken the city?"

"Look through the window. Nicolas, the Spatar of Peyris, commands the army of the Duchess."

"I thought I heard Nicolas," one guard whispered. "I prefer to serve Nicolas and Cleyre than Sandro and Albert." There was faint noise in the room, one man walking with care, going away, then returning. "We are coming out," the same guard spoke, loudly. "Our crossbows are down." He placed his weapon on the floor and pushed it in front of the open door. The second guard did the same.

Knight Dolen was the Master Guard of Peyris that night, and he was napping in his office, when the courier came to give him the news that the West Gate was under attack. He had a hundred riders on duty that night, but it took them half an hour to gather. They rode out just before a second courier came to announce that the gate had fallen.

"Who is attacking us?" Dolen asked, turning in the saddle to address the courier.

"Sir Nicolas. He has taken the gate in the name of Cleyre, the Duchess of Peyris."

"How many men does he have?"

"More than a hundred, and many of them are archers."

Nicolas and I never really got on, and that bitch shamed me in front of the court. "Sound the general alarm."

"Maybe we should talk with Nicolas and the Duchess," his deputy said.

"Traitor," Dolen growled and killed the man with a brief flourish of his sword. "We serve the Duke, not Nicolas and his bitch. Sound the alarm. Tardon, take five guards, and go see what's happening," he said to his most trusted man.

Tardon returned before the three hundred men from the barracks could be assembled. "Sir," he reported, "Nicolas has more than six hundred men, a hundred of them armed with crossbows. They have already taken over the western part of the city. And, Sir," he said in a low voice, "I saw that man from Poenari."

"What man?"

"Codrin. If you want my advice, we should leave. Nicolas is not our friend, and there is no way we can defeat them."

"Gather my men at the North Gate. Cancel the alarm," he shouted. "Go back to your beds."

Half an hour later, Dolen left the city, with a hundred men. During the night, the fugitives hid in a forest north of the city, and with the first light of day, they rode toward Amiuns.

Octavian and Reymont arrived at the camp between Peyris and Amiuns at noon, happy that they had escaped Albert's bigmouth and small brain, and Peyris was now close. A real city, not just a simple fortress. They went directly to Sandro's tent. The newly promoted first Spatar of Peyris was not busy; there were no pressing issues.

"Anything new?" Sandro asked his guests and sent his pages out of the tent.

"In Amiuns, the water is not good, the beds are too small, as are the rooms, and the servants are too old, especially the women. Shall I go on? Albert has a long list of complaints," Octavian said and seated himself, followed by Reymont.

"We should change places. How long will we stay here?"

"There are some rumors about soldiers gathering around Peyris," Octavian said, evasively. "We should know more in a few days."

"We have had a few desertions. Perhaps fifty men."

"Any news from Peyris?"

"Nothing urgent," Sandro said. "Nicolas is still camped outside the walls. What is he planning? He doesn't move without a plan."

"Perhaps he is trying to bribe his way into the city, but those we left in command are hostile to him. Like Dolen. He hates both Nicolas and Cleyre."

"Why do you mention Cleyre?"

"I think Nicolas wants to make her Duchess. He obviously doesn't know that she is already married and far from Peyris."

"Neither did I," Sandro said, and looked from one of them to the other, frowning.

"Only a few people know. You are now one of them. It was a political issue that was solved by the Duke."

"You may not enter," the two soldiers guarding the tent said.

"Mind your words, soldier," Dolen growled and pushed away the one blocking his path.

"Let him in," Sandro said, seeing the Knight's red face. "Dolen, why are you here?"

"Peyris has fallen."

"To Loxburg?" Reymont asked, and Octavian threw a murderous glance at him.

"Old Loxburg is in his bed. It was Nicolas who took it."

"How could Nicolas take Peyris with only eight hundred men? You had the walls and six hundred guards," Octavian said.

"Costa attacked the West Gate during the night, and Nicolas entered the city, but it was not he who led the attack. It was Codrin, and together, they had more than fifteen hundred soldiers. I barely escaped with a hundred men, and we spent the night in the forest, before coming here."

"You must be mistaken. Codrin is in Severin, and he disbanded his army more than a month ago."

"He *is* in Peyris, and they have taken the city in the name of Cleyre, the Duchess of Peyris."

"Cleyre is nowhere near Peyris." Octavian's voice lost some of its confidence, but he assumed a posture of disinterest, apparently distracted by a white spot on the floor.

"Look, Sage," Dolen snapped, "I don't care who's been telling you fairy stories. Codrin is in Peyris. I can bring you six men who saw him. They all fought in Poenari, where you sent us to die."

"Dolen," Sandro said sharply. "I trust you but watch your tone. We have to tell Albert. Would you return to Amiuns?" He looked at Octavian and Reymont.

"We will stay here for a few more days. We will need a tent. Send a courier to Albert." *How could this have happened?* Octavian stood up and left the place in a hurry. He wandered through the camp until he found the tent he was looking for.

"Clewin, we need to talk," Octavian said, his voice low. "I have an important mission for you. Very important. No one but the two of us should know what we discuss here. You have the full backing of the Circle, and I promise you a Seigneury when all this ends. Now, listen to me carefully."

Chapter 19 – Codrin / Cleyre

As was customary for the nomination ceremony, Peyris Council gathered in the Inner Council Room. There were fewer people than usual. The Secretary, the second Secretary and the new Spatar were missing. Nicolas, the previous Spatar, Paulus, the third Secretary, the Vistier, Costa and a few other councilors were there. There were guests too: Codrin, Vlaicu and Phillip, Devan's son. In front of the assembled councilors and guests, Cleyre accepted the scepter of the Duchy and raised it above her head.

"From now on, Peyris stands on my shoulders," Cleyre spoke the ancient words, and became the new Duchess of Peyris. "Things could be better," she sighed.

"Things can always be better," Codrin laughed, "But you will be a better ruler than Albert. Nicolas and Costa will defend Peyris. There is not much for us to do, and we should be able to leave in two days. I have my own challenge to solve now." *I hope I still have enough time; winter is coming.* He looked at Cleyre, and their eyes met. "In these strange times, perhaps Peyris needs a Duke too."

Nicolas and the councilors around the table breathed a collective sigh of relief – Codrin would be the new Duke. The only man who looked unhappy was Costa, but he was strong enough to keep his feelings hidden, and no one was looking at him anyway. Logically, he understood that it was the best solution for Peyris, but heart and mind do not always agree.

"Have you someone in mind?" *Why is he...?* Slightly irritated, Cleyre withdrew behind her tired blue eyes. She would have liked to postpone the decision, at least for a few days, and it was *her* decision to make, but she did not want to contradict Codrin in public. Cleyre owed him too much, and she liked him, even when she loved another man. *After everything that happened, his proposal was unavoidable. He will make a strong Duke.*

"I might have, but it's not for me to decide." Codrin smiled apologetically, making some people around the table a little confused and perhaps worried.

"Let's see what you have in mind." Cleyre gave a piece of paper to Codrin, who wrote down a name. Tense, she took the paper back, and raised her eyebrows, breathing deeply, before she read it. "Well," she said, and her eyes crinkled with mirth, "it seems that we are thinking the same thing, not for the first time." She moved her chair closer to the corner and to Codrin. "Costa, could you please place another chair here?" She gestured toward the empty space on her left.

Despite his wounds, both physical and mental, Costa stood up and brought a chair, then made to leave.

"Do you think he will agree?" Cleyre asked and gave the piece of paper to Costa. A wave of tension went around the table, and the councilors exchanged confused looks.

Costa took the paper. *Why is she doing this to me? The last thing I want is to announce her marriage to Codrin. Why did she asked me if he would accept? Perhaps it's not Codrin. Then who...?* He looked quizzically at her, though whether in agreement, disagreement, or some refined irony, no one around the table could tell. He suppressed a sigh and forced himself to read. It did not take long. He moistened his lips.

"Costa?" Cleyre asked.

"Yes," he breathed.

"Yes what?"

"Yes, he will accept."

Cleyre smiled and nodded at the empty chair. Moving slowly, Costa sat, and she placed her hand over his.

"Costa will be my husband," Cleyre said, "and the Duke consort, helping me to rule Peyris. We will arrange the wedding today. I hope that Codrin will be our guest of honor." *We will wed tomorrow. I never thought I would have three weddings in just a few months. The other two were... Forget about them.*

Feeling he had been cheated, Nicolas frowned at Codrin, who nodded to assure him. They had talked about Cleyre's marriage just before the meeting, and Codrin assured him that he will handle everything.

"That was the easy part. We now need a military council," Codrin said.

"Paulus," Cleyre gestured toward the third Secretary, "from now one you are the Secretary of Peyris. Nicolas, you are the Spatar of Peyris again. You can thank me after we defeat Albert." She laughed lightly when they bowed to her, and that chased all the tiredness from her eyes. "You need to cancel my marriage to Veres. No," she frowned, "you must *invalidate* it, Paulus; I did not agree in the church. They married me against my will, and they shamed Fate. Ask the Bishop to invalidate it and to unfrock the priest who married me against my will. Then ask for the Bishop's resignation. Mateus will take his place." She frowned, pondering if she had missed anything. "Bring them in," she said to the only page in the room, and in the general silence, Vlad, Boldur, Valer and Knight Emich entered the room. "So," she glanced at Codrin.

"Albert is more a nuisance than a threat."

When Codrin nodded discreetly, Vlad gave his report. "There have been some desertions from Albert's camp. Around fifty men. They happened before it was known that we had taken Peyris. I am expecting the rate to grow, but perhaps Nicolas can say more about this. Our scouts saw the deserters leaving Albert's convoy on the road to Amiuns, and we can only guess their reason."

"Albert had two thousand soldiers," Nicolas said, thoughtfully, "six hundred posted here. Four hundred are ours now. I have started negotiations with the Knights Endris and Clewin, who still consider Albert their Duke. They are camped halfway between here and Amiuns. We will know more in a few days. I doubt that Albert wants to move against us. He will prefer to remain in Amiuns."

"It's not what Albert wants; it's what Reymont wants." Cleyre frowned, and tightened her lips, a glint of white teeth pressing into a lower lip gone thin.

"Reymont belongs to the past now. I don't know why he convinced Albert to leave Peyris, but it suited us." Nicolas shrugged, then turned his palms out.

"That's a bit of a mystery," Codrin agreed, looking at Nicolas, and his brows drew down in thought. "I don't like this kind of mystery in general, but this one is driven by the Circle, and it may burn us later. Octavian is there too, and he is as intelligent as he is deceitful. Perhaps we will know more tomorrow."

"Do you really have to leave?"

"Yes, Nicolas, I must claim some blood debts, and time is short. Don't worry, I will not ask you for help. You have enough problems here."

"Maybe if you postpone it for a few days, we will know more and be able to give you some soldiers," Cleyre said.

"Everyone knows now that I am here, and that I did not disband my army in Severin. That was to be my advantage. Unfortunately. But today is not a day to worry. We have a wedding to celebrate."

"In the evening, we will have a small party for our friends from Severin and Deva." Cleyre smiled and looked around the table. There was a warmth in her that she did not feel for a long time. The meeting was now closed.

"Codrin, please stay," Cleyre said when most people had left. She nodded to Costa, who nodded back and left them alone. "How did you know about Costa? I hid my feelings for a long time, to protect him from my brothers and from Albert."

"I had no Vision, if that's what you mean, perhaps an intuition, the kind of thing people with the Light have from time to time. I apologize for forcing it on you, but it was urgent, and I did not have time to talk with you. Peyris needs stability, and some people have put pressure on me to marry you. They ambushed me this morning and wanted to propose it just now."

"Nicolas, I suppose. He appreciates you and fears for my future. You know," Cleyre said and laced her arms around his neck, "we are a strange couple. A couple that almost happened."

Codrin arched his brows. Then he smiled. "True. If it weren't for Saliné, I would have asked for your hand. You are a wonderful woman, Cleyre." *If I lose Saliné, there is no way to turn things back. I must find her.*

"And without Costa, I would have wanted you to ask me." With a mischievous smile, she pulled him closer and kissed him. Codrin swallowed his surprise and, embracing her tightly, answered her. "That was just so we know what we've lost," Cleyre said after they recovered their breath. "It was the last day we could do it. Tomorrow, I will be a married woman. Again. But this is the only marriage that counts. Thank you, Codrin. Without you, things would have been much worse for me."

"Peyris is in good hands again."

"Let's hope you that are right. Where do you want to go from here?" They were still embraced, her head on his shoulder, and she was playing absently with his hair, but once the passion of that one kiss had passed, they felt like brother and sister. It was a strange feeling that neither could explain, but they enjoyed it, nevertheless. For Codrin it was a reminder of better times, when his twin sister Ioana, Saliné or Vio embraced him the same way, a long time ago. For Cleyre it was something new, untested and even more valuable. Her brothers were always eager to beat her, not to embrace her.

"Arad."

"You want to free Jara."

"Yes, I owe her that."

"You are a kind man, Codrin of Arenia. The toughest man I know, but kind. And..." she said hesitantly, "there is something new. You've changed since we last met."

"We are almost one year older, and bad things have happened to both of us."

"It's not that. I can feel when someone has the Light. There is something new in you, a different sort of power."

"The Blue Light. I have both the White and the Blue Light."

Cleyre leaned her head back from his shoulder, frowning in surprise. "Are you a Seer?"

"Yes. I did not ask for it, but it came to me a month ago. Only you and Vlad know about it."

"Can he feel it too?"

"No," Codrin laughed, "but otherwise it was difficult to explain to him how I knew where Ferko or you were in the Nest, and some other things. How do you know about the Seer?"

"Dochia told me, and looking back, I think she knew about you becoming the Seer of the Realm. I'm glad to know such an important man. But all I can offer you is a small party."

"Without your help, I wouldn't have been what I am now. Each of us has a role to play in life. And it's for us to decide how to play it," he said and caressed her face as she disengaged from him.

"Codrin," she said gently, "even without a Vision, my feeling is that you and Saliné will be together. But not this year."

There were not many people in the room. Cleyre had invited Codrin, his captains and Phillip, and from Peyris only Costa,

Nicolas, Paulus, the Vistier and Emich were present. The party started early, and it was not going to last long. There were preparations for the tomorrow's wedding to make. They were still at war, so everything would be simple and unfussy. Nicolas and the new Secretary wanted her to postpone the wedding, to make it one fit for a Duchess. For them was a political issue, but Cleyre and Costa wanted Codrin to be present, and her most powerful people no longer insisted. The party was stalling; none of them was really in a good mood. Tiredness was taking its toll. Amid the quiet conversations, some noise came from the antechamber.

"You can't go in," a guard protested. "They are having a party in there."

"It will end now," a gravelly voice said, and the door opened with a bang.

A large Mounte entered, followed by the still protesting guards. He towered over anyone else in the room, except Boldur, but few men were larger than the Mounte Chieftain. Remembering he had seen the man before, with Vlad, Nicolas frowned, not knowing how to react, while Codrin and his men recognized their scout squad leader. In general, his scouts were small men – they needed to pass unobserved; but, at times, there was a need for strong ones, able to climb where the horses or weaker men could not go. Codrin used them mostly in the mountains, and this scout had come from the White Salt Mountains.

"I told him," the guard complained, keeping his distance from the large Mounte.

"My scouts have a free pass when something important has happened. Tell me, Jamet," Codrin said, knowing that he would not have entered without a good reason.

"Lenard of Dorna is coming this way with six hundred soldiers. He will be here tomorrow evening."

"Thank you, Jamet," Codrin said, nodding to Vlad, who filled a glass of wine and gave it to the scout.

Jamet raised the glass toward Cleyre, saying, "Salut," and drank the glass in one shot. He turned abruptly and left the room, followed by Vlad.

"My kin was a bit overwhelmed by your presence, Lady Cleyre," Boldur said, and bowed. "We don't see Duchesses often in our mountains, and such a beautiful Duchess, never. I apologize if he offended you."

"He did what he needed to do. Codrin is right that we should waive the rules for emergencies, however important the party. Well, we have all the soldiers here," she said, seeing Vlad returning. "We will switch from party to war council. We can still drink."

"Vlad," Codrin asked, "is Jamet sure that Lenard is coming here and not going toward Amiuns?"

"There is a crossroads ahead of them with a branch that goes north, but it's not the shortest road from Dorna to Amiuns. They would have been there already, using the other road."

"Maybe they have heard that we took Peyris," Nicolas said.

"Two days ago, our scouts encircled the city completely. No couriers came out, and no one went in. Dolen was able to sneak out, with his escort, because they outnumbered our scouts north of Peyris ten to one. We did not engage them, but a scout squad followed them north, and none of them left the troop. Lenard can't know."

"I don't like this." Codrin raised his glass against a candle, looking into the sparkling ruby of the wine.

"You mean that there is no *apparent* reason for his presence here." Cleyre looked at him, trying to understand if he worried for the same reason. She stretched her mind, trying to feel the Light. She felt nothing.

"Yes. There is no apparent reason, but there clearly is one, of course. Lenard is an old fox, and we need to solve this riddle."

"He has only six hundred soldiers," Nicolas said.

"That's part of the riddle, and we don't know how many parts are out there. Cleyre, we need a map of Peyris."

"Let's take the wine and go to the Council Room," Cleyre said, nodding at the young pages. "Its walls are filled with maps."

The room was close, and it did not take them long to move. They scattered inside, thinking thoughts that were not pleasant. Codrin stopped in front of the map of northern Frankis, at a distance from where he could see all of it without effort. His eyes strayed over Peyris, over Dorna, Arad and the three Seigneuries in the north. His gaze hovered over Loxburg. Then he closed his eyes, and Cleyre could see his demeanor change.

He is using the powers of the Seer. Cleyre discerned some small changes in the way she could feel him.

She was right, but after a while, Codrin gave up. He knew that his power was limited to less than two miles, but he had to try. Having no more tricks up his sleeve, he looked at the map again.

"There are three possibilities," he said after a while. "One, Lenard felt the need to see the beauty of Peyris and came to the wedding without an invitation." His eyebrow arched, he looked at Cleyre, who smiled wryly, and there was laughter in the room. *They are less tense now,* he thought. "Second, he is here to help Albert, or third, he is here to attack Albert. His army is too small to attack Albert, and why help Albert when Cleyre has only eight hundred soldiers? Lenard's raid makes sense only if there is another threat against Albert we don't know about. That means Loxburg. Others may be involved too, but nothing can move without Loxburg. He has the numbers."

"You just spoiled my wedding," Cleyre said, but she was smiling. She did not feel like smiling, but she was able to pull some smiles from the others.

"There is nothing more we can do now, so we can indulge more of your wine." Codrin sipped from his glass. *This will delay me, but I can't leave until things are clear. Fate.*

It was morning again when Vlad requested a meeting. In the corridor leading to the Inner Council Room, he briefed Codrin, who frowned deeply. In the room, he let Vlad reveal what the scouts had found out.

"Lenard and his six hundred men will be here late in the evening, but... Yesterday, Loxburg crossed the eastern border. In three days, he will be here with more than four thousand soldiers. They are moving slowly, as he has a thousand infantry with halberds and long spears. They carry the black eagle banner of Litvonia."

"I never heard of Litvonia interfering in Frankis before." Cleyre racked her brains but could find nothing.

"There is always a first time." Vlad's mind was half in the room and half in the house where he was born in Litvonia. "We could visit them too."

"Vlad is pining," Codrin laughed. "He was born in Litvonia. One thousand soldiers were not sent for territorial gain. They are here to help Loxburg. Perhaps they are paid mercenaries, as they are all infantry."

"Albert still has fifteen hundred soldiers," Nicolas said, thoughtfully, "but I don't think he will join Loxburg. Even his little brain can work out that Loxburg wants the Duchy for himself."

"No, he won't join any of us. In the worst situation, we have to defeat an army of four thousand five hundred." Codrin raised his forefinger. *They are three times stronger than us. And Arad...*

We, Nicolas thought with relief; he was not sure if Codrin would stay. "Will you lead the army?"

"I won't let Cleyre down. There are more links than you know between us. Political links." He smiled at Costa. "And the new Duke was our liaison."

"I always wondered where the Duchess got her information. It seems it was from the Wraith of Tolosa."

"Cleyre has more sources than you think, Nicolas. In fact, I received more information from her than I delivered to her. We will continue to help each other. We just need a new liaison, as Costa is no longer available for the position. Newly married men tend to stay at home. I still don't know why. The war now. I want the army to leave today before noon. Costa will stay behind to lead the garrison and guard his Duchess."

"Lenard?" Nicolas asked.

"He will arrive late today, and sleep well, because he will think we left in a hurry to meet Loxburg, and we will fight him in the morning. While he is still sleeping, I hope."

"You will hide nearby," Costa said.

"Yes, we will camp in the large forest south of Peyris. Most probably Lenard will camp in front of the main gate, the southern one. No one except us should know about this. Lenard or the Circle must have spies here. Everyone else in the city must know that we have gone to fight Loxburg. Don't even tell them that Lenard is coming. We must be *surprised*. And Vlad," Codrin added after a brief pause, "loosen the net of scouts. Let the traitors reach Lenard. It suits us to let him know of our hasty departure. Watch them, though, so we know who they are. It will be useful to grab them after the battle, too."

The morning dawned strange. During the night, a brief rain shower had sprinkled the ground, a few drops more than the usual dew, and fog had enveloped the valley. The sun was not yet in sight, but there was enough light to see. It was the mist which made everything strange. It spread across the land, a seven-foot-thick blanket, stretched almost uniformly over the flat bottom of the valley, and the gentle slopes leading down into it. As silent as the mist, Codrin's army moved out of the forest. An observer high above the ground would see rows of floating heads, arranged in a matrix, the distance between them almost regular. Having helmets of many different colors, the heads offered a striking contrast to the white-gray monotony of the mist. An army of floating heads. Unaware of their weird appearance from above, the heads continued their journey down, toward Lenard's army.

To an observer on the ground, nothing could be seen until it was too late. Lenard's sleeping soldiers woke up when the ground trembled to the rhythm of more than a thousand horses trampling everything in their way. They woke up, and they died. Some of them died while they slept. When the last cry died away, and the fog finally lifted, the surviving men surrendered. At the end of the clash, which became known as the Battle of the Mist, Codrin found that he had lost only fifteen men. Lenard had lost half of his army, his son and his life.

Chapter 20 – Codrin

Hooded, the man walked shoulders slumped, the scouts handling him ungently, followed by Vlad. They had come directly from the camp, so few in Peyris knew about him, and those who did had only seen a hooded figure on its way to be interrogated. The scouts sat the man in front of the long table opposite the six people waiting for him, and Vlad seated himself next to Codrin. The scouts pulled off the prisoner's hood and left the room.

"Vasso," Cleyre said after a brief glance toward Costa, "let's not make this more disagreeable than necessary. We found you in Lenard's camp. Who are you working for?"

"Reymont," Vasso said, despondently.

"And the Circle?"

"And the Circle."

"Why did you go to Lenard?"

"To let him know that your army had left the city."

"Tell me what I need to know. I will be more lenient if you cooperate."

"Thank you, Duchess. Octavian and Reymont planned to surrender Peyris to Manuc, the Duke of Loxburg. That's why they convinced Duke... they convinced Albert to leave the city. Octavian and Reymont were supposed to return and negotiate the surrender."

"Why did they want to give Peyris to Manuc?"

"I don't know, Duchess. I know only one more thing: they planned to marry you to Duke Loxburg's son."

"Manuc's son?"

"Yes, Duchess. I am sorry, but I know nothing more."

"You are in high demand, Duchess," Nicolas said.

Cleyre smiled briefly but kept her attention on the prisoner. "What accomplices do you have here?"

Vasso sighed and gave her three more names; all of them were from the lower ranks, and they knew less than he did, but at least they confirmed Vasso's version of events.

"Let's see the men from Dorna now," Cleyre said, and she nodded to Codrin. Together with Costa, they had agreed that morning on how to proceed; the Knights from Dorna were his.

"I have a surprise for you." Vlad looked, slightly amused, at Codrin.

"Long Valley?" Codrin asked, and Vlad nodded. "Bring him first."

Vlad came with two men instead of one: Lovrin and Balint.

"Lovrin, I did not expect to see you here," Codrin said, surprised, coming around the table, where they clasped hands. "My Knight of Long Valley," he presented Lovrin, "and Balint, his Chief Guard." He clasped hands with the second man. "Sit," he gestured at the chairs across the table, and went back to his place.

Lovrin was not a fighter, but he was a calm man, with a lot of experience. He glanced around the room, searching, evaluating, nothing visible on his face, before saying, "Lenard never liked me, after I took Boar's place; he forced me to join his army."

"You killed the Boars?" Nicolas asked, incredulous; Lovrin was maybe a third of Boar's size.

"I didn't, they did," he pointed at Codrin and Vlad. "And Codrin killed Sharpe, the Black Dervil, too." Lovrin felt the need to enhance Codrin's status even more. "Lenard learned that I had sent soldiers to you, in Poenari. On its way to Peyris, his army passed through Long Valley and surrounded my castle. I had to join him, but Lisa sent a courier to you, in Severin, after we left."

"Lenard is dead, his son too, and I intend to keep Dorna. You are my Knight, and I need a governor. You are a skilled Secretary. Are you willing to take over?" Codrin asked.

"The administrative part, yes, but army commander is not really my best part."

"Balint can be your Chief Guard there, and we will talk about a Spatar later. I may give Damian to you."

"Thank you, Codrin."

"How is Lisa?"

"As beautiful as when you left us. Our son is now almost one year old. I would like to talk with Damian and Lisandru. Lisa will ask me about Varia and Livia."

"Damian is in Severin. Vlad will bring you later to Lisandru."

Codrin knew only one of the other four Knights from Dorna, and he had met him in the past as the Wraith. They were men who understood their interests and agreed to pay allegiance to him. They did not cry for Lenard, but they would not cry for Codrin either, in similar circumstances. After what had happened in Leyona, Codrin knew that well enough, but he also knew that he was stronger and, after Poenari and Severin, his name was now known in Frankis. The Battle of the Mist would enhance his fame even more. All Peyris and the defeated Knights would know that he had lost only fifteen men. There were more than sixty wounded too, but nobody talks about the wounded after a battle; they talk about the dead. And glory.

"Codrin, in the past, I had a good relationship with Manuc. It may be worth talking with him before we go to battle," Cleyre said, just before the army was ready to leave.

"I would not say no. Who do you think that we can use?"

"Nicolas knows him well."

"I can't send Nicolas." Codrin frowned in thought and shook his head. "If things go badly, you may lose your Spatar. There are few men like him in Frankis. Only Pierre of Tolosa and Manuc are better commanders."

"And you," Cleyre smiled. "Emich knows him too."

"Emich, then. Our preparation for battle will still continue."

In the afternoon, the army moved east to confront Loxburg, a different kind of threat, both subtler and stronger. Codrin and Nicolas had seventeen hundred soldiers with them. An hour later, a column coming from Amiuns, and led by Knight Clewin, joined them.

"I hope that I am not too late," Clewin said, stopping his horse, in front of Nicolas. "I bring three hundred soldiers with me."

"Well, you missed yesterday's party against Lenard, but we have saved something for you. Loxburg is waiting for us. And he has almost five thousand men, at the scouts' last estimate. I am glad you accepted my offer. Cleyre's offer."

"So, it's true."

"Yes, and now we need to go, Codrin is waiting for us."

"Codrin?" Clewin reacted sharply, his thick brows knitting together. "From Poenari?"

"Yes, that Codrin. He is leading our army. Cleyre has a good eye for allies."

❧

"Loxburg will be here in four hours," Vlad announced in the military council. If not speaking about his mountains in Litvonia, he was sparse with words, and Codrin appreciated his way of passing concise messages that could be understood fast by everybody.

The campaign tent, which had once belonged to Duke Stefan, was three times as big as the one Codrin had inherited from Mohor. His own tent was being used by Vlad's scouts. Despite its size, the duke's tent was almost full. Codrin's army of two thousand had four times more captains and Knights than

Mohor or Codrin had had in the past. The army was drawn up at the entrance of a valley, three hundred feet wide, having two narrow ends.

"That's not enough time to finish our preparations," Boldur said.

"How much time do you need?" Codrin asked.

"Eight hours."

"I will return in half an hour. Vlad, come with me," Codrin said and left the tent, leaving behind some puzzled captains.

"He is a strange man," Clewin whispered to Nicolas.

"Well, he is, but in a good way. For years, I knew him as the Wraith of Tolosa."

"I thought the Wraith was a man called Tudor."

"Yes, Tudor is Codrin, and Codrin is Tudor."

"Strange." Clewin shrugged. *I was expecting Nicolas to lead the army. No one told me that Codrin was here.* "What is Boldur up to? I didn't see anything that looked like a trap."

"They left Peyris before us. We did not have much time to talk, but Codrin said that he is cutting some trees down. I think he wants to slow Manuc's exit from the valley." Nicolas pointed to the forest at the end of the field behind the tent. "If we can keep them in a tight field, they can't use their advantage in numbers."

A hundred paces away from the camp, Codrin stopped and hid behind an old oak, larger than six men tied together. "Guard me, Vlad." Eyes closed, he let his mind wander west, toward Loxburg's army. He flew over the forest, following the road, and soon found himself at the limit of his Farsight. *Less than two miles,* he thought. *It's not enough.* He came out of his trance, opened his eyes and fixed them on a lonely peak some twenty miles away. This time, for the first time, he entered in the trance eyes open, staying focused on the peak. His mind moved away, farther and farther. Pain lanced through his head, and he moaned, but he forced himself to continue. Almost at the foot of the peak, he could no longer endure the pain and stopped, then came out of his trance. Warm liquid ran down his face, and touching it, he found his fingers red with blood from his nose. Feeling weak, he leaned his back against the old oak.

"Are you well?" Vlad asked, his eyes fixed on Codrin.

"Yes. Give me two minutes. I have found a good place, twelve miles from here." He recovered and wiped the blood from his face with a handkerchief. Some blood had dripped onto the pelerine he wore over his ring mail, but the dark blue color more or less masked the spots. "Let's go back, some of them would think me crazy. Before a battle, every aspect is important."

"We will split up," Codrin said from the door of the tent. "Boldur will stay here, with all the men he needs, to finish the trap. We will leave now. There is a place, twelve miles from here, on the road from the west. We will wait for Loxburg there and delay him."

From the ground, things looked different than from the height Codrin had flown in his Farsight trance, but he recognized the place easily enough. Nature had played a strange game with the land. From above, the ridges looked like a giant fork with two tines, forty feet tall and three hundred feet long. The road led upward between the tines. There was a narrow, potholed saddle to the east, from which they entered between the parallel ridges. Five horses could ride abreast, and that was Codrin's main problem; there was no easy way to retreat. The place was mostly surrounded by forest and ridges. The lower, western part of the fork was a long stretch of grass that sloped away and down, for about six hundred paces.

"Not a bad place. Who found it?" Nicolas asked Codrin.

"The scouts. Nicolas, you will lead the right wing. Take Clewin, three more Knights and four hundred men. Vlaicu, you will lead the left wing. Valer will join you with fifty of his men. Take two hundred more soldiers from our men and a hundred fifty from Dorna. Vlad, place a hundred archers on the right-hand ridge, which is slightly shorter; and put couriers in place for the archers and both wings. You will stay with me. Our wings will hide in the forest behind the ridges, south and north of them, and they will attack their flanks after his army engages us in the center. This place is narrow, and they will have to stretch out in a long column. We need to make them retreat, and then we do the same. The terrain behind us is too rugged for a swift retreat, so we will make a detour to the right while the archers protect us. Get the wings in place now," he looked at Nicolas and Vlaicu, "and come back here. Then we just have to wait for Loxburg. Vlad, let his scouts come closer to find us. I am expecting him to stop and assess the battlefield. Maybe he will think his men are too tired and will wait for tomorrow to attack us, and we can go back without giving battle."

Duke Manuc of Loxburg halted his army three miles away from the fork; his scouts swarmed the area, followed at a distance by Vlad's.

"Emich," Codrin said, "take five men and Fate's banner, and go to Manuc. Here is a letter from Cleyre. You know what is written inside, and what to say. Let's hope that he is still the man she thinks he is. Now we must wait," he said, his eyes following Emich, riding away. The white flag of Fate, with hand and quill, waved in the wind. The hand and the feather were Fate's symbols; the goddess's hand, writing everyone's fate.

Twenty minutes later, half a mile down from Codrin's position, a squad of three scouts came out of the forest, onto the visible part of the road, riding at a full gallop. Codrin looked at Vlad, who frowned; it was not normal; usually the scouts stayed in the forest.

"Our delegation was slaughtered," the team lead said, without dismounting. "All six of them. A mile from here."

"Did you see what happened?" Codrin asked, a triangular crease burrowed between his eyebrows.

"Twenty men came out of the forest and attacked them. They wore no colors. There were two teams of scouts from Loxburg between us and Emich. Our second team is still in the area; maybe their team will leave, and we can look at the tracks."

"They wore no colors," Codrin said, rubbing his chin. "Strange."

"Loxburg attacked them," Clewin said, his voice angry, and his right hand gripped the hilt of his sword. "We have fought him for many years. A Duke without honor. He used men without colors to hide the fact he attacked a delegation under the protection of Fate's banner."

What reason could have Manuc to attack an embassy? "What do you think, Nicolas?" Codrin asked, and Clewin reddened at the polite snub.

"He is a tricky man, but to attack Fate's banner..."

It must have been the Circle, and they have a spy here, who passed information about our embassy. Well, he shrugged, *they have spies everywhere. They have soldiers too. Albert?* "Vlad, send two large scout teams, through the forest. Twenty-five strong. Take more men from Valer if you need to. Follow their scouts and see what you can read on the ground. When the main battle ends, we will hunt the assassins. I want them dead. Hanged with a traitor mark."

Vlad returned faster than expected, and he stopped his horse abruptly in front of Codrin. "Manuc is coming. He will be here in half an hour. The infantry is slowing him a bit. We had no chance to examine the scene, his vanguard was too close."

"Knights, captains, to your places," Codrin ordered, and took his place in front of the army, Lisandru and Pintea forming the Triangle behind him.

Manuc halted his army at the edge of the forest, and his thousand infantry moved to occupy the center. They formed a deep line, a hundred men in each rank, their halberds and long spears making them look like a huge hedgehog. On the sides of the hedgehog, two squads of riders took up position. There was space on each flank for about twenty riders abreast.

"I don't like this," Codrin murmured. "It will be a slow attack, driven by the infantry. That will force us to attack the spearmen. There will be too many casualties." He was pondering to sound the retreat while he still had time, when the sound of horses trampling the ground came from the right wing. They turned abruptly and saw three hundred riders cantering down the valley. On the tips of their raised swords, Codrin could see their helmets. The sign of treason. Clewin's men had betrayed them and joined Loxburg. *What kind of Seer am I if I could not foresee this?* "Send the couriers. Nicolas and Vlaicu must retreat now. The half rear of the main group will retreat too, through the saddle. Warn the archers to be ready. They will move back at the same time as we do."

Down in the valley, Clewin's men joined Loxburg. *They need to reorganize*, Codrin thought, following everything with his spyglass. *That will delay them, and give me my wings enough time to retreat. I need the right flank free, so we can leave the battlefield through there. The path around the ridge is narrow, and it will not allow more than ten riders abreast. That will take time. Manuc has reordered his forces, with Clewin on our right. He still plans to attack with the infantry. That suits us, now. I wonder what Clewin told him; he knows all our plans. Our old plans. They are advancing.*

"Vlad, take your bow, and ride behind Lisandru. See if you can take down Clewin. Be ready to ride!" he shouted, twenty minutes after the couriers had left with the orders for the wings and moved closer to the left flank of his army. "Follow my Triangle at a hundred paces. When I turn right, you turn too. I will raise my sword. Ride, now!"

He rode down at a slow canter, followed by Lisandru and Pintea, with Vlad behind them. The enemy infantry was more than a thousand paces in front from him. Going up the slope, Manuc's riders moved at the same slow speed as the foot soldiers. After three hundred paces, Codrin moved to a full gallop. One hundred paces more, and he raised his sword, turning abruptly to the right. A hundred paces behind him, the riders turned right too, in a wider arc.

Down in the valley, Manuc shook his head, trying to understand the maneuver. *What is Nicolas doing?* he thought. Clewin had misled him, not revealing that Codrin led the army. *He wants to kill Clewin. After I take Peyris, I will not keep Clewin at my court. He is the Circle's man. If he dies in battle...* "Send a courier to Clewin. He must attack now. Send a courier to the right wing. They should move out in front of the infantry. I want to catch Nicolas between my army and that small ridge on the left." *And I want Clewin dead. I did not ask them to betray Nicolas. There is no honor in winning like this. But I will win it,* he shrugged.

Tense and looking, from time to time, back at Manuc, Clewin waited until more than half of Codrin's cavalry had already turned west after their strange detour. He was wary of being in the vanguard and tried to delay his attack. When he finally understood that Peyris was running away, Clewin pushed his horse to a gallop, followed by his three hundred men. The last ranks of Codrin's riders were turning west, and Clewin was only two hundred paces away from them. He frowned, seeing that two soldiers had stayed behind the retreating riders, and then he recognized Codrin. "Kill those men!" he shouted at the people around him, pointing at Codrin and Vlad. He had to turn his troop slightly to the right, to meet them. The delay was not long, only fifteen seconds.

Calmly, Vlad nocked his bow and turned in the saddle, to look back, guiding the horse with his knees. "I see Clewin." He breathed long, tensed his bow and waited. The he waited more. Slowly, his fingers released the string. The arrow hissed like a hurried snake. Without looking, Vlad pushed his horse to a gallop. Down, Clewin's horse neighed in protest as the rider jerked backward and was nearly swept under its sharp hooves.

"Fine shot. You hit him in the neck," Codrin said. "One traitor less."

Codrin's and Vlad's Arenian horses were fast, but it took time to get to full speed. Six of Clewin's men were close, the rest spread out behind them like a paper fan. The six closed the distance: forty paces, thirty. Swords up, they shouted and spurred their horses. Twenty paces, and they were whooping confidently now, sure they would catch them.

The Arenian horses came to full speed and started to gain distance. Feeling that their prey was escaping, Clewin's riders shouted and spurred harder, and blood ran down the horses. Smiling at the heavy curses behind him, Codrin glanced to his right and saw the archers on the ridge, ready to shoot. *A few moments more*, he thought, and the first arrows flew with his last word, starting the kill. A second volley. A third one. Men and horses fell in the field. The wounded cried their pain. The dead were silent. Clewin's men chose to stay alive, and ran back, a disorganized wave of riders. Codrin and Vlad vanished into the forest. *That was tight*, he shook his head.

Clewin was not dead when the soldiers brought him, on a stretcher, to Manuc; Vlad's arrow had not struck the center; it was closer to the side of the neck, but the jugular vein was open. *He will not survive*, the Duke thought. "Call a healer to take care of him. We will camp here. They have probably all gone, but he sent a three hundred men to clear the ridges of archers."

Codrin's army gathered in one unit again and went back to their camp. Nicolas went with him in front of the riders. Bitter and sad, Nicolas shook his head at Codrin before saying, "I trusted Clewin. We played together when we were children. We hunted together. Why did he betray us?"

"He must have killed Emich too."

"I lost a good friend, because of my weakness." Nicolas's voice was a barely audible whisper. *And I have to tell his wife and children. His girl is only six-year-old*. He wanted to be alone and mourn Emich.

"You tried to help Cleyre. How much does Clewin know about my trap?"

I need to pull myself together, Nicolas thought. *The real battle has not yet started.* "Less than me, and I don't know much either. Do you think...?"

"Vlad killed him, but I don't know what Clewin said to Manuc. They did not have much time, though. Let's hope that my trap works; if not we will have to let them reach Peyris and lay siege. That will make Cleyre look weak." *And it will take time. There will be no way to attack Orban and free Jara before the bad weather comes. In spring it will be harder. Orban and the Circle will recover. Fate.*

❧❧

The scouts from Loxburg were in good spirits, a feeling the whole army shared. Peyris had lost three hundred soldiers through desertion and had been routed almost without a fight. Only eighteen men had died, killed by the hidden archers, and none of them was from Loxburg. Clewin had died too, but Manuc was not mourning for him. A squad of scouts was on its way toward the southern ridge overlooking the valley. There was another squad on the northern ridge. It was an easy path, and the valley did not look menacing at all. It was relatively wide. The southern and northern ridges were only twenty feet tall at most. In some places, there was no ridge at all, only a moderately steep slope from the plateau surrounding the valley. It was not difficult for the horses to negotiate it, both up and down. The scouts rode around a natural formation that looked like a tower, fifty feet tall and two hundred feet in diameter, guarding the entrance to the valley. There was another one, shorter, across the entrance. The leader scanned the tower on his side: no horse could climb it. He started when a horn blew, three times, somewhere to the north. He dismounted in front of what looked like a path toward the top and walked for some fifty paces. It was blocked by a fallen tree, which had died a few years ago.

"Nothing here," he said and mounted again. One of his men blew three times on a small horn, and Manuc's army moved into the valley. For the second time that day, the scouts went east along the ridge; they already had passed that way in the morning, but then they had ridden faster to check the end of the valley. This time, they moved just a little ahead of the army. The eastern end of the valley was almost identical to the western; it was as if nature wanted to create a pattern. The leader dismounted again and walked around the tower. This time, he found no path leading up. The tower was abrupt and tall, like a wall. He mounted and glanced back: led by Manuc, the vanguard was almost at the towers, ready to leave the valley.

From his position, Boldur observed the scouts at leisure. He could have killed them easily, but he did not reach for his bow, hanging on a stub of the old tree. *This is my easiest battle ever. The only thing I have to do is use my axe twice.* He poked his head out through the dense foliage, following the scouts riding away. *They will be dead soon.* He moved back and waited patiently. Five minutes later, a small white flag waved, in another tree across the valley. Few could see it. Standing on a thick branch, sixty feet above the ground, Boldur was one of them. He looked like a strange giant fruit of a dark green color. No one from the valley or from the ridges could see the flag. *Let's do it.* He cried three times like an owl, a signal he had learned from Vlad, and rubbed his palms together, before taking up the axe with one hand. He cut once at his feet, and a second time slightly above his head. Thump, thump, that was the only sound. The ropes reared like two swift snakes, with the sound of a giant popping cork. For a few moments, nothing happened. Then a crack followed, and another thump, thump, a hundred feet from him. *Now, I wait.* Boldur put down the axe away and took up his bow.

Cut most of the way through the day before, and kept in place by the ropes, the huge beech tree on Boldur's right inclined slightly, then more, until it fell on the next tree in line, then onto the ground, the sound of its fall thundering through the forest. Like in a giant domino, another massive tree fell with each thump; and another, and another. Down in the valley, the soldiers halted in confusion, and the horns sounded the alarm. Unsheathing their swords, shaking their spears, they looked around, their heads moving left and right, trying to spot the enemy. They saw only falling trees, everywhere around them. "Ghosts!" some of them cried. Feverishly, they touched their amulets and raised their left hands, fingers large spread, to attract one of Fate's many eyes. It makes sense to be in touch with her before the battle; when it ends, only the dead stir her attention. You won't want that. Soon, they realized that there was no immediate danger from the falling trees; they had been cut down only to block the route out of the valley for horses, in the places without a ridge. While Codrin was facing Manuc, the day before, another group of a hundred Mountes had arrived under the command of Boldur's cousin Dragos. With almost two hundred strong men under his command, Boldur had cut more trees than Codrin had requested. Hypnotized, the soldiers continued to watch, their heads turning to the next fallen tree. The last ones to fall blocked the extremities of the valley. Manuc found his army cut into three parts. He was already out of the valley with five hundred riders. The Litvonian infantry was caught in the valley with a thousand more riders. The rest of his army had not had time to enter the valley. The infantry began to force their way out of the trap, through the dense branches of the fallen trees. They were able, with a struggle, to take their halberds, but the long spears were left behind. The first volley of arrows came from the eastern towers when they were still climbing through the thick branches. After the second volley, they fell back into the valley, hiding behind the fallen trees. The third volley, coming from the towers and ridges, hit the riders, and they moved toward the center of the valley, giving up even the thought of trying to force an exit. They dismounted and placed the horses in front of them.

"Move away from the towers!" Manuc shouted, and pushed his horse to a trot, still looking back. "Faster."

"Sir," one of his Knights said, and Manuc turned only because of the fear in the man's voice.

"Prepare for battle!" Manuc cried and unsheathed his sword. From the forest in front, Codrin's riders had appeared. "Well," Manuc whispered to himself, "Peyris is as good a grave as any other. There is no shame dying in battle, but falling into this trap is not the proudest legacy."

The front ranks clashed, but to Manuc's surprise, the incoming riders did not press his men hard; they herded them into a tight group. Men still fell, here and there, and soon, his remaining riders were pressed as tightly together as the sand in an hourglass.

"Manuc, surrender!" Nicolas shouted, forty paces away from him.

I have never surrendered before. Well, there is a first time for everything. "Lower my banner," Manuc said to the soldier behind him. "I surrender!" he shouted. "Volker, sing that bloody song, they are still fighting in the valley; then go and tell everybody what has happened."

Shame in his eyes, the captain pressed the horn to his mouth. Three long notes filled the valley, then two short ones and another long one. Codrin's soldiers moved away, their ranks opening like two hard jaws, and the space between the army grew slowly. Nicolas and Manuc advanced and arrived face to face.

"You toothless toad," Manuc said. "Since when did you have the brains to lay such trap for me?"

"Since you had the brains to fall into it," Nicolas grinned, and they clasped hands.

"It's a pity. What is it like to kiss Albert's greasy hand? Such a strong Duke."

"I have no idea. I kiss a lady's hand, and the only pity is that I can't do it more often."

"Did he marry? Are you sure that she is a lady? A toad would be a better match for Albert. Don't ask me to kiss her hand too."

A scout approached Nicolas. "They are going after Clewin's men." He pointed toward a troop of six hundred riders, led by Codrin. "Our scouts found them riding north."

"Clewin is dead," Manuc said.

"I know. Let's talk." Nicolas took Manuc by the arm, and they walked away. "Cleyre is the new Duchess of Peyris."

"That little girl? She has more brains than all the surviving offspring of Stefan put together. I wish I had known. I came here after Albert. Well, I suppose I will meet her soon. How did she...?"

"She has good allies."

Manuc turned, checking the colors of the soldiers around him. "Dorna I recognize, even when they were supposed to join my army, but whose is that banner?" He pointed at a black raven on a pale-yellow background.

"You will meet him soon. He set the trap for you, not me. A tall man, dressed in black, wearing two swords," Nicolas said mysteriously.

"You always liked riddles. Is he the man I saw in our first battle? Well, almost a battle."

"Yes, that's him. And Lenard is dead."

"Then I can consider myself lucky. Did Clewin know about Cleyre?" Manuc looked at Nicolas, who nodded. "The bastard, he did not tell me."

"We send a delegation to inform you. They were killed on the road. Clewin," Nicolas spat. "Clewin's men killed Emich."

"We found a Fate's banner on the road and wondered who would do such a thing. Emich was a good Knight. I am sorry for your loss. Clewin worked for the Circle."

"I know."

"I suppose then, that I must pay homage to Cleyre. How many men do you want me to send home? There is no need for you to feed them all."

"Yes, you will. It's up to you if you want to kiss her hand or not."

"I would kiss more than her hand. What a pity that I am so old. She would have made a perfect Duchess of Loxburg."

"I am afraid that her hand is taken."

"Well, such ladies are quick to find a husband. They are in high demand." *That man with two swords must be the new Duke.* "So, how many soldiers?"

"We have some use for your cavalry. You can send home the infantry."

Clewin's deserters had the bad luck to use a road parallel to the valley and the trap. They met Codrin at a crossroads. The fight was short; they were disorganized and ran for their lives in all directions. That was their good luck, as Codrin could not surround them. He adapted quickly and pursued Clewin's deputy, disarming him in a one-to-one fight, and took ten more prisoners.

Codrin arrived in Peyris an hour after Nicolas and Manuc.

Chapter 21 – Codrin / Cleyre

"Cleyre, what a delight to see you again. You have grown into a beautiful woman. Last time I came in Peyris there was a little girl listening to stories on my knee. How old were you then? Thirteen? Who would have thought that little Cleyre would become the Duchess of Peyris?" Manuc asked. Some in the council chamber perceived subtle mockery in his words, reacted with brows arched over angry eyes, and even Nicolas considered intervening.

At sixty-five, Manuc was tall and muscular, and looked almost middle-aged, although his face, with its high, wrinkled forehead and wide-open eyes, betrayed his age. His hands were huge and calloused from the sword, and he was dressed in a dark green suit, accentuating his well-shaped body. Because of the unruly huge mustache and brows, there was something of the joker about him, but it was a foolish man who would laugh at him; his tall, straight body spoke of a hard center. As did his keen, metallic blue eyes.

Cleyre smiled and stood up, as he walked toward her. "You came to see that little girl again. How considerate of you. I hope to be a good host, and I still like to hear stories."

Manuc opened his arms, and to everybody's surprise, he embraced Cleyre, who reciprocated.

"I hope so too, niece, but it would be a lie to say that I came here to see you. I came to see that beacon of wisdom named

Albert," Manuc said, stirring laughter in the room. She was not his niece, but he used to call her that. He still liked to say it, and she liked it too. "Where is he? Hiding in the cellar? Preserved for posterity in jail? Tell me."

"Hiding in Amiuns."

"Not for long, I suppose. They have bad weather there, cold and rainy. I fear for his rheumatism. Where is Reymont?"

"In Amiuns, too. Story time now. What were you planning?"

"Whatever it was, it's not going to happen. Why stir up the past? Let's see what kind of future we can make now. I am, let's say, standing on the edge of unknown terrain."

"You know I like good stories, and even more so if they are true."

"Well, I came to find a wife for my son. He really needs a good woman; you know what I mean."

"Do you have someone in mind?" Cleyre asked. "Maybe I can help you." Her blue eyes glittered, her quick, intelligent face lit with amusement, and she sat again, nodding at him.

"I doubt that you will divorce just for my lovely son." Manuc shrugged, and his lips twitched in dry humor. Alof was his last son still living, the youngest one, and the one who had inherited few qualities from his father. *Both Stefan and I were cursed by Fate; our best sons died in battle, the worthless survived, but at least Alof is not as bad as Albert.* "It would have been a good political solution though," he sighed, and seated himself next to Cleyre.

"Did you agree this with Octavian?" Codrin spoke for the first time. He was standing in front of the window, leaning back on it.

"Ah, the lucky husband of our Duchess," Manuc said, and his eyes were amused, half-concealed by the mocking droop of his eyelids. "There was a plan. Two, in fact. Up to a point, my plans and the Circle's were similar. My plan was to unify the Duchies. Once Stefan died, I found myself thinking that Cleyre has enough intelligence for two people and two Duchies. They did not like that at first. They accepted it in the end. Or rather, Octavian's lips said the words, but they had something else in mind. Don't ask me what. I don't know. I played my game. I lost. What's your game, Duke of Peyris?"

"You are asking the wrong man."

Manuc blinked at him for a moment, then cocked his brows up, turning toward Cleyre. "My dear niece, indulge the curiosity of an old man. I thought this strange man, who sets many traps and speaks little, to be your husband and the Duke of Peyris. It seems that I am wrong."

"You are. My husband is not here, but he will arrive soon."

"If you found someone stronger than this fellow, I can't wait to meet him."

"There is no one stronger than Codrin, but Costa is both strong and kind."

"So, you are the young wolf of Poenari," Manuc said thoughtfully, looking at Codrin. "Strange, I have the impression that we have met before. I am not so old I should forget such a thing, yet I don't remember."

"Yes, we have met, but I was traveling as the Wraith of Tolosa at that time."

"Ah, then my brain is not so rotten. The Wraith was a strong man by himself. It would be interesting to learn how you could squeeze two strong men into that skull of yours, it doesn't look any larger than mine, but you don't seem to like talking. So, niece, what plans have you for me?" He turned toward Cleyre, his mouth curled up in a witty smile.

"Jail for the rest of your life, and three stories every day for me."

"Seeing you every day, it doesn't sound that bad. I hope that your husband will agree, but what a pity that I am not younger."

"We will meet again at dinner," Cleyre said, and people stated to leave the room. She glanced at Codrin, who nodded. "Uncle, please stay."

"So, you have some use for me after all," Manuc said, when they were alone with Codrin.

"For you? No." She shrugged with studied indifference, and her eyes glimmered. "But we need your soldiers."

"I don't know why you need more soldiers to take on that toad named Albert, but let it be. I expect to receive better meals in jail, for my cooperation."

"I don't need them for Albert, I need them for Orban," Codrin said.

"Ah," Manuc said, rubbing his chin. "Orban is a sharp one, something between steel and poison, but I still don't understand why you need so many men. After that melee in Poenari, he was left with less than a thousand soldiers. I don't see him winning a battle against you."

"I don't want to win a battle. I need to take Arad," Codrin said.

"That's a different kind of animal. A siege." He looked at Codrin and pointed at the window behind him – it was raining.

"There will be no siege; we will just pretend to lay one."

"Do you think that Orban will be scared? Perhaps enraged, but scared?" Manuc almost grinned, then stopped himself.

"He will not be scared, but many in Arad will be. I am counting on them."

"That could work." Manuc rubbed his chin again, calculating his options. "But niece, you must take my old bones out of jail and let me join the young wolf. I would like to see Orban's face after he loses Arad. You know how much I like him. As much as I like poison. I promise you a good story when I return."

"Agreed," Cleyre said, smiling, and placed her hand over his. "I think that you deserve to eat now."

Dinner was over, and on the tables remained only cakes and wine. There were more people than at the last dinner organized by Cleyre, and they were still talking in small groups scattered here and there, when she stood up and walked to the middle of the room.

"I have an announcement to make." Cleyre's voice was even and precise, carrying the tones of a commander on a battlefield, and she looked solemnly around the room. Everybody became silent as she walked toward Codrin, who was leaning against the window. "I Cleyre, Duchess of Peyris, pay allegiance to Codrin and recognize him as the King of Frankis. Your majesty," she said and made a deep curtsy.

Most people in the room were surprised, though they had expected her to pay allegiance to Codrin; they were surprised by her recognition of him as the king.

Codrin was surprised too. *She must have had a Vision*, he thought, understanding that there was now only one way open for him. He could not embarrass her and, by refusing this chance, he would block his own path. Such opportunities rarely come twice. *So be it.* "Duchess," he bowed slightly, then placed his right hand on her shoulder, "I accept your allegiance. Rise now." Codrin extended his arm, clasped her hand and pulled her up. They walked together, and he seated her, after kissing her hand.

Walking back, Cleyre looked at Phillip. She had spoken to no one about this, so he looked both surprised and undecided, but under her intense stare, he nodded briefly. She had inherited Stefan's trait of bending people to her will, just by looking at them with her expressive, deep blue eyes. Once Cleyre was seated, he went to Codrin.

"I, Phillip, the heir of Deva, speak in the name of my father, the Grand Seigneur of Deva. I accept to pay allegiance to Codrin, the King of Frankis. Your majesty," he said and knelt in one knee.

"I accept the allegiance of the Grand Seigneur of Deva," Codrin said, and repeated his previous gesture of acceptance, raising him up.

Manuc found Cleyre's eyes fixing him intently, and he frowned. Then he smiled. *This is my chance to be a player in the new Frankis. And my chance to lose if the Circle wins.* "The road to the kingdom is not easy, and the Circle is a strong enemy. They have another king in mind. Fate take the Circle, maybe you were born to break the curse of Frankis." Manuc stood up, went to Codrin, and proudly paid his allegiance.

The next morning, they interrogated Clewin's deputy, but he did not know much about the Circle's plans. One of his men knew Nicolas and told him that it was the deputy who had killed Emich.

"You killed a delegation under Fate's banner," Codrin said sternly. "Even the rope is too lenient, but luckily for you, I don't like torture."

The man was hanged in the main plaza and, in what had become his mark, Codrin placed a placard with *Traitor* and *The Circle's tool* on his chest.

There was a last meeting in the Council room, and Cleyre, Codrin and Costa met before it.

"Costa has a question about that night when you took the West Gate." Her face bore a pleasant smile that masked her thoughts, which Codrin took as a sign that she knew what had happened.

"It must be related to some arrows flying over the wall," Codrin smiled back. "Well, I think that it's about time to form the Council of the Realm." The idea had come to him the day before, and several times he had pushed it to the back of his mind. No one had told him, not even the Empress, but when there was a Seer of the Realm, there was a Council of the Realm too. He was evolving slowly. "A new Fracture is coming; the Lights of the Wanderers foresaw it in their Visions, and I will let Cleyre explain that to you. When there is a Fracture, there is also a Seer, and I was chosen by Fate to be the Seer of the Realm. I need your help to unify Frankis as fast as I can and gather the other kingdoms under my military command for the next nomad invasion. Together with Vlad, you will be the first members of my Council of the Realm. If any of you wants to stay out of this, speak now." He looked at them, and one by one, they nodded their agreement. "Before I leave, you will take the oath for your new position. Now let the others in."

It was a brief meeting; most things were already arranged, like Manuc joining Codrin with three thousand soldiers. Nicolas would stay in Peyris with Cleyre's army. Vlad would leave as soon as the meeting ended, going toward Arad with fifty scouts, the army following them at a slower pace.

"Codrin, be careful," Cleyre said and embraced him in front of the captains and Knights gathered in the Council Room.

"Who knows when we will see each other again?" Codrin said and kissed her hand. "But this time, I leave you in good hands." He looked at Costa.

In the afternoon, after they took their oaths for the Council of the Realm, Codrin left Peyris with four thousand soldiers; the largest army he had ever led.

Chapter 22 – Vlad / Codrin

It was almost dark when Vlad and his two men entered Arad. Ten more stayed at an inn just a mile away from the city, the rest spread in the forests around, watching the roads. It was dark, when he reached Panait's house, and a few moments later, he was at the table, eating with them.

"Codrin will be here soon," he said after the pleasantries were finished.

"That's dangerous." Panait's left eyelid was twitching, and he rubbed at it gently. Patterns of light flowed across his face from the candles. Playful, they made him look less worried than he was. "There are soldiers from Arad who saw him in Poenari. They even gave a description of him to Orban. Until two months ago, no one here knew what he looked like. For the moment, they have not made the link with Tudor, but soon they will. That's the worst moment." He gave a long sigh and rubbed at the bridge of his nose.

"Does he want to free Vio?" Delia asked, her voice less tense than Panait's.

"In a way." Vlad smiled, and his hazel eyes glittered. "He is coming to take Arad."

Panait swallowed, and with an effort he asked, "But does he have enough soldiers?" The vertical lines between his thick eyebrows deepened, and his left hand gripped the edge of the table. "Orban took some losses in Poenari, but he is still able to gather almost a thousand soldiers. And he kept most of his guard here, less than half of it fought against Codrin. His best soldiers are here, four hundred of them. And Orban is not without allies; even the Circle will try to help him, though I may be able to delay that. But not for long."

"Codrin has four thousand soldiers."

"What?" Panait was stunned, and his wide eyes settled on Vlad as if he was a kind of ghost.

"The Duchess of Peyris and the Duke of Loxburg have paid allegiance to him. The Grand Seigneur of Deva too. Lenard of Dorna is dead, and his city belongs to Codrin now."

"That's a hard blow to Orban. The Seigneur of Dorna cared about his granddaughter, Lanya, and was a strong ally."

"Things have changed, all the north is with Codrin. They have recognized him as the King of Frankis."

"What?" Panait let his knife fell on the table, and he stood up abruptly. "This is the strangest news I have heard in all my life. And the best since the day, a long time ago, when Delia agreed to be my wife. He walked quickly around the table and shook Vlad's shoulder. "Then we have a King. Bucur was demoted by the Circle, so there is nothing in Codrin's way. He will marry the little Duchess of Tolosa and all Frankis is his."

"Codrin is not too fond of the Circle's plans regarding Tolosa."

"The Circle doesn't mean only Maud and Octavian. I am the First Mester of Arad and part of the Circle too, Vlad. Cantemir is the Secretary of Arad and part of the Circle too." Panait shook his head, his mouth set in a tight line.

"There are few people Codrin trusts more than you two."

"What are you planning?" Panait went back to his place, and Delia placed a hand over his, gripping it gently.

"We don't want a siege. Too many people would die, and the city will suffer. The first hours after a city is taken are always lawless; you know that. With your help," Vlad glanced at them with a hopeful look, "and Cantemir's, we may be able to convince Orban to surrender. Codrin will leave him alive and in a good position."

"Orban is unpredictable," Panait said warily, and rubbed the tip of his nose while his brows knit tightly.

"Unpredictable but intelligent. He has only four hundred men in Arad. The other six hundred are with their Knights, scattered across the Seigneury. They can't come to Arad's rescue; we have blocked two third of the ways in. Or out. And most of them will not even try. Tomorrow, all the roads will be blocked, and the trap will close."

"It may work," Delia said.

Not yet fully convinced, Panait forced himself to be silent. To breathe long and slow. To hope. "I will talk with Cantemir tomorrow."

"So, you mean to say..." An accomplished speaker, Cantemir found himself at a loss for words. He had accepted Panait's invitation and now found himself in the First Mester's house meeting Vlad again after a year. "You mean to say..." he pointed abruptly at Vlad, "that Tudor is Codrin. And you mean to say that I was a fool all these years." He closed his eyes, tipped his face back, and he felt the warm sun through the window. It did not calm him.

"There was a certain necessity to his split identity, and very few people knew of this. That doesn't mean that the others were ... fools." Vlad set his glass down carefully, then looked up at him, eyebrows raised.

"I don't need your opinion on whether I was a fool. How many is a few?" Cantemir tilted back his head to catch the last trickle of wine and set the empty glass on the table.

"Three years ago, Dochia was the first to realize it. There is no need to explain how," Vlad chided softly. "A year later, my brother Pintea and I arrived here, and we lodged in his house in Severin. We fought for both Codrin and Tudor when the need arrived. Everything stayed within this little circle for a while. Jara and Cernat didn't know until we came here to free Vio."

Cantemir accepted the facts with a catlike blink of his eyes. "There were more fools than I thought," he mused and tried to smile, but it didn't come out naturally. "And you?" He glanced at Delia and Panait.

"Fools too," Panait laughed, "even when he stayed in our house. Delia figured it out when Codrin tried to take Vio away. He was badly hurt and hid here for almost three weeks. You know that. But it was not the wound which revealed his identity. It was Vio. She jumped into his arms when they met. Of course, she called him Tudor, so Delia worked it out only later."

"I feel better. A little better. And anyway, Codrin saved my life twice. He can fool me as much as he likes. So," he looked at Vlad, frowning in thought, "Codrin wants Arad, and you think you have enough soldiers to take it before winter. Four thousand soldiers, you said."

"We would prefer a peaceful solution. Sieges are bloody things, and conquering cities usually turns ugly, even with the most disciplined armies." Vlad turned his palms out, looking at Cantemir.

"You have a lot of experience."

"One siege in Poenari. Bloody. Perhaps fifteen hundred dead. Two years ago, Codrin took Mehadia. He negotiated, and no one was harmed. A month ago, we took Peyris. Half fight, half surrender. Less than a hundred dead, but dead, nevertheless. Arad is not Mehadia, and Orban is still alive, but that would be a good example to follow."

"Orban is indeed alive. That makes quite a difference, in fact."

"I am ready to negotiate with him."

"If things turn bad, you will end in a pyre, Vlad. Let me think of something. I need to talk with Jara too; she has a good influence on Orban. When will Codrin arrive?"

"In two days. The north of Arad should have been taken by now. I am thinking couriers will arrive today to bring the news to Orban – we will let them pass – and there will not be enough time for him to gather his army. He has only four hundred soldiers in Arad, if he chose to fight, and most of them will not be happy to fight against Codrin again. People in Arad will not be happy either."

Motionless, Orban listened in silence everything that Codrin, Cantemir and Panait had to say, his only visible reaction a slight arching of his left eyebrow. In his hand was a letter from Cleyre, the new Duchess of Peyris. *Are they betraying or saving me?* He glanced at his Secretary and First Mester. *Both, maybe? Manuc is silent, and usually he likes to talk. Phillip is silent too. And that young man, Vlad; I had him in my hands, but how could I know that Codrin and the Wraith of Tolosa were the same man?* When all was said, he closed his eyes and made his decision immediately, but chose to stay silent for a while. The old fox knew how the wind blew; it was not from his bellows, and there was no good spitting into it. All eyes in the Council Room were on him, and Orban knew it, though he could not see them. *How did Codrin convince Manuc? That man is more stubborn than a mule, and his pride reaches the Moon. And King of Frankis? Maud will swallow her tongue and praise him. That is something I would like to see. Some say that her tongue is bifurcated.* He forced himself to stifle a smile. "That sounds acceptable. I will give up Arad and hand all my Knights over to you. These are my conditions: I stay here, in the old wing of the palace. It's separate, and there is no need for us to see each other." A list of servants, guards, rights, even access to library, garden, stable and wine cellar followed. Orban's memory was as prodigious as his intelligence, and he filled almost three pages with his orderly writing. "I will keep the following lands and castles." He took another sheet and wrote five names on it. "That's enough to keep me a strong Knight, but you will grant me the title of Seigneur. My son will inherit everything, except my title. My daughter, Lanya, will be raised as a Signora, and she will receive a dowry from you, suited to her position. I am sure you will find her a better husband than I can. Cantemir will help you; he has a soft spot for Lanya. My Knights keep all their possessions. The Chief of the Guard, the Spatar and the Secretary of Arad keep their positions. The same for their men. There will be no siege, no battles and you get all my soldiers, losing none of yours. Or theirs," he added after a moment of thought, pointing at Manuc and Phillip. "With Arad, Dorna and Severin, you have a good grip on central Frankis. The north seems to be your ally. Take the south, and you will finally become the King of Frankis. My conditions are not negotiable." He frowned for a few moments. "Regarding my marriage with Jara; it's up to her to decide what's next." *My position is weak; I am like a dangerous beast that is not quite dead yet. The vultures that did not dare attack when I was strong, are circling over me now. Under the shadow of Codrin, Arad may be my sanctuary. The vultures will not come here; he is the strongest predator now.*

"That's quite a long list," Manuc said, to give Codrin more time.

To their surprise, Codrin reacted as fast as Orban and accepted everything. Almost. "But," he said after giving his agreement, raising his forefinger, "I will appoint a new Chief of the Guard and Spatar. Your men will become the second-in-command. They will be on probation for two years."

Orban frowned, and then he smiled. "It seems that we found common ground."

Codrin glanced at Jara, and it took her almost a minute to speak. "I haven't decided yet." *It was not as bad as I initially thought, but I can end the marriage after Codrin takes Arad. Should I?*

Everybody was expecting a few days of hard negotiations, but Orban was intelligent enough to understand that he would lose Arad one way or another; everything took less than two hours. The news spread fast in the city, calming the gnawing fear brought by the four thousand soldiers at the gate.

৵৹

"Lady Lanya," the servant, an old man, said, bowing slightly, "your presence is requested. Please follow me."

"Who has requested it?"

"I was not told, my lady. Perhaps your father."

Lanya flinched, as she was afraid of Orban, but she stood up and followed the servant. "I will return soon," she told Vio. As it became a habit, they were reading together in the library.

"I will finish the book before you." Vio grinned, raising her head, and returned to her reading. A few minutes later, she heard footsteps coming toward her, and she thought it was Lanya. From the corner of her eye, she saw men entering the room. She adjusted her position on the sofa and pretended not to see them.

"Grab her," Orban's son ordered when they surrounded Vio. This time, he had brought three strong soldiers with him. They had been paid in advance, one year of their pay, and they were to leave Arad, after Vio had been raped.

Two of them were already behind Vio, bending to catch her arms and immobilize her. She turned and slashed her small knife across the face on the man on her right. The tip of the knife cut through the man's left eye, and he howled in pain. It was the same type of Assassin knife Codrin had given to Saliné, and worked so well on Bucur. In his hasty retreat, the wounded one bumped into the second man behind Vio, and both fell behind the sofa. She rolled to the floor and passed behind the man in front of her, who tried in vain to stop her; Vio was too quick. Behind him, she slashed his thigh, and that stopped him running after her. She could not avoid the staff Orban's son hit her with.

"I've got you, bitch," he growled. "You will not escape this time. I will have you here."

Bent in pain, she rolled further, evading a second blow. The third one caught her arm, and the knife dropped from her hand. On her bottom, she retreated fast toward the fireplace, her eyes on him. Panicked for the first time, Vio stumbled as she attempted to stand, ending up on her behind again as he rushed toward her. Her hand chanced upon the poker lying beside the fireplace just as he descended on her like an animal. The combination of their rapid movements drove the head of the poker right through his chest, piercing his heart. Orban's son was dead before he hit the ground. Vio sat on the floor, gasping with shock and terror, while the three men tried to leave the room as fast as they could, painting the floor with small red spots. She closed her eyes and retreated inside.

It took Vio several long moments to realize that the man at her feet was no longer a threat, and she half calmed until realization came to her: she had killed Orban's son.

Trying to leave, the three surviving assailants bumped into Orban, entering the library.

"What happened?" Orban asked, and then he saw his son lying in a pool of blood on the floor. "Arrest these men," he ordered the guards behind him.

"I told you that Vio would kill him," Sybille, the Third Light of the Wanderers said, when they came to the other end of the room she had seen in her Vision.

"Yes, yes, you told me, but why should I have believed you? Last time she came here, Drusila told me only stupid things. Her Vision was totally false. Perhaps she tried to cheat on me." Walking slowly, he stopped when his foot almost touched his son. "You lived like an idiot. You died like an idiot. Take him," Orban ordered to the guards. He looked at Vio, and their eyes crossed. "So, in the end you did it."

"A servant came to take Lanya away, and then they tried to rape me."

"I didn't think they had come to read you a book, even though this is one of the finest libraries in Frankis. You killed a man. Well, I can't really say that he was a man. I can accept evil, but I can't accept stupidity. Even so, he was my son. You killed my son."

"He tried to rape me," Vio repeated, and moved half a step back.

"I would have done the same in your place, but I am the Grand Seigneur of Arad, and I must do my duty." He looked around and found a poker, lying alongside the body of his son. "You did not even use a weapon to kill him. I don't resent that; a sword would have been too noble a thing for this halfwit."

"I demand a council to judge me."

"That will take too long, and we are in a difficult situation. Arad will have new masters tomorrow. I've already passed judgment, and you will be punished now. Sybille, take her, and do what we've already agreed."

Vio stepped back until she felt two hands grabbing her shoulders. She wriggled, trying to escape, but the hands were too strong, and another grabbed her by the arm. Escorted by the two Wanderer guards, she was taken out of the room.

"Prepare the pyre for my son," Orban ordered his men. "Hang those three men you found here. Find the servant who made Lanya leave the library. Hang him too."

Silent, Orban stood in front of the pyres. They were almost consumed, no more flames, just thin stripes of smoke rising quietly toward the sky. The sun was close to its zenith, a huge red sphere. "Let them come," he said without turning.

The guards parted and allowed Jara, Cernat and Cantemir to come to the pyres too. Codrin was not yet in Arad.

"The one on the left is for my son; the other one is for Vio."

Jara already knew that Vio was dead, but the shock left her breathless. "Monster," she finally said, her voice cracked and loud. She tensed and stepped forward, ready to strangle Orban, who had his back to them. Cernat stopped her, seeing the guards prepared to intervene, weapons ready. At Orban's signal, the guards moved away, leaving only the three in front of the pyres.

Without turning, he spoke again. "I will tell you a story, Jara. I am sure you will find it interesting. I was still a boy when my mother was poisoned. My father was assassinated when I was sixteen. An arrow during a hunt. My first wife was poisoned too, only a few months after my first son was born. It was bad luck; she took my plate by mistake. I made a decision then, that I no longer wanted to suffer, that it was better for others to suffer in my place. A long time ago, a philosopher – I forgot his name – said that he had decided to be happy because it was good for his health. I decided to be evil because it was good for my health. With the next assassination attempt I was lucky. I captured the man myself, a well-trained mercenary. I was only twenty years old but good with a dagger. He had miscalculated. Then I captured his family and killed them all in front of him, children, wife, siblings, parents. All of them. He is still alive in my jail. An old man now, but I took good care of him. I did the same for the next one who tried to assassinate me. They share the same cell in my jail, so they can talk about the good old times. Guess what? Nobody tried to kill me again. So, you see? It served me well to be a monster. There was only one glitch, when my first born, Bernd, vanished without trace. Mischance, I suppose," Orban shrugged. "My second son was a failure, and he deserved his death. I even feel relieved that I will not see him again. He was my biggest failure, and it was hard to see that each day. My daughter is an intelligent girl who I love. She doesn't know that. Nobody knows that. It was my way of protecting her, keeping her safe from assassination, yet she hates me. I don't blame her. In all this world, you and Cernat are the only ones who know of my love for her, and that she is my only weakness. This is the gift I leave in your hands, Jara: my daughter. Tomorrow, I will lose my power. Your will rise, and my daughter will be in your hands. You will have the power to avenge Vio. It's a poisoned gift, isn't it? If I am still alive, in three years, I will tell you another story. You will find it even more interesting. You should not worry if I die; I have taken measures to ensure you will still hear it. My mourning has ended. If it helps you, it was not my son that I mourned. I will leave you alone, now."

"Did your decision, to live like that, made you happy, Orban?" Cernat asked.

"I can't say that. I can't say that at all, but you can't have everything you want in life. You know that well, Cernat. We are so much alike in our old sorrows."

Chapter 23 – Codrin

"I was within my rights as Grand Seigneur of Arad. Vio killed my son, and the punishment was appropriate." They were gathered in Orban's office on the day Orban was to hand Arad over to Codrin.

"You executed the victim," Codrin said. "Your son tried to rape her."

"I won't deny that, but it changes nothing. If she had not killed him, I would have taken the appropriate measures. We signed a treaty. Both sides suffered a similar loss. Almost similar, as I lost a son, while the new Duke of Arad lost only a family friend. Despite this, I will still recognize my signature on the treaty."

Codrin was caught on the wrong foot. Legally, Orban was right, even Codrin's allies were of the same opinion. Everybody knew that the treaty would avoid a siege, and everybody wanted to stay alive and go home. And as the newly proclaimed King of Frankis, breaking his first signed treaty would only weaken him.

"I need some more time for consultation," Codrin said. "Jara, Cernat, Manuc, Cantemir, Panait and Vlad will stay."

"Do you need any help?" Orban asked, dismissively.

"Don't push your luck, Orban." Codrin's voice was flat and menacing.

Vlad went out with Orban and returned with a man whose face was hidden. The man bowed before revealing his face. There was a stunned silence in the room, and the man flashed a large smile before saying, "A lot of familiar people, I see."

"Verenius," Manuc said, "I would really like to know how you escaped from that noose around your neck. It would be a useful trick in such an unstable world." *So, this is how Codrin has manipulated the Circle. He is quite sophisticated for his age.*

"I cut it with my teeth." Walking toward the place Codrin had pointed to, he flashed his smile again — Verenius had strong, large teeth.

"We are complete now. Almost. Cleyre and Costa are missing. We need to find a solution." He stopped, unable to find words good enough to soothe Jara.

In the end, Cernat was the first to speak. "My family has suffered a great loss but, legally, Orban is right. The treaty stands. Breaking it will not bring Vio back to us. It will bring nothing good. Only more death." He glanced at Jara, who nodded sullenly. "We agree to end this and move on."

Her eyes blurred, Jara thought back, filled with bitterness. *That night, Drusila promised me she would save Vio from Orban. I even allowed her to make to Vio a Wanderer. What went wrong? Did she let me down on purpose? Are the Wanderers so treacherous these days? Even if they are, that doesn't absolve me. Vio counted on me and I failed her. I failed Saliné too. I have failed everybody. I am a failure.* Unable to think straight, she stood up and went to the window, followed by all the eyes in the room. She met Codrin's stare and nodded at him.

"There is more," Codrin said, feeling Jara's pain, which mirrored his own, but he needed to continue. "Some of you already know that a Fracture is coming; the Lights of the Wanderers foresaw it in their Visions. I think all of you know what that means, and what we say now, stays between us. Only Cleyre, Costa and Vlad are aware of what will follow." He looked around until all of them nodded. "When there is a Fracture, there is also a Seer. This time, I am the Seer of the Realm. We must unify Frankis and gather the other kingdoms under my command for the next nomad invasion. No one knows, yet, when they will invade us."

"From what I know, that's more a burden than a favor. Since when are you...?" Manuc asked, rotating his forefinger a few times.

"Yes, it's a burden. It happened less than two months ago, the day after I took Severin. I suppose you want to know if my victories happened only because I am Seer. My power is limited. No, not my power, but the knowledge of how to use it. I am Seer only because I have the potential. It takes a few years to develop. You are the first ones to know, and the first to share my burden. As both your King and Seer, I am expecting you to act accordingly. Jara, Cernat, thank you for your understanding. Vio was dear to me too. Together with Cleyre and Costa, you will be my Council of the Realm. If any of you wants to leave, speak now." He looked at them, and one by one, they nodded their agreement. "Tomorrow, you will take oath. You will also keep secret the fact that Verenius is alive. Vlad, bring Orban here."

Verenius covered his face again, and when the door opened, Codrin said to Orban, while he was still in the doorway, "The treaty stands. You have two days to move to the old palace. You may leave now." He gestured at the guards visible through the open door.

"I know the way," Orban said and left the room for the second time.

❧

Walking absently through the palace, Codrin found the library. Still grieving for Vio, he was too troubled to read, and entered without realizing it, the result of a wandering mind and old habit. After a while, he heard a faint noise coming from a distant corner. Nothing dangerous; it resembled a muffled cry. In the farthest corner from the main door, he found a girl, sitting with her back against the wall, knees to her chest, clasped very tightly with her arms, her head leaning on them. She was sobbing.

"What happened?" Codrin asked gently.

The girl tried to answer, but her words were drowned in tears. He pulled the girl up and took her in his arms. Unconsciously, she placed her arms around his neck and embraced him tightly.

"What happened?" he repeated.

"Vio," the girl cried. "I lost my Vio."

Codrin bit his lip, pain returning to him. "I lost her too, and she was my friend. Was she your friend too?"

"Yes, she was my only friend."

"Would you tell me your name?"

"I am Lanya."

"Ah," Codrin said. "Would you walk with me?"

"Yes." But she only tightened her arms around his neck, and he walked away, carrying her in his arms.

In the corridor, people moved aside, making space for them to pass. Behind them, they looked both surprised and pleased. They liked the shy and furtive Lanya, though they tried to hide it when Orban still ruled Arad, afraid of him. Codrin gestured toward a woman he had spoken with before, asking her mutely how to find Lanya's room. He pressed a finger to his lips. Silent, the woman curtsied and gestured to follow her. Just when he was about to enter, another woman came out of Lanya's room.

"Your majesty," she whispered, "I was looking for Lanya. We lost... We haven't seen her since yesterday." Codrin did not like to be called majesty, but Cantemir had a different opinion. He had instructed all the servants to act that way, and they all were accustomed to obeying the Secretary, who was now the Chancellor of Frankis.

"You didn't search too hard," Codrin said coldly. "Lanya, I think that we should go and eat something."

"Yes," the girl said, and Codrin carried her into the kitchen, where she ate for almost half an hour, everything the Chef put on her plate.

In the evening, upset about her behavior, Codrin asked Cantemir to replace the woman who took care of Lanya.

"She cares about Lanya. I understand that you are upset, but her father died two days ago. The funerals were this morning. Give her another chance."

"I did not know that, and you know her better. From now on, Lanya will move to the S'Arad suite and will eat with us."

Jara and Cernat were the closest people to Codrin and, in the new arrangement, Jara and her toddler son, Mark, kept the suite of the Signora while Cernat took the one which had belonged to Bernd, Orban's son, a long time ago. They ate together, each trying to reenact their past in the hunting house at Severin but, without Vio and Saliné, it was just a pale imitation. To their surprise, Lanya recovered well, and soon, a strange thing happened, as both Jara and Codrin started to act as if they had adopted Orban's daughter. She became a kind of replacement for Vio. Even though Lanya was a year older, she was smaller than Vio, and there was not much physical resemblance between them, apart from their large blue eyes. The year the girls had spent together in a palace where both felt unwelcome, and Vio was a prisoner, pushed them together, and each learned from the other. Unconsciously, both Jara and Codrin found those similarities, and their longing fed on them.

It took Codrin two weeks to decide that Jara was ready to hear the news about Veres.

"He did that to Cleyre?" she asked, incredulous. "I can't believe it. Well, yes, I can believe it, yet I can't believe it. Codrin," she said, taking his arm, her voice pleading. "What do you want to do? Please don't execute him. Veres has a simple mind, and most of his sins are only because Aron perverted him. And he may be the only child I still have from Malin. Give him... No, give me a chance..."

"A chance for what?"

"For a grandson. Keep him in jail while I try to find him a wife. She will know everything about him, and she will lead the house until their eventual son will be old enough to take over. Malin was too good a man to lose his line. Tudor's line has also vanished, and they don't have other siblings alive."

"We can try," Codrin said, not really convinced, but he did not want to upset Jara even more.

The caravan from Poenari entered Arad a month after the city fell to Codrin. People moved both ways, in and out of the city. This reorganization kept Codrin occupied and his bad memories in the back of his mind. Sava came to take over the Guard of Arad; Boldur returned to Poenari – his clan was now settled in the mountains around the fortress, and he was both Chief of his clan and of the Chief Guard of Poenari. Varia was named governor of Poenari, and she kept Livia with her. Valer left to take over his fiefdom, Cleuny, and the governorate of southern Mehadia. Vlaicu returned as governor of Severin and remained the Spatar of the kingdom. Damian went to Dorna as the Spatar of the province.

Mara, her children and her father came too.

"You have grown," Codrin laughed, and raised his son up in his arms. He was greeted with a loud cry that made him frown.

"Radu is just hungry." Mara laughed at the helpless look Codrin threw at her and took the child in her arms. "But is also afraid of this big stranger." She sat in a chair and put the child to her breast. That gave her some respite, as she did not know how to handle Codrin. On the road, she had learned about Vio's death, and she knew how much Codrin was attached to the little girl. *She was no longer a little girl*, she thought, *but for him she still was, and that will hit him even harder. It's all about perspective.* And she had her own worries, about her relationship with him. *He is vulnerable now. Saliné seems to be lost, and if I get too close to him, he may become too attached to me. He may even propose marriage again. This must be avoided.* Little Radu finished his meal and fell asleep, a moment later. She placed him in his bed and spent much more time than was needed to arrange his small body. Codrin watched them from close proximity, a smile on his lips – the first one in more than a month. When she could no longer pretend, Mara turned to face Codrin. She embraced him, hiding her face in his shoulder, so he could not kiss her. He embraced her too.

"I am glad that you are here."

"Yes," she laughed nervously, "You need your Secretary."

"I need you more than the Secretary."

"Well, I am here." She gently pulled from his embrace and went to check Radu in his bed. "Have you any news about Saliné?"

"No." *I am cursed to lose most people I love.* He shook his head, his eyes straying away, around the room.

"You will have. I suppose your men are combing Frankis for her."

"I have sent scouts everywhere, but..." He shrugged and coughed to mask the weakness in his voice.

A month later, after midnight, Radu woke Mara, and she fed him. After making him sleep again, hungry herself, she left her suite and entered the saloon. Head in hands, Codrin was sitting at the table. There was a bottle of wine in front of him and a glass. The glass was full, and it seemed that he had not touched it yet. Her first thought was to leave him alone. Undecided, she hovered in the doorway. At the table, he was as still as her. Breathing deeply, she walked toward him, and laced her arms around his neck. Without speaking, he pulled her slowly into his lap.

"I failed her," he rasped. "Vio. I failed Vio. I failed Saliné too. It's like Fate is laughing at me. I am cursed. I lost my family and now this. Why, Mara? Why?"

"We have had bad moments in life. We have had good ones too."

"Of everything, you are the only happy thing that has happened in my new life."

"You are..."

"Do you think that winning battles and being almost a King can compensate for my losses? I would have preferred to be just the Wraith of Tolosa and have Vio still alive."

"I know, but you have to move past it." Before he could answer, she kissed him, and that moved them back to a time when the world around them was simpler and less demanding.

❧

The excitement of taking over Arad faded, and the Winter Solstice was coming. Codrin cancelled the festival, but the people both nobles and servants understood his decision. After most of the important things were settled, Codrin found more free time than he needed, memories he wanted to keep away burdening him. Reading only recalled his time with Vio and Saliné, but it was not possible to avoid the library completely, as he promised Lanya he would read with her from time to time.

On one of those evenings, she was reading to him, in her pleasant voice. After a while, Codrin's mind wandered, and Vio's face came to him.

"What do you see?" Lanya asked, sensing that he was no longer with her.

"Vio."

"You see Vio in me. You want Vio, not me," Lanya said, fighting hard not to cry.

"Vio? No, I will never see Vio in you."

"You don't want to see me," she cried, feeling betrayed, just when she had started to be happy, and ran away.

Startled, Codrin reacted slower than normal, but he still caught her in the doorway of the library.

"Let me go," she cried, trying in vain to free herself from his arms.

"Lanya, listen to me," he said gently. "I will never see Vio in you. I will always see Lanya in you. Understand? You are an intelligent and kind girl named Lanya. You don't need to be anyone else. You need to be you."

She was still sobbing, but no longer tried to escape his arms. Codrin lifted her thin body, and walked with her, through the large library, until she stopped crying. *You will always have a place here, Lanya, and when the time comes, I will find a good husband for you and make you a Signora. Not because I signed that bloody treat with Orban, but because you deserve it.*

She put her arms around his neck and leaned her head on his shoulder. "I want you to see me," she whispered.

Chapter 24 – Dochia

"Someone just entered the Sanctuary in Hispeyne," Ai said, a slight tone of worry in her voice. "No one has been in there for more than eight hundred years; the place is well hidden. It's not possible to find it without an ancient Talant map or a copy."

"Hispeyne... That's so far from here. How do you know that?" Dochia asked more eager than she had intended, unable to feel the irritation in Ai's voice. She jumped to her feet, and moved around the room, hands clasped at her back.

"The Sanctuaries are linked together."

"Like the Map is linked to the world?" *This kind of magic I enjoy, but like the Maletera it can be used both ways, good and bad.* Dochia had started to reevaluate the Sanctuary and everything she had found between its walls. She would have enjoyed talking at a distance with her sisters in the Hive, or with Codrin and Jara. News was scarce, even from Arenia, and nothing came to her from Frankis. She was completely cutoff from her home, and she would stay at least a few years more in Nerval. "Did they reactivate the Sanctuary?"

"No. They could only open one small gate. You don't need much blood to open it."

Ada was right, Codrin has the blood. "Can we see them?"

"Why do I get the impression that you were expecting this?"

"Because I was expecting it." Dochia smiled coyly, wondering how powerful Ai's magic could be. "Can we see them?" she repeated with the eagerness of an exuberant girl.

Saying nothing, Ai projected an image in Dochia's mind, and two people appeared in a hall that looked vaguely familiar. Across the large room, two sets of footprints were visible in the deep dust. "My feeling is that you expected somebody else, not those two."

"One of them is unexpected indeed." *What is Aron's son doing there with Siena?*

"Does this mean bad things will happen?"

"It may do." *What happened to Codrin? I was expecting him to discover the Sanctuary. Is he still alive? He is the Seer of Fate.* She had had a Vision about this just a few weeks earlier. *He must be alive.* "Can you hear them too?"

"That's a bit more tricky, but I will try."

"What I see there seems similar to the halls of the main gates here."

"In each Sanctuary, there are several main entry points, a round hall. There are three Sanctuaries on the continent, and all of them were built by people having similar skills." Even before she could end her phrase, Ai sent some new images to Dochia, and this time, there were voices too.

"See, Nard? What did I tell you? This is magic." Siena waved her hand, and a door opened, the one linking the first hall to the second, larger one. They walked inside, and the door closed behind them. Startled, they turned as one, and tried to open the door with their hands. They couldn't.

"We are trapped here," Nard whispered.

Siena frowned, and waved her hand again. Nothing happened. Beads of perspiration ran down her face, and she closed her eyes, hoping for some trace of Light to help her. Instead fear came, and she stepped back instinctively and waved again. The door opened.

"Uh," she said and wiped perspiration from her brow. "I have the magic to open the door, but I need more time to learn how to control it. Now let's go to find the magic weapons."

"That's why you sent them there? To find magic weapons?" Ai asked, deception filing her voice.

"I sent people there to find a solution to the Fracture, but the person I counted on is missing. I don't know what has happened."

"What is a Fracture?"

"Something that will destroy civilization on the continent. We have had two in the last six hundred years. The first one destroyed the Alban Empire. Some parts were salvaged, but we are still less developed than we were six hundred years ago."

"And now?"

How can I tell her? She belongs here. Her parents are what we call the nomads, though the people here are less like the nomads than I expected.

"Dochia?"

"It's difficult to explain. It's..." *I can't call them nomads...* "We are afraid that the Khadate will invade the continent."

"It's what Nabal wants? To restart civilization?"

"Well, we don't think that they will be able to restart anything. We are afraid that everything will be ruined. Baraki brought only misery to Arenia. He killed two kings and their children. He killed even their girls."

"Is Nabal so wrong?"

"He may be right in some respects, but killing so many people, during the invasion, makes them wrong. And the combination of the Khadate and the Serpentists brings nothing good. They are using magic for evil purposes. I don't want Meriaduk to conquer the continent with his Maleteras."

"You should have told me before."

"I am sorry. It was just too difficult for me to talk about this."

"You call me your friend, yet you hid your real plans from me."

"I apologize, if that has offended you."

"I have to think," Ai said abruptly, and Dochia understood from the following silence that she was alone in her room.

For almost two weeks, Dochia remained on her own in the Sanctuary; Ai refused to speak with her. She could talk to Meriaduk or to other priests. But that was duty. And loathing.

❧

"I had a Vision," Dochia said, looking straight at Meriaduk. They were alone in the High Priest's office, the place from where he was governing the Sanctuary.

"Do you still see yourself as a Wanderer?" he barked and moved closer, his eyes on her. His hand went into the pocket of his large purple robe, gripping the Maletera that he always carried with him.

Dochia knew well what was in his pocket and, recalling the pain that the Maletera inflicted to her brain, she froze for a moment, her face stretched tight. She let out a short hiss of air, heart pounding in her ears, then she counted to five, and lowered her eyes. That pleased him. "My life belongs to the Serpent, but I still have Visions. They are not related to Fate, they come from the Serpent. Baraki has Visions too. You know that. And they bring useful information."

"Such as?" Meriaduk voice was still angry, but there was a slight tone of expectation in it. His fingers relaxed on the Maletera. A little. He fought a sudden impulse to rub away the twitching of his left eye.

"Baraki is planning to move against you."

"He plans. I plan. This is politics." Meriaduk shrugged and stretched his neck from side to side. "I don't need your Visions to know that."

"Baraki plans to kill you."

"He wouldn't dare," Meriaduk growled, and he stepped forward until they were face to face, their noses almost touching. He breathed in her face. "He wouldn't dare." A few drops of saliva left his mouth, then he swallowed, unable to calm his breath. He smoothed his brown hair back from his temples and fumbled with the thin ends of his moustache.

Dochia wiped her wet cheek with the back of her forearm and stepped back. "You are too nervous. Killing is part of politics too. You have to get used to it." *A frightened chicken.* She noticed that his left hand was trembling slightly and felt the urge to spit into his face.

"He wouldn't dare."

"Then my Vision is false," she said coldly and turned, trying to leave.

Meriaduk grabbed her elbow with bony fingers that felt like claws, and she turned back to him. "Tell me." This time his voice was calm. And his lips dry. His cold eyes locked with hers.

"Some of his Royal Guards got uniforms similar to your Priest Guard. Each month, you go to preach to the main temple of the Serpent. The day is still short, and you return in the Sanctuary after the dark comes. I saw them attacking you." Dochia had no Vision about Baraki trying to kill Meriaduk, but she had learned from Ai about some uniforms being sold by a greedy priest; they were good clothes.

"They are too weak to attack me or a Vicarius. We have powerful weapons." Meriaduk clasped his hands at his back, chest out, chin up, head cocked. A lopsided smile crept up on his face.

"I believe you, and I wish to see them working, but are they able to stop an arrow?"

Meriaduk pondered, then swallowed his pride. "No. I can paralyze the aggressors, if they are less than fifteen paces away from me, but I can't stop an arrow."

Another kind of Maletera? Ai refused to inform me about the magic weapons in the Sanctuary. Dochia said nothing, hoping that Meriaduk will speak more.

"What would you suggest?"

"Perhaps making the prayers shorter, but they can attack you even in daylight; there are many tall buildings in Nerval, and enough places to hide an archer."

"I can't stop the prayers. Nerval needs them. It needs me too."

Nerval needs you as much as I need poison. "You can't stop an arrow either. But you can make Baraki feel your power."

"Should I use the Shot on him?" He opened a cabinet and grabbed a dark brown tool that had an L shape. The shortest part of the weapon fitted well in his palm. "We have seven such weapons." He gestured with the Shot, a wicked grin spread on his lips.

So that's the weapon... Dochia forced herself to take her eyes from it. *Meriaduk has enough blood to activate and use it. Can I use it too?* "Perhaps is better to let a Vicarius perform a test in front of Baraki and let him know that your ... Shot is much stronger."

"You have an interesting mind. I still don't know why the Maletera could not fully take over it, but it suits me."

"It must be a reason for that. I serve the Serpent." Dochia bowed. "And you."

"You serve me better than I thought."

"I will serve you to death." *Your death.* "Perhaps you can also postpone Baraki's coronation as the new Khad. Nabal will not be happy, but..." Dochia shrugged and turned her palms out.

"We need a Khad to conquer the continent for the Serpent. The path is open for glory."

The path is open for blood. "We are not fully prepared for the invasion, and one year delay is not much. The Serpent is wise and patient. So are the Serpentists. Baraki may have the crown and the army, but it's the High Priest who must have the last say. I am not sure that Baraki understands this."

"I have to think about it," Meriaduk said abruptly, and gestured to Dochia, making her know that the audience had ended. She bowed and forced a grimace into an unfelt smile.

Alone, he took out the Maletera from his pocket, and rubbed it until the tool reacted, pulsating faintly in his hand. *Dochia may be useful, but she may be dangerous too. There is something still untamed in her. Should I use the Maletera on her again? Perhaps later, after I will be able to fully control Baraki. Nabal will make problems, but the Serpent will guide me.*

"I should have watched you more closely." Nabal appeared abruptly in Dochia's vision. She was alone in a secluded part of the secondary dome. Like the Last Empress, he used his power at his own convenience, but he liked to surprise his interlocutors.

"Why should I require such attention?"

"You convinced Meriaduk to postpone Baraki's coronation."

"Why are you so sure that it was me?"

"Am I wrong?"

"I don't make decisions for Meriaduk, he is the high Priest of the Serpent, but if you want to know what I think about the coronation..." She looked at Nabal, who nodded for her to continue. "We need a swift conquest of the continent to spare as many lives as possible we can. We want to replace the rulers but keep the people. You have already agreed to this. Meriaduk and Baraki don't work well together. Don't ask me why, I am still new here, and you know better. Their lack of collaboration will make the conquest a painful and protracted process. You have the power to make them understand that each has his own place, in the new world you are building. Why are you not working on this?"

Is she testing me? Or she is just too new here to understand that we are both allies and competitors? "What would better collaboration look like?"

"They don't need to love each other. But the Seer should not lose a battle because two grumpy old men can't stand each other."

"Who can defeat Baraki? He is a Seer; Arenia belongs to him; Frankis is still in state of civil war, and there are no capable army commanders in the other two major kingdoms."

"The nomads are still split in various tribes which are ready to jump at other's throat, and the army of the Khadate is not yet ready. The continent has always unified to face an invasion from the east. The dogs fight each other for a bone, but when a wolf arrives... It's the same here. And they must have a Seer too."

"Yes, they have, and you know him, but he is still young and without a kingdom."

"If you mean Codrin, his father defeated the nomads, and he is a capable army commander. Don't underestimate him. One more year of preparation will only help us."

"Then?"

"If you can't convince Baraki and Meriaduk to collaborate better in one year, then no one can. We go with what we have. Do you have your own order of the Wanderers that I can join?"

"The Church of the Serpent plays the role of the Wanderers and the Circle here."

"They rely on the magic of the Sanctuary, and they mostly use it to get young girls in their beds. I don't really know what makes you think this will create a new civilization. An order must have some discipline. Why are you not creating one here? You can find another name if the Wanderers doesn't suit you."

"I will think about that, but, Dochia," Nabal extended his arm, his finger pointing at her, "in one year we will have a new Khad. Baraki."

"Yes, I have already agreed to that. Will you agree with me about a new military order? To bring some discipline?"

"I will have to think about that," he repeated and vanished from her vision.

Well, Dochia mused, leaning against the wall. *We have one more year to plan our defense. How I wish to have news from Frankis. I miss my sisters. I miss Jara. Codrin... It's strange how the distance enhances your loneliness.*

Chapter 25 – Saliné

Wandering through the library of S'Laurden, Saliné found a lyre sitting on a table, in the corner next to one of the large windows. Two feet tall, it was an expensive instrument, its frame painted in gold. She glanced around and, seeing no one, took the lyre in her hands, her fingers caressing the strings. After a while, she sat in the only chair at the table, the lyre between her knees. The song rose into the room, and shy at first, Saliné warmed herself slowly to the music. The room vanished from her mind, then the walls, Laurden and everything else. She was only a young woman, dreaming through her songs, and her lyre. When she finished, eyes closed, she leaned against the frame, a faint smile on her lips. For the first time in more than two years, Saliné forgot everything and felt happy. With a sigh, she lifted her head and opened her eyes. In front of her, Foy, Eduin and a few servants looked at her, no one willing to disturb her tranquility.

"That was my mother's lyre," Eduin said, "and no one has touched it since she died."

"I apologize." Saliné's voice was barely more than a whisper, and she set the lyre back on the table. "I will not touch it again."

"My dear Vio, if you don't play again, I am afraid that I will instruct the servants to keep you locked in the room, with no food. Why do you think we've been standing here for half an hour? Just to be sure you don't touch the lyre?" He come closer and took her hand in his. "Come, it's dinner time, and you just won the right to eat more than any of us."

"My impression is," Foy said thoughtfully, as his son still stood hand in hand with Saliné, "that your voice matches the skills of your fingers."

That evening, Foy moved the lyre back to the saloon where it had stood years ago, and his thoughts moved back to a time when his wife was still alive. *In some ways, Vio resembles her, gentle and intelligent. Is this what Idonie meant about her being special? That she will replace my wife in Laurden's life? Vio and Eduin... No,* he shook his head, *there will be too many political issues. Laure is pressing for the marriage between my son and her niece. We can't afford to ignore her. Spring is still far off, and there will be no negotiations until then.* He closed his eyes and fell asleep, Saliné's last song still playing in his mind.

From that day, once a week, Saliné played for them and for herself, in the evening, when the logs were singing in the fireplace too.

~၄၅~

"The Winter Solstice Party is in less than a month," Foy said, throwing an amused look at his son. "Are you ready with your preparations?"

"More or less."

"What about Vio?"

"Hmm," Eduin smiled. "You are testing me. I have already asked Martha to make her a dress."

"Good, and I think that we can move Vio into a suite. The one that belonged to your sister. She will not return soon. Her husband wrote that they will not come to the party. They will go to Tolosa. Matilde will be Vio's maid." *This is another step in an uncertain direction,* Foy thought, *but I feel that I must do it. Damn, Idonie, I am not a Wanderer who can see the future, but*

I have the feeling I am creating a new one that was not in the cards just weeks ago, and I have no idea where it will bring us. It is both great and dangerous. Why can't you tell me more? "Let's talk to her." Still weighing his thoughts, Foy frowned heavily, under Eduin's inquiring stare.

They found Saline in her room, and Foy was more succinct that he would have liked when talking to her. *I was almost rude*, he thought. *What's wrong with me?* He rubbed gently at his own temple, as though his own thoughts were giving him a headache.

"Thank you, Sir Foy," Saliné said. She wanted to add more, but the shadow behind his eyes locked her tongue. Her eyes flicked away from the man who seemed to act strangely, back to the window. She frowned slightly.

"To my friends, I am Foy." He blinked at Saliné for a moment, then he smiled, avoiding to look at Eduin, who struggled to suppress his amusement.

"Thank you, Foy," she repeated, unable to say more, and made a curtsy.

Guests started to come to Laurden weeks before the Winter Solstice Party. Most of them were from the valley, as most of the passes were now blocked. Some were from other corners of the Seigneury, or even from outside it, and they were the first to arrive, when the snow was still manageable on the high roads. Part of the inner circle of S'Laurden, Saliné found herself the center of the attention of several young men, but mostly of Eduin and his cousin Arnauld, who competed in a friendly manner. She enjoyed their jokes and that exuberance so typical of the south of Frankis. They gave her a strange feeling of being at home. She was not fully aware of it; she just felt at ease. Her only concern was that Idonie could not come.

In the evening everybody had been waiting for, she took her place at the main table, next to Eduin, who was next to his father, at his right. Remembering Idonie's warning, Foy settled Arnauld at his left, so the Seigneur of Laurden could act like a fence between the young man and Saliné. He thought that everything was settled well when the Majordomo made his call for the first suite of dances. Caught in an argument between his guests, Eduin saw too late that Arnauld had asked Saliné for the first dance of the evening. *My bloody cousin was quick to take advantage*, he mused, and turned his back on them.

"There is nothing more enjoyable than dancing with a beautiful woman during the long winter nights." Smiling, Arnauld lent Saliné his arm and led her to the floor. He could not stop looking at her.

Saliné was dressed in her new dark-green velvet gown, showing her shoulders, which looked as though they were carved in old ivory, and her slender arms. She had no ribbons on her clothes, the only woman in the hall without them. Her simple dark dress was not noticeable on her; it was only her frame that captured the view – simple, natural, elegant, and that attracted the eye of both men and women. Her coiffure was not striking, most of her hair being tied in a long ponytail tied with a single dark-green ribbon, the same material as her dress. There were some little willful tendrils of curly hair free at her temples. Her auburn hair contrasted in a strange way with the dark velvet. That was striking. She felt the pressure from their eyes and fought to control her breath.

"It may be, if the woman knows how to dance. The rhythm is strange to me, the stranger from the north." *I will dance with a stranger. In Severin, I was forced to dance only with Bucur. I never danced with Codrin.*

"Who worries about dancing? It's the easiest thing in the world. I saw you walking. You were born to dance," Arnauld said, encircling her waist, ready for the start. "With me," he whispered, looking amused at her. "Let's try a few steps." Taking her left hand, Arnauld laid it on his shoulder, and led her to the left, then to the right, and her feet began to move rhythmically over the slippery marble of the floor, in time to the music. "What did I tell you? It's easy. Rotation now." He took his hand from around her waist and turned her two times, then two more. At the end, he took her waist again.

"You want to make me lose my head."

"From only four rotations? At the end of the dancing suite, we should make a diagonal of rotations. Like this." Arnauld tightened his arm around her waist, and they turned together this time.

"That was much better." Saliné laughed, and finally let the party take over. It was so different from the two she had had in Severin.

Arnauld was both a good dancer and a good teacher. He also knew his business, and in every dance, he still found something to correct, to keep her attention. He did it jokingly, so Saliné did not feel pressured, and she did not notice how fast time passed; she spent the entire first suite of five dances only with Arnauld.

"It's such a pleasure to dance with you," he said, during the fourth dance.

"You will soon empty your bag of compliments." Saliné's laughed a bit tight, yet she was strangely pleased by his words. "And I may never learn to dance your southern dances properly, if you don't criticize me too." She was in the middle stage; she was pleased, and at the same time she had sufficient self-awareness to be able to observe: Arnauld was exaggerating, but he was doing it in a natural, exuberant and almost childish manner. The only young man from her past with whom she could make a social comparison was Bucur, and all the men she met in Laurden were *not* Bucur.

"You have nothing to worry about; I will always find more compliments for you."

From one corner of the hall, they started the fifth dance with measured steps, then he began the rotations, straight towards the group in the center, continually saying, "Excuse us, excuse us," and steering their course through the sea of lace and ribbons, until they made a full diagonal. "We've made it," he laughed.

"Yes, we made it," Saliné breathed, suddenly thrilled, now that her fear was gone.

"I hope you will allow me to invite you again." Arnauld kissed her hand, and then he led her back to her place.

Traversing the room, she saw many couples hiding behind the columns or leaving the hall. There was a closeness between them that she envied without realizing it. They were young and exuberant, and some did not even care that people saw them kissing.

Arnauld dark eyes glittered with amusement as he said, "That's something normal at our parties," and he pointed to one of the many kissing couples. "Are you different in the north?"

"Thank you for the dancing lessons, and of course I would like to dance again with my teacher," she said abruptly. *Mother told me the same. She was doing that too...* A hint of desire to be a normal girl and enjoy everything passed through her, but she did not feel fully at ease with Arnauld or with anyone else.

Under Eduin's intense stare, Arnauld pulled back her chair to let her sit. He was doing the same, with another girl, two tables away. Arnauld, his eyes crinkling at Eduin, whispered something to Saliné, who laughed in delight. Deliberately, he placed his hand on the rail of her chair, without touching her. From his place, Eduin saw his hand on Saliné's shoulder. Arnauld winked at him and went to his place.

Vio is both intelligent and innocent, Arnauld thought, leaning back against his chair, *and sometimes she looks strangely at me, like she is dreaming. Maybe there was no one to teach her such things at their court. Her father was a Half-Knight. I doubt that they really had a court. More probably they just had a large house. In two weeks, I should be able to convince her to come with me. My place is closer to Valeni, and she knows it. She wants to leave Laurden, and I want to keep her. Father will not be happy, but I like Vio. She is so ... different.*

From her chair, Saline observed the effervescence in the hall, and a serene smile settled on her lips. *How I wish Codrin were here,* she suddenly thought, and her smile became tighter.

When the second suite of dances was about to start, Foy kept Arnauld in a talk so Eduin could invite Saliné, but the tempestuous young man broke with etiquette and, jumping up from his chair, he stood behind Saliné. "I am sorry, Eduin, but

Vio promised me these dances too. Please, my dear," he said and lent his arm to her, "the second suite is the best."

Saliné felt the hidden tension behind the smiles of the two young men; her senses were much better trained for bad feelings than for good ones. "Of course, I will dance again with you, Arnauld," she said with a charming smile, and Arnauld grinned, satisfied, at Eduin, who fought hard to conceal his disappointment, just to avoid giving even more satisfaction to his cousin. "You are a wonderful dancer, but Eduin invited me first, so this is his dance." The corners of Saliné's mouth twitched, and she bit her lip to keep from smiling at Eduin; his grin was quite devilish. *I must give Arnauld another dance later.*

From that moment, she took care to change partners after each dance, and it happened that Arnauld got the last one in the second suite. "It's becoming too hot here, and I have a surprise for you," he said mysteriously when the music stopped. "Please allow me to show you."

Reluctantly, Saliné agreed, and he walked her through a small hall into an adjacent room that she never saw open before. Music and laughter followed them through the darkening air. The moment Arnauld opened the door, a strong scent of orange flowers came to Saliné, and she walked toward the six trees in full blossom, long forgotten memories from her childhood in Midia stirring her – they had a small orangery there too. Briefly, she thought that perhaps Eduin would have preferred to surprise her, but it was already too late.

"Thank you, Arnauld, this *was* a surprise." She touched the flowers and buried her face in them. She shivered from both pleasure and cold. While the frigid air outside could not get in, the room had no heating. Resembling some friendly ghosts through the large windows, high clouds moved across the first stars. Round and mysterious, the moon was sending its silvery tentacles across the room, playing gently on Saliné's face.

Arnauld came closer, almost touching her. She sensed warmth radiating from his body and felt better. Slowly, Arnauld came even closer and his chest touched her back. It happened so gently that Saliné only felt more warmth coming to her and involuntarily, she leaned back a little. His breath stirred a stray strand on her neck, yet she did not move away. She turned her head, though, to meet his glance. Arnauld smiled and whispered, "One day, when you have time, I will invite you to see an orange orchard. Here, in the mountains, it is too cold, but there is one in the garden of my castle. It flowers at the spring equinox. You must come."

Saliné thought for a while and calculated that his place was closer to Valeni.

He moved his mouth even closer to her ear, and placed a hand on her shoulder, turning her a little. "Your aunt, Agatha, is a good friend of my father, and from there, you can easily reach Valeni."

"Thank you, Arnauld, you are a kind man." *I have to keep this option open, if Foy doesn't want to help me.*

"I am glad that you agree," he said and, turning her even more, kissed her. Arnauld caught her with her mouth open, as she tried to speak, and he misinterpreted her stance. His strong arms tightened around her, one over her waist, the other behind her neck, and he pressed further, parting her lips even more. Saliné tried to stop him, but his embrace was so tight that she could not move, and she was losing both breath and mind. He stopped for a moment, and she breathed deeply, her eyes wide. A memory of Jara telling her that kissing was normal at a ball came back to her. All the girls and young men did it.

This is so different from Bucur, she thought, a trace of desire passing through her. There was something primal in this man, force and passion, something that Bucur lacked. Another burst of memory came to her, the only time Codrin had kissed her. That kiss was powerful too, leaving her breathless, but somehow her mind wanted to forget it now. Arnauld was not playing with her; he wanted her, and she felt it. And it was a ball after all. "Arnauld..." she tried to speak, but he kissed her again, and his hand behind her neck did not allow her to pull away from his mouth, and his embrace was strong, almost melting her body into his. *I have to solve this calmly,* she pondered, not realizing that her lips were already answering him, and her thoughts fully dissolved.

He let her free for a moment, and she finally breathed. "I love you, Vio," he whispered. "I never wanted anyone as I want you. Come with me, tomorrow. You will be the queen of my castle."

She was in an awkward position, her left shoulder pressed on his chest, his arm still around her waist. *This is more than a kiss at a ball. I need to think and stop him, before...* "Arnauld, let's go back now. We can talk again later when things are calmer. People may come here." Talking gently and keeping her eyes on his, she moved away from him.

"They won't. I've stolen the key. No one knows that the room is open." Arnauld leaned forward, ready to kiss her again. He was totally lost.

Oh, no... Did he lock the door? "Arnauld, please stop." Overriding her lingering thrill, Saliné tried to move further away from him, before his strong arms could immobilize her, but he was too excited now and ready to risk everything. *I need to stop him, before it's too late.*

"I can't," Arnauld said, his voice edgy. "I want you, Vio."

Before he could embrace her again, she panicked and slapped him, but not in the formal way a woman would normally do to escape from such situations without harm. In a split second, her fighting skills took over, and she reacted like a trained Assassin. She flexed her knees slightly, lowering her center of gravity. Then her body rotated, springing up at the same time. Powered by the swift move, her spine and shoulder passed the whole force of her whirling body into her arm. He was pushed a step back, and blood flowed from his nose. The shocked moments of silence that followed were baffling for both.

What have I done? That was the Assassin Whirlpool. It could have broken his nose or worse... But her instinct had chosen a light form of the Whirlpool and caused little damage. "I am sorry, Arnauld," she breathed, trying to calm him and herself, her wide eyes watching the blood pooling on his face and neck.

Unconsciously, he had reacted in a similar way and moved into a fighting stance, ready to hit her. He restrained himself a moment later, their eyes locked. They were stunned, and neither of them knew what to do next. Maybe Arnauld deserved some form of punishment, but nothing so serious. Even though he had lost control of himself, he was doing what other young men and girls were doing at the ball, but something broke in Saliné in that moment. Her reaction was not against Arnauld, not really; it was against the two years of misery Bucur had inflicted on her. It was Bucur she was punishing, not the man in front of her. Even though he was dead, that evil man still haunted Saliné.

"I am sorry," she repeated. "I did not mean to react that way, but you scared me. I will go now, as Eduin or Foy may be worried by our absence. What happened here stays between us. Arnauld, I am not upset at you, and I should not have reacted so strongly. Compose yourself and return a few minutes after me. I will enjoy dancing and talking to you later. You are a wonderful dancer."

"I must apologize." Arnauld finally recovered from the shock, and his mind was normal again. "I lost myself because of your beauty. It has never happened before, and I feel ashamed. Forgive me." He bowed and stepped aside, to let her pass.

What happened to me? Strange, she thought, *I resent him less than I resented Bucur. Arnauld was too insistent, but he was not wicked. In fact, I don't resent him at all. Mother was right about dancing and kissing...* She shook her head nervously, unable to understand herself. At that moment, she wanted to be an eighteen-year-old girl, free of worries. She wanted to be exuberant and enjoy the party as any other girl could enjoy it, even let some young men kiss her. She couldn't. At least not fully. Her tormented life did not leave much childhood in her, and there were too many bad memories restricting her freedom. They acted like shackles on her mind. Out of the room, which had not been locked by Arnauld as she had feared, Saliné arranged her dress and walked away through the small corridor toward the dancing hall, as if nothing had happened. At the main door, she met Foy, who was walking out briskly. Without understanding it, she felt the tension in his stare and a sudden relief too. Saying nothing, he stepped back, his eyes on her, letting her enter. Arnauld was nowhere to be seen.

"I have a surprise for you." Eduin smiled at Saliné when they met in the middle of the hall; he had been searching for her. "Please come with me."

She panicked, and the tension in her body seemed almost to constrict her breathing. *No, Eduin is even more ... different.* She thought of Bucur again, shook her head, to force his evil memory away, and followed Eduin. Saliné never tried to compare them with Codrin – he was unique to her, and they lived in kind of parallel world suspended between their beloved cherry tree, books and her lyre. They did not live in a court. In the orangery, she worked hard to look enthusiastic about the beautiful scent of the delicate flowers, and she almost physically felt Eduin's delight.

While she touched the flowers, Eduin stood close to her, looking over her shoulder. He was tempted to rest his lips on the nape of her neck, where her hair, lifted into that ponytail, revealed the pale skin. Reluctantly, he restrained himself, and stepped back a little. They stayed there for more than fifteen minutes, talking in pleasant intimacy. Strangely, his presence calmed her, and Saliné left on his arm, all dimples and bright green eyes, her long hair bouncing as she moved under Eduin's scrutiny. She offered him almost half of the dances in the two last suites.

Caught in the effervescence of the dances and the chatter that followed, she forgot about Arnauld, who did not return to the hall. For the first time, Saliné discovered what a court really meant. She was too young when she left Midia, and Severin, while not much smaller than Laurden, did not have a real court. Mohor did not care about such things, and there were no people of value to entertain Saliné. Bucur was always methodical and calculated, and a bad character. Arnauld, for all his wrong steps, was still a normal young man, and Eduin was an even better one. Her mind absorbed by the party, Saliné looked distractedly around the hall, looking for both of them. She was never alone; five more young men surrounded her with their well-mannered attention. Saliné also had her first glimpse of courtship that evening. Codrin was her *brother*, then her love, but he did not court her, the relationship simply blossomed between them. She let the young men of Laurden swarm around her, and encouraged them, both deliberately and unintentionally. Caught in the celebration, she did not realize that she was more mature and intelligent than the young men around her, even though some were five or six years older. She simply led them along, except for Eduin, who was the only one who matched her for wit, and their encounter was delightful. She had decided to enjoy the party, and she did.

Discreetly, from near or far, Eduin watched her through the whole evening – the party here did not stop at sunset, as was the habit in Severin. He did not chase away his competitors and tried not to force himself too much on her. He saw her delight, the flashing light in her green eyes, and the smile of excitement playing on her lips, the deliberate grace and lightness of her movements. From time to time, eyes closed, Eduin imagined things. With her.

Late in the night, Saliné went in her room, tired, but filled with a strange exuberance that she had never felt before. There was also an even subtler undercurrent: though Eduin's mother had died five years before, the S'Laurdens were a normal, joyful family, as she had had in Midia, before her father was killed, and they were forced to leave their home, into exile. Their stay in the hunting house had its good moments too, but it was marked by the ubiquitous fear of an unstable future, and in Severin all her dreams had been shattered. Deep in her heart, she craved to be part of such a family. *I wish Codrin and Mother could be here.* Her last thought, before she fell asleep.

The next morning, Arnauld discovered that he had an urgent errand and left Laurden when most people were still in their beds. Hearing this, Saliné felt both relieved and uneasy – and perhaps sad, as she guessed that he had left Laurden because of her – until Foy sent a page to request her presence.

"Please sit," Foy said, his face serious, but a faint glimmer in his eyes. "Now tell me what happened when you *first* visited my orangery." He waited patiently, but Saliné did not know what to say. "To help your memory, you were not alone.

Arnauld of the broken nose was there with you." He could no longer hide his mirth.

Coyly, Saliné smiled at him. "I think he got too close to the flowers and fell against the trunk of the tree. There was no reason for him to leave Laurden. He was entertaining, and he taught me to dance. I will miss him. Did he really break his nose?"

"No, I was just playing with you. Some flowers know how to defend themselves. This story will stay between us and the servant who warned me that you were in … danger. He could not have been more wrong. Not even Eduin knows about this." Foy stood up, came to her and took her hand in his. "You are indeed a rare flower, Vio," he said and kissed her hand. "I think Eduin wants to talk to you now."

With the same mysterious look, he had the evening while taking her to the orangery, Eduin led her into another room she had never seen before. He opened an armoire, and a long row of dresses came into view. "I am sorry that we were a bit unobservant and made you only one dress. In Laurden, the Winter Solstice Party runs for five days. We know how to party in the south. Please take whichever dresses you like."

Saliné looked at him, then at the dresses, and found that they would indeed fit her, with some minor changes, then again at Eduin, who was smiling. "To whom do they belong?"

"They were Mother's."

"I apologize for asking. Eduin, I will survive fine with one dress, I am not that fussed about them."

He said nothing, just took one dress, and pressed it against her body. "Dark red, it suits you well."

"What would your father say if I...?"

"He suggested it; I had no idea about this wardrobe. Take whatever you want. Martha will come and make whatever adjustments are necessary." He placed an arm behind her shoulders, and pushed her gently, closer to those tempting clothes.

She looked once more at him, and then picked three dresses: the one Eduin gave her first, a pale yellow one and a black one. Without knowing it, she smiled each time she took a new one, while Eduin watched her.

After five days full of parties and joy, Saliné woke late in the morning. She felt lazy and not hungry at all. *I will skip breakfast today.* The room was warm, and a log was singing in the fireplace, spreading a pleasant scent of resin. *Matilde came in the morning to restart the fire.* She left the bed and moved toward the window, leaning forward against the sill. A sun of impossible brightness was almost at the roof of the sky, its vivid blue as impossible as the brilliance of the large yellow orb. Fresh snow was glittering all over Laurden, almost blinding her, yet she forced her eyes to stay open, absorbing a vibrant world she had never seen before. There was frigid cold too. Warmed by the sun playing on her skin through the window, and by the wood burning the fireplace, Saliné did not feel it. *I am happy.* Memories of the past days came to her, all at once, fighting for her attention. Like any woman with a trace of Light, Saliné had a good visual memory, and she was able to recall with surprising clarity most of the things that had happened to her. For half an hour, she drowned herself in a collection of dances, sparks of brilliant conversations and jokes. And even in that weird and pleasant moment of closeness with Arnauld. The memories came and went at their own will and, slowly, Arnauld's figure morphed into Codrin, then Jara's face came to her. Saliné had been humming one of her favorite songs, and now she felt tears sting her eyes. Her throat was tight, and she couldn't sing any more. *Mother is still a prisoner,* she thought bitterly, and all her happiness vanished as if it never had existed. *Spring is not so far off, and I must prepare for leaving Laurden. Valeni is not that far and, from there, Aunt Agatha will help me to reach Severin. Codrin...* Thinking of him brought a bit of calm to her mind.

Chapter 26 – Saliné

When the last month of the winter was almost spent, Saliné found the courage to ask Foy and Eduin to help her leave for Valeni.

"The roads are still unsafe," Eduin said, his voice suddenly edgy. "We don't want to put you in danger. The earliest time for safe passage to Valeni is in the middle of spring. I am sorry to delay you, and I am ready to make amends by taking you for a ride. It's sunny, and soon the snow which fell last night will become dirty. It would be a pity not to see the white valley from the mountains."

She nodded awkwardly, and they went out together. It was her first ride outside snowy Laurden, and after a while, she found herself caught up in the beautiful landscape. Eduin was right; the endless pure white had both a cheering and romantic appearance. Feeling the power of the coming spring, the chill seemed cupped within the valley, pressed down by the white mountains, as if trying to hide from the radiant sun. They ate together at a small inn and drank spicy hot wine, which warmed their blood. Outside the inn, Saliné made ready to mount, when a snowball crashed into her face. It was fluffy, and did not hurt, but she remained stunned for a few moments. It was Eduin' laughter which woke her up, and she started to chase him, throwing snowball after snowball. Most of them missed the target, but even when he was hit, he still laughed. He jumped down a slope and slid on his back all the way down on the three-foot-deep snow. Like a child, Saliné followed him and inadvertently landed on him before he could move away.

Eduin gasped from the shock, but then only laughed louder. "You attacked the Seigneur of Laurden. There will be a price to pay for that." He filled his hand with snow and rubbed it in her face.

This time, Saliné was no longer stunned and paid him back. She was still sitting on his chest, like she was in the saddle, and she had the advantage. When the laughter shook the breath from them, they lay down in the snow, her head leaning on his extended arm.

"You have never played snow games before," Eduin said, and pulled her closer, her head resting now on his shoulder. It was so natural that Saliné did not object.

"There was not much snow where I lived." *And not many children to play with. Strange that we did not play like this in Severin.* The snow in Severin was thin and the land lacked the wide white spaces here. Half of Laurden was a land of pastures more than forests. And in the winter, Severin rarely saw the sun. Here, it was as sunny as it was cold.

"Look." He pointed abruptly, up into the sky.

"It's that an eagle? I never saw one before. It looks so big."

"Southern eagles are larger. They can reach twelve feet in wingspan. Some of them can carry a goat or a sheep. Or a child."

"No, don't say it." Saliné covered his mouth with her hand. "I don't want them to carry off a child."

"Do you know what we need now?"

"Hot spicy wine," she laughed, as she felt the cold seeping into her.

"Yes." Eduin laughed too, and standing up, he stretched his arms to pull her up, and it was almost dark when they returned home.

༺༻

With the first days of spring, change came to Laurden. The first chain of mountains around the city was not tall, and, from the ocean, warm winds chased the cold away. The last snow was already three weeks old, and now the first rain came. It was always the same here; today was winter, tomorrow was spring. This year, spring came in the same abrupt way, two weeks before the equinox, and Saliné's thoughts went even more often to Severin and Codrin. Hiding her actions, she started to prepare for her departure.

She made an inventory of her money and thought she had enough to reach Valeni, but her first difficulty was to leave Laurden. She compared it with Severin and found that Foy was a much more organized man than Mohor. The gates were better maintained, and there were patrols too, keeping peace in the city, though Laurden was not a dangerous place. *If they allow me to leave, everything will be easy. If not... Why would not they not let me go? I have to be prepared for both cases. In the worst case, my main problem is leaving the palace*, she thought. There was a gate there too, manned by five guards. *The gate I can handle, but how can I get my mare? I can't leave on foot. Then I have to pass through the main gate. Without Foy's or Eduin's approval, I can't sneak out through the main gate alone. The small gate is even more difficult; few people use it, and I will attract more attention. I will need a diversion.* She shook her head and decided to gather more information.

Each spring, Foy and his son made a tour of their fiefdom, to see how people had fared over the winter. There were two differences this year, though; Foy went alone and two weeks earlier than usual. After two days on the road and bad weather, going from one village to another, he cursed himself and his idea of going earlier. The soldiers said nothing, but a simple look at their faces betrayed their feelings and hidden curses. *We have very colorful curses in the south*, he almost laughed.

On the third day, Foy finally came to the place he had wanted to see from the beginning, Passin village, which was higher in the Pirenes Mountains. There were more villages scattered even deeper in the mountains, like Valis, but they were small, and their wardens usually came to Passin to meet the Seigneur.

The large village was finally in sight, and Foy wiped his wet palms on his clothes. It did not help. The steady drizzle, which had persisted for the last two days, had soaked through every layer of clothing he wore. And from his helmet, water dripped into his eyes. Pale and larger than usual, the sun, wreathed in thick patches of mist, soared far above. He suppressed a groan at the stiffness of his limbs and pushed his horse faster through the mud. *I am getting older...*

In Passin, they stopped at the only inn, and he decided to pay for the soldiers' wine, to stop their faces getting any longer. Warned by earlier couriers, three of the four wardens were in the inn already, and Foy went to a separate chamber to talk with each of them. He finished quickly with the first two, and then it was the turn of Guiscard, the warden of Castis and Valis, to meet the Seigneur.

"Sit," Foy said, and gestured toward the carafe of wine. He sipped some wine too, but his glass was still almost full. "What's new in Castis? Did the Knight of Silon arrive there?"

"Yes, he came later than we expected him, in mid-autumn, with his son, a young lady and nine more soldiers. A storm had delayed his ship. As I already informed you, five soldiers came three months earlier."

"That's quite a lot of soldiers for a small place like Castis. Do you know why he needs them?"

"He did not say, but he acts like a hunted man, and..." Guiscard sipped some wine for the first time, "his son, Claudin, was killed. It happened during the night before his wedding."

"You said something about a girl. Poor thing, to lose her husband like that."

"Well, Sir, it was she who killed him."

Foy accepted the news with a catlike blink of his hazel eyes. "Do you know why?"

"From the beginning, I had the impression that the girl had been kidnapped. On road from Sebastos to Castis, she was watched by two guards, day and night. The priest had the same impression, and he did not like the Knights, especially the son."

"That's a way of saying that you dislike them too."

"I am the warden of Castis, it's not my task to judge my Knight," Guiscard said, letting a wry smile cross his lips.

S'Laurden smiled back in tacit agreement. "Did you talk to her?"

"Not much, but at the crossroads where the road to Castis divides, she asked me where the main road led."

"What happened to her?"

"She left Castis during the night, just before the Mother Storm came."

"I see," S'Laurden said, thoughtfully. "She must have a name, this girl."

"Vio. She looked a fine lady, educated, polite, proper speaking, but Sir Bernier was not very communicative about her. Understandable after what happened. I learned more from his soldiers though, after I poured enough wine into them. Some things were contradictory, but I have a kind of story now." Guiscard took his time and sipped some more wine.

You like to talk, Guiscard, and you want me to ask. Foy smiled inside, even an intelligent man like Guiscard had his small flaws. "Do you know who she really is?"

"I'm not certain, but I think that her father was the Seigneur of Severin, a place far to the north, close to Arad. He was killed by Sir Bernier, who took over the Seigneury."

"I know where Arad is on the map, but I have never heard of Severin. What happened to her mother?"

"She disappeared, and no one knows if she is still alive. Probably not. At the end of the last summer, someone else took Severin – the Knight of Cleuny, who was a family friend of the former Signora of Severin, the one who vanished. Sir Bernier managed to escape and took Vio with him, against her will. From what I understood, she was promised to another man, but his son wanted her instead. It's a strange thing, but the soldiers were afraid to speak about that man. I have no idea why. Perhaps he is dangerous, or vicious; their minds seemed to freeze."

I have to send a courier to Pierre, in Tolosa. Maybe he knows something. "Did Vio escape?"

"Sir Bernier set off after her the next morning, and the last time I saw her was on the road out of the high mountains. One of those long hairpin curves. You are face to face with someone, a hundred paces from you, but you need to ride for three more hours to meet."

"Should I understand that Bernier did not get her back?"

"That's right, but I can't tell if she escaped the Mother Storm. I hope she did, Vio was a fine lady."

"Anything else worth knowing, Guiscard?"

"Sir Bernier wants to rebuild the walls and even make a new one to surround the barn too."

"You said that he acts like he is hunted. What is he scared of?"

"I don't know, Sir, but it's true, there is someone hunting him, three or four times a day he climbs the wall too search the road. And his mood did not improve much after his son... Maybe it is the man who took Severin, or the man to whom Vio was promised. The soldiers fear both. I may be able to learn more in time."

"Thank you, Guiscard. You may go now," Foy said, and placed a small purse on the table – it was more than Aron paid Guiscard in half a year. Alone, he leaned his head back against the wall behind the chair and closed his eyes. *Vio, Vio, you are full of mysteries. I wish that you had not come to Laurden, but there you are. I can't change that. It's too late. Even this old grumpy man likes you. At least you are a woman of character and a Signora. I would like to know who the man you were promised to is. He doesn't sound like the one you mentioned to us; that commoner in Valeni. Could he be a danger to us? Idonie, I will curse you, if you don't tell me more... I don't know exactly what that might be. I am afraid that I will both like and dislike it. And fear it. La naiba!* He used the damnation words that would have made Dochia laugh.

When he came back from the spring tour, Saliné found Foy cold and distant. He was polite and did not avoid her, but something had changed. Fortunately for her, Eduin was still the same, sometimes even too eager to please her, for all Saliné's efforts to temper his enthusiasm. Not that she did not enjoy his presence and courtesy, but even she had started to understand what everybody else in the palace knew already, that the son of the Seigneur of Laurden had fallen for her, and she was walking on thin ice, trying to be friendly to Eduin, without encouraging him. With all her effort the plans for leaving Laurden were stalling.

A day later, Foy sent Carlo, his Spatar, to Tolosa, to learn more about Severin. It happened that Pierre was not there; he had taken his family to Nimea, his fiefdom. By chance, Carlo met the Duchess, and he asked her about Severin.

"A small place," Laure said, coldly. "There was a battle last year, and the city has a new Seigneur. Nothing of great importance. I heard that you have a guest in Laurden. A girl."

"Eduin saved her when the savages attacked Siecle. She is good looking," Carlo said, his eyes glimmering.

"So Eduin was not bored this winter."

"Not at all, Duchess."

"What about his wedding?"

"A new round of negotiation will start in a month or two. Some clauses in the marriage contract are still not ... fully agreed."

"I hope that they will be cleared in time. We support the marriage between our niece and Eduin." *Poor man, I won't scold him for having mistresses. My niece is a shrew, but she will help me to keep Laurden under control. Foy is too independent, sometimes.* "Have you some news about the Candidate King and Queen?"

"Lady Maud wrote us about this situation, but they did not appear in Laurden. What happened to them?"

"Inform us when you have news." The Duchess dismissed him.

≈≫≈

It was the sixth day after the equinox, and spring was more advanced than Saliné ever remembered for that time of the year. Life was different in the south; both people and nature were more exuberant and ready to take everything that could be taken. She was in the small park in front of the palace, on one knee, to take in the scent of a famous plant: lavender. She knew it was the source of the best perfumes in Frankis, but it was so different to actually to see the plant instead of drawings, and even better to enjoy the scent. Even for the area around Laurden, it was too early for lavender to flower, but this patch of ten small bushes was covered during the winter, and only a few days before, the gardeners had taken off the glass cover that protected them from the cold. At the corner of her eye, she saw movement on the small road, which divided the park in two, leading to the main entrance to the palace. *Octavian...* She froze, yet some faint vestiges of preservation pushed her head lower until it was almost buried in the lavender bush. Sixty paces from her, the Primus Itinerant was walking briskly, without paying much attention to the girl in the park, and that interest focused on her lower back, which was generously exposed, and not on her half-hidden head. He noticed en passant her auburn hair, but sometimes men of the south married girls from the north. That was all.

When Octavian and his two guards entered the palace, Saliné breathed deeply and stood up. As if at her leisure, she left the park by the same road Octavian had used and walked directly to the stables. The men already knew her from riding out with Eduin. She went directly to the man who was in charge, and smiled warmly at him.

"Baldo, it's a wonderful day, perhaps the best of this spring until now. I feel the need for a short ride around the city. The orchards in the valley must be full of flowers now." She waited patiently, but the man seemed flustered and searching for an answer, likely a polite refusal. "Please give me three guards too. I am still a stranger who doesn't know the land. And bad people may try to harm a lone woman."

The man's face became lighter, but he was still inclined to refuse her. S'Laurden had forbidden her to leave alone and without approval.

"Please, Baldo, don't spoil my pleasure. Look how nice the day is."

Three guards... "I will make it five guards," he finally agreed.

"Thank you," Saliné said, and placed her hand on his arm. "Please help me to saddle and mount my mare." *I have no money with me... At least I have my dagger. In four days, I can be in Valeni.*

Out of the city, she felt half free, and studied her guards carefully. Their leader always rode beside her. Two guards rode in front and two behind her. *Without a diversion, there is no way to escape.* "Let's gallop," she said, filling her voice with joy, and pushed her mare faster, then as fast as she could race. The guards followed her, keeping the same tight formation. *They have good horses too.* Saliné led them up a small hill, and for the last part she dismounted and made it on foot. Three guards followed her while two stayed behind with the horses. She gave up on her thoughts of escaping. *At least I will not meet Octavian*, she sighed and sat on a warm stone. Polite, but keeping a keen eye on her, the guards sat too, thirty paces away from her.

Feeling almost alone at the top of the small hill, Saliné was dreaming. Her thoughts were going more and more to Severin, going back in time too. A time when she was an almost happy child in the hunting house. A time when Jara, Codrin and Vio were there too. A time when she sat in Codrin's arms under their cherry tree. Eyes closed, she did not feel the tears on her face. And she did not see or hear five riders approaching like a storm. They stopped at the foot of the hill, a hundred paces away. Foy and Eduin dismounted in a hurry and walked briskly toward her. She did not hear them coming closer, on foot, either.

They saw her, and they saw the tears too. They looked at each other, then stepped back and seated themselves on some warm stones, thirty paces from her, leaving her alone with her feelings.

It took Saliné a while to gather her thoughts and realize that the sun was now past noon. *They must be worried by my absence*, she sighed, remembering what had happened when she ate alone in the kitchen, and no one knew where she was. She stood up and turned to climb down from the ridge. Her eyes fell on Foy and Eduin, who were staring at her. "I am sorry if I worried you," she said and bit her lip. "I just felt the need to see the valley and be alone."

"You must be hungry, by now. Let's go back." Both Foy's voice and stare were neutral, but Saliné still felt uncomfortable.

I hope that Baldo will not get in trouble for this. "You had some guests, and I did not want to bother you with my request to go for a ride," Saliné said, tentatively, testing if Octavian was still in Laurden. "Baldo took care to give me five guards."

"They were visitors, but not guests. Nobody likes to be visited by the Sages of the Circle," Eduin said. "They are already gone."

Well, she thought, relieved, then kept her mouth shut, letting them to discharge a tension that was well hidden, but not well enough for her keen senses.

"Yes, Baldo was right to provide the guards, but I prefer that you don't leave the city without letting me or Eduin know." Foy still had the same neutral appearance.

"I apologize, and it will not happen again, but I did not know that the rules were so strict for me. Am I a prisoner?" Saliné asked, no longer able to contain her bitterness. "I am sorry; I should not have asked that," she added quickly. *They will not let me leave soon. Why? Octavian? No, he would have taken me with him.*

"It's just that we were worried. Let's return now." Foy pointed down the hill, toward the horses.

The next three days passed without incident, and Saliné calmed down eventually. Eduin even went with her for another ride in the valley. She was thinking to ask again for permission to leave Laurden and go to Agatha in Valeni, when a page came to tell her that Foy wanted to talk with her. The page did not know the reason, and in the long corridor, she tried to imagine what the problem was, one scenario more fantastic than the next. *I am becoming childish*, she thought, with a trace of amusement. *Maybe he will tell me that I can leave Laurden.*

In his office, Foy gestured for her to sit while he finished reading a paper. *He looks in a good mood*, Saliné thought, folded her hands in her lap and waited patiently.

"Sorry for making you wait. This document came after I sent for you." He waved the paper in front of her. "With spring, news comes from everywhere. Some of it is bad, some of it is good. Every spring we make bets which will be more plentiful. What do you think about this year?" Foy asked, his eyes fixing Saliné with an amused stare. "You are new here, so give me something from your instinct."

"The good ones."

"Youth is always optimist. Don't misunderstand me, I consider that a bonus. I was like that too. A long time ago. Time passes so fast. Unfortunately. Last week, during my journey, people reported six crimes committed over the winter, or said they heard from other people what had happened, and as the Seigneur of Laurden I have to listen and take measures. Five of them seem to be easy to solve. There are no doubts about who the perpetrators are. What should my first step be?"

Slightly confused, Saliné frowned, trying to find an acceptable answer. "To verify if the crimes really happened; sometimes people like to make up stories."

"Then." Foy gestured loosely, encouraging her to speak her mind.

"Well, verify both witnesses and facts. Sometimes witnesses are trustworthy; sometimes they have an interest in presenting a different story."

"One crime seemed to have happened in Castis," S'Laurden said absently, looking away, yet the corner of his eye was on Saliné, and he saw her biting her lip. "The person who told me, learned about it from another man, who learned it from another man. A young man, his name seems to be Claudin, was killed by his future bride, just before their wedding and before the Mother Storm came. There are rumors that the girl was kidnapped and forced to marry him, so you are right, more information is needed in such difficult cases." This time, he looked straight at Saliné yet, knowing that she was observed, nothing transpired on her composed face. The years when she had to hide her feelings from Bucur had schooled her better than most. "But let's talk about more pleasant things. What do you think of my son?"

"He is a kind and intelligent man."

"Yes, he is a kind man, more romantic than I would have preferred. He is in love."

"I have heard about his coming wedding."

"It will not happen." Foy gestured carelessly. "He loves another woman. Did you not feel anything?"

"No." Saliné shook her head, desperately trying not to think of Eduin, and to keep a certain distance in their talk.

"Tomorrow, he will ask for your hand. What with your strange appearance during the Mother Storm on the road from Castis, I have had enough time to learn that you are an interesting woman. Beautiful, intelligent, cultivated. You have had good teachers. My servants like you, and there is no one to say a bad word about you in all Laurden. You remind me of my dear wife. So," he said and came in front of her, "I would be glad to welcome you into my family. I don't want to make noises about him being the future Seigneur of this or that. As you said, Eduin is a kind man, and my feeling, that you two would get on well together, should be enough." He underlined his words by taking her hands in his.

Saliné felt suddenly trapped. *Why is he pushing me into marriage, if he knows that I killed Bucur in Castis?* "What if you learn that I don't deserve to be the wife of your son?"

"We have learned enough about you, Vio. In times like these, there is no one without some unpleasantness in their past, and whatever happened and wherever it happened, there must be a good explanation. Why should we look for more? I am sure you will not disappoint me." He looked at her, his eyes serious.

Idonie's premonition about the important event in spring came to her, and there was also a sudden surge of Light in Saliné, pushing her in the same direction. *Why?* The Light did not answer, and feeling that there was no other choice, she nodded, unable to speak. The next day, she accepted Eduin's proposal, and he put a very old ring, of strange beauty, on her finger.

"It belonged to my mother and to my grandmother and so on, for twelve generations," Eduin said, his voice proud and gentle, and the wedding was arranged for one month from that day. "Last night, the Light came to me, and I dreamt the date of our wedding. I even saw the color of your dress, but I will not reveal it to you." He smiled, an enigmatic glimmer in his eyes, and gave her a sealed letter. "Open it after the dress will be ready."

He is a much better choice than Bucur, a much better man and, in time, I may love him too. I already like him, she thought when she was alone in her room, yet she still cried until an uneasy sleep finally came to her. Through the night, she dreamt of Codrin, yet in one dream Eduin visited her too. They were again fighting in the snow, laughing and drinking hot spicy wine, which by the magic of the dream was served to them by invisible hands, in the middle of the snowy plain. They enjoyed each other.

In the morning, Saliné woke with the feeling that everything was just a dream. She rubbed her fingers, hoping to find nothing. The ring scratched her skin and, slowly, she took her hand out from under the blanket, and stared at the ring as a hundred thoughts gathered behind her eyes, and she couldn't figure out which to seize first. *Old and beautiful. Why did they choose me? I am just a stranger.* Her mind went back, recalling time and events from the first day she had cast her eyes on Eduin's face and pleasant smile. She also recalled her Vision about that particular event – it had happened just before she lost her consciousness in the snow, during the storm. *Is the wedding what Idonie meant about waiting for the spring? Did she know this already? Why did the Light pressure me to accept?* Saliné went further, almost day by day and week by week, and every memory of some importance came back to her. *I feel like they are my family.* The strange idea startled her, but the more she thought it, the more she believed it. *I was a chance guest, saved by Eduin from the storm, and after a month, they treated me like family. They never treated me like a nobody they found on the road.* She let her mind roam free over Laurden, but after a while it went back to Severin. To Jara. To Codrin. Saliné shook her head. *My future is here. Eduin loves me, and I can love him. I am sure I can.*

❧§❧

The first time Saliné played the lyre again, after she had accepted Eduin's engagement ring, Idonie was there too. Whether because of the Wanderer's visit or because the proposal was still fresh in her mind, she played like a goddess. Her songs became stories, fragments of her own life rising and falling with the notes. Her longing for her family and Codrin; her bitterness that her mother and sister were Orban's prisoners. Everything came to her unconsciously and, in her trance, she was not aware of the sadness filling the cascade of notes from the strings, and their effect on the people in the room. There was happiness in her playing too: memories of what had happened at the party, her thrill, her exuberance, and her feelings of being almost at home. The anticipation of the wedding was there too, a whirlpool of assorted sensations and feelings.

In her chair, Idonie turned her head slightly, so no one could see her tears. They were moved by Saliné's playing and by the two Visions that filled her mind. When Saliné had finished and become as quiet as everybody else in the room, Idonie came up behind her, embracing her and leaning her head on her shoulder. Her tears were already dry. *I saw Cosmin, your first born, Saliné; the son you will give to Eduin, and that filled me with joy. Then I saw him dying, falling on some rocks. Perhaps from a cliff, or from a tree. He was still a boy in my Vision, and he looked so much like young Foy in that painting, when he was only ten years old. There was an unknown man there too, who tried to save your son. Though I could not see his face, the man was tall and strong and dressed in dark blue; he was not Eduin, and I think that he died too. There was so much blood on the rocks around his head. There was a strange, curved sword too. I wonder if they had been attacked by an Assassin. One day, soon, I will tell you about the birth of your son, and each day, I will pray to Fate to give me an accurate Vision, to learn where and when the accident will happen, so I can save him. I promise that to you, dear Saliné. To you and to Eduin.*

Chapter 27 – Codrin

With the end of winter, the days were now longer, and Codrin found more time for reading. He did not like to read in candlelight, and his favorite spot was a small terrace that looked like a greenhouse with its large windows covering the curved half circle of a wall, adjacent to the library. Orban was a refined thinker; his library held over five thousand books, and the terrace was built to his specifications. In his first months in Arad, Codrin had avoided reading as it reminded him painfully of the time he had spent with Vio and Saliné in the library. With the coming of the long winter nights, he forced himself to forget and read. He needed it, and there was Lanya too, who enjoyed it when they read together. After so many years of neglect, she was blossoming into a young woman, under Jara's and his care. That winter she grew fast, almost catching up with the girls of her age, and the young men, visiting Arad, started to turn her heads to look at her. Some, more daring, even complimented her. At sixteen, she promised to be as beautiful as her mother had been. Not accustomed to the sudden increase in interest around her, she felt uneasy and, as in the years before, she tried to sneak unseen along the corridors and to hide. The terrace was oriented west, toward the large park, and there was no other building in front of it. Each evening, the last sunshine shone deep inside, painting the wall with fire. Codrin enjoyed that, but now he was so absorbed in a seven-hundred-year-old book, dating from the time of the Alban Empire, that he did not notice the mischievous light playing on his body. He did not observe Lanya either. She had been on the terrace for ten minutes already, and stood there, looking at him. She was happy; Codrin was closer to her than anyone else had been before, including her own father, Orban, and while for Codrin and Jara the last months had not been easy, for Lanya it was the best time of her life. Slowly, she came even closer, until she almost touched his shoulder. She stood there, looking intently at him, as he turned the page, still unaware of her presence.

"Father," she whispered and walked in front of him.

"Yes, Lanya," Codrin said absently, without realizing what she had said.

Saying nothing, she smiled, tears on her face. The yellow orb in the sky changed to hues of tangerine, and her tears caught the light, in a strange radiance. Kneeling on the sofa next to him, she out her arms around his neck, and her head on his shoulder.

"What happened?" he asked gently and circled her waist with one arm, then pulled her into his lap. Inadvertently, Codrin caught her scent, neither perfume nor sweat but almost grown woman, sweet and fresh. His hazel eyes widened, and he exhaled briefly to dismiss the strange sensation.

"You are the only father I have ever had."

"Lanya, you have a father," he said, and suddenly realized how she had started the conversation.

"No, he was never my father. He never cared for me. Please be my father."

Codrin closed his eyes, and the memory of his twin sister, Ioana, came to him; that and his late, lonely childhood without parents or siblings. "Very well," he said tentatively, "I will try, but what should I do differently to what I've done before now?"

"Nothing," she said happily and nestled herself in his arms, like Vio might have done, and Codrin forced himself to ignore her memory.

That evening, after dinner, Lanya stopped next to Codrin. "Good night, Father," she said and kissed him on his cheek.

"Good night, Lanya."

"I could not refuse her," Codrin answered to the mute questions from Jara and Cernat when she had gone. "Well, I have a daughter," he said and smiled coyly.

Jara and Cernat smiled back, saying nothing. A few days later, in a similar way, Jara became Lanya's *mother.* The girl had inherited both Orban's intelligence and his stubbornness, but her version of those traits was gentle and persuasive. She was intelligent enough to realize that Codrin was haunted by bad memories and persuasive enough to disturb his habits, helping him, if not to fully forget, at least to feel better. Codrin sensed that the girl kept his ghosts at bay, and he let Lanya have her way. After a while, he came to enjoy her presence as much as she enjoyed his, and they spent more and more time together.

The large backyard of the palace was half park and half botanical garden, and the first signs of nature claiming its rights were already there. Every day, Lanya dragged Codrin out of the palace, and they both let the exuberance of spring fill their minds. Sometimes Jara joined them. One day, just after lunch, Orban, who knew by heart where and what plants were blossoming, was there too, and they met suddenly, face to face, walking around a large bush spread with white flowers with a scent like a lemon tree. As had happened many times in the past, Lanya froze on seeing her father, and she gripped Codrin's arm. She tried to hide behind him, and it was only his firm arm that stopped her.

"Ah, Codrin, would you leave me alone with my daughter?" Orban asked, his gaze measuring Lanya, a muted pleasure showing in his eyes. She was planning to ride after the walk, this afternoon, and she wore a riding habit with a jacket dyed dark blue traced with copper thread, and black boots peeping from the hems of her split skirts. Her blonde hair was tied back and bundled in a crocheted net at her neck. Jara's hand showed in her choice of clothes, and everything suited Lanya well. "Just for a few moments."

Silent, she gripped Codrin's arm even tighter.

"I will be around, Lanya," Codrin said and gently pulled his arm from her stiff fingers.

"Let's walk a little." Orban lent his arm to her, and a baffled Lanya obeyed him. "You have a good relationship with Codrin."

"Does that displease you?" Lanya asked, her voice brittle. Her mouth tightened in a tough line, a glimpse of white teeth pressing into a lower lip gone pale.

"Why? Codrin is the best thing that has happened to you in a while. He is like a ... father to you." Orban swallowed the lump in his throat and nudged his daughter to walk faster. "You've blossomed during this winter, and you are safe." He was now composed again, apart from the tightness in his voice, a faint vibrato that disconcerted Lanya. Her keen senses felt his well-masked uneasiness, and she was uneasy too; she had never sensed even the slightest trace of emotion in her father before.

She looked uncertainly at the signs of spring around them. "Yes, I am safe."

"One day, I will tell you more about what safe meant for you in the past. But not now. You have inherited both the beauty and the intelligence of your mother. They will serve you well in time. Codrin may be like a father to you now, but you are no longer a child, and he might make a good husband too. There are very few men like him in Frankis. Well, he is waiting for you." Orban nodded at his daughter, patted her hand and walked away at a brisk pace, followed by her puzzled eyes. Unseen, he smiled at the ambiguity of his words.

Lanya was supposed to ride with Codrin that day, but he was confined to the palace by one of the first embassies of the spring. Orban's words still rang in her mind and, for the first time, she did not dismiss her father. Even though she was tired from the ride, that night, Lanya found it hard to fall asleep.

With the first month of spring, an embassy from the Circle arrived in Arad. It requested free passage for Octavian, the Primus Itinerant, and an audience for him with Codrin. The interdiction on Sages entering his lands was still in place, and none of them had risked being hanged wearing a placard with the word Sage written on it, Octavian the least of all. During the winter, Codrin sent emissaries to some of the Seigneuries in Frankis asking them to recognize him as the new King of Frankis. Only two groups, in neighboring Peyris and Loxburg readily gave their allegiance, and they did so mostly because of the pressure from Cleyre and Manuc. All the other Seigneurs and Grand Seigneurs asked for more time to make their decision. This was the Circle's work. Baldovin, the Duke of Tolosa, wrote that his allegiance depended on the marriage of his daughter to Codrin. Due his deteriorating health, he offered to step down as Duke and pass his title and lands to Codrin, on the day of their wedding.

Spring, and not only nature was blossoming; new intrigues were weaving their way into the political tapestry of Frankis.

Octavian waited patiently at the border between Leyona and Severin until he received approval to enter Codrin's lands. It came with five soldiers, who escorted him to Arad. A day later, they met another troop going south. The soldiers knew each other, and they stopped for a friendly chat. One man, the only one wearing no colors, walked away from the group and came to Octavian, who did not feel the need to stay among the soldiers. The rain had stopped some minutes earlier, but the man who came toward the Sage still had the hood tight around his head. When he reached Octavian, he pulled back his hood and smiled broadly.

Fate, no, Octavian groaned inside, and his face crinkled up. *Can't be.* His eyes went wide. Then wider. He stepped back in shock.

"Have you lost your voice?"

"No, this is a nightmare. I am dreaming." Octavian squeezed his eyes shut and shook his head, but when he opened them the ghost was still there. "You are dead."

"Am I?" The man laughed and slapped the Sage. "See? Feel?"

"How...?"

"How what?"

"I saw you hanged."

"Did you? How could I be hanged and alive at the same time? You wanted me dead, so you could take my place as Primus Itinerant. Which you did." Verenius pointed at the insignia on Octavian's chest. "But you are a fake. I am the true Primus Itinerant." Verenius opened his pelerine, to show his own Primus Insignia. "While you are in Arad, I will have a word with Maud. I have the feeling you have sold her many false trinkets since that day in Severin. My death was only one of them. I doubt that she or the council will be happy. In fact, from what I've heard, no one appreciated your services during autumn. The Duchess of Peyris and the King of Frankis the least. How could such an experienced Sage like you make so many mistakes?"

"There is no King," Octavian growled, then he recovered. "Don't you see what Codrin wants? He wants to weaken the Circle. He kept you alive and told me that you are dead."

You are right, but why do you think that I still care about the Circle? That's wrong; I still care about the Circle, but not the swamp you've made of it. "I don't know, Octavian. I don't know. Maybe it's what you want us to believe, to hide your betrayal and failures. When you return to Leyona, you will know what the Circle thinks about them. I wish you good luck in Arad. See? I am not such a bad man as you think." Verenius laughed and walked away, leaving Octavian alone with his ghosts.

As he neared Arad, Octavian's ghosts became more and more restless. All his failures of the last year came to him, one by one, and the disaster that happened at Eagle's Nest was particularly jarring; it ended with a long list of strong enemies. Half of Frankis was now against him, and that hindered his moves. A restricted Primus Itinerant is of no use for the Circle. He scowled, and the muscles round his jaw tightened under his skin. In a burst of rage, he cursed Codrin, Cleyre, Manuc and even Maud and the Circle. He was intelligent enough to realize that the encounter with Verenius had not happened by chance; Codrin wanted him to know that Verenius was alive and on the road to see Maud and the Council of the Circle before they met. Passing through the southern gate of Arad gave him shivers.

The evening sun pierced the swirling clouds with bright red, and the Sage shivered even more. Ten guards surrounded him and walked him through the narrow streets of the city, the gate of the palace and even through the long corridors inside, the strict cadence of their boots fraying his nerves. None of them spoke to him, and they finally left Octavian alone only when he passed through the door to Codrin's office. He gritted his teeth while the silent door closed behind him. *Fate, be kind with me.*

Codrin received Maud's letter, then fixed his eyes on Octavian, his face showing the sharp expression that usually made men step away from him. Silent, he massaged his shoulder. "I took a bolt at Eagle's Nest." His stare became harder. "From here to Peyris, you left behind a trail of evil intrigues. And blood. And failures. They will haunt you."

Octavian's face had gone white, and he looked down at his feet, which had started to shake under the table. "I..." he managed to say, though it was hard to understand exactly what he was trying to say.

Codrin read Maud's letter twice – it was the same offer Baldovin had sent just weeks before: his daughter for the kingdom. "The Circle gives with the left hand and takes back with the right. Its right hand is always stronger and always greedy. You crave too much control, and that's the only reason Frankis was so long without a king. As Baldovin is too weak to ride, in one month, I will visit Tolosa, and we will settle everything. Make sure that Maud is there too. I have no other answer for them now." He stood up, and went to the window, leaning against the sill. "Sage, find a den to hide, and never cross my path again." His voice was flat and strangely more menacing than a burst of rage. *Am I becoming too weak and predictable? A few months ago, I would not have spared this snake for political gain.*

Octavian left the room, silent, bowing, even when Codrin was ignoring him. A cold trickle of sweat slid down his forehead. His mouth tasted salty and bitter. Like blood. Perhaps he had bitten his tongue.

Codrin looked through the window, seeing nothing until gentle, familiar figures came to him, one by one: Saliné, Marie of Tolosa, Lanya. Their faces formed a carousel before his eyes, rotating, coming and going, increasing and decreasing, replacing each other by turn. *What kind of Vision is this? It shows me no future. Several futures?* he asked tentatively. *Lanya is too young, and how can I choose between Saliné and Marie? Politically, Marie is the best choice, but...* Even his most trusted people were discreetly pushing him to choose Marie as his spouse, and make the crown a fait accompli. Not only Cantemir, Panait and Verenius, who were Sages of the Circle, but Sava, Valer and Boldur too, and the latter hated the Circle. Vlad, Mara, Vlaicu and Cleyre abstained; they knew Codrin better, and Jara did not interfere either. *I am the Seer of the Realm, and I must act in a responsible way. My decision will have an impact on the Fracture. Marie will bring me Tolosa and help me unify Frankis. Tolosa...* He tapped on the letter from Maud. *Then why this feeling that Saliné is still my future? Am I blinded by my love for her?* Abruptly, the carousel Vision returned, as if it were sensing that he did not understand the hidden message.

Frustrated, he shook his head to end the Vision, and threw Maud's letter on the floor. His mind drifted to Severin, to a time long gone, yet everything was still fresh inside him. Vio was sitting on his shoulders, trying to reach some cherries, and Saliné was looking at him with her large green eyes, and that smile he would give anything to see again.

"Up, Codrin, up," Vio said in her crystalline, cheerful voice. "I want those big cherries, there."

Chapter 28 – Codrin

As usual, the Vision came to Codrin when he least expected it, and he gazed angrily at the priest who was speaking to Saliné and a young man, who looked quite handsome. He would have killed both the priest and the young man. Especially the young man, but there was no way to interfere in a Vision – it was going to happen in some nebulous future, after all. In one hour, or in one year.

"They came here as two people; they will go as a family. Does anyone have an objection to this marriage? Speak now," the priest said.

It's not a large city, though perhaps a bit larger than Severin. Somewhere in the south, Codrin thought, seeing a tall cypress. *Spring... Spring comes earlier there. Still, it has not happened yet. No Vision shows the past.*

"I declare you husband and wife," the priest said, and the man kissed Saliné.

A name, give me a name! Codrin shouted inside, but the Vision ended as abruptly as it had come to him. His hand gripped the pommel of his dagger.

"Lanya, I must leave now." They were in the park, their last promenade before Codrin went south to Tolosa. Unhappy, she kept her feelings hidden and nodded with the understanding of a girl already stepping into the adult world.

He went upstairs, taking three or four steps at a time, then ran through the corridor toward the council room, baffled people stepping back to the walls to let him pass. He stopped in his Council Room, in front of the large map of Frankis he had taken in Mehadia, as a spoil of war, made by the former Royal Cartographer more than fifty years ago, one of the few still remaining after so many years of civil wars and disasters. He traced a path across the map, over the southern lands.

I was in Grenble, and it's not there. Genvas, he tapped on the map, *Nicea*, he tapped again, a little further west. *It's not Nimea. Pierre is its Seigneur. Massala, Montpell, Laurden, Bardaux.* The land and the map ended at the border of the ocean. *I would need more than a month to visit them all. I don't have that time. The wedding may be tomorrow;* he shook his head, struggling to overcome his bitterness.

Unconsciously, he recalled the last part of the Vision. "I declare you husband and wife," the priest said, and the man kissed Saliné. Her warm response unsettled Codrin, and he passed a hand through his hair.

Is everything lost? Does she love that man? Who is he? Confused and angry, Codrin left the map, threw himself in a chair, and placed his elbows on the table, his chin on his clasped hands. *What should I do now?*

"What happened?" Jara asked as she came in. She was the first arrival for the last council before he left for Tolosa.

I've lost Saliné. "Nothing."

Jara inclined her head in acknowledgment, thinking if it was something personal that she could inquire later. One by one, people entered in the room, glanced at Codrin, who was looking nowhere, absently, then at Jara, asking mutely for a clue. She shrugged.

"We will leave tomorrow," Codrin finally said. "As already agreed, we will take the road through Valeni; the last thing I want is to meet Maud on my way. We may bite each other, and the road is long. There will be some changes, though. Sava, you will come with me, too, and we should take two hundred fifty soldiers instead of a hundred."

"Will they try something against us?" Sava asked. "Should we take more archers?"

"I don't think that they will but bring fifty archers. That's a good idea. I had a strange Vision, and I may need to dispatch some companies to a few towns in the south. I don't have a clear picture yet. Vlad, bring twenty extra scouts."

A Vision of Saliné? Jara wondered. *That could explain his mood. Bad news?* "Would you tell me more about your Vision?" she asked when they were alone. "Was it about Saliné?" she insisted, when Codrin did not answer.

"Yes, it was a wedding."

"We already knew that she would be forced to marry Bucur." Her voice was uneasy, though she tried to calm him and herself. "At least we know that Verenius was right, and Bucur took Saliné to the south. We will cancel the marriage."

"It was not Bucur." *And she did not look like she was being forced at all.*

No one could be worse than Bucur. "If not Bucur, then..." Jara arched her brows, struggling to hide a sense of relief that Codrin would not have appreciated.

"I don't know."

"Would you mind if I join you? And perhaps Father too. We will go as far as Valeni. It's not far from Tolosa."

"Are you fit to ride?" Cold, his eyes opened a little too wide, then looked away. Recalling that kiss transferred some of his bitterness toward Jara too.

Jara though for a moment. *Codrin needs me.* "I rode there two years ago; it should not be much harder. I won't delay you. Perhaps I will return in a carriage. I will send one tomorrow."

❧❧

"Joffroy, you need to calm down. I understand that you and Marie love each other, but for a Duchess marriage is political. And for you too. The fate of Frankis depends on Marie and Codrin. I can see him now. Codrin doesn't know about you and Marie. Let's keep it like that."

"Yes, Father," Joffroy said thoughtfully, without looking at him. *Three years ago, I lost Idonie, now Marie. I must be cursed.*

The sound of many hoofs hitting the ground focused the men waiting at the crossroads. The cadence slowed and, in a few moments, Pierre, the Spatar of Tolosa, and his son, found themselves in front of Codrin. It was their first meeting since the siege of Poenari.

"I'm glad to see you in good shape," Codrin said, clasping hands with Pierre. "What's new in Tolosa? Don't tell me about Maud," he laughed and clasped hands with Joffroy too. Sava and Vlad dismounted too, and they greeted the two men from Tolosa.

"It's spring. The wedding season. We have to attend three in Tolosa, one in Laurden and another one in Montpell. All in just ten days."

"Don't complain; you have good food here in the south and the best wine in Frankis. Where does that road lead?" Codrin shielded his eyes against the bright sun with one hand, to see better. He did not see the pain reflected on Joffroy's face.

They were at the Sealand crossroads, one of the most important in the south; the road from the Pierens Mountains in the south to Rhiun's Mouth in the north was the main artery of Frankis. The road from Genvas in the east, going toward Bardaux in the west, was important too. The ocean in the west and the sea to the south were faraway, and no one knew who had called it Sealand, or why, a long time ago. The crossroads was west of Tolosa.

"That's the Arrow Road; it goes to Laurden. The road is safe, it's just that it goes straight south, like the path of an arrow. There are almost no bends in the road."

"To the east are Montpell and Grenble. I was once in Grenble. Is there any other large town in the south?" Codrin asked only to make Pierre talk. Sometimes a new Vision could be stirred like this.

"And they called you the Wraith of Tolosa," Pierre laughed.

"I still don't know why, but it suited me at the time."

"There are two more Seigneuries in the south: Massala and Nicea."

Codrin glanced up at the still climbing sun and stretched his mind like when he was using his Farsight, but no Vision came to him. "It's early, and I am not in a hurry to see Maud. Let's make a half day detour. I want to see the land south of Tolosa, and we need to talk." He mounted Zor and let his Farsight go east toward Tolosa. It was easier now, but he still felt slightly lightheaded when his mind returned to his body. His weakness was masked by the horse's movement, and Zor did not need Codrin's eyes to ride. *Fifteen miles from here to Tolosa*, he estimated. "Come with me, Pierre." He stayed silent until they were far from their men. Behind them, at thirty paces, rode Joffroy, and Codrin's captains: Sava, Vlad, Valer and Boldur. Pintea and Lisandru followed them.

"The Lights of the Wanderers have predicted a Fracture," Codrin said after a while.

"Yes, Idonie warned us. She is a Wanderer from the south, the niece of a friend."

"Did she tell you about the Seer?" Codrin looked at Pierre, who shook his head. "When there is a Fracture, there is also a Seer. I am now the Seer of the Realm. I need to unify Frankis and gather a strong army before the next nomad invasion."

"I understand. Marriage to Marie will help you consolidate the crown."

"We will talk about that later. I am forming a Council of the Realm too. I need someone from Tolosa in the council. Will you join it? It brings you no wealth, no titles, nothing, only hard work and unexpected danger."

"I would be honored."

"Now tell me everything that's happening here. The weddings included." Codrin laughed, a bit edgily, but Pierre did not realize it. "I need to know my people."

After their long detour, they arrived in Tolosa in the evening. Laure greeted Codrin, and guided him to his suite, where a bathtub was waiting. An hour later, the meeting finally started, and Codrin was irritated to discover that Pierre was not invited. He was surprised to see that Drusila had traversed Frankis to be there, and their eyes met for a few moments. He could not read much in the Wanderer but did not feel her hostile.

Being the last to enter the Council Room, Codrin nodded curtly and seated himself, saying, "We know each other well, there is no need for introductions. Although Marie was still a girl when we met last; and I was an unknown quantity at the time." Their eyes locked, and they exchanged a smile. It was genuine on both sides, and that did not escape to the women in the room, who watched them like some hungry predators.

"We will decide the future of Frankis today," Maud said, and Baldovin, the Duke of Tolosa, and his wife, Laure, agreed with a solemn nod. Drusila did not react in any way, and Marie merely blushed.

"Let's resolve something from the past, first." Codrin looked at her, his face locked in a slight frown of dislike.

"Ah," she smiled, "is this issue from the past related to Leyona?"

"You paid allegiance to me, when I took Leyona." He looked around and saw that only Marie did not know that he had taken Leyona and how Maud, who was both Secretary of Leyona and Master Sage of the Circle, convinced Garland to proclaim himself Grand Seigneur and replace Codrin.

"Yes, the Secretary of Leyona paid allegiance to you, but was it the Secretary who ordered Garland to take the city from you? Or it was the Master Sage of the Circle?"

"It's hard to say where the Secretary ends, and the Master Sage begins. I suppose that both find shelter in the same person." Codrin inclined his head more in acknowledgment than clemency, and Maud was sharp enough to understand that the matter was closed; but she did not see further into his thoughts.

"Thank you for understanding my position," she said, her lip curled just slightly in relief. "Should we return to the future?"

Codrin took the treaty he had signed in Severin, with Verenius from the Circle's side, and placed it on the table in front of her. Maud took her time to read it, and tension mounted inside her, but nothing could be seen on her face.

"I think that the man who signed this was ... punished, in some way that I don't yet understand," she said, tentatively.

"Verenius signed, as the Circle's man. What happened there was the effort of a team. The team included Octavian and Laurent."

"What would represent a satisfactory solution for you?" Maud asked, and only her eyes did not share the calm of the rest of her.

"They must suffer my judgment."

"In the past, your judgment against the Circle's men has carried a severe punishment."

"As severe as their sin."

"Would it be so hard to draw a line under it and start everything anew, without looking at the past? Perhaps we should look more into the future," Laure said, trying to shield Laurent, who she wanted as her husband after Baldovin's passing away. Judging by the parchment texture of his skin and his deathly gray color, it was not far off.

"There is no future for the ten men Laurent killed in Severin. I was his liege, and he betrayed me."

"We should continue after dinner," Laure said, relieved that she could delay an answer, when a page came to announce that the meal would be served in half an hour.

"I need to talk with Marie before that. Alone," Codrin said.

"There is a room there." Baldovin pointed at a closed door, and both his daughter and Codrin left the office.

The room was not large but had the same beautiful view toward the mountains. Codrin took a chair and placed it in front of the window. "The light is better here," he said, looking at Marie.

Her black hair, contrasting with her fair face and blue eyes, made her one of the most beautiful young women in Frankis. She blushed under his stare, and let herself be seated, then waited, unmoving, but for her hands. She held a handkerchief, which she commenced to fold, over and over, into smaller and smaller squares.

"I don't bite." Codrin smiled briefly and took her hands in his, undecided. He was feeling the pressure of a choice which would shape his future, Frankis and the Fracture.

Still staring at her hands, Marie spoke, her voice barely more than a whisper, "You bite hard, but you don't bite women." As she spoke, her voice became more confident, and a smile transformed her beautiful face.

"You could say that. Tell me about Tolosa."

"What can I tell you that the Wraith of Tolosa doesn't know?"

"You might be surprised how little I know about your city, or about you. Three years ago, I saw you for the first time, the kind of beautiful girl men find hard to forget."

"You were with Joffroy." Her voice stumbled a little at the young man's name.

"You were quite an observant girl as I recall. What's between you and Joffroy?"

"Do you really need to know?"

"I would not have asked otherwise."

"We grew up together. I like him. This has nothing to do with our marriage. It's a political thing, but perhaps it can be more than that. You are an attractive man, and I trust I am not a complete fool or an ugly woman."

"You are as beautiful as you are intelligent. Do you love him?"

"Perhaps like you love Saliné," she said, quietly. "I thought that we could talk about more pleasant things, about what can bring us together, not about what pulls us apart."

"What's more pleasant than love? I will let you choose the man you want to marry."

"Why are you treating me like this? Pierre told me that you are different. He told me about the kind man under the tough skin. Our marriage is necessary for Frankis, and I don't see why we can't love each other. Please stop this, Codrin."

"I am not mistreating you, Marie," he said gently. "I had a Vision about you and Joffroy, and whatever decision you make, I will accept it."

"Please," she whispered, too anxious to ask what he meant by Vision.

"Then I will make the decision for you. I will announce that my wish is for you and Joffroy to marry."

Marie pulled her hands from his and stood up so suddenly that her chair fell back on the floor. She flew toward the other window in the room. Silent, she set her brow against the cold glass. The bright setting sun flashed through the branches of a large pine and struck playful sparks through the stained glass. She did not see them.

Codrin placed his hands on her shoulders, turned her slowly, and seated her again. "Do you agree with me?"

Marie breathed, tried to speak, but all she could manage was a graceful nod.

"I think that we have an agreement." Codrin kissed her hand, and then he pulled her up. "Let's go and announce our decision."

For a while, they looked at each other, face to face. "Thank you, Codrin," she said, raising her hands, which were still in his, until they reached the level of his chest. With a sudden impulse, she embraced him. "I did not plan that," she said, a pleasant touch of redness on her fair face, when they separated. "But neither do I want to take it back. There is such strength in you. And kindness." She smiled and touched his face with her delicate fingers. "Now let's go see Grandmother." Her voice sharpened, and Codrin recognized Maud's strength in the girl in front of him.

She would have been a strong queen, he thought, and his mind went back to those Visions of Saliné kissing the unknown man. Teeth gritted, he shook his head, furrowing his brow and struggled to ignore them. Walking in front of him, Marie saw nothing. *I may lose both Saliné* and *Marie. And Tolosa too. Many will consider me weak. They will challenge me. What is left for me, if Saliné loves that man? Lanya?* His mind recalled the carousel Vision, in which all the three girls danced for him by turns, a glimpse of the future that he was still unable to understand. *She is still young, but she would be a fine wife too. Fate.*

They returned to the silent Council Room, the atmosphere heavy with expectation. The future of Frankis will be finally set on the right tracks. Marie struggled to hide both her happiness and fear at disobeying her parents. Maud said nothing, expecting Codrin to announce their agreement. Codrin simply waited to raise the tension in the room. His tactic failed, because Marie's joyful eyes had deceived both Maud and Laure. Both women had been in a position of power too long to imagine that things might take a different path, against their will.

"Did you tell them?" Codrin asked Drusila.

Maud has put the cart before the horses, the First Light of the Wanderers thought, *and Codrin wants me to play along with him.* "No." *I can play too, Codrin.*

Codrin arched his brow, and a little grin flashed across his mouth. Without speaking, he leaned against his chair, his sharp eyes urging the Wanderer.

"What should we know?" Laure was the first one to cede and break the studied silence.

Drusila's brows rose, though whether in annoyance, or polite irony, Laure was not sure. *You should know that the marriage will not happen. Codrin only wants me to prepare you.* "For this occurrence of the Fracture, Codrin is the Seer of the Realm. His duty and power go beyond Frankis." *And his actions ruined the Prophecy. Again. Grand Master Tudor died before his time. This stubborn young man refused to play his part. Fate knows what will happen now.* She forced herself to breathe long and slow, the Wanderers' equivalent of the Assassin Cool. *Perhaps I am overreacting. Perhaps we are misunderstanding the Prophecy. Codrin* is *the King of Frankis.*

Her face composed, Maud drew a deep breath, looking past Codrin. "Seer of the Realm, and soon King of Frankis. Things could not have gone better for you."

"I am already the King of Frankis, Maud, and I expect the Circle to acknowledge that. One way or another." His cold smile was hard as a razor. "And I am expecting the Circle to behave appropriately from now on. Baldovin," he turned toward the Duke. "I require your allegiance. Now."

Laure breathed angrily and tried to intervene. Under the table, Drusila gripped her hand and squeezed it hard. Maud just squinted her eyes — she was more experienced than her daughter.

"Your majesty," Baldovin bowed in acknowledgement. He was ill, not stupid, and he was tired of Maud's schemes.

"Can we talk about the marriage now?" Laure asked, her voice even, and Drusila released her hand slowly.

"Yes, of course," Codrin said. "It is my pleasure to announce the marriage of Marie and Joffroy. It pleases me, as I am fond of them both." He placed a protective arm around Marie's shoulders.

I had no Visions about Saliné, Codrin, she seems lost in a serpent hole, but right now, there is a shortage of quality brides in Frankis, Drusila thought. *You will learn that soon. Since Rochil and her trip on the ship, I had no Visions about Saliné. Isn't that strange?*

Chapter 29 – Saliné / Codrin

"I think everything is ready. You look beautiful, my lady," Martha, the dressmaker said. Saliné's dress was a very pale green, a pastel reflection of her eyes, with a belt of dark cerulean, the color of sunset reflected in coastal waters. She would wear no other color on her.

"Yes, it's beautiful," Saliné agreed, turning in front of the mirror, her dress rustling faintly. "Thank you, Martha, you have done a wonderful job."

To a less sophisticated observer, there was apparently nothing striking in Saliné's dress. Everything was made bright by her way of moving; her smile that shed light around her; her straight, elegant body. As at the Winter Solstice Party, the simple dress was not noticeable on her; it was only her frame which captured the view – simple, natural, elegant.

"I agree," Eduin said from the door, his eyes absorbed in her.

"Sir," the dressmaker protested, her face turning red, "you should not have seen it before the wedding day."

"I am afraid that is now too late for that," Eduin laughed. "I could not wait another two weeks. Let me see you better." He took Saliné's hand and walked her closer to the window, in the bright light of the morning sun. Discretely, Martha left the room, closing the door after her. "The dress is beautiful, but it can't compare to you, Vio."

The compliment reminded her that she was to marry in two weeks, and she smiled. It was half genuine. "Thank you, Eduin. That was kind of you."

"What if you open my sealed letter?" he asked, a playful glimmer in his eyes.

"Hmm," Saline said and went to her cabinet; the letter was there, untouched. *From his smile, he must have guessed it well.* "Light green dress with a blue belt," she read, and smiled coyly. *It was meant to be family.*

Looking at her, desire reflected in his eyes, Eduin pulled her toward him. Slowly, his mouth searched for hers. Saliné stayed still for a moment, then her arms laced around his neck. He parted her lips, and the kiss became more demanding, followed by a second and a third one, all answered by her. When their passion calmed, he held her in his arms, her head leaning on his shoulder. Saliné acknowledged that Eduin knew how to kiss a woman, and he took every opportunity to prove that to her in the days that followed and, day by day, a pleasant intimacy built slowly between them. She both enjoyed and feared it, but she felt quite different from when Bucur pestered her, pretending to love her. Eduin *did* love her.

Most of the evening before the wedding, Saliné did little but stare through the window. Her future husband, relatives and servants left her alone; brides were always shy and nervous before such an event. She set her brow against the glass and closed her eyes. It was cold and refreshing, but it did not help much to calm her emotion.

"How is my beautiful wife?" Eduin had formed a habit of slipping unseen in her room, to claim a kiss, and it was happening more and more often.

She turned her head and smiled, saying nothing, afraid that her voice would betray her emotion. He embraced her from behind and kissed her neck. She shivered without realizing it, yet he noticed, and his lips moved over her sensitive skin. Her shoulder blades tightened but, this time, Eduin was the unobservant one, desire mounting in him; he did not hurry, and slowly Saliné abandoned herself to his lips and touch. His hand moved up her body, finding her breast.

"Eduin," Saliné protested, but her voice was feeble, as her body had already started to answer him, and his lips pressed on her mouth.

Her bathrobe slid down, and she no longer resisted when he pulled up her night gown.

"You are so beautiful, Vio," Eduin said and gently laid her on the bed, pressing his face to her belly, his lips moving slowly up until he found her breast. She breathed faster, and her arms tightened around his neck. After a while, he tried to move up, parting her legs. Unconsciously, she stopped him and moved his head over her other breast. Then she could stop him no more.

"Oh, Eduin," Saliné whispered, tilting her head back. Her hands moved along his back, answering him with the same passion, and soon they found their twin rhythm. At the end, they lay on their backs waiting to recover their breath, until he turned toward her.

"Vio, please don't think badly of me. I should have waited until tomorrow, but I lost my head. I apologize for my happiness." He caressed her face gently. "Perhaps it was easier like this, without the pressure of the wedding night." This time there was a mischievous glimmer in his eyes.

Saliné blushed, and she pressed her fingers to his eyelids, closing them.

"I like that color." He laughed quietly and kissed her fingers, which moved slowly over his face, across his lips, learning him. When she rested her palm on his chest, feeling his heartbeat slowing down, Eduin pulled her over him, her head resting on his shoulder. They stayed like that, drowned together in a pleasant silence, almost asleep.

"We lay like this after that battle in the snow," he said after a while.

"I was a bit better dressed then," Saliné chuckled, and he pulled her over him completely. They were now face to face, eyes locked. Slowly, she lowered her mouth over his.

They made love once more, and at midnight, Eduin left the room when almost everybody was sleeping in the castle, just to keep up appearances.

Alone, Saliné embraced a pillow, pleasure still murmuring in her body. *I think I can love Eduin. Perhaps it has started already.* The pleasant memory of his body leaning against hers stirred and made her blush at the same time. *He is a good man, kind and intelligent. Well,* she sighed, *tomorrow I will become Signora of Laurden. Codrin was not meant to be. Fate.* She could not sleep for a while, and when it finally came, her dreams moved her back in time, to Severin, talking with Codrin under their cherry tree, but Eduin appeared in her dreams too, saving her from the storm, then in Laurden, dancing in the castle, under the high starry sky, his lips and well-built body pressed against hers.

Walking toward the church, Saliné was at the same time content, afraid, elated and resigned. If asked what was weighing more in her mind, she could not have answered. Once the memory of the night had vanished, nostalgia for a past that could not come back had consumed her. She was equally consumed by her future with Eduin. Her thoughts went again to Codrin and, this time, she forced herself to stop thinking of him. *It was not meant to be,* she said to herself for the hundredth time. *And love may come to me again.* She looked at Eduin, who all the women in Laurden considered to be a handsome man. Saliné had acknowledged that too, on that first day in the castle when she woke up in a strange room. She had thought herself dead until the young man smiled gently, comforting her. *I like him,* she thought, recalling that gentle smile. *And this is my wedding day.* Her mind started to settle down, and she straightened her body.

Eduin felt her turmoil and assumed it was the tension of the wedding. His hand covered hers, resting on his arm. He smiled, and Saliné smiled back. "You have nothing to worry about, wife, you look so beautiful." Still smiling, she nodded and swiped her thumb over his hand.

"My dear girl," the older priest said and, feeling her unease, he came closer to Saliné, taking her hand in his. "It's a pleasure to marry such a good-looking couple. Today, you will become a wife and a Signora. It's an important moment in your life, and I promise you a beautiful ceremony, though I don't know if it could be as beautiful as you are." He patted her hand, then let it free. "Ready?" he asked the other four priests, who all nodded. "We are here to make a new life for Vio and Eduin. They came here as two people; they will go as a family. Does anyone have an objection to this marriage? Speak now."

"I have," a man said, raising his hand, his voice more powerful than his small stature would indicate. His shortness was even more striking as he stood next to a very tall man. The short man would barely come up to the nose of an average man, but the chin of the tall one would rest comfortably on the head of most people in the yard, and many were gathered there to witness the marriage of the future Seigneur of Laurden. The odd pair stepped a few steps closer, pushing some people aside until there was no one between them and Foy. Discreetly, five more men followed them. "I apologize for speaking so late, but we've just arrived in Laurden."

Foy looked darkly at him, struggling to keep his irritation under control; he knew both men. He had invited them to the wedding and did not expect such interference. "Speak," he snapped.

"The bride is the daughter of a Grand Signora. Did you receive her mother's approval?"

A ripple of surprise passed through the crowd. Most of them wondered how the foreign girl who Eduin had saved in the mountains could be the daughter of a Grand Signora. Such noble ladies don't walk alone through the forests, and they thought her a commoner, or at most a Knight's daughter. Some, mostly young women ripped for marriage, even whispered that she had seduced the heir to advance her status. For the first time, Eduin and his father began to understand some aspects of Saliné's behavior that had eluded them until now, or that they had perhaps chosen to ignore.

Who is that man? Saliné looked at him, and their eyes locked. The man smiled briefly under his large salt and pepper moustache. *I don't know him, but if he stops the wedding... I wish it had happened earlier. It may be too dangerous now. Both Eduin and Foy are upset.*

"I have known you for a long time, but why should I believe you?" Foy rasped. "We found Vio alone in the forest."

"He speaks right," the tall man said, "but you can just ask lady Saliné."

"Her mother?" The name felt known to Foy, but his anger overcame his knowledge. Maud's imperative letter, asking news about the Candidate Queen, was now forgotten.

"My real name is Saliné, and my mother is ... the Grand Signora of Midia."

"Midia belongs to Orban."

"Orban has lost both Midia and Arad," the tall man said. "Orban has lost everything bar his life."

Mother is free, and only Codrin could have defeated Orban. Saliné bit her lip to repress a smile that did not match the seriousness of the situation.

"I can confirm that," another man, who stood on the opposite side, said. He was tall too, but where the other tall man was just tall, this one looked like a bear, and behind him were five other men, almost as big as him.

He is a Mounte, and I saw him once, Saliné thought but, under the pressure of the moment, she could not remember where or who he was.

Foy frowned, his eyes moving from one group to another, and he realized that there were tough soldiers in both. There was also coordination between the groups. He did not like that and turned to observe the yard: another group of armed men were walking in a leisurely way toward a place, a hundred paces behind the priests. All the men, in the three groups, wore the same colors: a red, yellow and blue diagonal, and an embroidered raven, which he did not know. He nodded to his Spatar, who made his own assessment. Both reached for the hilts of their swords, but they were unarmed. Foy nodded at his closest group of ten guards, and they came even closer, but the signal for violence had not been given, so they walked calmly. Twenty more guards around the plaza were signaled discreetly by the Spatar, and they were ready to intervene. Before the flurry of glances, gestures and moves ended, three men dressed all in dark blue appeared at the edge of the crowd, some distance behind Saliné. Without a word, people made way for them, and they advanced silently until they arrived at the edge of the small, almost empty, circle where the S'Laurden family, the bride and the priests stood.

"Lady Saliné is my betrothed," the man at the front said; the three formed a wedge that looked menacing, and all carried two swords. *Now, I will know if she...*

Foy and his son turned abruptly and measured the stranger with angry eyes. Saliné's words about her betrothal resurfaced in their minds, but this man did not look like the commoner in her story at all. He was a tough soldier and had the stance of high nobility. Saliné closed her eyes for a moment, then turned slowly to face Codrin. Their eyes met. There was such happiness on her face; she was elated. That did not escape Eduin. She also recognized Pintea, behind Codrin. All his inner demons suddenly vanished, and Codrin let out a breath he hadn't realized he had been holding.

"If she is indeed Lady Saliné of Midia, then she is betrothed to Bucur, the Candidate King," the Secretary of Laurden said before Foy could stop him.

"Foy, you must let her go," Idonie whispered in his ear. "I am sorry to disappoint you, but things have only just become clear, even for me. And you, keep quiet," she snapped at the Secretary, who clamped his mouth shut.

"Greetings, S'Laurden. Allow me to shed some more light on this issue." A man walked forward from behind the three strangers and bowed slightly.

"Sage Verenius." Foy nodded, surprise reflected in his stare, as like many others, he knew the man had been hanged by Codrin, the year before.

"By the treaty of Severin, Lady Saliné was taken from the Candidate King." Verenius thought for a moment and decided to leave for later the news that Bucur had been demoted by the Circle.

"Who are you?" Foy turned toward Codrin.

"Codrin is the King of Frankis," the tall man said.

The young wolf from Poenari... A trace of understanding filled his mind, but his anger threw it away. "I trust you, Pierre of Nimea, but why should I believe you? Frankis has no King."

"Because it's true."

"What about Bucur, the Candidate King?"

"Bucur is dead," Saliné said, before Verenius could answer. "I killed him when he tried to rape me, before forcing me into marriage." Her voice was flat, but her eyes glimmered when she glanced at Eduin, and a moment later at Idonie.

Eduin's eyes widened and, for a while, he stared at her in stunned silence; Foy had kept the story about Claudin and Vio from him. "So, should I consider myself lucky that I have escaped?" *She accepted me during the night, and I am still alive.* "Because of the marriage proposal?" he added swiftly, unwilling to put her in a bad position because of what had happened between them.

"Eduin," Saliné said, touching his face, "you are not Bucur, you are a kind man who saved my life during the Mother Storm. If not for Codrin, I could have seen myself as your wife, but he is the man I have loved from the first day we met, the day when he saved Mother's life, a long time ago. I think that you ... already know what I think of you." She blushed, as the memory of their night together came to her. She also thought of the possible consequences, but she was too happy now to blame herself for making love to another man, in that strange situation. "This belongs to your family." She pulled back her hand, but Eduin caught it and kissed her fingers briefly, before releasing it. Slowly, she took off the old ring that Eduin had given to her when he proposed and returned it to him.

"We knew you as Vio," he said, a touch of disappointment and irritation filling his voice.

"The day I woke in Laurden, after you had saved me in the mountains, your father received a letter from an important person, *your relative*, who asked about me. You were both in my room when it happened, and I pretended to be still asleep. That person had tried to kill me just a month before. I was afraid. I am sorry that I deceived you."

"You did well to hide your name," Foy said, his voice level. "If I had known the truth that day, I would have delivered you to that person. We did not know about the assassination attempt, and it would have been hard to believe it. A month later, you were safe no matter how many letters we received." Strangely, his voice warmed to her at the end.

"I know that, and I felt as if I was adopted by your family, but it was difficult to change my story. I want to thank to both of you for being so kind of me, and I apologize for any harm I have caused." She looked at Eduin and smiled gently, trying to soothe the man who still loved her, a man for whom she cared. Swallowing his pain, he returned the smile, and Saliné was finally free to greet Codrin. Caught in his arms, she leaned against his chest, sobbing quietly, watched by Eduin and his father.

So, it seems that a Vision can be changed, Codrin thought. *The marriage didn't happen. A kiss didn't happen; the other one... The other ones? The other one is past.* "We need to go, Saliné," he whispered, and she raised her head, smiling at him through her tears. "Seigneur Laurden, I thank you and to your son for saving Saliné and taking care of her. You did not know who she really was, so no offense is taken for the marriage proposal. I can even say that I understand you, for wanting a woman like Saliné. I want her too." Unconsciously, Codrin pulled Saliné closer to him. "In one month, I will expect a letter of allegiance from you. We will leave now, hopefully in peace."

Foy clasped his hands at his back, uncertain how to react. He looked at Pierre, the Seigneur of Nimea and Spatar of Tolosa, then Sava, men he had known most of his life. *If Tolosa is already in this...* "I will send the letter, your majesty." Then he turned toward his Majordomo. "Take care of lady Saliné's horse and clothes."

"Give me one moment," Saliné said, and she pulled away from Codrin. She went to Idonie, and they embraced. "Thank you for everything, Idonie. You were right to make me wait until spring. Take care of Eduin, and if he feels bad, tell him that apart from Codrin, he is the only man for whom I feel anything. One day, when things will calm down, I will expect him in Arad, and every day, I will expect you."

"I was right that you are different," Idonie laughed. "I will come to see you. Dochia told me good things about Codrin, but I am a cautious woman, and I want to make sure he deserves you."

Saliné went next to Foy, and they looked at each other for a while. "Thank you, Foy," she said, making a curtsy, and returned to Codrin, after the Seigneur of Laurden had kissed her hand.

Seeing Codrin and his men leaving, Foy realized the trap that had been laid for him. Around fifty armed men moved out of the crowd, or appeared from behind the church and the closest houses, and followed Codrin, some of them archers. One group was led by Valer, the famous Black Dervil of Tolosa, another by Joffroy, Pierre's son. He did not know the other two leaders, Vlad and Boldur, but there was no need to read them for too long. *All strong men, and Codrin has the reputation as the strongest...* "Carlo," he whispered to his Spatar, "I am glad that we did not try to use force, but I want to know how so many armed men could enter Laurden without us knowing."

"I apologize, Sir, but it was the wedding; people from everywhere came to see it."

"It seems so, but we should be more careful at the next wedding; I don't want to lose another daughter-in-law. Son, let's take a little walk." He grabbed Eduin's arm, and they walked for a while in silence, the father thinking how to appease his son. "It seems that I was right, and you had a new mistress." He laughed quietly at Eduin's confused look. "Do you really think I don't know where you spent the night? Vio did not lie about liking you, but I am relieved that we did not have the wedding sooner. We could have a powerful enemy by now."

"Do you want to restart the marriage negotiations for...? Eduin asked, his voice edgy. He tried to say more, but clamped his mouth shut, and his jaw set, if possible, even more tightly. Even with the political advantages, he did not want the woman.

"No, son. Laure's niece is not the woman you deserve, and after Vio, she would be a drink too bitter to swallow. As it looks, I think that we can trust Pierre; we have a new King. And I think that we have a friend at court now, and I intend to use that to escape from Laure's tight grip. Vio... I think that I should get accustomed to her real name. Saliné is intelligent, knows you well, and likes you. And after that Mother Storm, she is in your debt. I think she will not disappoint you. She knows that I like her too, so she will not disappoint me either."

"I have much to learn about what happened in my absence," Saliné said to Codrin, as they walked away.

"We have all the time in the world." He placed an arm around her shoulders and pulled her briefly against him.

"What about that young Duchess of Tolosa?" she asked with a wry smile.

"That one? Unfortunately, she loves another man, so there was no place for me in her heart. I had to renounce the marriage."

"Ah, that explains your presence here," Saliné laughed. "How did you find me? In the last days, I lost all hope."

"I am sorry that it took so long. Verenius learned that you had been taken somewhere in the south, but the south of Frankis is quite large."

"Did the Circle have a change of mind?"

"Only Verenius, Cantemir and some Mesters; most of the other Sages still hate me, and I had a tough time with Maud in Tolosa, until I convinced her that I would not marry Marie, her granddaughter. Fortunately, Marie was my hidden ally, as she is in love with Joffroy, Pierre's son. They will marry in a few months."

"Who are they?" Saliné gestured at the unfamiliar people around them.

"Pierre is the tall man who spoke, together with Sava, the short one, against the marriage. He is the Spatar of Tolosa. Both are my friends, and Sava is the Chief of the Guard in Arad. It's a long story; he was the Chief of the Guard in Leyona and delivered the city to me, and then he followed me in Poenari, after Maud stirred that coup to replace me."

"Verenius betrayed us in Severin, but he also helped me."

"The letter and the marking ribbons, I know. I don't know why he did it, but he is no friend to Maud, and he is in my council now. The ribbons helped us to follow you until Aron boarded that ship in Rochil."

"I left two marked sticks in Petronius's grave. I scratched Dog and Pirenes on them."

"That was a good idea, but we found only the one marked Dog. Some men from the Circle were there before us. Let's forget about it. When I came here, the day before leaving Arad, I had a Vision about your wedding. Bloody Vision. I hated it, as I did not recognize the place, and had no idea where the wedding was. On the road to Tolosa, Pierre told me that there would be a wedding in Laurden, and he was invited. Tolosa is not far away, and I asked him to show me the land south of the city. We rode to a place from where I could use my Seer Farsight to search for you." His voice wobbled a little, but Codrin didn't tell her that he saw her kissing Eduin. Twice. "We arrived here this morning. I planned to take Laurden if I had to, but I hoped that it would not be necessary."

"Seer?" *How much did he see?* she wondered, and her mouth tightened in a worried line.

Codrin pretended not to notice her reaction. "Yes, it seems that we will have a Fracture, and I was chosen by Dochia, the Last Empress, to be the Seer of the Realm. It took us two days to prepare my strategy to stop the wedding."

"You brought enough men," Saliné nodded at the soldiers behind her, "but I am glad that everything was peaceful. Eduin is a kind man, and he saved my life."

"I will always be grateful to him for that, and I always pay my debts. There are two hundred more soldiers hidden in the forest, less than a mile from here."

Four days later, on the way back toward Arad, they arrived in Valeni, where Jara and Cernat were waiting, and they stayed there for a week. They arrived at noon, and by the evening, they were already husband and wife. Agatha was older, but her wit had not left her, and she insisted on marrying them under her famous statues. The priest complained at the beginning, but there was no way to bend the old iron lady to his will. There was also a strange feeling, when the couple stood in front of the side niche, where the two marble statues stared down at them: a huntress tensing her bow, and a swordsman. While everybody knew that Saliné and young Agatha looked alike, they also noticed a resemblance between the now mature Codrin and Agatha's long dead husband, and no one saw the tough old woman hide her tears. She, who had never shed one for more than thirty years, since her husband was killed.

Their last night in Valeni, Codrin and Saliné dreamed the same dream. The hordes of the Serpent God moved like a wave across the continent, leaving the land fractured behind them. The hordes vanished, and the land froze over, its features disappearing under a thick blanket of ice; now it was nothing more than a huge iceberg and, as they watched, it split into two great frozen blocks. Codrin and Saliné found themselves on opposite sides of the widening chasm. Struggling to keep their footing on the shuddering, moving ice, they stared, helpless, at each other as they drifted apart; it seemed only moments before they were both out of sight.

Neither spoke of the dream; each kept it stored away, in a secret chamber of their mind. And nine months later, in Arad, they realized that their son, Cosmin, had been conceived in Valeni, in the room that Codrin had entered by climbing the wall, only two years earlier.

Appendix

Poenari

Codrin, son of the slain King of Arenia and the legitimate King. After his father's death, he finds sanctuary in the former kingdom of Frankis, sometimes using the name Tudor to conceal his real identity. Seigneur of Poenari in Frankis

Mara, the Secretary of Poenari

Vlaicu, Spatar of Poenari (commander of the army). Former Chief of the Guard of Severin before Severin fell to Aron.

Sava, Chief of the Guard of Poenari, former Chief of the Guard of Leyona

Ban, Chief of the Archers of Poenari and Sava's right hand. Former Chief of the Archers of Severin before Severin fell to Aron.

Bernart, custodian of Poenari before Codrin took the fortress.

Vlad, born in Litvonia, he followed Codrin to the former Frankis Kingdom. Chief Scout of Poenari

Calin, former Secretary of Mehadia and Mara's father

Laurent, Knight of Faget, Garland's brother

Pintea, Vlad's brother

Julien, Sava's son and captain

Neira, Sava's wife

Nard, Aron's second son, taken prisoner by Codrin after the conquest of Faget

Siena, Bernart's granddaughter

Amelie, Bernart's granddaughter

Mihail, Mara's son

Severin

Jara (Stejara), Signora of Severin, former Grand Signora of Midia. She lost her castle to Grand Seigneur Orban after her first husband, Malin, was slain in battle. She lost Severin to Aron when Mohor was killed.

Mohor, former Seigneur of Severin and Jara's second husband, killed by Aron

Cernat, former Grand Seigneur of Midia and Jara's father

Saliné, Jara's daughter

Vio, Jara's daughter

Veres (Snail), Jara's son

Mark, Jara and Mohor's son

Aron (Big Mouth), Seigneur of Severin after killing Mohor, former Spatar of Severin (commander of the army)

Bucur, Aron' son, and new Candidate King of Frankis

Karel, Spatar of Severin (commander of the army)

Martin, guard

Geo, guard

Gria, servant of Aron used to keep Saliné under control

Milene, servant in Jara's house

Ferd, mercenary from Valer's army

Senal, Secretary of Severin

Frankis Wanderers

Dochia, the Fourth Light of the Frankis Wanderers

Valera, the First Light

Livia, the Second Light at her death

Drusila, the Second Light after Livia's death, the First Light after Valera's death

Derena, the Second Light

Splendra, the Third Light, converted Serpentist and High Priestess of the Serpent in Frankis

Sybille, the Fifth Light

Olmia, the Eight Light

Chloe, the Ninth Light

Viler, Drusila's nephew, and Chief of the Men Guard of the Frankis Wanderers. He was killed by Codrin in a duel.

Arenian Wanderers

Ada, the Second Light of the Arenian Wanderers, and the strongest Light of all the Wanderers

Litvonian Wanderers

Ingrid, the First Light of the Litvonian Wanderers

Salvina, the Fourth Light, converted Serpentist

Mared, the Fifth Light, converted Serpentist

The Circle

Cantemir, former Master Sage

Maud, the new Master Sage

Aurelian, Sage and Primus Itinerant, killed in Severin

Belugas, Sage and Primus Itinerant, hanged by Codrin

Verenius, Sage and Primus Itinerant

Octavian, Itinerant Sage

Dog, the best assassin of the Circle

Eric, the Chief of the Circle's assassins

Petronius, Itinerant Sage

Hadrian, Itinerant Sage

Paul, novice Sage

Arad

Orban (the Beast), Grand Seigneur of Arad

Cantemir, Secretary of Arad and Master Sage of the Circle

Panait, the first Mester of the Merchants Guild in Arad

Delia, Panait's wife

Doren, the Spatar of Arad (commander of the army)

Vasile, Jara's agent in Arad

Leyona

Garland, the new Grand Seigneur of Leyona

Leyonan, former Grand Seigneur of Leyona, slain in a battle against Codrin

Maud, Secretary of Leyona and the new Master Sage of the Circle

Sava, Chief of the Guard of Leyona

Bartal, second Secretary of Leyona

Lina, Garland's wife

Farcu, Chief of the Guard of Leyona's castle

Dobre, governor of Orhei in Leyona Seigneury

Peyris

Stefan, Duke of Peyris

Cleyre, Stefan's granddaughter and member of the Council of Peyris

Albert, Stefan's son

Nicolas, First Spatar of Peyris (commander of the army)

Reymont, Secretary of Peyris and Hidden Sage of the Circle

Gilles, second Secretary of Peyris

Paulus, the third Secretary of Peyris

Emich, Knight

Mateus, priest

Vasso, secretary

Nerval

Meriaduk, the High Priest of the Serpent

Ai, the young, invisible woman helping Dochia in the Sanctuary

Kasia, sixteen-year-old girl having a strong Light

Iovon, chief of a strong band of robbers in Nerval and Kasia's brother

Gresha, Iovon's deputy and cousin

Mesko, merchant

Krisko, merchant

The High Sphere

Dochia, the Last Empress, founder of the Order of the Wanderers

Nabal, the Last Emperor, he joined the Serpent God

Castis

Guiscard, the warden of Castis

Tolosa

Baldovin, Duke of Tolosa

Leon, the old Duke of Tolosa

Laure, Baldovin's wife, and the real ruler of Tolosa. Maud's daughter.

Marie, Baldovin's daughter, promised to Bucur, and the Circle's real choice for the Candidate Queen

Pierre, the Spatar of Tolosa (commander of the army)

Celeste, Pierre's wife

Joffroy, Pierre's son and captain of Tolosa

Masson, Secretary of Tolosa, Hidden Sage of the Circle

Deva

Devan, Grand Seigneur of Deva

Filippo, Devan's son

Balan, the first Mester of the Merchants Guild in Deva and Sage of the Circle

Mona, Balan's wife

Dan, Chief of the Guard of Deva

Long Valley

Matei, Half-Knight and mercenary in Valer' army

Varia Matei's wife

Livia, daughter of Varia and Matei

Damian, elder son of Varia and Matei

Lisandru, son of Varia and Matei

Boar, Knight

Sara, Boar's wife

Little Boar, Boar's brother

Balint, Boar's second Chief of the Guard

Sharpe, Black Dervil, mercenary captain, slain by Codrin

Valeni

Agatha, Signora of Valeni, Jara's aunt and Hidden Sage of the Circle

Bran, Chief of the Guard of Valeni

Maxim, Bran's right hand

Mercenaries

Valer, Black Dervil of Tolosa, mercenary captain

Eagle, Black Dervil of Peyris, mercenary captain

Bear, Black Dervil in south if Frankis, mercenary captain

Sharpe, Black Dervil for north-west of Frankis, mercenary captain, slain by Codrin

Assassins

Scorta, Assassin Master

Dorian, Assassin Master

Arenia

Tudor, an Assassin renegade and Codrin's mentor

Ioana, Codrin's twin sister

Radu, Codrin's brother

Baraki, Chief of the Royal Guard of Arenia

Iulian, captain of the Royal Guard of Arenia

Gaspar, Knight, Baraki's nephew

Loxburg

Manuc, Duke of Loxburg

Others

Dolgan, one of the most famous ship captains, an Io Capitan

Dragos, Mountes Chieftain and Boldur's cousin

Konrad, Knight

Boldur, one of the Mountes' chieftains

Iaru, the third Mester of the Merchants Guild in Dorna

Lenard, Seigneur of Dorna

Miscellaneous

Spatar, Chief of the Army

Vistier, administrator of a castle and coin master

Wraith, most successful Lead Protectors (only four in Frankis)

Black Dervil, mercenary captain (only four in Frankis after Codrin killed Sharpe)

Vicarius, the most powerful priests of the Serpent

galben (galbeni at plural), gold coin, ten grams weight

turn, alternative time unit of measure, equivalent of one hour

cozonac, cake from Arenia

Months of the year:

Gerar, January

Florar, May

Stove, July

Wanderers ruling councils

Inner Council of the Three

High Council of the Seven

Printed in Great Britain
by Amazon

78962236R00201